THE PERFECT MAN

"I'm a peaceful man."

"Are you?"

He raised his shoulders, but there was something close to a denial in the movement, something strong, driving, vital, the promise of a conquest that was as violent as it was removed from violence.

"And it's just possible, MacGillvray," he continued, "that on some fine day, the man of your dreams will appear out of the mist. He might not be what every woman would consider the finest example of manhood on the face of the earth, but you'll know he's the one for you. And you'll never be the same again."

She froze in her chair. She didn't know she had been holding her breath until it escaped in a soft gasp. She had seen him appear out of the mist this afternoon and she had known, somehow, that he was the man she had been dreaming of all her life.

A Case Of Nerves

Angie Kay

LOVE SPELL BOOKS   NEW YORK CITY

For Alan, for everything.
To remember my inspiring Scottish forebears
and Gene Kelly.
I'll be seeing you in Brigadoon.

LOVE SPELL®

June 1999

Published by

Dorchester Publishing Co., Inc.
276 Fifth Avenue
New York, NY 10001

ISBN 0-505-52312-4

The name "Love Spell" and its logo are trademarks of Dorchester Publishing Co., Inc.

Printed in the United States of America.

ACKNOWLEDGMENTS

Thanks to my husband for his unwavering support and confidence, to my mother for her impressive store of Scottish proverbs, and other things, to my brother for his daunting knowledge of history, to C.M. for advice on tantric sex, to W.G. for encouraging his wife to read it, to A. C., his wife, for reading it. You know who you are.

A Case Of Nerves

The soger frae the wars returns,
The sailor frae the main,
But I hae parted frae my Love,
Ne'er to meet again, my dear,
Ne'er to meet again.

When day is gane, and night is come,
And a' folk bound to sleep;
I think on him that's far awa',
The lee-lang night and weep, my dear
The lee-lang night and weep.

—Robert Burns

Chapter One

The fog was thick on Culloden moor, the sky above it gray, pregnant, threatening rain. The wind was raw, and the flags at either end of the battlefield— the colors of the Jacobite army, the colors of the Hanoverian army—twisted, wraithlike, in it.

Kate surveyed the vista, hugging her voluminous all-weather coat around her, pressing her guidebook against her chest. A low-pitched wail echoed in her ears. *It's just the wind*, she told herself, though she had never heard wind blow so monotonously, with such insistence. As she listened, it became the back-beat for a symphony of other sounds, first bagpipes, then drums, then finally the staccato report of gun-fire. In the next moment, a man lunged out of the mist, reared up on his toes, his back arched, his arms open wide, and crumpled at her feet. Before she could dislodge the scream that stuck in her throat, he vanished, leaving her with the impression of height and seething urgency, wrapped in dark plaid that was oddly weightless, like gossamer, nearly transparent; leaving her with the realization that the wind had stopped howling. Dead silence.

She suspected she was going to faint.

She stumbled toward one of the benches the National Trust had thoughtfully placed beside the graveled trail that ringed the field. For occasions such as these? she wondered as she sank down onto it, dropping her book. She squeezed her eyes shut. *Breathe deeply and steadily*, she coached herself, laying two fingers of her right hand against the pounding pulse in her left wrist. She was rewarded by feeling the beat begin to slow, by feeling the tightness in her chest begin to lift. She had never fainted in her life and wasn't going to start today, she concluded finally. She was a physician, after all, trained to expect the unexpected and respond to it calmly, a physician who was respected for the cool and level head with which she approached the hundred minor and major catastrophes that were thrown her way each day in the big city hospital where she was Chief Medical Resident. She never got hysterical—or hadn't before Tuesday. She wasn't prone to flights of fancy. "You have no imagination," Evan had often told her, in the soft and sympathetic tone that he seemed to reserve for enumerating her quirks. And she had rarely doubted Evan's judgments. But here, in twentieth-century Scotland, on the site of the last battle waged on British soil, she had seen the ghost of a slaughtered Highland warrior meet his end yet again. Either

her imagination was improving or she was losing her mind.

She was just overwrought, as her mother would say. Stressed out, not crazy. Setting foot in a place that was the centerpiece in the family lore was bound to give anyone an attack of déjà vu, she assured herself. She had found it particularly unsettling to lay her hand on the weathered boulder with MAC-GILLVRAY etched on its front. The man it immortalized was her kinsman, two centuries removed but a MacGillvray nonetheless, starving and bone tired before the *coup de grace* that laid him low, buried in a ragged plaid that bore the blood and dirt of a battle he never could have won, should never have been made to fight. Yearning. His pain was almost palpable here. It wasn't strange that she could empathize with her long-dead relation's wish for solace, for food, and, in the end, for oblivion.

Seeing him, or one of his compatriots, however, was a different matter.

She opened her eyes reluctantly, in time to observe a gaggle of tourists gather around a youthful tour guide in period dress. *That's who I saw!* she decided, studying the man, pouncing on the explanation. He had just been participating in some kind of historical tableau, and in a certain light . . .

In any light, the man she'd seen was taller than the guide.

Don't go there! she warned herself. She had come to Scotland during the inhospitable second week in April to escape her fears, not add another to the list. Ghosts. She closed her eyes again, but couldn't block out the image of the place where one Mac-Gillvray had faced his demise—with more courage

11

than she had faced the departure of her fiancé, no doubt. He had probably accepted the loss of a hundred of his men with more courage than she had *one* of her patients.

They were so very young, every one of them, soldiers in the war on the streets, and many of them were dying as they were wheeled or carried into the emergency room, amid swarms of paramedics and police, their bodies shattered by bullets, torn by knives, broken by bats. You could tell whether a particular boy had fought for the Huns or Diablos if you took the time to read the name stenciled on the back of his jacket. But there wasn't any time. . . .

"It can't help but affect you. It can move you to tears, but you'll feel better for them."

Kate considered these words, then nodded in concurrence. She had every right to cry over the senseless loss of life—at the Battle of Culloden, or the Battle of North Philly. She had every right to mourn the defection of Evan Hall, the man she loved and had expected to spend her life with, no matter that the touch of his hands made her feel indifferent, at best. She had long since come to terms with the fact that fate, or genetics, or some forgotten psychological trauma had left her with loopholes in her libido. But Evan had asked her to marry him in spite of this small stumbling block on the road to happily ever after, and she had unhesitantly agreed. She had longed to be married. She had wanted the kind of companionship her parents had found in each other, though she had resigned herself to never knowing their kind of intimacy. She had needed someone to come home to at the end of days spent elbow-deep in blood and human misery. What Evan had wanted from their union was never quite as clear. In the end, his reasons for breaking up with her had made more sense than his reasons for pursuing her in the first place.

Cry! she urged herself silently. *You'll feel better for it.*

The best she could manage sounded like a hiccup.

Though she had grown up in an enlightened era, surrounded by friends who favored let's-pretend games featuring women astronauts and doctors, she had been happiest when they relented and agreed to play wedding, with herself in the coveted role of princess-bride. She could still see herself, swathed in the kitchen curtains, carrying a bouquet of blooms pilfered from her mother's prize rose bushes, promenading proudly toward the prince, portrayed by her mortified oldest brother, while her playmates looked on and giggled. The little girl who had dreamed of marrying Prince Charming was going to wind up an old maid.

"Cry!" she ordered herself. Then she stiffened, realizing that the original suggestion hadn't been made by her own battered psyche, but had been spoken from without, in a deep, melodic voice. Ghosts. Do they speak? More likely, it had been an auditory hallucination, a complex but scientifically explainable phenomenon involving a short-circuit in the brain's temporal lobe, she decided, raising her head slowly.

She jumped to her feet, stepping on the guidebook. This auditory hallucination was accompanied by a visual one!

A beam of sunlight broke through the clouds, touching the dark auburn hair of the apparition. He was very tall, an impression exaggerated by the fact that he was standing on the path, a few inches uphill

13

from the patch of grass on which she stood. His hair was clipped short, and it did nothing to soften the angular lines of his face. He was wearing corduroy slacks and a heavy sweater, both in shades of brown, under a shiny yellow rain slicker. His boots were similar to her own, she noted, allowing her gaze to travel down the length of him—definitely L. L. Bean, or the Scottish equivalent.

This man was oddly familiar. He was certainly a stranger, yet she felt as if she had seen him before, somewhere. She suppressed the impulse to touch him, to convince herself that he was, indeed, cor- poreal, and not the fog-cloaked phantom she had seen right on this field. "Were you wearing a kilt a few minutes ago?" she asked suspiciously.

He glanced down at his trousers. "I don't think so. But I'll run home and put one on, if you'd like," he answered, smiling.

The smile was beautiful. His teeth were white and straight. She placed a shielding hand above her eyes, attempting to determine the color of his through the glare. "Green," she said.

"Pardon?"

"Never mind."

"Your first time?"

"What?" Synapses. Everything in life could be reduced to the synapse, she decided, to that infini- tesimally small space between the ending of one nerve and the beginning of the next. Impulses were passed across this chasm in tiny chemical packages called neurotransmitters, permitting orderly trans- mission of data to the appropriate way-station in the brain. She nodded resolutely. A scientific explana- tion. A logical one that required little imagination on

14

her part. Too many neurotransmitters in the synapse could result in hallucinations, misperceptions. Confusion.

"Is this your first time to Culloden?" he asked.

One bold brow was arched quizzically, and he seemed to be trying to control the very slight Scots burr to his words, as if he believed her failure to comprehend him was due to his accent. He repeated the question, slower this time, deciding, perhaps, that English wasn't her native tongue. Or perhaps he suspected she had left her white-coated attendant tied up behind one of the distant trees.

She shook her head, to clear it. The tortoiseshell barrette that had been anchored at the nape of her neck fell to her feet, allowing her hair to tumble to her shoulders. "It's my first time," she whispered, staring at the barrette, suddenly more frightened by the possibility that her head shake might have driven him back into the neurochemical twilight zone from which he had come than that she might look up to find him dressed in plaid.

"It can't help but affect you."

Something was affecting her. The sound of his voice, however, assured her that he was still standing his ground. She sighed in relief, raised her gaze, found that he was still wearing brown cotton and machine-carded wool, yellow vinyl. But now his gaze was intent, with an unmistakably earth-bound appreciation. She felt her face flush. The wind was whipping her hair against her cheeks, into her eyes. She pushed it back impatiently, not wanting to lose sight of him again, guessing she would be content to bask in the warmth of his appreciation for the rest of the afternoon. He rescued the barrette and extended it to her. She took the far end of it, carefully, leaning forward to do so, keeping two arms' lengths and three full inches of plastic between them. Yet she still jolted back when she touched it, feeling as if it had conducted fifty thousand volts of electricity from his hand to hers. She stared at him in surprise. A shock to the nervous system. A faux tortoiseshell bridge across a synapse.

"Bonnie Prince Charlie could have saved his loyal followers by admitting defeat and fleeing. Instead he had five thousand of them stand here, outnumbered, starving and ill-armed, to be slaughtered by a legion of Redcoats in the futile effort to put his father, James Stuart, on the British throne," he said.

"The terrible waste of it," she murmured, wrestling her hair into a tail and securing it with the barrette. "History has painted it too romantically."

He nodded. "Death isn't romantic. Highlanders were trained to fight in the hills. This place is wide and flat with no cover. Their rations had been cut to a biscuit a day for at least several days before the battle, and they hadn't had much more than that for weeks before. They were armed with broadswords and dirks and small pistols, no match for King George II's firelocks and grapeshot. But they were brave and proud. It was the last day of a romantic year, *Bliandna Thearlaich*, Charlie's Year, the last day the people of the Highlands believed in miracles and the first one in which they understood that blind devotion to a person, however *bonnie*, invariably ends in disaster."

"Does it?" she asked. Blind devotion. Evan was

16

bonnie. Undeniably beautiful. And he knew it. "You're careful with your devotion?"

"I've never offered it easily."

"And you can't see yourself marching headlong into the enemy's gunfire in the service of it?"

"No," he said. He glanced over his shoulder, toward the towering cairn that had been raised, rock upon rock, to honor the men who fell on the field behind it. "The 16th of April, 1746. The English started the day with a steady barrage of heavy artillery, for which the Scots had no reply. Then Prince Charles Edward ordered the Highland charge, and the first wave rushed forward. 'Like hungry wolves, they were,' one witness said: the MacDonalds, Alexander MacGillvray and his Clan Chattan, the Camerons, MacLeans, MacLachlans. They ran willy-nilly into a forest of bayonets and the crossfire from two lines of big guns. They never stood a chance."

She stared at the desolate field, could almost see the charge, could almost hear the gunfire.

"Next week, descendants of those men will gather here to commemorate the 250th anniversary of the battle. As long as they're all kitted out in their *breacan*..."

She lifted an inquiring eyebrow, needing a translation.

"... dressed up in their tartans," he clarified, "carrying targes and pikes and facsimile claymores, I say they might as well have another go at the fighting. Rumor has it the odds favor the Scots this time around, since the English won't be attending."

"Neither will you," she guessed. She would have

called his tone contemptuous if it hadn't been so sad.

"I don't care much for battle lore or battlefields. In fact, I'm not certain why I came here today . . ."

It wasn't the first time an unfathomable impulse or a random twist of fate had brought a man to this place, she supposed. Or a woman.

He stepped off the path toward her, throwing off what little poise she had managed to marshal. She wasn't petite, yet even from her new vantage point, her chin barely reached the bottom tip of his breast-bone. She had to tilt her head way back to meet his eyes. He was lean, but broad-shouldered, and he seemed to radiate a strength and power that drew her toward him, that filled her with the desire to relax against him, to lay her face against his sweater and listen to his heart beating under it.

"American?" he asked.

"What?"

"Are you an American?"

He was speaking slowly again, looking at her oddly. She noticed that his long, straight nose sported the faintest dusting of freckles. She found herself wanting to count them, the way a child would, one by one, laying a finger on each before adding it to the tally. She raised her eyes to his. "I'm American. From Philadelphia."

"Will you walk on the moor with me?"

It seemed an intimate question, one full of subtext and possibility. She would have been less surprised if he had asked her to go to bed with him. But she suspected the answer to either question would be the same. "Yes," she said.

She retrieved her guidebook, then hurried forward

to catch up with him. He walked like a warrior, contradicting his professed aversion to warfare, she noted, with long, purposeful steps, his gaze directed straight ahead, his chin held high. She could almost see the folds of a kilt flapping against his knees in the brisk wind.

He headed away from the path that circumvented the battlefield, along which the clans' mass grave markers were sited, toward one that cut right through the middle of it. The field on either side of the path was much less solid than it looked from a distance, she discovered. It was spongy, covered with clumps of coarse, dark scrub and tangled brush, with pools of water between the clumps—difficult terrain to fight on, she imagined.

"The sun doesn't seem to shine on this place often," he said finally.

"I've heard it doesn't shine on Scotland often," she answered.

He laughed. "American propaganda! But somehow Culloden always seems shrouded in fog, chilly and impossibly desolate. There are many stories about illusory clan brigades appearing out of the mist. One tourist, an American I believe, swore he found himself in the middle of a pitched battle here. Culloden House, over that way," he said, pointing, "was Prince Charles Edward's headquarters. The present structure is built atop the original cellars. Some people say he haunts them still. . . . You don't believe in ghosts, do you?" He stopped short and turned to her.

She stared at him, speechless, wondering if his perceptive eyes could read on her face the truth about her recent departure from reality. "No, of course not," she managed finally, defensively. "I'm a scientist."

He grinned. "A scientist, are you?"

She nodded.

"Then you're of the opinion that there's a rational explanation for everything?"

She raised her shoulders. She would have been better able to answer in the affirmative a scant half hour before. But suddenly the world seemed filled with mysterious things, with mist-shrouded moors and phantom Highland warriors, with this man's lips and her almost irresistible need to kiss them until she uncovered all the clues.

They continued on in silence, looping around the Stuart flag, passing plaques that marked the positions held by various clans in the ill-fated charge. The MacGillvrays had been front and center, she noted.

Just before they reached the bench from which they had started out, she felt compelled to step off the path, to lay her hand on an etched boulder to her right. Her companion seemed to feel the same compulsion, at the same instant, because suddenly his fingers were touching hers. And she was shaking. *Swooning*.

"Are you all right?" he asked.

Was she?

He gestured toward the Visitors' Center at the end of the path, a low, modern building whose display of artifacts and brief film had done little to prepare her for her reaction to setting foot on the field where so many men had lived their last, had been laid in death. "Perhaps we should go inside," he said.

Perhaps they should. She nodded.

"The 'Well of the Dead,' " he said enroute, pointing.

She stopped, crouched down, scooped up a handful of the cold, peaty water and let it trickle through her fingers for the second time today. She touched her fingertips to her cheek. " 'Here the chief of the MacGillvrays fell,' " she quoted, without looking at the stone beside the small pool.

"You've already seen this one?"

"Yes." She stood up, turned to study it again. "My father's name is Alexander, too," she added, speaking to herself more than to her companion. Alexander MacGillvray. Dr. Alexander MacGillvray. He was the chief of his clan as surely as his namesake had been.

He watched her. "And the other one?"

She knew which one he meant. She hadn't quite reached that boulder the first time she approached it; she had seen a ghost and the world had begun to career out of control before she could do so. The touch of this man's hand had caused similar sensations, and kept her from studying it the second time. She shook her head, listening for the sound of neurotransmitter slashing against her cranium. "It was almost as if someone I knew was buried there . . ." she whispered.

His words were measured. "Odd sentiments to be voiced by a scientist. The men put in the earth under that stone have been dead for nearly two and a half centuries."

"Yes," she said, agreeing with both statements.

His green-eyed gaze held her rooted to the spot. He raised his hands slowly, as if in supplication, or

21

to cup her face. But he appeared to reconsider the action and thrust them into the pockets of his slicker instead, lifting his shoulders into a questioning shrug. "I don't suppose Americans have a taste for our good Scotch whisky."

"This American has never had any."

"Ah," he said. "It's the highlight of a Highland tour, and a damned sight better at warding off the weather than the weak tea they serve in the Visitors' Center."

She held up her guidebook in a hand that was visibly trembling before she pushed both into the pocket of her overcoat. "That's why they recommend 'frequent stops at quaint local pubs,' I guess."

"No doubt," he said, grinning boyishly. "And I find it an excellent remedy for a case of nerves."

"Then I need a double dose," she said.

Kate had always envied people who could toss caution to the wind and leap full-tilt into an adventure. She had told Evan as much once.

"It's not you, Katie. You're so . . ." He searched *for a diplomatic adjective, gesturing with his graceful surgeon's hands.*

"Boring?"

"Reliable," he assured her, his voice soft and *sympathetic.*

Her decision to follow this Highland warrior—and she had dubbed him so despite his thoroughly twentieth-century attitudes and lack of kilt—over fences and across fields, past assorted members of the bovine and equine species, in search of a glass of whisky, was one she would have considered madcap in an impetuous person. She was breathing heavily from keeping pace with him, admiring the easy length of his stride and cursing it at the same time, wishing she hadn't so readily agreed to abandon her rented car in the parking lot in favor of a hike. He was way ahead of her now, standing at a line of trees, motioning her onward with a wide sweep of his arm, looking as straight and solidly rooted as any of them.

"It's just there," he said, as she halted at his side.

She nodded breathlessly. She followed the line of his finger to view a cluster of stone houses at the bottom of the hill, built on either side of a paved road. Civilization. One of them appeared to be a pub, with a sign mounted over the door that swayed in the wind. She had been listening to the squeak of those rusty hinges for several minutes, she realized, along with the high-pitched whistle of the wind through the trees, and the occasional soft lowing of a cow. They were peaceful sounds, far removed from runways and motorways, from the tourist attractions and traps she had seen since she arrived in Scotland, from the more familiar sounds of the hospital she had left behind: public-address pages, beepers, alarms. Screams. Moans and sobbing. She had heard laughter in the hospital on occasion, of course, usually in the cozy medical staff lounge to which she would escape for a cup of coffee and a few minutes with Evan. He would invariably sweep into the room like a conquering hero, dressed in surgical scrubs, self-effacing despite his latest victory in the operating room, tossing a lock of dark, shining hair back from his milk-chocolate eyes with a quick movement of his head. And he was usually surrounded by an adoring covey of medical students who hung on every pearl of wisdom that fell from his lips. . . .

She didn't want to think about the last time she had watched Dr. Evan Hall with his entourage.

"A good surgeon's got to have 'one hell of a nerve,' " Evan said, *addressing his audience with exaggerated arrogance. "He's got to have 'nerves of steel.' " He held forth an imaginary scalpel in a theatrically shaking hand.*

"And he's got to have steel balls, I suppose," the beautiful girl responded, her laughter irreverent, mocking.

"It doesn't hurt."

She'd never noticed this student before Tuesday, but as Kate had watched the girl toss her mane of tawny hair, plant her hands on her slender hips, she had wondered how she'd managed not to.

"I think balls are an overrated commodity, Dr. Hall," the girl challenged, raising her chin, arching her back so that her generous bosom was shown to an advantage, in spite of the loose, unisex lab coat she was wearing. She turned so that the ID badge clipped to her lapel could be read by anyone in the room who cared to read it.

Jenna Marcus. M.S. III.

"We'll have to arrange for you to examine a surgeon's . . . in situ, of course," Evan answered, chuckling sexily as he qualified his statement with the Latin term for studying something in its anatomically correct location.

And Kate had suddenly wanted to examine the spectacular specimens in question herself. *In vitro*, of course. On a dissecting tray.

"Allow me to introduce the lady who just aced her board certification exam and is the leading contender for the plum job of Assistant Director of Emergency Services come July—don't let her catch you sleeping when you're on call! That's Dr. Kate MacGillvray over there. Internal Medicine."

His tone had been conciliatory, apologetic, but Kate had suspected he was simply sorry she was in the room.

"Surgeons say: 'When in doubt, cut it out.' Internists say: 'When in doubt, q 2 obs. 'til you lay 'em out.' Right, Katie?"

"Q 2 obs." was the shorthand way of ordering the nursing staff to monitor vital signs—pulse, blood pressure, respiration, temperature, level of consciousness—every two hours. Surgeons prided themselves on boldly leaping into a problem with both feet, and both eager hands, while their non-surgical colleagues opted for more conservative treatment and regular observation. It was usually a lighthearted rivalry, an insider's joke.

But on Tuesday, Kate had felt like an outsider, looking in.

"Time heals all wounds, Evan."

"So does death, Katie."

He had grinned at the students around him, his eyes lingering on the exquisite Jenna in much the same way they had once lingered on a zealous young intern named Kate MacGillvray.

And Kate had known the truth then, many minutes before she demanded that Evan dismiss his cortege and tell it to her in private.

"You're fond of Latin phrases, Evan. Try this one on for size. In flagrante delicto."

She had caught him red-handed, with the smoking gun, so to speak. Evan hated conflicts, avoided them at all costs, but she had been determined not to let him shrug and joke his way out of this one.

"The better woman has won."

"Jenna's not better than you, Katie. Just more passionate, much more passionate. . . . I've given up trying to break through your suit of armor to get at a little emotion."

And it had all come pouring out, his coerced confession giving way to confessions she hadn't wanted to hear.

His words had still been echoing in the silence of the room, settling in the pit of her stomach like underbaked bread, when the P.A. system crackled to life and the urgent summons came.

"Code D. Emergency Room. Code D. Emergency Room."

"D" was the designation reserved for Disaster—train wrecks, airplane crashes. Nuclear war. Gang war in the community that surrounded the hospital, a part of town where it sometimes seemed as if every male under eighteen had taken up arms and chosen sides.

Instinct had kicked in, and she had leapt up, realizing that while her own small disaster had been unfolding within the confines of the medical staff lounge, a much bigger one had been unfolding somewhere beyond it.

But she hadn't realized her fiancé wasn't the only thing she was going to lose that day.

Kate shook off the shiver that coursed through her, forced her mind back to the present, returned her attention to the peaceful Scottish hillside in front of her. "It's so beautiful," she offered.

Her companion's gaze was solemn, reverent, and he looked around slowly, as if he had never seen this place before, or had been gone from it for a long time. "Aye," he answered.

"There aren't many people living around here," she commented.

"And the population gets sparser as you go north. The Highlands suffered after Culloden; some say they never recovered. There were vicious reprisals by the English after 1746. There was famine and starvation. People were forced to move south, or to emigrate—to Canada, to America."

Her own ancestors had arrived in America in the mid-eighteenth century. She had never really stopped to wonder why they left Scotland.

"And then there were the clearances," he continued.

"Clearances?"

"Entire villages were leveled so that the land could be used for grazing. Sheep were more valuable than people, you see."

"How awful!"

His smile was sad. "But those awful things helped to keep the Highlands the way you see them today. The greater the number of people in a given area, the greater the number of roads and motorcars and factories, not to mention disposable nappies and razors, plates, cups, and cutlery." He was surveying the valley around him again.

"And you like this place just the way it is." It wasn't a question.

27

"I do."

He motioned for her to follow him, and she did so, allowing the stiff wind at her back to propel her downhill. She stumbled on a knot of half-frozen grass at the bottom. He held out a strong hand to steady her, allowed her to hold it for the moment it took her to regain her footing, then withdrew it. He continued on to the pub, and she stared after him. His hand had been solid and warm. Her body was suddenly ripe, expectant. He was no specter or hallucination, but something even more frightening: a flesh and blood man whose touch could make her ache with need.

Lust!

Kate considered this, her first experience with the sensation, in awe. It was a powerful sensation, she realized, one that could drive even a reasonable, proper man like Evan Hall into the arms of a voluptuous redhead.

How far could it drive Kate MacGillvray?

She watched her Highland warrior approach the pub's door and halt there, turn and wave. What she was feeling now was quite elemental, but it was also tender and unaccountably familiar. She wasn't a person given to easy confidences, or even to ones more dearly bought. But she suddenly wanted to share her past with this stranger, to tell him about her almost forgotten fantasies, her secret dreams. She wanted to tell him about soaring, snow-capped mountains, painted in acrylic on the back of a black leather jacket by an unusually gifted hand.

She wanted to tell him about the dead boy who had been wearing that jacket on Tuesday.

Or did she?

She bit her tongue to keep from demanding that he not take another step until she had told him every detail of her life, and had heard every detail of his.

Was this love at first sight? she wondered. She had stopped believing in such things a long time ago. Or was it insanity? She nodded her head. She still believed in insanity. She had witnessed a wholesale display of it in the E.R. on Tuesday, the day she lost her fiancé, and her nerve.

She often thought it ran in her family.

Anne MacGillvray had shown appropriate, albeit skeptical concern on Tuesday night when Kate announced she was quitting medicine and getting on the next plane bound for Scotland. She had behaved like a candidate for a straight jacket when she first learned her daughter intended to marry Evan Hall.

"Are you crazy, Kate? You can't marry Evan! You don't love him!"

"I do love him, in my way. I'm not like you, Mom. I don't think I'm capable of loving a man the way you love Daddy."

"That's because you haven't met the right man!"

Kate smiled slowly. Had she finally met the right man?

Chapter Two

Kate passed under the hinged sign that identified the pub as "Walker's," into its low-ceilinged common room. It was dimly lit, smelled of beeswax and old wood mingled with a rich, smoky aroma she couldn't identify.

"Ailig, my boy! Welcome home!" The barman leaned over the counter and extended his hand to her Highland warrior, who pumped it heartily and addressed his greeter as Niall.

"Ailig," she murmured behind him, not to summon him but to feel his name on her lips. *Ailig*? He turned, though he couldn't possibly have heard her.

"Alec," he said, with a smile and a small bow. "Alec Lachlan."

"Kate," she said, her lips suddenly parched and

inflexible. She ran her tongue along them, but it was just as dry. "Katherine MacGillvray."

"Ah, MacGillvray," he said, as if this answered many questions.

He saluted Niall, then extended his arm to indicate that she should precede him. But as his hand grazed her back, she became dizzy again, found herself standing on legs as sturdy as rubber bands. She felt as if she was going to sink to the planked floor in a quivering, insensible heap.

"Let's sit down," he said, when she made no effort to move in the direction he had indicated.

"What?" Confusion.

Alec Lachlan shook his head in amusement, then pointed to a small table in front of the fireplace. She walked toward it, surprised, even as she reached it, that she had been able to cover the distance without falling on her face. She couldn't bring herself to sit down. What in the world was wrong with her? She sensed him standing behind her then, his hands hovering above her shoulders, and she jumped.

"May I take your coat?" he asked.

She swallowed. "Yes. Thank you." She shrugged it off and handed it to him, watched him hang it, and his own, on a hook near the window. When he turned and started back toward her, the room began to spin again. With each long stride he took, the thumping in her chest grew louder and more forceful. She clutched the back of the chair, squeezing until she was sure the old wood was going to splinter under her fingers. Pain. Conveyed along a lengthy pathway of nerves and synapses: brainstem to spinal cord to fingertip. Accompanied by the primitive survival reflex that jumps into overdrive in all mammals in the face of stress: excitation of the autonomic nervous system causing adrenaline release, causing a body-wide sensory high-alert. It was a reflex very appropriately called *fight or flight.* . . .

"Where are you going, MacGillvray?" he asked.

"What?"

"Sit down right here," he said, pulling out the chair and settling her into it in a decidedly custodial manner.

Niall delivered two glasses filled with sparkling amber liquid, retreating with a grin and a pleasantly spoken salutation that was completely incomprehensible to her! What was wrong with her?

"Where are you going?"

She shook her head. She had no idea.

"Slainte Mhath!" Alec offered, tilting his glass toward her before he took a sip from it, repeating the words the barkeep had spoken. "It means 'good health.' You don't speak Gaelic, I take it."

Gaelic! She sighed in relief and sank back down into her chair. She had been afraid she'd developed an inability to understand the spoken word. "Do many Scots speak Gaelic?" she managed.

"Not many," he answered. "Though I'm told it has enjoyed a resurgence of late, people rediscovering their roots, that sort of thing. My father insisted we learn it."

She nodded mutely.

"At one time, it was the language of the Highlands, but the English discouraged the speaking and teaching of it. After Culloden, they made it illegal to wear a kilt or own a tartan. It was all done in the name of assimilation. They also made it illegal to bear arms, though the reasoning behind that one was a bit more straightforward. We Scots are a feisty lot. They knew we were ever eager for a tussle and wanted us unarmed when we indulged ourselves.''

"You?" she croaked.

He leaned toward her, coming an inch closer, maybe less, but suddenly her teeth were chattering and she was sure he could hear them.

"The nature of the tussles has changed, Mac-Gillvray. I find more socially appropriate outlets for my feistiness," he said, pushing her glass toward her. "You're trembling and as pale as a sheet. I insist you drink that. For medicinal purposes, of course. Doctor's orders.''

She was on her feet again. Doctor's orders? It was a figure of speech, nothing more. She didn't want Alec Lachlan and Evan Hall to have anything at all in common! "You're not a physician, are you?" she begged.

"Guilty as charged," he answered. "I'm a general practitioner. I treat kiddies, old folks and everyone in between, I deliver a baby now and then, perform light surgery, in a pinch. I've just moved up from Edinburgh, though, and I'm in the middle of a couple of weeks off—to get settled.''

She groaned and dropped into her chair heavily.

"I share your opinion," he assured her. "I'm not overfond of physicians myself. Particularly female physicians . . .''

This last sentiment was spoken in a mumble as he hoisted his glass in what appeared to be another toast, then took a healthy swallow from it.

"A swing and a miss," she said.

"Pardon?"

She shook her head. It wasn't a good time for a discussion of baseball and its peculiar lingo. She lifted her own glass instead, swigging a mouthful of what it contained. She gagged and the Scotch cascaded onto the table in a great amber explosion.

"Whisky must be sipped, MacGillvray," he said blandly, blotting the table with the handkerchief he extracted from his pocket. "Like life."

"OK," she gasped, in embarrassment. She didn't feel like sipping either one at the moment, wished wildly that she could sink under the table and disappear. "So you don't approve of female doctors," she said, forcing herself to step up to the plate, ignoring her internal batting coach who was insisting she bunt.

Alec tilted his head, as if giving her question the consideration it deserved, then he answered: "I don't. I intend to avoid them like the plague, for the rest of my life."

"OK," she said again, lifting the whisky and gulping it. She could feel it burning its way down the right pipe this time, down her esophagus and into her stomach. But from there it was going straight to her head. She studied Alec over the rim of her glass. She wanted him, very badly, despite the fact that he was a physician, and a sexist one, at that. The heroes from the novels she had devoured as a teenager had all been sexist—sensual, brooding misogynists to a man. Although on an intellectual level women might despise them, on a more primitive one, deep inside, they found such men irresistible—sensual, brooding challenges just waiting to be shown the errors of their ways. But somehow, she doubted this one would be as easily swayed from his opinions as his storybook brethren.

What would Alec have said if she *had* told him about their similar calling, about her recent crisis of confidence and flight from the brotherhood of healing? *Women are no more cut out to be physicians than they are to be artillery gunners*, perhaps. Or, *it's against the laws of nature for women to act logically and decisively in an emergency*. Or even worse, *you must have had your period that day*. And then he probably would have avoided her, like the plague.

He didn't want to hear the truth.

She was suddenly very glad she had squelched the odd impulse that had insisted she tell him every bit of it, just a little while ago.

And they could undoubtedly find more interesting things to discuss, anyway. Was it this Highland warrior or the Scotch whisky that was filling her mind with words of surrender and promises of forever? She squeezed her eyes shut for a moment and savored the very explicit visual fantasy that played behind them. Her experience with men was modest, impoverished in fact, virtually limited to Evan. And she had never felt this way toward him. She opened her eyes. *Warrior or whisky*? she asked herself again, glancing from one to the other. In either case, she wasn't going to allow something as trivial as his dislike of his female colleagues to foil her investigation into this conundrum. "You were subjected to some kind of malpractice at the hands of a woman doctor, I presume. Took out your tonsils to cure a hangnail, right?"

"Her scalpel was directed a bit lower," he corrected.

Her gaze dropped to the table over his lap. "I see," she said, keeping a straight face with an effort.

He threw back his head and laughed. "She tried for those, MacGillvray, but I was too fast. The injury inflicted was to my heart."

"And you're still suffering?"

"Time heals all wounds. It only pains me now when I think about what I nearly got myself into. Fate had her play me false well before we reached the altar so I wouldn't be tempted to take a horsewhip to her afterwards."

"You don't look like a wife-beater."

"No? Well, I almost took it up at one time."

"There hasn't been anyone since?" she asked softly, hopefully.

"My humiliation occurred two years ago and we've already established that I'm not a eunuch. Of course there have been other women, more than a few of them, I'm afraid, but . . ."

"Yes?" she prompted.

He raised his glass. "Well, Tess did cure me of one thing. I'll never fall in love again. And I'll certainly never get married."

"Strike two," she muttered.

"What's that?"

She shook her head. "So you brought me here

because I appeared to need medical attention.''

"I approached you on the moor because you appeared to need medical attention. I brought you here because . . ."

She watched him carefully. The fire's light behind him made a copper halo of his hair. Its warmth had banished the chill from his skin, which now glowed bronze. "Yes?"

He narrowed his eyes. "Surely you possess a mirror, MacGillvray."

She raised a self-conscious hand to her disordered hair, glanced down at her oversized cableknit sweater. If a mirror were to magically appear in her hand right now, she would be afraid to look in it. But even at the best of times, she wasn't the kind of woman to whom men were drawn at first glance. She had what Evan called an *athletic build*; she had long-since decided this was a euphemism for a flat chest. Her eyes were a nondescript blue. Her hair was a nondescript light brown that could be upgraded to dirty blond with liberal highlighting. She couldn't remember the last time she'd had it highlighted. It was curly, unruly, and benefited greatly from skillful cutting, another luxury for which she hadn't found time in years. Instead she opted to draw it back with a barrette or scrunchie, or, when her patience with it ran out all together, to wield the scissors herself.

"Don't you care what you look like?"

Evan had been appalled by this last time-saving measure.

She cared very much what she looked like today for reasons that were as obvious to her as they were unfathomable.

37

"I liked the way you looked out there on the moor, like a woman from another time. Lost. Vulnerable. And very feminine."

So those were the traits he now required in his women. They weren't ones typically found in female physicians.

"There's something so honest about you. It's as if I can read what you're thinking by the expression on your face. Even before I spoke to you, I had the oddest sense that I could trust you with all my secrets."

What kind of secrets did he have? And why couldn't he read *hers* on her face? Evan had once made a similar observation about her inability to hide her thoughts.

"Don't play poker, Kate," he said, rolling onto his back and squeezing his eyes shut. "It requires a skill you'll never learn. It's called bluffing."

She suspected bluffing wasn't a skill she would need to cultivate with Alec Lachlan. "I'm not into swooning," she assured him.

"What are you *into*?" he asked, leaning across the table again.

"Musical theater. The Phillies—they're a baseball team. Szechuan food," she mumbled. And a bona fide, full-fledged nervous breakdown! She was hyperventilating, panting like a dog in a heat wave, and her cheeks felt as if they were on fire.

"It has been a long time since I've seen a woman blush."

It was probably longer since she had done so. Blushing: the rush of blood into the superficial capillaries of the malar prominences, cheekbones, in response to a stimulation of the autonomic nervous system by stress, excitement, desire. Or all of the above.

She took another sip of whisky as she watched humor flicker across his fine features, creasing the corners of his eyes. What was going on? She really was behaving as if she were demented, or incompetent, or falling in love.

"You've never acted like a woman in love."

"How do women in love act?"

Evan had raised his shoulders, she recalled, not yet ready to expound on his latest experience with the species.

"I'm told they giggle. And blush. And look at their men longingly. They can't wait to get them into bed. . . ."

Right again, Evan. She had never done any of those things. Until today.

What would Freud say about the odd symptoms she was experiencing? Kate found herself summoning up her med school psychiatry. *Psychoanalytic theory holds that if the root of a symptom can be explained, the symptom will disappear.* It was worth a shot. "Do you know the Willie Nelson song 'My Heroes Have Always Been Cowboys'?"

Alec considered this with a baffled expression. "I think so," he said.

"Well, my heroes have always been Highlanders."

"Ah, cut your teeth on tales of Rob Roy MacGregor, did you?"

She nodded. "And I love *Brigadoon.*"

"Brigadoon?"

"It's a Scottish village that appears for one day every hundred years."

"Is it around here?"

"You know, it's a musical. It had a long run on Broadway, before I was born, of course. But I must have seen the movie version two dozen times. In it, Gene Kelly plays Tommy, an American businessman who happens upon Brigadoon on the morning it appears. As soon as he steps into town, his past and the future he had planned fade away—he forgets about his high-pressure job and his selfish, shallow fiancée. He falls in love with a beautiful woman named Fiona—Cyd Charisse—who lives there. They spend an incredible day together, singing, dancing, picking heather, that sort of thing."

"That's my idea of a good time," Alec agreed.

"Anyway, he finds himself living the day from moment to moment—as if it's the first one of his life and the last. But at nightfall, the local wise man, Mr. Lundie, tells him it's time to decide whether he wants to stay forever, or return to America and never see Brigadoon again."

"What a dilemma," Alec said. "Ah, well, there's a Mr. Lundie at every party, no?"

"I guess so." This was getting her nowhere fast. She took a long draught from her glass. But the whisky was tasting better and getting easier to swallow with each mouthful.

"Sip it. You're a slip of a girl, but I don't relish the idea of having to carry you back to your car on the off chance you're up to driving it."

"There are no cars in Brigadoon."

"This is Inverness. You're daft or drunk, Mac-Gillvray."

"One or the other," she agreed, abandoning her quest for other explanations and draining her glass.

Kate managed to walk back to the car without having to be hoisted into her Highland warrior's arms, though she toyed with the idea of faking a swoon to encourage him to do it. Her personality had certainly undergone a make-over. She was blushing, giggling. She couldn't wait to get Alec into bed. She longed to touch him, to have him touch her. And the future she had planned, the flashbacks that had been dogging her since Tuesday, had all but faded away.

"Are you sure you want to drive?" he asked.

She looked at the car, then back at him. It wouldn't be right to prolong this interlude with a lie, though she seemed to recall a truth or two she already should have mentioned. How was she going to keep Alec Lachlan from vanishing like the fleeting fantasy of Brigadoon? Short of throwing herself at his ankles and hanging on for dear life, she had no idea. If he was really the man she had been waiting for all her life, fate would intervene on her behalf, she decided finally. Heaven would give her a sign. It would happen as magically, as inexplicably, as everything else had today, as everything was supposed to happen in places like Brigadoon. *You're a scientist*, she reminded herself. "I want to drive. Can I drop you somewhere?"

"I'll just walk. May I take you out to dinner tonight?"

He seemed to mistake her surprised glance toward the sky as an indication of indecision.

"I'll wear my kilt," he coaxed.

"Yes!"

He laughed. "I'll call for you at seven."

She watched him stride away, realizing only then that she hadn't told him where she was staying. She started to call out, but stopped herself before she spoke his name. Fate would no doubt draw him a road map.

The Munro House was an old Georgian inn south-west of Inverness. It was luxurious, the amenities were modern, but it had the ambiance of a more gracious time. Kate paused at its wrought-iron gate, admiring its smoke-gray roof against the steel-gray sky. She crossed the front lawn slowly, surveying the burlap-covered flower beds, guessing they would be magnificent in bloom. Masses of thorny branches grew up around the building's foundation, suggesting that its weathered bricks would be decked in roses in a few months' time. She would love to see this place in the summer. But she wouldn't be able to finagle a summertime vacation for the rest of her career if she continued on the course she had laid out for herself. New residents started every July. If she left them to their own devices during their first few months in the E.R., all hell would break loose.

She had fought death, tooth and nail, on many occasions. She had immediately acknowledged its preeminence on many others. She could spot it at ten paces. This time, she could also see it reflected in the eyes of the hardened middle-aged cop and the

*tiny teenage girl who flanked the stretcher on which
the lifeless boy lay. The girl's face was beautiful and
exquisitely sad under the coarse woman's makeup
that covered it; her voice was filled with guilt and
grief as she repeated the same words, over and over:
"It's my fault he's dead. He wanted to paint, not
fight. He joined the Huns to prove himself to me."*

The flashbacks had returned.

She hurried into the hotel, waving to its loqua-
cious proprietor, Mrs. Munro, as she crossed the
wood-paneled entry hall, hoping to forestall a
conversation.

"There's tea in the front sitting room, Miss
MacGillvray," the landlady called, trying to catch
up.

Kate suspected another whisky might be more the
thing. She dashed up the stairs to her room, neatly
evading her pursuer, then into her bathroom, turned
on the tub's hot tap, and sprinkled the inn's com-
plimentary scented salts under the gushing stream of
water before she removed her coat. Suddenly the
room was filled with the smell of what was alleged
to be Highland wildflowers. She took a deep breath,
hoping to ease the tension in her neck and shoulders.
Aromatherapy. Then she heard the music. Bagpipes.
The Munro House featured a piper on the lawn
everyday at sunset, she recalled from the brochure
her travel agent had shown her. She sighed. Bagpipes always made her emotional.

*"I've given up trying to break through your suit
of armor to get at a little emotion,"* Evan said.

She had experienced emotion enough for any two

women during the past few days: self-doubt, panic, fear . . .

Lust!

A small smile curled her lips as she recalled the intensity with which she had experienced that last one this afternoon. Perhaps she didn't suffer from some rare neurological-psychiatric syndrome that prevented her from responding sexually, some neurotransmitter deficiency in her limbic cortex, aggravated by faulty toilet training and her parochial schooling, that rendered her incapable of feeling passion.

"Your rigid Scottish forebears have done their worst by you, Kate. You don't enjoy sex much, do you?"

"It's pleasant."

"Is that all?"

"I'm frigid, Evan! Go ahead and say it! I hear you not saying the word every time we make love."

"A man likes to feel his woman melt under him. He wants to have his back gouged with her nails as she screams his name! Can you understand that, Katie?"

She hadn't understood it.

"I'm in love with Jenna."

She had laughed in distress and disbelief, feeling this betrayal more keenly than the sexual ones Evan had already acknowledged, glancing around the medical staff lounge to make sure none of his nosy students had hung back to witness her mortification.

"Let me guess. She melts under you and screams your name as she gouges your back with her nails!"

"Yes! Maybe someday you'll find someone who can make you feel that way."

Evan's reply had started on a contrite note, but had ended on a bitter, accusing one.

"Can you even imagine feeling that way?"

She finished undressing, leaving the discarded clothes in an uncharacteristically careless heap in the middle of the room. She shut the window, but couldn't shut out the music. She went into the bathroom, sank into the tub, guessing she wouldn't be any more successful at shutting down the relentless camcorder in her head that kept replaying the same scenes, over and over. The image that greeted her was unexpectedly pleasant, however, and she smiled again. Alec Lachlan. She could see him as clearly now as she had an hour ago. She dropped a finger through the fragrant suds over her thigh, sketched the line of his profile there, relaxing as the water lapped softly, rhythmically, against her belly in answer. Then suddenly her breasts felt heavier and her nipples were hardening into tight little nubs.

"Can you even imagine feeling that way?"

She hadn't been able to imagine it, then. But here, in a bathtub by herself, three thousand miles away from the man who had framed that all-important question, she could more than imagine it. She could sense it lurking just beyond the scope of her vision, just outside the partially open door. She could feel it tugging at her, jolting her upright, encouraging her fingertip to venture up to caress it. . . .

She could hear it rumbling inside her, swelling toward full volume and screeching, like the bagpipes.

But then she balked, with uncertainty and something close to fear. She settled back in the tub with a groan of disappointment, leaving herself aching and tremulous. And very surprised.

Kate had packed only one outfit that might be considered remotely suitable for a first date because she hadn't imagined she would need one. Though the events of this afternoon remained something of a blur, she had no doubt that Alec would be taking her out to dinner tonight and that she would look devastating when he arrived to do so.

She touched the lightweight wool suit reverently. It had cost her a month's salary. It was black, distinguished by the simplicity of its lines, by the quality of its fabric. Its skirt was short and tight. Its jacket was long and sleek. She donned delicate black hose and a lacy silk camisole. She pulled on the skirt, smoothed it down over her hips. She eased into the jacket, buttoned up the placket. She slipped her feet into black high-heeled pumps.

She regarded her reflection in the mirror on the inside of the closet door. She seemed to possess new curves tonight, and she felt no need to disguise the subtle valley of her décolletage with the blouse she had bought to serve that purpose. Her hair was drying into a cloud of curls, but for once she liked the feel of it, heavy and soft on her shoulders, and she decided to wear it loose. She applied mascara and lipstick with a light touch, but it was more than her usual none-at-all. There was a glow on her cheeks that made blusher unnecessary. And there was something in her expression that hadn't been there when she brushed her teeth this morning.

She took the small square of tissue paper out of the drawer. She held it in the palm of her hand for a moment before she unfolded it. Then she studied the pin she had uncovered for much longer. It was a filigree circle pin, in heavy beaten silver. She ran her finger over its worn, intricate pattern. It had been a gift from Gram, handed down two days ago, just before Kate boarded the plane bound for Scotland.

"It's very old, Katie, two hundred years old, at least. My grandmother gave it to me on my wedding day and her grandmother gave it to her on her wedding day."

"It's a pity I'm your only granddaughter. I'll never have a wedding day."

Kate had felt very sorry for herself as she stood at the boarding gate Wednesday morning and bid her family farewell. She had seen the uncertainty in her mother's eyes, the confusion in her father's. Only Gram, who knew all the details of her granddaughter's harrowing past eighteen hours, had behaved as if Kate was embarking on the greatest adventure of her life, rather than fleeing Philadelphia with the demons of perdition nipping at her heels.

"I'm giving it to you now, Katie. Every woman who has worn it has been lucky in love. I believe it will lead you to your heart mate."

Had it?

The filigree was not simply an interesting design, Kate realized suddenly. There were words formed by the cutouts in the silver and they ran continuously around the brooch's perimeter. *"Fortis et Fidus."*

She traced the words with her fingernail, attempting to recall her high school Latin. "*Fortis*: strong, brave or courageous. *Fidus*: faithful," she murmured finally. Brave and faithful.

She pinned it to her lapel quickly, grabbed her wrap and handbag, descended to the inn's elaborate but comfortable sitting room. She sank into the large couch in front of the fireplace. She glanced at the slender gold watch on her wrist. The clock on the mantel chimed seven times.

"Ah, MacGillvray."

Fate was punctual. She stood up, keeping her eyes focused on the fire. She turned to him slowly, afraid her face might betray the secret she had learned this afternoon. She met his green eyes finally. She held her breath as she let her gaze drop to his broad shoulders, cloaked by a gray tweed jacket, to travel down his starched white shirt-front to his kilt. She struggled not to stare at his sporran. She was panting by the time she viewed his knees. And she was trembling before she got past strong calves, under beige knee-socks, a flash of ribbon under their folded tops, to his feet, which were shod in what looked like black wing-tips, without the tongues, their laces tied around his ankles. "Nice shoes," she said.

"Ghillies," he offered, with a smile and a shrug. "You look lovely."

"And you . . ." She looked up into his eyes again. Yearning.

"And I?"

"You look magnificent," she answered softly. There was no point in being circumspect with a man she intended to seduce, whose ghillies she hoped to find under her bed in the morning.

"Like Gene Kelly?"

"He was the American businessman. He never wore a kilt."

"Ah," he said, nodding in understanding. "And how long did he have before the whole thing disappeared?"

"One day."

"Then we'd better get going, MacGillvray."

The huge cashmere shawl was an extravagance Kate hadn't been able to pass up during her brief stopover in Edinburgh. It was exquisitely soft and warm and brightly hued in the blazing MacGillvray plaid. She watched Alec pick it up off the back of the couch. It would be impossible for him to drape it around her without touching her. . . . He handed it to her with a smile, with careful fingers that came nowhere near her own. Yet as she flung it around her shoulders, she could feel the heat from the place where he had held it, and it was as if his long, slender fingers were touching her just beneath her left collarbone. She sighed audibly, then coughed to cover the sound.

"Recovered from this afternoon's excitement, are you?" he asked.

She felt her face flush in the moment before she realized he was referring to her visit to Culloden. He didn't know that her afternoon had been filled with excitement, and she hadn't recovered from any of it.

"I hope you're hungry," he said.

"I'm starving," she said, more aware of the aching emptiness inside her than she had ever been of anything, more aware of the large man at her side than she had ever been of anyone.

"I know where we can remedy that nicely. And afterwards, there's a lovely place I want you to see."

"Is it near here?" she asked.

"Aye. But I'm afraid it's as close to Brigadoon as I can take you."

He drove a Range Rover, very fast. The vehicle was solid and heavy, sure-footed, a latter-day warrior's stallion. She watched his profile, straight-nosed and proud, his eyes narrowed as they intently scanned the road ahead of him, his full lips pressed into a pensive line. She groaned when his hand suddenly dove for the stick shift between them, easing it down and toward her expertly. His stallion answered with a low-pitched whinny. She watched his hand in the flickering light supplied by other people's headlights. She longed to reach forward and lay her own hand over it, softly, quickly, just long enough to feel his pulse beating in it. Now! It moved back to the steering wheel.

The road was deserted now, the car a dimly lit island in the endless blackness. Where was he taking her? Did she care? "I'd go to the ends of the earth with you," she whispered with certainty. Or stay in Brigadoon. Forever.

"What was that, MacGillvray?" he asked, keeping his eyes fixed on the road.

"It's like the end of the earth here," she murmured. She saw the corner of his mouth twitch in answer.

50

"It's off the beaten track, as you Americans say."

Two hundred and fifty years off the beaten track, she guessed.

A car bore down on them from the opposite direction, lighting his face and the folds of tartan that covered his thighs—a bold plaid, dark stripes on a red background, much like her own. She grinned. Despite the many miles and generations that separated her from such a claim to clan allegiance it had occurred to her quite naturally. And she thought of the man at her side as her own despite the briefness of their acquaintance and his earlier assertion that he would never belong to a woman, in love or marriage. Well, she would make him hers tonight, she decided with a resolute nod, in whatever way he would allow. Or she would die trying.

Chapter Three

Alec pulled into a graveled parking lot outside a single-story building with a roof of well-maintained thatch. Candlelight flickered through the lace curtains at its windows. Soft music greeted Kate's ears as he helped her out of the car with a quick, light touch. She looked up into his eyes, gray in the dim starlight, in the soft light from the windows behind him.

"Brigadoon?" she asked.

"Later," he said, gesturing her onward.

As they neared the building's door, the rich savory smell of onions and herbs and carefully cooked fish filled her nostrils.

He held the door open and she stepped through it. A handsome middle-aged man in a kilt rushed forward to greet them.

"Welcome home, Ailig!" the man said, hugging her Highland warrior familiarly.

"I've missed you, Aonghas," Alec said.

"Well, you won't be wandering off again."

"No, I won't be," Alec said. He turned to her. "This is my uncle, Angus Campbell. Uncle Angus, this is Kate MacGillvray."

"*Allo, a* Cheit," Angus said, bowing.

"Aloha," Kate improvised. "Is this your restaurant?" She looked past him into the beautifully appointed dining room.

Angus followed her gaze proudly. "It's mine. I've saved a special table for the two of you."

They followed him to a table in front of the fireplace, comfortably removed from the musicians who were playing at the opposite side of the room. The table was draped in crisp white linen. Candlelight heightened the luster of the silverware and crystal that adorned it. Angus held out a tall tapestry covered chair and pushed it in when Kate was seated. She thanked him with a smile, shrugged off her shawl.

"American, are you?" Angus asked.

"Yes," she answered.

"Staying awhile?"

Forever. She glanced across the table at Alec, who was seated now and watching her carefully. "A week," she said. *Forever.*

"Well, I hope you're enjoying your holiday."

"I am," she assured him.

She saw an indecipherable glance pass between Alec and his uncle before the latter bowed and backed away.

"He's the second person I've heard welcome you back. You're from around here?"

Alec nodded. "I was born and raised about three kilometers from here—my brother and his family, and my mother, still live there. I came back for my father's funeral six months ago, and I decided I didn't want to leave. So I returned to Edinburgh to clean up my affairs. And now, I'm back to stay."

"I'm sorry about your father," she offered.

"I'm sorry too. He was a good father, strong and loving. It was quick and unexpected, a heart attack. He died the way he would have wanted to, in his wife's arms. I wish I had been there, though. They say the only thing harder than watching someone you love die, is not watching it." Then he smiled. "He would have liked you, MacGillvray."

"How do you know?"

"I like you."

She was blushing again. "Was your father a physician?"

"He was a farmer."

"But he wanted you to be a doctor?"

"He often pointed out the advantages of a career in veterinary medicine. He was a practical man."

Angus arrived with a bottle of white wine, which he opened and poured out with a flourish before discreetly disappearing.

Alec raised his glass. "To Brigadoon," he offered.

"To Brigadoon," she agreed, gulping the wine, finding it to be dry, woodsy and quite delicious.

"Sip it, MacGillvray," he said.

She nodded, took a long sip. She looked away

self-consciously, toward the solitary couple who
were dancing, holding each other close, moving together rhythmically, easily, alone in a room full of
people. She wanted Alec to hold her in his arms.
She needed to touch him. She looked back at him,
watched him take off his jacket, revealing broad
shoulders and firm biceps muscles covered by white
broadcloth. She realized that she was staring.

"It's warm in here," he explained.

"Hot," she murmured, feeling her blush deepen.
The tone of her voice seemed to have stepped up an
octave. "Do you dance?"

He grinned, glanced toward the dance floor. "I'm
no Gene Kelly."

She laughed, took another sip of wine. "You
know, I've never had a problem accepting the prem-
ise that Brigadoon disappears for a hundred years at
a stretch and all its citizens wake up in a new century
feeling as if it's the next day. I've never had a problem believing that every one of them is kind and
decent and blissfully happy. I've never even flinched
when Mr. Lundie says, 'If you love someone
enough, anything is possible,' and he must say it ten
times during the course of the movie."

"Ah," Alec said.

"But the last time I watched *Brigadoon,* I had a
hard time believing Fiona could fall in love with
Gene Kelly at first sight."

He threw back his head and laughed. It was a
joyous sound, full and uninhibited. "Not your type,
eh?"

"I must admit I had a shameless crush on him as
a teenager."

He leaned toward her and she shivered in the warmth of the room, like someone with a spiking fever. "What's your type now, MacGillvray?"

She gulped her wine for fortification. *You. A Highland warrior. Tall and strong. In a kilt.* "At this point in my life, I suppose I'm attracted to men who are a bit more macho. I'd take a soldier over a sashayer, any day."

He narrowed his eyes. "A soldier? Leaves me out of the running, then. The objectives of soldier and healer are diametrically opposed. I'm a peaceful man."

"Are you?"

He raised his shoulders, but there was something close to a denial in the movement, something strong, driving, vital, the promise of a conquest that was as violent as it was removed from violence.

"And it's just possible, MacGillvray," he continued, "that on some fine day, the man of your dreams will appear out of the mist. He might not be what every woman would consider the finest example of manhood on the face of the earth, but you'll know he's the one for you. And you'll never be the same again."

She froze in her chair. She didn't know she had been holding her breath until it escaped in a soft gasp. She had seen him appear out of the mist this afternoon and she had known, somehow, that he was the man she had been dreaming of all her life.

"Trust me. Stranger things have happened," he said, his tone matter-of-fact.

But not to her. Alec Lachlan undoubtedly spoke from experience, an experience that had soured him on commitment. But she would have him tonight, in the only way he might ever allow her to have him. He was cynical and well defended, with nothing to give her but the heat of his body, with a heart so thoroughly bandaged that nothing could seep into it, or out, but perhaps it would be enough. At least, she would have the memories of tonight to warm her through all the cold days ahead. "I trust you," she said.

Their food was delivered pleasantly and competently by a handsome young waiter, also in a kilt. They ate soft, sweet cheese baked in a pastry crust and delicate fillets of smoked trout. There was a stew of lamb and tiny onions, redolent with wine and fresh rosemary. They sipped French chardonnay and chatted easily, laughed often, as if they had known each other for a long time. After the main course was cleared away, Alec leaned back in his chair, unbuttoned his cuffs and rolled his shirt sleeves midway up his forearms, revealing auburn hair over bronzed skin over finely delineated muscle. He laid one arm on the table, fingers flirting with the midpoint that couldn't have been more clear had it been painted on the linen. She watched his strong fingers open and close, hypnotically. Beckoning . . .

"Tell me about yourself, MacGillvray."

The spell was broken. She looked up in confusion. "What?"

"Tell me about yourself," he repeated. Slowly and distinctly.

"What do you want to know?"

"Everything."

She guessed her face was reflecting the horror that was knotting her stomach because he laughed, shook his head, then narrowed his request down considerably. "How old are you?"

"I'll be thirty on my next birthday."

"Which is when?"

"June 15th." *That's two weeks before the end of my residency, if I can work up the nerve to go back and finish it. I'm on the short list to become Assistant Director of Emergency Services come July, which is a great job, if I can work up the nerve to go back. . . .*

"Ah, a Gemini. And an older woman. I won't be thirty until the beginning of August."

She nodded. He was a Leo. A lion. Fearless and strong. King of the jungle. He would never run scared from the work he was trained to perform.

"What kind of research do you do?" he asked.

"Research?" She coughed. "Medical. I work in a large university teaching hospital," she managed finally. Withholding the whole truth was different from telling a lie. Wasn't it?

"Ah. So we have something in common."

Something more than he suspected. "Yes."

"Comfortable with doctors, are you?"

She lowered her eyes and nodded. "My brother Dale is a surgeon. The other, Colin, is a flutist with the Symphony—he takes after my mother, who is an accomplished pianist. My father is a pediatrician." *Dad encouraged me to be a doctor, too, when it became clear that I had inherited his tin ear and steel nerves. I can still hear him bragging about my mettle. "My baby girl has guts," he always said. I couldn't bring myself to tell him how wrong I proved him that last day. I made my grandmother promise not to tell him. . . .*

"Alexander MacGillvray," Alec said, remembering.

"Yes. His friends call him 'Sandy.' His patients call him 'Dr. Sandy.' "

"I'll have to marry you, MacGillvray."

She stared at him, her discomfiture abandoned on the banks of the warm, caressing quicksand pool into which she was suddenly sinking.

"I've heard that doctors' daughters make the best doctors' wives."

"I've never heard that," she whispered.

He grinned. "I imagine there's quite a bit I could teach you."

He had already taught her something today. He had taught her that she could ache for a man, that she could burn for a man. Without laying a hand on her, he had taught her that his body and hers would be complementary, curve for curve, and that the unexpected sensations she had experienced in the bathtub this afternoon could be duplicated, and intensified, in his arms. Her shoulders moved back, just a bit, as if of their own volition, forcing her breasts forward slightly, forcing the shadow between them to his attention. She saw his gaze drop to it, saw his tongue touch his lips for just an instant before he met her eyes again.

"MacGillvray," he murmured, extending a rescuing hand, palm side up, toward her, ready to yank her back from the brink, onto familiar, solid, unyielding earth.

She studied the creases on his palm, wishing she could read his future and her own there, wishing she could alter the future that was surely etched there. Then slowly, tentatively, she curled her fingers through his and he lifted her hand off the table, drew it toward his mouth, kissed it. She realized, as it was happening, that her savior was only hastening her demise, that her heart had stopped beating, that the quicksand had flowed into her mouth and she had stopped breathing the instant his lips touched her skin.

"I want you." His voice was gruff. "I want you more than I can ever remember wanting a woman."

The words felt dry and slurred in her mouth, confused in her brain. "I'm yours," she gasped. *Forever.*

He signaled the waiter.

Angus had pressed a flat wicker basket on them before they departed, speaking a word Kate hadn't understood. "Leftovers," Alec had explained. It was sitting on the back seat of the car that was once again hurtling forward into the night. There was a gentle intimacy between them now, a fragile bond composed of the words they had spoken, and the ones they hadn't, forged by a hand-kiss that had been as brief as it was passionate. They pulled off the road and stopped abruptly. Where were they? she wondered, as she peered through the car window, found no clues. All she could see was shadows in the blackness.

He was out of the car and opening her door in an instant. He leaned across her to reach the glove com-

partment at her knees and extracted a large flashlight.

Where in the world were they?

He helped her out of the car. He took off his jacket
and draped it around her shoulders. Then he gripped
her hand firmly in one of his, held the flashlight forward with the other. The light cleared a narrow trail
in front of them. The ground was uneven, littered
with small stones and hard clods of earth. She faltered several times, but Alec was there to steady her,
to urge her on. Finally, a large gray mass loomed
before them.

"Come on, then, MacGillvray," he said, shining
the beam on a rough wooden door, pushing it open,
pulling her through it.

It was even darker inside the structure, if such a
thing was possible, and colder. She hugged his
jacket and the shawl under it around her. The only
part of her that was warm was the hand he had so
recently surrendered. She touched it to her chilled
cheek. "Alec," she called, suddenly feeling alone,
without a reference point, hearing a rustling noise
behind her. Why had she come here without a question, without a moment's hesitation? She was God
knows where, with God knows who, and his intentions were . . . Seduction? Then they were of a like
mind. Madcap and impetuous. Yearning.

"Here," he said.

She heard a match being struck. She watched the
light of a small lantern move in the darkness. She
followed it to another lantern, then to a tall brace of
candles. Then the room was filled with pale yellow

light. She saw Alec kneel down in front of an ancient fireplace.

"I heard something behind me," she managed.

He looked up and past her. "Mice, probably," he said.

Mice! She stifled a small shriek and hurried toward the fireplace on her tiptoes.

He looked up from his task and grinned. "Afraid of mice, are you?"

She raised her shoulders. Terrified was closer to an accurate description of her attitude toward them. Alexander MacGillvray's brave baby girl had grown into a nervous wreck.

"I have a foolproof way of ridding a house of vermin, MacGillvray. Do you have a bit of paper and a Biro in your bag?"

She considered this in confusion, then opened her bag, ripped a page out of her address book. Biro? Well, unless he was planning to eat the paper, she had to assume he meant to write on it. She handed him a pen. He watched her for a moment and she could see the corners of his mouth twitch mischievously as he laid the paper on the stone at his knees and began to write. A moment later, he passed it to her.

She squinted at it in the dim light. " 'Ratton and moose, awa' frae the hoose, awa' ower tae the mill, an' there tak' yer fill!' " she read aloud, in disbelief.

He bowed his head. "Now lay it on the floor, MacGillvray, and you'll have nothing to worry about."

"Mice can't read!" she laughed.

"The literacy rate in Scotland is very high," he

said, turning back to the kindling and logs he was piling on the grate. She grinned happily as she looked down on his broad shoulders, followed the line of his spine to his kilt. She allowed herself to consider his backside, the powerful gluteal muscles hidden, but somehow not disguised, by this drape; then her gaze drifted down to his stockinged calves against the rough floorboards. He lit the fire and stood up, his body uncoiling, his muscles rippling as he did so. He brushed his sooty hands on his tartan plaid and looked into the fire for a moment before he turned.

"You'll be warm soon," he said.

She was feeling warmer already.

His eyes were embracing her, stripping away her defenses, searching for the truth inside her. She was dizzy again, and breathless. She broke away from his gaze reluctantly and scanned the room, which seemed to be made entirely of whitewashed plaster, in crying need of more whitewash. The ceiling was low and dark and beamed. The few pieces of furniture were of grossly disparate style, but seemed to belong together: the massive, ancient sideboard against the west wall, a lantern burning atop it; the broad and deep couch in front of the fireplace, fashioned from bright, polished wood and covered with pillows in a Native American motif; the tall, silver pole topped with an elaborately crafted candelabrum, footed in tiny, silver animal claws. There was a long table against the east wall, dipping precariously at one side, its finish gouged and chipped between the large boxes that had been piled atop it. There was another lantern hanging on a wrought-iron hook near the door through which they had entered.

She met his eyes again. "Whose house is this?" she asked.

"It's mine," he answered.

The room was warm in a few minutes, cozy in fact, and Kate discarded her wraps, settled down into the comfortable couch and watched the blazing fire. Alec appeared with two fine crystal glasses shimmering with amber liquid. Scotch. She knew the color and smell of it now, and she took a tiny taste from the glass he handed her.

"Do you have a boyfriend back at home, MacGillvray?" he asked, sitting down beside her, not looking at her.

"Not anymore. Evan left me for a buxom redhead earlier this week."

"So you decided to run off to Scotland to ease your broken heart."

Evan had wounded nothing more vital than her pride, she realized in that moment. If her heart had been badly damaged by Evan's betrayal, it wouldn't have healed so quickly, so thoroughly, during the hours since she'd met Alec Lachlan. She studied his profile. "How do you know I wasn't planning this trip for a year?"

He raised his shoulders. "I just know it. You're strong-willed, MacGillvray. And passionate. You decided to do it and you did it. Am I wrong?"

"No," she said, returning her attention to her drink. Strong-willed and passionate? Evan would disagree with that assessment. But Evan's opinions were no longer of much importance.

"Was he your first?"

She gagged on the sip of whisky she had just swallowed. "My first?"

"Your first lover," he said softly.

She grinned, felt her face begin to burn. "Technically, he was the second. I had a good friend in college, Tim. One evening we were sitting around lamenting about being the only two virgins in the Ivy League, so we decided to remedy it."

"Where did you go to school?"

"University of Pennsylvania." Undergraduate.

"Ah, Penn. I've heard it's a good school," he said. "What was your major?"

"Biochemistry."

"A scientist," he said. "So what happened with Tim?"

She raised her glass to her lips, then thought better of risking another sip. "Well, it was the blind leading the blind, I suppose. But by the next morning, we weren't so innocent. And I don't think we ever spoke to each other again."

He laughed. "You're still innocent. Again, don't ask me how I know it, but I do. You lost your hymen to Tim. You lost your self-confidence to Evan, perhaps. Neither one touched your innocence. Or your heart."

The sound of his laughter rumbled between her thighs. The glowing warmth from the Scotch fled her stomach, settled in the same place. "I don't know what you're talking about," she murmured, guessing she really did. "I haven't been a virgin for quite some time."

"I guess it all depends on how one defines virginity," he said. "Have you ever lost control with a man, MacGillvray? Have you ever stopped knowing where you ended and he began? Have you ever been taken out of yourself?"

"No," she gasped. And she had never clawed a man's back with her nails as she screamed his name.

He laid his finger on her hand. "When I touch you, the sensation is conveyed along peripheral nerves to your spinal cord and up your spinal cord to your brain, where it is processed and experienced. Your response is conveyed back down the spinal cord and along the peripheral nerves. . . ." His finger moved up to rest on her forehead. "This is your most important sexual organ," he finished.

"Is it?" she asked breathlessly, closing her eyes as his finger slowly traced the line of her nose, then briefly settled against her lips.

"The true barrier of innocence resides between the ears, not the legs."

She looked up at him now. "Does it?"

"You've got to want to lose it, you've got to be ready to lose it . . ." he began. Then he chuckled. "Women and men are built differently. . . ."

"No! I wish I'd consulted a doctor about this sooner."

He turned toward her, putting one bent knee on the couch between them. She glanced down at the narrow expanse of furred leg between kilt hem and stocking top. He certainly was built differently! The kilt emphasized the long quadriceps muscles in his thighs in a way his trousers hadn't. *What does a Scotsman wear under his kilt?* she asked herself silently, considering the oft-repeated question, but now it wasn't rhetorical, or amusing. She couldn't stop thinking about what Alec Lachlan was *not* wearing under his kilt. And she was suddenly more aware of the thinness and smoothness of her own legs, and of the delicate black nylon that covered the place where they met.

His grin was sheepish. "Women are rarely fully awakened the first time they make love. Many aren't fully awakened the thousandth." He sighed. "You must let it swallow you whole, MacGillvray. And it requires a certain . . ."

"Yes?"

"A certain angle, a certain posture. The man must have a certain . . ."

His bare knee touched her wool-covered thigh for an instant and she swallowed a groan.

". . . awareness."

Her cheeks were blazing and she was suddenly, painfully shy. She had been quite ready to seduce him, but now that he had become the seducer, she felt unsure, hesitant. Frightened. And she was bothered by his unspoken contention that his experience with women was so vast, he was qualified to make blanket statements about their sexuality. She didn't want to be one of dozens. She couldn't bear the idea that Alec had ever touched another woman.

"You've already assured me that you possess the necessary equipment, Alec, but do you possess the necessary awareness?" she asked, with forced bravado.

"I don't know, MacGillvray."

She met his eyes in surprise. There was no arrogance in his voice now, and the smile that curled his lips was wry.

"You don't hang around ancient battle sites looking for tourists who have never lost control so that you can help them do it?"

He laughed. "Lord, no."

She couldn't resist pressing her advantage. "So men are much more fortunate than women. The first time or the thousandth, it's the same."

He studied her face. "No, it's not. A man can usually reach a climax whenever, and with whomever, he chooses. But it's probably even more difficult for him to lose control than it is for a woman. Maybe in my own way, I'm as innocent as you."

"It takes one to know one," she quipped, but there was no humor in her voice. The raw desire she saw on his face wasn't funny.

"I always believed I'd recognize the woman who could do it for me at first glance. I always thought something in my brain would click when I laid my eyes on her—a distortion of the senses, ringing bells, flashing lights, the sensation of spinning, falling. . . . I always supposed it was chemical. Like pheromones in animals. Do you know that the olfactory cortex in the brains of lower mammals is more highly developed than ours, making them more sensitive to the secretions of sexually receptive animals of their kind? Perhaps human beings haven't totally lost that faculty, maybe it has simply become more refined, more selective."

It was an interesting idea, but not a very romantic one. He was cynical indeed. Though hadn't she blamed her synapses for the symphony of bells and whistles she had experienced this afternoon? She had since amended that theory. She didn't know what it was, but she was certain it *wasn't* anything that could be named, quantified or synthetically duplicated in a laboratory. "Tess didn't do it for you?"

He shook his head. "She always claimed I was aloof, afraid of intimacy. She attempted to draw me closer by making me jealous, by going off with another man, a good friend of mine. But that just hurt me, made me walk away and never look back."

She considered this. It was a story very similar to her own. And it was maddening to want to get closer to a person who wouldn't allow you any closer, she supposed. Maddening, humiliating and frustrating. She didn't blame Evan for dumping her. What made her so sure it would be different with this man?

"Perhaps that kind of light show means you're falling in love . . ." she ventured softly, needing to say it out loud, surprised to hear such a statement coming from her own lips.

He took a long sip of his whisky, appeared to be weighing the merits of her idea. Then he shook his head. "Only in Brigadoon," he said with a snort.

The warmth of the fire, the depth and softness of the cushions on the couch, the wine, the whisky and the lateness of the hour all contributed to the drowsiness that suddenly overwhelmed her, that rendered her eyelids too heavy to hold open. For all his rather explicit discussion of the rapture she might find in his arms, her Highland warrior hadn't even kissed her lips. And now she was only dimly aware of settling back against his chest, of having his sinewy forearms lock around her while his lips touched her hair. As if from a great distance, she could hear his soft voice saying: "Sleep."

"What about my awakening?" she murmured, struggling to sentience the way one struggles to the surface of a swimming pool after a deep dive, amid a distortion of time and perception. Her voice sounded as if she were speaking through water.

He chuckled. She could feel the vibration of it against her back. "You have to be awake to be awakened. Besides, being awakened abruptly isn't often a pleasant sensation."

She knew that. She had been awakened by ringing telephones and buzzing beepers many times during the past six years.

"I intend to do it slowly," he continued. "I don't intend to consummate our relationship until we find we have no other choice."

"How will you know when it's time?" she whispered.

"You'll tell me, MacGillvray. You'll tell me."

Chapter Four

Kate awoke to sunlight pouring through a latticed window. Alec was asleep, sprawled into the corner of the couch, and she was still tight in his arms. The cashmere shawl was tucked around the two of them. He was as beautiful in the harsh morning light as he had been by candlelight the night before, she noted, as she turned and watched his face. She regretted the necessity of waking him.

"Alec," she said.

His green eyes opened slowly and the smile that curled his lips was as slow. "Good morning."

"I need to use your bathroom."

"I don't have one."

She pulled out of his arms and stood up, the shawl tumbling to the floor. She hadn't relieved her bladder since she'd left Angus's restaurant. The situation was nearly critical. "What am I going to do?"

"In the old days, they used to sprinkle urine on the door posts to keep ghosts out of the house."

She wasn't amused. "What am I going to do?" she pleaded again.

He grinned broadly. "You *have* a led a sheltered life, MacGillvray. Am I going to have to teach you everything?" he asked.

There was a portable toilet stall set up amid construction materials at the edge of a gaping foundation hole to the rear of the cottage. She was able to figure out how to use it without instruction, though she reckoned it would have been easier if she had been a contortionist. Then she picked her way through a minefield of plumbing supplies to an ancient well. A bucket of water had obviously just been drawn up. It rested on the well's edge, a dipper beside it. She filled the dipper, took a long drink of crisp water. Thanks to her father's influence, she always carried a toothbrush in her handbag. She brushed her teeth, rinsed her mouth. She plunged her hands into the frigid bucket, but patted them against her face more gingerly, dreading the prospect of air-drying this chilly morning. She drew a comb out of her bag and attempted to bring some semblance of order to her hair.

Then she stood back to admire the cottage's simple and beautiful lines. But for its crumbling roof and peeling walls, it could grace a postcard in an Inverness gift shop. She rounded its corner and pulled up short, found herself at the top of a hill that rolled down, green and lazy, to a shimmering lake.

She caught her breath in awe. Alec was standing halfway down the hill, barefooted and bare-legged, his white-shirted back to her, his hands on his kilted hips, watching the water. Sunlight glinted on his auburn hair. He must have felt the intensity of her scrutiny, because he turned suddenly and held his hand out to her. She started down the hill, her high heels sinking into the soft ground. She stopped and pulled them off, continued on toward him in her stocking feet. She took his hand and allowed him to pull her against him. She whimpered softly as he bowed his head and found her lips.

She was limp and liquid, with bones that had melted in the heat of the fire he stirred in her. The arms that held her upright were strong and solid, the chest against which she found herself pressed was hard. When he levered his hips forward just slightly, she felt the hardness there too, against her soft parts. It was over in a matter of moments, he pulling back abruptly, as if he had thought better of kissing her in the first place, but he kept one arm curled around her waist when he turned back to the water.

"What is this place, Alec?" she asked finally, forcing her gaze away from his profile to watch a pair of geese land on the lake with a splash.

"Maybe it's Brigadoon, after all," he said.

"But it's a new day and we're still here."

"We are," he said. "Will we still be here tomorrow?"

She nodded. *If you love someone enough, anything is possible.*

*   *   *

Alec laid the cottage's blueprints out atop the sideboard and Kate studied them with interest.

"It's small, but eventually it will be very comfortable," he said.

"Well, a man who never plans to take a wife doesn't need much space."

"True," he said. "I won't need a place to sleep when she tosses me out of the bedroom."

She couldn't imagine any woman tossing Alec Lachlan out of her bedroom. "And you won't need a nursery."

He nodded, somewhat sadly, she thought.

"But how do you live here without a bathroom? That Porto-San is rather . . . cramped."

"I don't live here yet," he said in surprise. "For the past few days I've been staying at the Munro House."

"You have?"

"I didn't recognize you on the moor, though I sensed something familiar about you. Then later, in Walker's, I realized I had seen you at breakfast, in Mrs. Munro's dining room, that very morning. How did you imagine I knew where you were staying?"

Daft or drunk, she thought. She couldn't tell him she had decided that fate had led him to the moor, then later to her door. "You don't want to know," she assured him.

The basket Angus had packed for them was bountiful indeed and included a tin of pâté, a wheel of cheese and a bottle of wine that didn't qualify as leftovers. They breakfasted on the side of the hill, on raisin bread and smoked trout, along with mugs of strong brewed tea.

"I do believe you brought the sunshine to Scotland with you. How about a swim, MacGillvray?" Alec asked.

A swim! "It's barely April," Kate said. And, as close as she could figure, barely fifty degrees. Despite the fact that the sun was shining brightly for the first time since she'd arrived in Scotland, despite the fact that crocuses were beginning to push through the soil around the cottage, she couldn't imagine plunging bodily into a lake that was probably freezing cold in the middle of July.

"I'm in need of a good bath myself," he said, standing up and stretching.

He peeled off his shirt without self-consciousness, and she stared at him, unable to look away. He was even more magnificent out of his shirt than in it. When he unbuckled his kilt and it fell to the ground, she learned for sure what at least one Scotsman was wearing under *his* this morning. Her cheeks were suddenly red-hot. Her breath was coming in rapid gasps as she allowed her gaze to drift from his face, down . . .

"Are you sure you won't join me?" he asked.

She stood up slowly. Join him? She wanted to meld with him. "I will," she whispered.

He grinned and stepped toward her. She felt herself beginning to sway. His fingers were approaching her buttons. She averted her eyes to keep from staring at the other part of him that was fast approaching her, as well. He made short work of the buttons and peeled the jacket back off her shoulders, laid it atop his kilt. He eyed the camisole he had uncovered. "Pretty," he said. "Do you want to leave it on?"

"No." Her voice was barely audible, but she was surprised she had been able to speak at all.

He nodded in approval. "We need to feel completely comfortable with each other before we go any further, MacGillvray," he explained, as he gently grasped the hem of her camisole. "We need to strip away all the barriers, as it were. Arms up then." When she obliged, he peeled the silk shell up over her head and dropped it atop her jacket.

"Ah," he said softly, more like the intake of a breath than a word. "They're beautiful." His open hand hovered over her breast for just a split second before he closed it, lowered it to the waistband of her skirt. He attended to hook and zipper, carefully, not touching her skin. He eased the skirt down over her hips.

"Pantyhose," she said.

"I see," he answered. His eyes were indeed roving down the length of her nylon-clad legs. "You take them off."

"Ah," he said again, when this was accomplished. "You're perfect, Kate. If I were an artist, I'd paint you like this. Come on."

She felt little embarrassment at having a man see her naked now, she realized in amazement, though this had never been the case before. Evan had often called her a prude. She placed her hand in Alec's and they ran down the hill to the lake's edge.

"It's best taken in a single, bold plunge," he offered.

Most things were, she supposed.

"Now," he said, and they dove into the water together.

The lake was ice cold. She felt a shock as she broke its surface, thought she heard an urgent, unfamiliar voice call her name: "Katherine!" as she went under and its frozen fingers closed around her. She forced herself to swim forward quickly to increase the circulation to her numb limbs. When she surfaced, Alec was beside her.

"Enough, MacGillvray," he said. "I'm risking frostbite in parts of my body that are essential for the rest of this interlude."

She laughed, her teeth chattering.

They retrieved their clothes and tea mugs on the way back up the hill and hurried into the cottage. She settled down on the couch, hugged her shawl around her body as she watched him build up the fire, return a battered kettle of water to the hook above it, presumably to make more tea. He drew his kilt around his hips before he sat down beside her. She stared at his bare chest, covered with auburn fur, still wet from his swim. Then she looked up into his eyes.

"What are you thinking about, MacGillvray?"

"I . . ."

"You're my honest lady, remember?"

She raised her chin. She could give him this truth, but not the others. She couldn't tell him she was a physician, yet, and risk having him recall his odd vow and throw her out of his house before she had a chance to explore the sexual mysteries he presented. Her body wouldn't allow that. She couldn't tell him about the cowardice that had driven her away from Philadelphia and risk having him greet it with disappointment, or worse, disgust. Her ego wouldn't allow that. She couldn't tell him she believed she was falling in love with him and risk having him laugh at her. Her heart wouldn't allow that. "I'm thinking about what you looked like without your kilt on," she said.

"Ah," he answered. "It was apparent that I wanted you, very much."

"Yes," she whispered. It had been abundantly apparent, wonderfully apparent, and she ached with the knowledge.

"Well, I've just had my first of what I would guess are going to be several cold dips in the loch this weekend."

She raised a questioning eyebrow.

"I want you, very much," he explained.

"Ah," she said, not really understanding. *I'm yours,* she had offered in the restaurant and she meant it more surely now than she had then. *I'm yours. Forever.*

He smiled, and she knew he had read her quandary on her face. "You're still afraid of me, Kate. You'll never be able to lose control with me until you lose your fear of me."

The mention of losing control with him made her afraid she would never find out if she could.

They spent the rest of the morning talking and laughing, exploring the cottage and digging through the boxes that were scattered around the main room.

"Have you read all these books?" Kate asked, opening yet another crate packed to the top with them. There were the expected medical texts, but also books on philosophy and art, myths, legends and religion, collections of poetry, classic and best-selling novels, thrillers, mysteries.

He looked up from his own crate. "I would guess so. I can think of only one or two things I enjoy more than a good book."

She met his suggestive smile and chuckled. "Is this everything you own?" she managed, changing the subject, gesturing to the rest of the boxes.

He followed the sweep of her arm. "Pretty much, except for my clothes. There's a Scottish proverb: 'If ye ha'e little gear, ye ha'e less care.' "

"That's like the American proverb 'He who travels lightest, travels fastest.' "

He nodded. "But my traveling days are over. And I suppose I'll need to do quite a bit of shopping. Which reminds me of another proverb: 'A sillerless man gaes fast through the market.' Refurbishing this place is bound to bankrupt me."

"But it will be the most beautiful place in the world when it's finished."

"I think you mean that."

"I do."

He studied her face for a long moment. Then he said: "Time for another dip," and captured her hand.

"Oh, yes?" she asked knowingly, dropping her gaze to his kilt.

He pulled her against him and touched his lips to hers. "That, too, MacGillvray. But the primary purpose of this plunge is to freshen us up a bit—for the wedding."

"The wedding?" she whispered. *"I'll have to marry you,"* he had said the evening before. Maybe he hadn't been kidding. More likely, she was going to wake up in about thirty seconds and find herself back in Kansas, trying to hang on to a dream as fragile as the steam that was rising up from the kettle. Or the gaffers were going to descend on her back-lot Brigadoon and start carting away the sets.

This was better than any movie she had ever seen.

She was reminded of a book she had read during her romance-addicted adolescence called . . . *The Duke's Deception*, perhaps. In it, a sensual, brooding misogynist met, wooed and married a beautiful, innocent girl, all in one evening, never telling her that he was heir to a magnificent estate and title if he was married at the time of his uncle's demise, and that his uncle happened to be on his deathbed on the evening in question.

Had the Duke been motivated by greed, or—sigh—love at first sight? She couldn't remember. But she was pretty sure it had been the latter.

Was Alec next-in-line for a title? Perhaps Angus wasn't his only uncle. Or, dare she hope . . .

This was better than any book she had ever read.

"My best friend, Duncan Knox, is getting married in about"—Alec consulted the heavy, stainless steel watch on his wrist—"one hour."

"It's your friend's wedding," she said, ashamed of the ridiculous fantasies that had momentarily steamrolled her logic. Her voice was still tremulous.

He nodded and watched her inquiringly. "Whose wedding did you think I was talking about?"

She grimaced.

He lowered his face to hers. "Be patient, Mac-Gillvray," he said. "I haven't even asked you, yet."

They ran full-speed down the hill toward the loch. "If you slow down, you'll never go in at all," Alec cautioned, feeling her hesitate as the freezing water loomed ever closer.

Kate let go of his hand in answer and ran ahead of him, dove in neatly before he reached the banks. He surfaced beside her a moment later.

"You're fearless!" he crowed, drawing her shivering body against his.

And courage was a trait he valued above all others, she suspected. "I'm afraid of 'mooses and ratton,' remember?" Among other things.

"Well, you haven't seen any since I bid them *be gone*, have you? And I intend to find myself a great marmalade tomcat as soon as my cottage is fit to house him."

She laughed, plunged under the water one more time, then raced back up the hill to the cottage and the blazing fire in the grate. She was drying her hair in front of this, swathed in her shawl, the chill almost gone from her skin, when he wrapped his kilt around his hips, crouched down beside her, and held his blue fingers out toward the flames a minute later.

"There's a lot to be said for indoor plumbing," he muttered, shivering.

She moved behind him, wrapped her arms around his chest in an attempt to warm him. "There's a lot to be said for not having any."

He groaned as her breasts pressed into his back. "Spare me. Please. I'm not up to another dip yet."

She laughed. She stood up and extracted the comb from her bag. She settled down in front of the fire and struggled to pull it through her tangled curls. "I'll be barely presentable for your friend's wedding," she said finally. "I slept in my suit, and my hair's beyond combing."

"You'll be the most beautiful woman there," he assured her, taking the comb out of her fingers and plying it with slightly more success than she had. He finally raised his shoulders in resignation. "Your hair is lovely, but is it always this much trouble?"

"More or less."

"I would seriously consider taking clippers to it if I were you, MacGillvray," he said with a laugh.

They were dressed in their finery from the evening before in short order, and they surveyed each other. "A wee bit rumpled, but quite passable," Alec said, walking around her. He lifted her shawl and smoothed it out, then folded it neatly. He laid its widest section atop her left hip and drew its ends up to meet on her right shoulder. He considered this for a moment, then unpinned the ancient silver brooch from her lapel and secured it to the place where the shawl ends overlapped. "An *arisaid*," he said. "It suits you."

"A what?" she asked.

"It's the way the Highland women used to wear their plaids."

She glanced down at it, feeling oddly comfortable with this odd style. "Now you," she said, strolling around him and eyeing him critically.

"Well?" he demanded. "I wish I had been able to shave."

She brushed off the folds of his kilt, picked an imaginary bit of lint off his tweedy coat sleeve, then laid her hand on his jaw. The short, auburn whiskers there were soft and bristly at the same time. She liked the way the nap of his beard changed as she stroked it, up and back. "You can't improve on perfection," she said.

Alec was pressing his pedal ever closer to the metal and, as the car shot around a blind curve, Kate tightened her grip on the overhead strap that Rover Motorcars had thoughtfully provided. "There's a wonderful wedding in *Brigadoon*," she managed.

"That's a bit of an oxymoron, eh, MacGillvray?" he chuckled.

"What?"

"Wonderful wedding. Never mind. Whose is it? Gene Kelly and Fiona's?"

Kate glanced at him, saw that his lips were still twitching in amusement. "No. Fiona's younger sister, Jean, is the bride. We're given the impression that Fiona has been waiting for the right man for a long time. While the women are preparing Jean for her wedding, they tease Fiona about being an old maid. She tells them she'd rather wake up alone every morning than sleep next to the wrong laddie."

"Ah. So we're given the impression that she has never—"

"Alec! Before marriage? In Brigadoon? Mr. Forsythe would turn over in his grave."

"*Who* is Mr. Forsythe?"

"He *was* the village minister. He made the deal with God that resulted in 'the miracle'—you know, the one-day-every-hundred-years thing. He paid for it by not being able to partake in it."

"Makes sense," Alec said.

"Anyway, back to Jean's wedding. . . . Just as the sun is beginning to set, each clan descends from the hills, single-file, torches held high, chief at its fore, to the sound of the pipes. When the chief reaches the wedding site, he shouts out his clan's name, you know, 'Campbell!' a roll-call sort of thing."

"Not so loud. I get the idea."

"Mr. Lundie has to officiate, of course, because Mr. Forsythe is gone, but he assures everyone that the laws of Scotland require just a statement of intent and a witness for two people to be married."

Alec threw back his head and laughed. "If they hadn't toughened up that law, MacGillvray, there wouldn't be a single man left in the country," he said.

Alec parked his car along the side of a narrow lane, got out and helped Kate climb down. He took her hand and they joined the stream of people who were heading into the church in the early afternoon sunshine. Alec's name was called out often and he seemed to be the object of much hand clasping and back slapping as they moved down the aisle toward a pew near the front. Kate was not unaware of the appraising glances that were cast her way, but she felt no self-consciousness, held her chin proudly, feeling at ease at Alec's side. They slid in beside a tall, strong man with chestnut-colored hair and a pretty blond woman. Two little boys were rolling on the floor at their feet, hitting each other.

"Kate MacGillvray, this is my brother, James Lachlan, his wife Isabel, and two of their three beasties, Andy and Michael."

The couple offered smiles and pleasant greetings, but the two boys were more concerned with pummeling each other than with introductions.

"Where's Mum?" Alec asked.

"Wee Maggie was feeling a bit under the weather. Our mother stayed home with her. And I don't think Mum's quite recovered from the visit of Clan MacLeod either," James offered.

"Jamie!" Isabel said, smacking his forearm. "I was a MacLeod before I became a Lachlan," she explained to Kate. "And one of those two names can be dropped as easily as it was taken," she added, grinning at her husband. "My family just paid us a short visit."

"Not short enough," James laughed. "And what exactly would you do without me, dearie, a stubborn and disagreeable woman like yourself with three ill-mannered beasties?"

Isabel became quiet then, backing down from his challenge, dropping her gaze. Kate was surprised by this, having already sized Isabel Lachlan up as a woman who was capable of defending herself. James seemed surprised too, and he curled his arm around his wife's shoulder, kissed her ear. "What is it, my love?" he queried.

"Stop calling my children beasties!" she said, her tone ending the conversation.

Alec looked from his brother to his sister-in-law

questioningly. When no explanations appeared to be forthcoming, he excused himself, went to the two handsome young men in Highland regalia who were waiting at the altar. He hugged each of them, then whispered something that made them guffaw. He slid in beside Kate again and took her hand. He leaned forward and looked past her to James and Isabel, who were both still sitting in silence, their eyes trained straight ahead. He raised his shoulders in bewilderment.

"The best man is Duncan's brother, Hugh. They're both friends from Edinburgh," Alec told Kate finally.

"And the bride?"

"Ah, sweet *Ealasaid*. Elizabeth MacDonald. She's as close to a sister as I have. We grew up together. She was the first girl I ever kissed and almost the last."

"What?"

"Her brothers came upon me while I was at it and beat me until I swore I'd never touch her again. I still hear ringing in my ears when I get too close to her. How many brothers did you say you have?"

"Two."

He groaned in dismay. "Anyway, we eventually went off to medical school together. I introduced her to Duncan. She and Tess used to share a flat when Dunc and I came courting."

"She'll be here, then?" Kate asked, keeping her voice light and unconcerned with an effort.

"Elizabeth? She had better be here or those two chaps have dusted off their sporrans for naught."

"Tess."

86

His eyes widened, as if the thought hadn't occurred to him before. "It's possible, MacGillvray," he said.

Elizabeth was a beautiful bride, dressed in white with a sprig of white heather in her bonnet, moving gracefully to the sound of the pipes, smiling and nodding to people as she walked down the aisle on her father's arm. She winked at Alec and blew him a small kiss as she passed. Kate's heart quickened when she caught the loving look that passed between bride and groom as they joined hands at the alter. As if aware of her thoughts, or in response to some of his own, Alec squeezed her hand at that moment. She turned and met his eyes.

"What kept you from getting married, MacGillvray?" he whispered, bending to her ear.

His breath was warm and sweet against her face. "I'd never met the right laddie," she said.

The ceremony was far from solemn. The minister was a jolly, philosophical soul and his remarks were liberally spiked with his own observations, and those of Robert Burns. "He's funny," Kate whispered, leaning in close to Alec.

"You mean Mr. Forsythe? Close your mouth, MacGillvray. I'm joking!"

Elizabeth and Dunc recited poems of their own choosing. When they were finally pronounced husband and wife and they kissed happily, Kate's eyes blurred with tears. Alec joined in the cheer that went up and hugged her against him. Then, amid the joyous wailing of bagpipes, he led her out into the bright sunlight. He introduced her to the families of both bride and groom, and finally to the newlyweds themselves.

"Kate MacGillvray, this is Elizabeth. She's a psychiatrist." The bride offered Kate a broad smile and a hearty handshake.

"Alec told me I needed a psychiatrist," the groom said, "and, as usual, he was right." He squeezed his new wife's waist.

Alec laughed. "And this is Duncan—now a Heilandman by marriage—the famous Dr. Knox."

"I'm the not-so-famous Dr. Knox," Dunc said, grinning as he took Kate's hand. "You know about the infamous Dr. Robert Knox, I'm sure."

Kate shook her head.

"He was a popular professor of anatomy in early nineteenth-century Edinburgh. He hired two gentlemen by the name of Burke and Hare to scour the less prestigious areas of town and bring him the newly deceased for anatomical research. Well, the get was so good that Burke and Hare decided to *urge* people, shall we say, to serve in the noble quest for scientific knowledge."

" 'Up the close and doun the stair, but and ben wi' Burke and Hare. Burke's the butcher, Hare's the thief, Knox the boy that buys the beef,' " Alec quoted helpfully.

"Later I'll tell you about another of my illustrious ancestors, John Knox. He, too, was sadly misunderstood."

Kate laughed. "Mary Stuart's John Knox?" she asked.

"Aye, that's the one, though I'm quite sure neither he nor the Queen of Scots would appreciate being mentioned in the same breath.''

''And does Alec know a poem about him as well?''

''I'm under the impression he knows one for every person and occasion,'' Elizabeth said. ''Alec, I don't suppose you've yet regaled Kate with your bawdy version of 'My Love Is Like a Red, Red Rose.' ''

''It's a little soon yet for that one,'' Alec said.

''I gave you the best five years of my life and I've never heard that one,'' a soft female voice interjected.

They all turned to the new participant in the conversation. Kate found herself looking into the cornflower-blue eyes of the most beautiful woman she had ever seen.

''Hello, Tess,'' Alec said.

Tess. Kate swallowed a groan. The woman was tall and slender, willowy, Kate decided. Tess's silky blond hair hung to her tiny waist. She was wearing a loose velvet dress in a little-girl style, white tights and black patent leather shoes, yet she looked light-years away from the schoolroom.

''Hello, Alec. You always did know how to fill out a kilt,'' Tess said, smiling and surveying him with approval.

''And you're as pretty as always.''

Kate suddenly felt wretched, underdressed and overweight. Alec's hand was on her back, urging her forward. ''I'd like you to meet Kate MacGillvray. Kate, this is Tess Boyd, another of my classmates from Edinburgh.''

"Hello, Tess," Kate managed.

Tess's smile was pleasant. "Hello, Kate," she said.

"We're holding up the receiving line," Alec said, glancing back. "We'll see you all later." He took Kate's hand and led her away.

The silence in the car was interminable. "Tess is beautiful," Kate said finally.

"She is," Alec answered, concentrating on the road in front of him.

"Was it uncomfortable for you to see her again?"

He appeared to be considering this. His hand dove for the stick shift as they approached a curve in the road. "Only because it seemed uncomfortable for you."

She shook her head. "Why in the world should it be uncomfortable for me? I'm just a girl you picked up for the evening, a one-night stand."

"A one-night stand?" he asked, apparently unfamiliar with the term.

"You know. Just for sex."

He grinned. "I'll admit my memory is growing faulty with my advanced years, MacGillvray, but I don't recall having sex with you."

She laughed.

"When it happens, Kate, we'll both remember it," he assured her.

Chapter Five

The reception was in a large heated tent on a grassy knoll in front of the MacDonald family's home. Because the weather was unusually cooperative, drinks were also being served from tables outside. The band was playing and a few couples were already dancing when Alec and Kate arrived. He quickly fetched them both a glass of punch.

"Cheers, MacGillvray," he said, raising his glass.

"*Slainte mhath,*" she attempted. Her effort was rewarded with a beaming grin.

They strolled around inside the tent, and outside it, talking to so many people that Kate couldn't remember their names. They all seemed to know, and be glad to see, Alec. He was quick to introduce her, proud to introduce her, she sensed. He seemed oblivious to the longing glances directed toward him by an assortment of pretty women, including the incomparable Tess. Kate wasn't as oblivious.

"So many of the women seem to know you," she ventured.

He looked around in surprise. "Most of them do, I suppose."

"You're popular with the ladies."

He laughed, drew her into his arms and kissed her lips lightly. "Right now I only care about being popular with one lady," he said.

Tess descended on them and invited Alec to join her for a walk. He looked at Kate with a cocked eyebrow, and she nodded her head in concurrence. She wandered off to nibble delicacies from the bounteous buffet tables with as much aplomb as she could muster, struggling with another powerful emotion: jealousy. Dunc came toward her several minutes later and presented her with a fresh glass of punch.

"Where's Alec?" he asked.

"He went for a walk with Tess," she answered.

Dunc laughed. "Tess never gives up. She refuses to believe any man is immune to her charms."

"Are you sure Alec is immune to them?"

"Absolutely!" he said, nodding his head. "Now," he added under his breath.

Kate was staring off into the distance considering this information when she saw a small girl at the far table pick up a delicate champagne glass, which somehow shattered in her hand. Kate sprinted forward and was swiftly at her side, with the little limb elevated and a napkin pressed against the bleeding palm.

Dunc was kneeling next to the girl in the next

moment, holding her against him, comforting her while Kate attended to the wound. He looked up at Kate, who was picking glass out of the cut, patting the back of the hand she was holding. "This is my sister, Helen," he said.

Kate managed a smile for the little girl, despite the sudden nausea that gripped her, and when she returned her attention to her task, it was with a mounting sense of trepidation.

"Alec didn't say you were a physician."

Kate studied her trembling, blood-caked fingers for a moment before she met Dunc's eyes. "Then how do you know I'm a physician?"

He grinned. "There's method to the madness of the purveyors of medical training, Kate. They make us work thirty-six-hour shifts for a reason. When the average person sees an accident in progress, he freezes for a period of time, seconds to a minute or more. They make us work until we can't stand up, long past the time when our brains have stopped functioning, so that we learn to respond on instinct alone. I saw the instinct in the way you leapt to Helen's aid."

She swallowed heavily, afraid she was going to vomit. "Don't tell Alec."

Dunc's eyes widened. "You mean he doesn't know?"

She shook her head. "Before I could tell him, he launched into a diatribe against female physicians. Timing is everything, I'm told, and that seemed a poor time to enlighten him." It was the easier part of the tale to relate.

Dunc snorted. "That was merely and purely a diatribe against Tess. Alec doesn't have a chauvinistic bone in his body. Ask Elizabeth. She's known him longer than any of us.''

But the point the groom made in that moment, without intending to, was that Alec still needed to hide his true feelings for Tess behind a wall of chauvinistic bluster. ''At any rate, the longer I let it go, the more difficult it became to explain why I didn't just tell him in the first place.''

Dunc stood up, removed the napkin from Helen's palm and looked at it appraisingly. ''I believe our crisis is over. A couple of steri-strips should do for this, don't you think?''

Steri-strips were tapes that often made stitching a laceration unnecessary. Kate explained this to the girl before she forced herself to examine the gash again. But as she watched a drop of blood well up in it, she began to sweat.

''Move him onto the table at my count of three. One, two, three.''

''He's dead, Dr. MacGillvray,'' the medical student at her elbow murmured, watching incredulously as she cut away the front of her patient's shirt and pounded on his still, cold chest.

''Get me a thoracotomy tray! I'm going to open his chest!''

''It looks like someone has already done that for you,'' Rose Lefarge, the charge nurse, said, pointing at the ghastly pool of congealing blood on the stretcher from which the boy had just been moved.

''I've got to do something!''

''Do it for someone who has a chance, Katie.''

A gloved hand touched hers for just a moment then, but it couldn't have been more effective at bringing her to full, stunning awareness had it shaken her shoulder, or slapped her face. She returned her gaze to the table to find that the medical students had levered the patient onto his belly and were studying a gaping hole in the back of his black leather jacket. But her eyes were riveted on the blood-smeared painting beneath it. Mountains. Rugged, soaring mountains, capped in snow. So real that the air she was breathing suddenly seemed thinner and icy-fresh and she could almost hear the cry of a circling hawk. The Gothic letters over the scene confirmed the boy's affiliation: Huns, despite the fact that the middle two had been blown away by the bullet. And the graceful script under it supplied the only name by which anyone in the room would ever know him: Attila.

"A couple of steri-strips should be fine," Kate replied.

"Well, I'll take Helen in the house and attend to it," Dunc said. "Why don't you find Alec, dismiss *la belle* Tess and tell him all about yourself? Honesty is important to him, and I can tell by the way he looks at you that you're important to him. Despite his protestations to the contrary, I believe our Alec is falling in love."

She bowed her head, doubting Dunc's conclusions, but garnering no satisfaction from the small possibility that he was correct. Even if Alec was falling in love with her, he was falling in love with a fraud, a two-dimensional, picture-perfect woman conjured up with smoke and mirrors, whose neuroses had been made to disappear courtesy of the Brigadoon magic show. He was falling in love with a coward, a woman he never would have endured beyond the first glass of whisky in Walker's pub, had he known the truth. A flush crept up her cheeks. "There's more to it, Duncan . . ."

Her free hands were quickly commandeered to help with the staggering number of someones in need of attention. She dutifully attended them, proceeding on automatic pilot, fighting to ignore the mounting sense of trepidation and uncertainty that gripped her, working until she couldn't stand up, until disaster gave way to the controlled debacle that was a routine evening in the E.R. But throughout the interminable night, the boy's name remained on her lips: Attila. And his girlfriend's litany repeated itself over and over in her head: "It's my fault he's dead. . . ."

"I've lost my nerve. I'm not sure I'll ever practice medicine again." It was a difficult admission to make, but Kate had to make it to someone; the incident with Helen had reminded her just how far she had fallen.

Dunc was the wrong person to tell, however. He broke into a guffaw that turned her embarrassment into anger, and she raised her eyes in accusation.

He held up one hand, begging for her patience while he composed himself, and he attempted to muffle a chortle with the other. Helen was grinning at his side, looking from adult to adult, her injury forgotten. "When did this happen?" he asked finally.

"Tuesday," she said.

"Tuesday!" He laughed again. "And you're still adamant about it four days later! You're a stubborn lass, Dr. MacGillvray. Is this the first time you've quit?''

"Of course!" she said, offended.

"Ah. I remember my first time—"

"Your first time!"

He nodded. "I discovered I had a comatose gentleman on my service when I arrived to take it over, my first year out of school. Maybe he reminded me of my grandfather or something, I'm not sure. But I felt a special need to save him. When he died, as he was bound to do, I decided I'd given him too much IV fluid, or too little, that I'd calculated his hyper-alimentary solution wrong. . . . Anyway, I blamed myself, despite the fact that his treatment was no different than it had been for years, and I vowed never to darken the door of a hospital ward again."

Kate stared at him, moved a step closer to him, knowing, somehow, that it was vitally important she hear every word he was saying.

"And it's not always the patient himself who evokes these feelings. Sometimes it's the circumstances. You can ask Elizabeth to recount a few of her adventures in the land of *mea culpa*, if you have a taste for melodrama. Self-doubt plagues every rational human being—why do we expect ourselves to be above it? Repressed memories and associations move us to react, and overreact, the way we do—to everything in life. It's the soft underbelly of medical swagger, Kate—but you can't be a good physician if you pretend it isn't there. These eruptions serve a vital function, much like loosening the cap on a motorcar's radiator. If we don't break the seal from time to time and let off a little steam, we'll boil in our own arrogance.''

Kate shook her head in wonder. ''Why didn't anyone ever tell me this before?''

''You've never been to Scotland before. We're a humbler lot than our American colleagues—comes from getting paid so much less, I imagine.''

Kate watched Duncan and his sister walk toward the house. How had Alec reacted to his friend's admission of fear and fallibility? Or had Dunc known better than to share it with him? At any rate, if Dunc was right, she wouldn't be able to go back to her work until she uncovered the associations that had caused her to run from it, that had caused her to react so dramatically to the death of one young street warrior named Attila.

The bride rushed toward Kate in a flurry of rustling satin and petticoats. ''Is Helen all right?'' she asked.

Kate nodded. ''She broke a glass and cut her palm. There was more blood than damage. Dunc is seeing to it now.''

''They always managed to spill a bit of blood at Highland weddings in the old days,'' Elizabeth laughed. Then her gaze became assessing. ''Alec didn't say you were a physician.''

''How do you know...'' Kate began, then stopped. She already knew the answer. ''So do you leave on your honeymoon tonight?'' she asked, changing the subject.

Elizabeth shook her head. ''We're both due back at work on Monday morning. We couldn't get the time off until June. But June's not so very far off, is it?''

Kate smiled vaguely, filled with the oddest sense that she existed apart from the flow of time and had lost the capacity to judge its passage.

There was an early sit-down dinner, punctuated by much toasting and ribald humor. Alec stood up and offered an eyewitness commentary on the courtship of the bride and groom, which had all the guests doubled over in mirth and wiping tears from their eyes.

Dunc responded by raising his glass. ''May I live long enough to offer a toast at Alec Lachlan's wedding,'' he said.

'' 'It's ill wark takin' the breeks aff a Hielandman,' '' Alec responded. This was greeted with appreciative hoots and chuckles. Kate looked up at him for clarification and he gestured to his knees, delightfully free of breeks, in answer. The meaning of another of Alec's Scottish proverbs dawned on her.

After dinner, everyone, it seemed, from the oldest guest to the youngest, joined in the dancing. Alec was the one exception. Kate was in great demand, and she found herself in James Lachlan's arms for just a few minutes before she was claimed by the bride's father, then the groom's. She danced several times with Dunc, and finally with his brother, Hugh. Hugh was a large, handsome man, and Kate responded easily to his considerable charm. He swept her around the dance floor and she laughed up at him as he plied her with jokes and compliments. Then he escorted her to the table from which the delicious and potent punch was being served. He handed her a glass, raised his own. "To Alec's taste in women," he offered.

"Thank you, sir," she said, bowing her head in gratitude.

Alec was at her side then. He obviously didn't appreciative Hugh's gallantry as much as she did. "We share similar tastes," he said dryly.

"It's an odd man who doesn't enjoy intelligent, beautiful women," Hugh offered.

There seemed to be more to this conversation than what was being said, and Kate looked from one man to the other.

"Well, you're finished enjoying this one," Alec said, taking her hand and drawing her away.

"What was that all about?" Kate asked in surprise.

Alec shrugged.

They left the tent and walked silently for a few minutes. The sky was very black, despite its peppering of stars, and the air was chilly.

"Are you cold, MacGillvray?" he asked finally.

"A little," she said.

He peeled his coat off and helped her into it, over her protests. "I have a high tolerance for cold."

"But not for Hugh Knox."

He raised his shoulders. "Hugh is one of my best friends. I don't suppose I was being very reasonable in there, but suddenly . . ."

"Yes?"

He stopped walking, laid his hands on her shoulders and watched her eyes. "Hugh is the friend Tess went with two years ago. It only happened the once, and every time he's in his cups, he begs my for-giveness for it, but I was suddenly afraid of seeing history repeat itself. As odd as it seems to say this after knowing you just over a day, I don't want to lose you.''

His hands were moving on her shoulders now, massaging her muscles through the multiple layers of fabric that covered them, yet it felt as if he were touching her bare flesh. *"Our Alec is falling in love,"* Dunc had said. Was it possible? *"I'll never fall in love again,"* Alec had said. Had that claim just been the bravado of a man who was terrified of being hurt again, of losing someone he loved again? "You won't lose me," she whispered, unable to keep herself from saying the words, despite the small voice inside her that cautioned against them.

He buried his fingers in her hair, drew her head back and settled his lips against hers. His kiss was alternately soft and firm, gentle and probing. She wrapped her arms around his broad shoulders to keep from sinking to the ground. His mouth was at her ear, then against the pulse at the angle of her jaw, then at the valley between her breasts. She couldn't contain the whimper that rose to her lips as he did this, and she wished they were back at the cottage, unclothed, alone. She wanted him to touch her breasts, to hold them. The thought of his mouth closing around their tips was making her tremble uncontrollably.

"You're cold."

She shook her head.

"We'd better go back inside," he said.

*   *   *

The celebration continued until after midnight. Kate didn't dance with Hugh again, but she noticed that he seemed very content to dance all the remaining dances with Tess. The traditional breaking of the shortbread over the bride's head was accomplished, and when the pieces were handed around to the gathered women, everyone insisted Kate had snagged the largest piece.

"That means you'll be the next bride," Tess offered.

Kate turned to face her. "Does it?"

Tess nodded. "Take your piece of wedding cake home tonight and put it under your pillow. You'll dream of the man you're going to marry."

"Then all I'll have to do is figure out what I'm going to wear."

"I hope you'll dream about Alec because I venture he'll be dreaming about you."

Kate considered this in surprise. There was no rancor on the beautiful woman's face, her laughter had been genuine. "You don't mind?"

"If I thought I had a chance to get Alec back, I'd fight you for him for all I'm worth. But I don't. So I wish you joy of him. Love him well. He's a good man."

"You're already marrying us off. I just met him."

"It's not up to me," Tess said, gesturing to the shortbread in Kate's hand. "You got the biggest bit."

When they finally departed from the reception, Kate had her tiny piece of rich, dark wedding cake wrapped in a napkin and tucked in her bag. She

102

leaned back in the car's seat and watched Alec's profile in the dim light. She sighed with pure contentment. "I had a wonderful day," she said.

He glanced at her and grinned—she could see the flash of his white teeth. "I'll endeavor to make tomorrow as good," he promised.

Arriving back at the filthy, cold cottage was like arriving home, Kate noted in surprise as she stepped through its door. Alec quickly lit the lamps and set to work at the fireplace. Soon the chill was gone and the room felt comfortable.

"We'll sleep better tonight," he said, digging through boxes until he came up with several large, fleecy blankets.

She rearranged the pillows on the couch, surreptitiously slipping the slice of wedding cake out of her bag and under one of them. "We won't sleep with our clothes on," she said quietly, not turning.

"I would suggest you take yours off."

She glanced at him and nodded, then began doing so, folding each piece carefully as she removed it, laying it on the floor. She knew his gaze was on her and she quivered under his scrutiny. Finally she peeled away her pantyhose and added them to the pile.

"Look at me," he begged.

She turned, raised her eyes with an effort, feeling like a reluctant virgin suddenly, shy and uncertain. He had seen her without a stitch on several times this morning. But this was different. The circumstances were almost impossibly intimate now. They were on the verge of becoming lovers. And she was afraid.

103

"You're the most beautiful woman I've ever seen, Kate," he said.

She dropped her gaze again. What if she couldn't respond to him? What if she disappointed him? *"A man likes to feel his woman melt under him."* Was she capable of melting?

"Maybe if we try different ways of making love it will help."

She had resisted that suggestion, just as she had resisted all of Evan's other efforts to improve their sex life, hiding behind the safe shield of her modesty. She had always possessed insight enough to recognize the passive aggression in her behavior. Only now did she realize how little effort she'd actually put into overcoming it. She didn't blame Evan for dumping her. In fact, it seemed unbelievable that their relationship had gone on as long as it did. And now, she was about as accomplished in bed as she had been before it started.

Was she capable of pleasing Alec Lachlan? Would she be able to look at herself in the mirror again if she wasn't? *You're an innocent, MacGillvray,* she reminded herself. A frigid innocent? she wondered.

"Look at me," he said again.

She looked at him, saw that he was smiling in understanding as he stripped off the last of his clothes. He moved to the couch, sat down, held his arms out to her. "Relax, Kate. Just let me hold you."

She nodded, sank into his arms. And he just held her.

"Now tell me everything I need to know about baseball," he said.

"What?" she asked in surprise, raising her head.

"It's played with a ball and bat, like cricket, no?"

"For all I know about cricket, it might be played with a big, green bug."

He chuckled. "I'll take you to a match someday. But this baseball—what's the object of the game?"

"To knock the horsehide into the cheap seats . . ." she began, settling her face against the crisp, dark hair on his chest and relaxing.

The dream came late in her sleep cycle, Kate knew this much for sure. She awakened briefly, feeling the warmth of sunshine on her face, seeing its light through her closed eyelids. Her head was nestled into the crook of Alec's arm, her leg was stretched across his groin. His hand was stroking her hair, gently, slowly.

"It's morning. I'd better get up," she murmured, but her body made absolutely no effort to cooperate.

"Go back to sleep, Kate," he whispered. "You had a late night. Remember?"

Remember.

And then she was far away.

The moss was soft and very green, like a velvet blanket on the banks of the lake. Sunlight sparkled on the surface of the water. The man and woman were holding each other and kissing. Then he eased her back against the ground. She looked up at him through narrowed eyes. Her long, thick braid had been drawn over her shoulder, and it appeared golden against the brown bodice of her gown. Her breasts were rising and falling in tempo with her rapid breathing.

"I must ha'e ye," he whispered, studying her, then he lowered himself on top of her. "Yer father is taking uncommonly long in considering my troth."

"Ye're no my only suitor."

"But I am yer only love."

"If I gi'e ye what ye want before ye take me to the church, ye'll take a maiden there in my stead," she laughed.

"Ne'er," he said gruffly. *"I'll ne'er tell ye a lie. I'll be true to ye fore'er."*

"Fore'er is a long time, Alasdair."

"No near long enough for us."

She ran her hands through the lush dark hair that hung to his shoulders. "And what's to be done if ye put yer bairn in my belly and my father chooses in favor of the fine young Mackintosh?"

He chuckled. "Mackintosh will likely withdraw his offer once he learns I've put my bairn in yer belly."

"Ye might withdraw yer offer once ye learn ye've put yer bairn in my belly!"

It was an odd dream, vivid and brightly colored, without blurred edges. *I'm dreaming*, Kate reminded herself. But it was more like seeing a photograph of herself taken at a place she couldn't recall visiting. *Is it me? Is it Alec?* The emotions and sensations experienced by the dream's protagonists were resonating in her own sleeping body.

She thrust up under him, feeling his need against her belly. "I ha'e only yer assurances," she teased.

"Ye ha'e my heart and my promise, as well as my assurances," he said, laying his hand against her cheek. Then he reached for the large leather sporran on the grass beside him. He rifled through it, extracted a silver circle pin. He handed it to her. *"And ye ha'e my mother's brooch."*

She sat up, studying the pin in delight.

"Wear it near yer heart, always," he said, reclaiming it and pinning it onto her plaid.

She spread her arms wide to welcome him and he sank into them with a softly spoken word: *"Catriona."*

"Alasdair?" Kate murmured, opening her eyes, sitting up abruptly. That was the man's name. He was Alec and yet not. Alasdair.

Alec was making tea at the fireplace. The sun was high and strong through the windows. She knew she had slept late. "What time is it?" she asked.

He turned and smiled at her. "Good morning, MacGillvray, or perhaps I should say good afternoon." He glanced at his watch. "It's ten past twelve."

"Ah," she said.

"Pleasant dreams?" he asked.

She raised her shoulders. That last one had disturbed her in a way she couldn't name, but it hadn't been unpleasant. She could blame it all on the nonsense about the cake under the pillow, she decided, glancing down sheepishly at the place where her head had been settled just moments before. Had she dreamed about the man she would marry? The man with the long, dark hair had to have been Alec, changed slightly, skewed in the manner of a dream image . . . Alasdair.

"Perhaps you'd fancy a bite of cake with your tea," Alec said, holding up a napkin. "It's a wee bit flat, but I'm sure it will be delicious."

She laughed and blushed, wrapped herself in her shawl and made her way out to the Porto-San. Then she sat down beside him in front of the fire and they shared the flat piece of wedding cake.

Alec announced that he was going fishing, holding up a length of string, a bit of pâté and a hook that looked as if it had been fashioned from a stray piece of construction debris. "Will you do me a favor?" he asked before he stepped through the door, wearing only his kilt.

"What's that?"

"Don't get dressed," he laughed. "When I come back, I want to find you just the way you are now, *mo breagha* Cheit."

"Who?"

"My lovely Kate," he said softly. "For so you are."

She wasn't comfortable exploring his house in the nude, so she remained wrapped in the shawl. The cashmere felt itchy against her bare skin, but she found that she was reveling in the sensation. She checked the plans on the sideboard and walked into the long, narrow room behind the main room's west wall. It would be the kitchen someday. She tried to visualize it with long, gleaming counters and state-of-the-art appliances. She walked back across the main room, pausing at the sagging table. She ran her fingers over its veneer. It would be beautiful when it was repaired and refinished. Tall-backed chairs were piled one on the other nearby. She tried to visualize them polished, cushioned in a brocade fabric. She walked through a low archway into the large room beyond it—the bedroom. It was bare and thick with white dust from the wall that was being torn down to make way for the bathroom. It was dark, sunlight denied entry by the filth on the long, latticed window on the wall opposite her and the tarp over the hole to the outside. She tried to imagine it with polished floors and wide-open windows, dominated by a bed draped in a handmade quilt. It would be a haven, an oasis into which they could retreat at the end of each day. . . . She shook her head. Alec would certainly entertain female guests in his bedroom. But this female guest would be long gone before the bed was delivered.

Chapter Six

Alec returned with a fish that he identified as a pike. "I'll cook it for dinner," he said.

Kate looked at it askance, nodded her head grudgingly.

"You don't catch your own food in Philadelphia, do you, MacGillvray?"

"No."

He wrapped the fish in newspaper and laid it on the sideboard. "I required a dip, you know," he said.

She noticed only then that his hair was dripping wet.

"I had a fantasy about you out there, while I was waiting for the fish to bite. I could almost see you lying on the banks of the loch, as naked as you are under that plaid, the sunlight making your fine skin gleam, your hair spread out on the moss behind your head. Your knees were bent and parted just slightly. Then a wind blew up and you didn't move a muscle, didn't blink an eye, but it caused the tall grass to bend and wave, to touch you here . . ." He stepped toward her and brushed the inside of her thigh with his fingertips.

She hadn't seen his fingers coming a moment ago, but now she couldn't take her eyes off them.

He drew her shawl off her shoulders, spread it on the floor in front of the fireplace. "Lie down here, MacGillvray. Close your eyes and bend your knees. Listen to the wind blowing."

She could hear it above the thumping of her heart, and his fingers swayed in it, bending forward and receding, touching the aching heaviness between her thighs, over and over. She heard a whimper of need, realized only afterwards that it had come from her own throat. She looked up into his green eyes. "Alec?" she begged, needing more.

He shook his head. He took her hands and pulled her to her feet. "Let's sit on the couch," he said. "There's something I need to say first."

She sat down on the couch. Every fiber in her body was on edge, in need. She stared, ashamed, at her knees, afraid he would see this hunger in her eyes.

"Look at me, Cheit," he commanded.

She raised her eyes slowly and met his, knew that the hunger in his eyes mirrored her own. "What is it?" she asked.

"I'm the one who's afraid now. I suddenly find that I don't want to be a casual holiday tumble for

111

you. I want to possess you, Kate. I want to imprint my touch on your body, like a brand, so that no matter where you go, who else you make love with, you'll remember me.''

Was this male vanity, a you've-tried-the-best-now-try-the-rest macho thing? Or could it be something else? "I'll remember you," she assured him.

He shrugged, in doubt, or in lieu of speaking such a promise of his own, she couldn't tell which, but it didn't matter. She moved into the circle of his arms, wrapped her own around his sinewy shoulders. The hair on his chest tickled her nipples, caused them to thrust forward eagerly against him. He recognized this invitation and bowed his head to them, traced one tight bud with the tip of his tongue, then the other. She trembled as he did this. She groaned as he captured one between his teeth, took it into his mouth. He began to suckle, gently at first, then more urgently. She tangled her fingers in his thick soft hair, drawing him closer against her, drawing him harder against her.

"I have my own fantasy, Alex," she said, suddenly wanting to give as good as she got. "I see a figure standing at the edge of the loch, motionless; a man covered in ice, after an ill-advised swim, perhaps, or a life-size George Segal sculpture, dressed in plaid. The wind ruffles the surface of the loch, causes the folds of his kilt to flap, forward and back . . .''

He groaned against her breast.

He was robbing her of her ability to speak, but she had to do so, had to tell him the rest. "The wind grows fiercer then; it blows his kilt up about his waist. He's not frozen under there. I see that he's warm and firm and pulsating with life under there. And I realize how I can thaw the rest of him. I pluck a handful of grass, and I touch him with it, here . . .'' She eased her fingers up under his kilt, brushed them across the sensitive orbs between his legs. She felt him shudder, draw on her breast more forcefully in answer, and she cried out.

"And then?" There was agony in his voice.

"He still can't move by himself, but I can move him now. I unclasp his kilt and let it fall to the ground. I ease him back onto the moss . . ."

He whispered a word she couldn't understand but which she guessed wasn't particularly polite.

"I gasp when I recognize his face. And I grow frenzied with the need to save him—to save you. I straddle you. I allow my shawl to fall back. I hover . . .''

His mouth moved abruptly from her breast to her mouth, silencing her, taking away her breath and her train of thought. *"Have you ever forgotten where you end and he begins?"* It was happening now. His tongue was in her mouth, his hands were in her hair, he was pulling her closer, closer, ever closer. . . .

"Save me, MacGillvray," he begged.

She laughed against his mouth. "I think I'll let you suffer for a while."

They packed a lunch and carried it out to the hillside. Alec took a quick plunge into the loch, then stretched out in the sun, drinking it into every un- covered pore of his body. The cold water had re- duced the boiling need inside him to a simmer, Kate

113

guessed, as she crooked her elbow in the grass, rested her face in her hand and watched him. He looked like a huge cat, oblivious and perfectly relaxed.

"What are you looking at, MacGillvray?" he asked suddenly, not opening his eyes.

She laughed. "How did you know I was looking at you?"

He cracked an eyelid. "I could feel it, as surely as a touch."

She bowed her head in acknowledgment of this. "I love looking at you. And I love it here, Alec," she said.

He sighed and sat up. "My brother and I used to ride our horses over here when we were boys. Even then it felt like my place, my private, special sanctuary. I didn't know it was Lachlan land until my father died and left it to me."

She looked at him, then back at the lake. "I feel as if I belong here too, somehow . . ."

"Do you?"

She nodded. "It's like I've been here before, though that's impossible. I've never been to Scotland before. But I can almost picture myself tending the garden and managing the house and caring for the children—two of them."

"You have quite an imagination, MacGillvray," he said, settling back on the grass again.

And it was getting better all the time.

"I think I was dreaming about Brigadoon," Alec said, awakening some time later from a nap Kate had been perfectly content to watch. "How does

Gene Kelly happen to be there when it appears?"

She smiled. "He's shooting grouse with his friend Jeff—Van Johnson—a cynic with a drinking problem."

"I've never understood why men enjoy doing that."

"Drinking?"

"Shooting grouse."

"Uhmm. Well, if it makes you feel any better, they don't bag a single one in the entire movie. Toward the end, Van Johnson thinks he's finally got one in the cross-hairs and fires, but it turns out to be Harry Beaton."

"I went to school with a Harry Beaton. Nice chap."

"This one takes a bullet in the heart and dies."

Alec bolted upright, looking thoroughly betrayed. "In Brigadoon?"

"If any inhabitant of the village goes beyond its boundaries—the stone wall, the old Kirk Road, the bridge, and . . . something else, I forget . . ."

"The loch."

"How did you know?"

"Good guess."

". . . the miracle is rendered null and void and everything disappears forever. Anyway, after Harry sees Jean marry Charlie Dalrymple, he's so distraught he announces his intention to blow it for everyone and takes off for the border. All the village men try to stop him, but Jeff finally does it, by accident."

"So nobody blames Jeff for shooting Harry Beaton?"

"Jeff blames himself."

Alec appeared to be considering this for a long moment, then he gave a dismissive snort and stood up. "Let's walk over to that hill," he said, pointing.

The hill he indicated was covered with patches of green and sheep, whose winter coats might have been fashioned from pieces of the low clouds in the sky above them. They looked harmless enough, Kate supposed, though looks could be deceiving. "It's kind of far," she hedged.

He pulled her to her feet. "Don't worry. It's this side of the old Kirk Road," he said.

They ate thick sandwiches of pâté and cheese on raisin bread as they walked. Alec's bare feet seemed to avoid the rocks Kate's found unerringly, and his kilt didn't require the periodic adjustments propriety demanded of her toga. She stopped to do this yet again. He took the brooch out of her hand to lend his expertise. After he had settled the toga it to his satisfaction, he drew her against him.

"You look lovely in your arisaid," he said.

She glanced down it. "I assume my ancient kins-women wore something more underneath it."

He laughed. "I like your style better." He met her lips and kissed her for a long time, probing and caressing her mouth with his tongue.

"Another fantasy," she murmured, glancing up the hill they were about to climb. Sheep were bigger than she expected.

"You're getting good at this."

She nodded. "You're walking across the hills and you come upon a small flock of sheep. They're all white and fluffy, but for one. It seems odd to you that one sheep was shorn so early, when it's barely spring, when there's still a brisk, chill wind—''

"Ah, the wind," he whispered.

"You come close enough to run your hand down the spine of the odd sheep and you realize only then that it has always been this bare, this smooth. Your hand moves to its bowed head. You touch curls there—''

"But they're silk not wool," he murmured, understanding, stroking her hair.

"You kneel behind the animal, determined to know just what manner of beast this is. Your questing hand moves between its hind legs and you find—''

"Wool. Golden brown wool," he groaned. "Stop, MacGillvray, you're killing me."

She laughed. "Then the wind springs up, begins to blow fiercely, causing the folds of your kilt to—''

He stilled her lips with a kiss, laid a silencing finger there after he pulled back. "Don't say another word about it, unless you're ready to get down on all fours, here and now, so I can determine what manner of beast you are."

"I'll let you determine *that* back at the cottage."

He retreated a step, eyeing her skeptically. "You're stalling!" he accused. "You don't want to go up that hill. Are you tired?"

"No."

"My feet are as tough as shoe leather. Are yours paining you, then?"

"Not really."

He glanced past her, his expression perplexed,

then he nodded in understanding. "You don't like sheep!"

She felt her cheeks heat up. "I can't say I've ever been close enough to any to have formed an opinion. Do they have teeth?"

"Of course they have teeth, MacGillvray. But they're herbivores." He grinned wickedly. "At least most of them are. You'll know the carnivores by the blood dripping from their muzzles. It's best to avoid that lot."

"Can't you be serious?" she demanded.

He narrowed his eyes and studied her appraisingly. "I'm beginning to think I can," he said.

After Kate survived her close encounter with the sheep, Alec advised her that it was time for one with a dead fish. He sorted through the treasures packed in one of the boxes atop his wobbly dining table. He finally found a large cast-iron skillet and held it up in triumph. He handed it to her while he dug deep in another box and found a sharp knife. Then he retrieved the newspaper-wrapped fish in question from the sideboard. "Come, MacGillvray," he said. "I'll teach you how to clean it."

She followed him to the loch's edge, laid the skillet in the grass and settled down beside it. She watched him cut and bone the pike, quickly, expertly, laying each fillet in the pan as he prepared it, tossing the inedible parts in the water. But as he rinsed the knife, it nicked his thumb. "Damn," he said, studying the digit for a moment before he popped it into his mouth.

She gasped, guessed her face had blanched because he looked up at her in surprise.

"Don't tell me the doctor's daughter can't stomach the sight of a little blood."

She shook her head. "I've seen plenty of blood in my lifetime," she managed. Gallons of it. And fully half that amount had seemed to be pooled on the stretcher from which one dead boy had been lifted.

"Uhmm," Alec said, sucking on his bleeding thumb.

"Alec?"

"Uhmm?" He looked up.

"Have you ever been afraid to do your job?"

He grinned. "Afraid?" He shook his head. "I've been in plenty of situations when the adrenaline started pumping and I was in a state of what you might call *high anxiety*."

"Like a runner at the sound of the starting gun?"

"Exactly! And I've second-guessed my share of decisions, lost my share of patients."

"But you've never . . . panicked?"

He laughed briefly as he washed his hands. "A physician prone to panic attacks would be a public menace."

Somehow she had known he was going to say that.

"We have no butter for the pan," he noted, as he lifted the pan off the grass. "The fish is bound to burn."

"We can poach it in wine," she ventured.

"Good thinking. You have all the makings of a Highlander."

Except for courage under fire. "Speaking of which, I've signed up for a hike to Lairig Ghru on Thursday."

He squinted up at the sky. "It's too early in the season to be completely safe in the mountains. I think I read that forty hikers died in the Highlands last year. The weather can be so fierce and changeable."

"And so windy," she murmured.

He grinned. "I'd hate to think of you up there without a doctor close at hand. I'm going with you."

She didn't argue.

They returned to the hillside to watch the sun set. The chattering of the birds seemed to be rising in a fevered crescendo as the low croaking of night frogs joined the din. The sky was streaked with purple and pink. Alec sat down, settled Kate between his thighs, drew her back against his chest.

"I don't want this day to end," he said.

"It's just beginning." She turned her face and lifted her chin, inviting him to kiss her.

He touched his lips to hers with infinite tenderness. "I want to taste you, MacGillvray," he said.

"You just did," she answered.

"No. I did not."

She watched him questioningly, but allowed herself to be pressed back into the grass. He unclasped her shawl and pulled it off her. He stroked her trembling thighs until they parted, until she wasn't able to hold them closed.

"Alec!" she protested, as he proceeded to do as he had promised.

He looked up at her face. "He never did this to you," he said, with certainty and satisfaction.

"No," she gasped, arching up involuntarily as he returned to his task.

She was aching. Yearning. She was moving closer to something warm and compelling, something that was drawing her toward it. She wasn't quite close enough to see it. But she knew she couldn't turn back now, that she had to pursue it, understand it, embrace it.

"Are you ready?" he whispered.

She spread her arms wide in answer, whimpered wordlessly in answer.

He was out of his kilt and between her thighs in an instant, poised, ready to plunge.

"Do it," she begged.

And he did. Again, again. Finding a rhythm and maintaining it, despite her pleas that he free her from the tension that was building inside her, climbing toward the darkening sky and growing unbearable.

"I need . . ." she gasped.

"I know what you need, *mo breagha*," he said through gritted teeth. He balanced himself on one arm, eased her legs up around his waist with the other, then plunged deep again.

She pressed up against him, pulled him closer with her arms and her legs. She was vaguely aware that her head was thrashing back and forth on the grass as the swelling tide buffeted her, battered her, leaving her limbs numb and useless, leaving her chest hollow with a scream she couldn't allow herself to voice, must keep herself from voicing.

"Let it go, Kate," he groaned. "Let it come."

And it did.

She screamed his name and clawed his back as her core convulsed, over and over.

Where do I end? Where does he begin?

She was floating upward now, anchored to the earth by the strong hands that were clasping her buttocks, by the long, hard pinion between her legs as he thrust forward once, twice . . .

She heard him cry out. She forced one heavy eyelid open in time to see his face contort in ecstasy and release.

He fell forward against her and she held him tight. She might never let him go, she decided. She listened as his breathing slowed. She lay still as the thumping of his heart grew softer against her breast.

They were much less innocent now, both of them. She knew this for sure.

"How do you feel, Cheit?" he whispered finally.

"Branded," she answered. "And you?"

"As if I just hit a home run."

She lay silently in his arms, the warmth of his large body warding off the chill of the evening. She closed her eyes and dozed. Then suddenly she saw them again, the people from her dream, as familiar as a reflection in a mirror and as clear.

The darkness was gathering around them as they lay entwined, unclothed, silent, on the banks of the lake.

"My father has decided to favor Mackintosh's suit," she said softly.

The man bit back a curse. "I'll no gi'e ye up," he answered. *"Steal away wi' me now."*

"Like a thief in the night..."

He tangled his fingers in her hair, drew her head back, searched her face in the dim light. "Ye'd wed wi' him, then?"

"It's likely he'll no ha'e me once he learns ye've put yer bairn in my belly...."

His eyes widened and his hand slipped down to caress his child. "I love ye, Catriona," he whispered.

"I never asked you about protection," Alec said suddenly.

She started, looked up into his face in surprise. He was unerringly close to the subject of her daydream. "I take the pill. After taking it every day for the past four years, it has become a habit. I forgot to stop taking it after Evan broke up with me."

"Planning on not ever having sex again, were you?"

"Well, I wasn't planning on having it, that's for sure. Sex was never very important to me." The next words were more difficult to say. "I thought I was frigid," she finished in a whisper.

He stroked her hair, laid his lips against hers, making a dismissive noise deep in his throat. "You're the most responsive woman I've ever known," he assured her.

She rolled on top of him, studied his face. "It never happened before, you know, the thing that happened inside me when we made love...."

"An orgasm," he supplied.

She nodded. "I've never had one before."

He laughed. "Well, then, MacGillvray, we have a fair amount of catching up to do, no?"

*   *   *

They retrieved the bottle of wine from Angus's basket. It was the same vintage as they had enjoyed in his restaurant on Friday night, the last of their leftovers. It was nearly chilled by the ambient air temperature in the far corner of the cottage. Kate crouched next to Alec in front of the fireplace, watched him remove the bottle's cork and splash wine into the pan, which he then set carefully into the fire.

"Alec . . . have you ever seen a ghost?" she asked.

He glanced at her. "Been into the whisky again, have you, MacGillvray?"

She shrugged, smiled sheepishly.

"If you have—"

"Been into the whisky?"

"—seen a ghost," he continued, "you're in good company. Some of the most sensible people I know take precautions to keep wandering spirits from wandering into their houses."

"Like urinating on their door posts?"

He laughed. "A bit messy, that. But they're not beyond nailing a horseshoe above it—the detouring power of iron is well known, you see—or tacking up a sturdy branch of rowan. My kin in Kingussie still tell tales of the Witch of Laggan, who was reportedly dispatched to her master in Hell hundreds of years ago. They keep a horseshoe outside the door and a rowan branch inside."

"The Witch of Laggan?"

"She was a very evil woman who was forever wreaking havoc on the poor locals—drying up their cows' milk, causing their bairns to be born dead and a' that. She could turn herself into a cat or a rabbit or a crow at will, so she was difficult to spot.''

''I would imagine so.''

''I'll tell you an incantation guaranteed to protect you against the evil eye: 'I make to thee the charm of Mary, The most perfect charm that is in the world, Against small eye, against large eye, Against the eye of swift voracious women, Against the eye of swift rapacious women, Against the eye of swift sluttish women.' ''

'' 'Swift, sluttish women'?''

He wrapped his kilt around the pan's handle and removed it from the fire, laid it on the hearth. ''Aye, MacGillvray, but not to worry,'' he said, ''we take a kinder view of female sexuality these days.''

He went to a velvet-covered box, salvaged two crystal goblets from it and brought them to the fireside. He filled them with wine and handed her one.

''You were quite extraordinary out on the hillside,'' he said, raising his glass to her.

''So were you.'' she said.

''We were extraordinary together,'' he amended.

He went to his stores again and returned with napkins, ancient silverware and two fine china plates. He dished up the fish and they sat on the floor and consumed it happily.

''I firmly believe food tastes better when you catch it yourself,'' he said.

''I'll have to take your word for that. I can't believe this would taste better if I had caught it.''

''You'll see someday, MacGillvray,'' he said. ''I'll teach you to fish.''

Would he? There were so many things he could teach her, so many things she wanted to learn, but there wasn't time. In time, she might even have been able to teach him something; she might have been able to teach him that love didn't have to hurt. She collected their plates and cutlery, deposited them on the sideboard. "Where can we wash the dishes?"

"We'll have to take them out to the well in the morning," he said. "But in two months' time, I'll have a fine dishwasher and we'll be freed from these primitive inconveniences."

They weren't so very inconvenient, she realized. She was enjoying herself immensely. But then she wouldn't be here for the era of the dishwasher.

She smoothed out her arisaid, settled back down on the floor beside him and watched the fire. She raised her glass, ran her finger over the laurel branches etched on one side of the ancient crystal, the aristocratic long-nosed man's head-in-profile etched on the other. Alec noted the gesture and nodded.

"Two hundred fifty years ago, a MacLachlan sat here with his wife, a lovely MacGillvray, I believe, toasting the King Over the Water, James III of England and Scotland, with these glasses." He studied the etching, his voice quiet and solemn. "The tide had long since turned and MacLachlan knew that Prince Charles Edward's troops would be marching to slaughter shortly. He knew his clan would be in the front line. He had stolen home for a few hours to bid his wife farewell."

Kate sipped her wine pensively. "What do you think they talked about?" she mused. She could see the scene clearly in the flames in the grate: a man in kilt and sark, his dark hair brushing his shoulders, a woman in homespun skirt and vest, her light hair bound into a long braid.

"How does one say good-bye to the love of one's life?"

She raised her shoulders. It wasn't the first time tonight she had considered the question.

"The children were already tucked into their beds. MacLachlan and his lady had shared a meager meal, but the conversation was stilted. Then they sat here, in front of the fire, and sipped wine."

"Ye swore ye'd ne'er leave me, Alasdair." Her voice was soft and bitter.

"I'll always be wi' ye, in yer heart," he said.

"But who will fill my arms and my bed? Who will our sons turn to when they need their father?"

"She begged him not to go," Kate said with certainty. "Then she told him she would rouse the children, pack a few of their possessions and they could be far away from Culloden field, from Scotland even, before the battle was joined."

Alec nodded. "And he told her he was a soldier. He told her they could never get far enough away. He told her he could die a brave fool, but never live a coward, a traitor."

"And she asked him who had his first loyalty, his family or the Bonnie Prince."

"You should write books, MacGillvray," he laughed.

She smiled vaguely. She would certainly consider putting all this to paper if she didn't lose her mind before she got a chance to do it. Why could she feel these people's emotions as surely as she did her own? Where were these images coming from? Perhaps she was simply remembering scenes and dialogue from another of the thousand romances she had read. She rejected this explanation immediately. They were too sharp, too detailed, too *personal*, for that.

Alec stood up and moved behind her, drew her back against his strong legs. "But he needed to see her skin gleam like alabaster velvet in the firelight. He needed to bury his hands in her soft, golden brown hair, one last time."

He untied the lace with which she had bound her hair, pulled his fingers through the length of it, to loosen it, to feel it against his skin. "Yer hair is the finest, softest thing I've e'er touched," he whispered, his voice breaking.

Alec pushed the shawl down off Kate's shoulders, lifted her hair up off them. "He needed to sink into her, to have her hold him until it was time for him to go."

"Hold me," Alasdair begged.

Kate turned and laid her face against Alec. He drew her to her feet, into his arms, and met her lips. He kissed her until she was weak and unsteady in his arms, soft and ripe against him. Then he carried her to the couch, laid her down on it. He kept his gaze focused on her as he unfastened his kilt and let it fall to the floor. He lay down beside her.

"Hold me," Alec asked softly.

She closed her arms around him, wrapped her legs around him.

He sank into her. He moved against her, fast and

slow, deep and shallow, but with infinite gentleness, until she was trembling and crying silently. They found release, and a link with eternity, together. And she continued to hold him.

She broke away from his embrace, finally. He groaned in protest, but his exhaustion drove him back into sleep immediately. She studied his thin, drawn face in the darkness and tears trickled down hers. She would never see him again, not in this life, she knew. And she would die on the battlefield as surely as he did, no matter how many years God forced her to endure after he was gone. He might suffer before he died, without warmth or comfort, she thought, her heart aching. "Lord, let it be quick and merciful," she prayed softly. She shook his kilt out and laid it across a chair. She hugged his sporran against her for a moment. She lifted his dirk, turned it this way and that, watching moonlight glint on its steely edge. She went to the washstand and sluiced her face, sponged her body, with the icy water in the basin. She dressed quickly. She brushed her hair, drew it over her shoulder and braided it. Then she nodded. It would be a small gesture, but one that might mean something to him in the end. She needed to send something along with him, something that he would find in the bottom of his sporran, that he could hold onto in the hour of his death and know he wasn't alone; something that would symbolize the part of her that would rest beside him in his grave. Forever. She reached for his dirk.

The words occurred to Kate as clearly as if they had been spoken in her ear. It was a strange phrase, one she didn't understand, in a language she could swear she had never heard, wouldn't have been able to name, until two days before. She spoke it in a whisper as she cradled Alec's head against her breast.

He stiffened. "Why did you say that?" he murmured, awakening abruptly.

She shook her head. "I . . ."

He relaxed back then, chuckled and squeezed his eyes shut. "I must have put too much wine in with the pike, MacGillvray. I could swear I heard you say 'till we're together again'—in Gaelic!"

Chapter Seven

Kate awoke in Alec's arms. She stretched happily against his long, strong body, feeling warm and sated, very lazy. Cared for? She considered this. It was difficult for her to believe that Alec had shown the same kind of tenderness, the same kind of passion, to every one of the women he had known since Tess. It was difficult for Kate to believe he hadn't felt at least some of what she had the night before. She stroked his hair back from his forehead, then laid her lips there.

He opened his eyes with a start, lifted his wrist and glanced at his watch. "Better get up," he said brusquely. "This Scottish idyll is over."

A one-night stand. *Three nights*, she corrected herself.

She couldn't keep the tears from welling up in her

eyes, but she could keep him from seeing them. She stood up and pulled her shawl around her, turned her back on him, wiped her cheeks impatiently.

"It's a wee bit late for modesty, no?" he asked.

She wasn't feeling modest. She was feeling bitterly ashamed. She had entered into this Scottish idyll with her eyes wide open, with an agenda that was perfectly clear, even when nothing else was: seduce him, get him into bed, find out if he can make it an entirely different experience from what it was with Evan. She had dressed it up, after the fact, gilded it with fantasies about destiny and true love, but the truth was clear and unavoidable. She had behaved like a *strumpet* and it was hypocritical for her to assume the role of offended *maiden* now. She managed a brief, unhappy grimace at her thoroughly antiquated choice of words, and a string of more up-to-date ones sprang readily to her mind. She wasn't the first woman in history to have behaved as she had, she supposed, and they had always been called *something*. Their idylls had probably been as short-lived as her own.

Suddenly his arm was curling around her waist from behind, his hand was brushing aside the hair on her nape so that his lips could settle there, warm and soft. She shivered. He turned her to him, looked down into her eyes in surprise.

"Tears, MacGillvray? Why?" he demanded.

She blinked to clear her vision. She couldn't recall the last time she had cried in another person's presence.

"Tell me, Cheit."

She forced herself to smile. "It was fun, Alec. I

132

thank you for an idyllic weekend. Now let me go. I have to use the Porto-San."

"Piss the floor, if you must. But I'll not let you go until you tell me why you're crying."

His strong fingers were digging into her shoulders. She sighed. "This is the first time I've ever . . ." she began.

"Slept with a stranger," he supplied irritably. "I know that. I'd have known it even if you hadn't told me so yourself."

"I don't blame you, Alec. You never misrepresented yourself. I knew it was just sex for you. But somehow I didn't imagine it would end this abruptly, this unpleasantly. Or that I would feel so . . ."

"MacGillvray—"

". . . cheap. I've heard other women talk about it, of course: the shame you feel the next morning, his desire to get rid of you quickly and pretend it never happened—"

"MacGillvray—"

"But 'get up, it's over'? Isn't that a little harsh, Alec, knowing that I had never done anything like this before? Maybe you could have said something like—"

"The workmen will be here in a quarter hour."

"Nice try!"

He bowed his head and silenced her with a kiss. He pried her shawl out of her fingers, pulled it off her shoulders, watched it puddle at her ankles; then his gaze moved up from her feet in a leisurely manner. "I can't bear the thought that another man has ever seen you like this, *mo breagha*. Do you imagine I'd enjoy having six rough workmen do so?"

"Workmen?"

He sighed. "It's Monday morning. There's wiring and plumbing to be installed, a foundation to be poured. They should be here in"—he checked his watch—"ten minutes."

He was holding her tight. She could feel him, hard and ready against her belly. "That's long enough," she said.

She had barely managed to struggle into her skirt before she heard the workmen unloading their tools, chatting loudly outside the window. She peeked out at them. She grinned at Alec, who was buttoning up his shirt. "We did everything but the dishes," she said.

He glanced over at the sideboard. "We'll take them with us. There's a place nearby that serves a fine breakfast and washes up a mean dish."

"What?"

"You'll see," he said.

After the delicate Jacobean goblets were wiped clean and stowed away in their case, Kate and Alec stole out of the house like two truant schoolchildren, giggling, loading dirty pan, plates and cutlery into the back of the car. "Fasten your safety belt," he warned, before he floored the gas pedal and sent the Range Rover plummeting down the rocky driveway in a cloud of dust, whipping onto the narrow, twisting, single-lane road at breakneck speed. She marveled, and cringed, as Alec tucked neatly into a bay in the face of an oncoming vehicle, then resumed his previous speed without flinching. He drove as confidently as he did everything else, she noted. It was admirable, and disconcerting.

Several minutes later, they pulled into another dirt road. It was thickly edged in trees. Though the trees were still bare, she could imagine their leaves forming a thick green canopy over the road. The car streaked down the pitted trail without slowing, Alec negotiating it as only one who knew his terrain well could. Where were they heading now?

Finally the woods gave way to open space, and a large brick house came into view in the clearing. It was fronted by gardens that were obviously well cared for, backed by rolling green hills. In a few months' time, this place would give the Philadelphia Flower Show a run for its money, she guessed. He pulled up to the front of the house, sprang to the ground, then dashed around to the opposite car door to release her.

"Where are we?" she asked, looking around in appreciation as he lifted her to the ground.

"It's called 'Dun Buie,' from *dun*, a fortified hill, and *buidhe*, yellow. This is where we'll have breakfast."

She glanced down at her beloved designer suit, which was certainly the worse for wear now, crumpled and not particularly fresh-smelling. Her stockings had obligingly sprouted several runs when she attempted to pull them on this morning and she had opted to toss them out. She was conscious of her bare legs beneath the short, tight skirt and of her mud-caked high-heeled shoes. There hadn't even been time to brush her teeth or take a comb to her hair this morning. She certainly wasn't up to dining at a fancy inn. She grabbed her handbag. At least she could nip into the ladies' room and take care of those two essentials before anyone saw her. "I look like something the cat dragged in," she murmured.

"And I'm the cat," he said, taking her hand and dragging her toward the door.

He let himself into the house familiarly. He glanced around the large paneled foyer for a moment before he shouted something in Gaelic.

Where were they?

"I'll be right back, MacGillvray," he said. "I forgot the dishes."

Before she could protest, he was out the door, leaving her standing alone, self-consciously, in the foyer. A plump middle-aged woman appeared then, wiping her hands on the flowered apron she was wearing. She met her visitor's eyes in surprise.

"Did I hear Alec's voice?" she asked.

"He forgot something in the car," Kate said, gesturing toward the door. "I'm Kate MacGillvray." She held out her hand.

"Ah," the woman said, taking it. "You're even prettier than I had heard."

"You've heard of me?"

"My brother Angus gossips like an old woman. He had me on the phone before you'd finished your soup on Friday night," the woman laughed. "And Jamie and Isabel have been singing your praises since they met you at Dunc's wedding on Saturday. I'm Violet Lachlan."

"Mum!" Alec said, coming forward, curling one arm around his mother's shoulder, hugging her, then presenting her with the pan and dishes he held in his other hand.

"For me?" Violet Lachlan asked.

He laughed. "We've been staying at the cottage. For all its charm, washing up there isn't easy."

"I can tell," she said, surveying her son, not his gift, critically.

He laughed. "Aye, Mum, I'm a bit ripe. And this kilt might be beyond cleaning. I suppose Kate and I could both use a hot bath, as well as a few of your bannochs. We dined on Uncle Angus's largess through lunch yesterday. I caught fish for dinner. I'm fairly certain I speak for Kate as well as myself when I ask, *when do we eat?*"

"You were always blessed with a healthy appetite, Ailig."

"I'm a growing boy," he protested.

"Full-grown, I'd say," Violet laughed, looking past her son. "Eh, Kate?"

"Overgrown, perhaps," Kate offered.

The older woman nodded, craned her neck in an exaggerated manner to meet Alec's eyes. "He's a big 'un, all right," she agreed. "But then, when I first saw his father, my James, I thought he must surely be the biggest man in Scotland."

Violet hooked her free arm through Kate's and led her through a maze of beautifully paneled and polished halls. They finally emerged into a massive kitchen whose appointments suggested its mistress was a serious cook. There was a long marble counter for rolling out pastry. The stove was starkly industrial, and an assortment of carefully polished copper pots hung on hooks above it. A well-used butcher block stood in the middle of the room.

"Sit down, Kate," Violet said, gesturing to a long planked table at the far end of it.

The table stood in front of a bank of bowed windows, and Kate glanced out at what appeared to be a vegetable and herb garden. Violet was a serious gardener as well, Kate guessed. "Your home is beautiful," she said.

"Thank you," Violet and Alec said in unison, and they both laughed.

"Of course, my brother Jamie is the *laird* here now," Alec offered. "But he has never seriously ordered me banished."

The plumply pretty Isabel came into the kitchen and flung herself against Alec. "I'm ashamed that my kin drove you out of your own house, into a hotel," she said.

He laughed. "It was purely coincidence that I decided I needed a few days away when the entire Clan MacLeod decided to descend on us. I hope you didn't mind."

The young woman grinned. "Jamie has to put up with them, thanks to the obligations of matrimony. You don't." She turned to Kate and smiled. "It's good to see you again, Kate."

"It's good to see you, Isabel," Kate said, realizing that it was.

Isabel took Kate's hand. "Do you ride?" she asked. "My husband is out in the fields somewhere, but he'd hate to miss seeing you this morning."

"I think I was riding before I could walk," Kate said. "But I'm not exactly dressed for it."

"I'll lend you some clothes!" Isabel looked pleased with her inspiration. "Alec can show off Dun Buie."

"The bannochs first," he said to his mother.

"The bathtub first," Violet directed.

He glanced around the kitchen then, as if suddenly remembering something. "Where are the beasties? I knew it was too quiet around here."

Isabel laughed. "They're all three in school now."

"Ah, aye, I forgot."

Isabel blanched, thrust the platter of bannochs she had just lifted off the sideboard at her brother-in-law and fled the room with her hand over her mouth. He stared after her in surprise, then looked inquiringly at his mother.

"Aye. There's to be another bairn. Jamie doesn't know yet."

Kate considered this, remembering Isabel's moodiness at the wedding.

Alec's eyes widened. "I believe I'll hide out at my hotel until after she tells him. I distinctly remember him saying two was his limit, and three his penance."

"Jamie's full of hot wind," Violet said.

Kate glanced from mother to son. The tone of their words told her that James Lachlan, the young laird of Dun Buie, was not a man who liked having his plans disrupted by unexpected turns of fate.

"Might we have a cup of tea before we hit the showers, Mum?" Alec appealed plaintively.

The older woman appeared to be weighing the pros and cons of allowing two such ill-kempt people to handle her teapot, then she laughed and gestured to it. "Help yourselves," she said.

Kate couldn't help but gape at the beautiful house as Alec dragged her behind him, up the wide oak staircase to the second floor. He raided a linen closet, emerged with a tall pile of fluffy towels. He divided the pile in two, handed her one, and gestured to another door. "I'll see you in a few minutes," he said, bending to lay a small kiss on her nose.

The hot water felt wonderful. Kate let it run on the back of her neck for a long time before she reached for the soft, fragrant soap and botanical shampoo and began scrubbing away the reminders of her Scottish idyll. It wasn't over, she decided with a smile. Was it just beginning? It was Monday, and she was scheduled to fly out of Glasgow early Friday morning. She shook her head before she doused it liberally with conditioner. She wasn't going to think about leaving yet.

She was wrapped in a towel, had just finished using her toothbrush, was combing her hair, when there was a knock at the door. She opened it to find Isabel there, bearing a pile of clothes.

"My boots may be a wee bit big for you," Isabel said, glancing down at Kate's feet. "You might have to put tissue in the toes."

Kate smiled and thanked her. "Violet told us about the baby," she added.

"Jamie isn't going to be pleased," Isabel said.

Kate hugged Isabel impulsively. "He'll just need time to get used to the idea."

"He's got seven and a half months," Isabel answered with a laugh as she turned away. "I doubt that's long enough."

Kate closed the door and surveyed Isabel's offerings. She had obviously worn these riding clothes before the first of the bairns came along, Kate decided, pulling them on, as they fit their borrower comfortably. There were well-cut buff breeches, a blouse with cravat, silky underpants, and a large hand-knit sweater. The socks seemed similarly homemade and Kate guessed Isabel was the knitter. The boots required just a small wad of tissue in each toe. Kate folded up her suit and camisole, retrieved her bag and shoes, took them out to the car. When she closed the hatch and turned around, Alec was behind her. He drew her into his arms, laid his face on her damp hair.

"I thought you were trying to escape," he said.

She laughed. "Why would I do that?"

"Lachlans are best taken one at a time, I suppose. And my brother and his beasties aren't even home yet."

"I can't wait to meet the third of those beasties," she said.

He watched her for a moment. "I think you mean that."

She didn't tell him she had been thinking about how it would feel to be part of his family, like Isabel was. She had experienced a definite twinge of envy when she learned Isabel was going to have a fourth beastie. And now, for the first time in her life, Kate allowed herself to consider the possibility of having a few of her own. "I'm not sure I'm brave enough to bring children into this world," she said, remembering the unwelcome revelations that had bombarded her after Attila died. She had suddenly seen the world for what it was: a violent, ugly place populated by violent, ugly people. . . .

She looked up into the beautiful face of the man who was holding her, an understanding smile on his lips, then past him to the peaceful pastures that seemed to roll on forever. "Even if you're a good parent, you can never completely shield them from the rest of life, from the horrors beyond their safe little nest."

"No parent has ever been able to do that, however much he has wished he might. All he can do is make that little nest a place where his children learn right from wrong, learn to love, gain the confidence to take on the world, and perhaps change it."

She smiled slowly.

"What the world needs is a good dip in your gene pool, MacGillvray," he said. "Now, come along. I'm starving."

Violet was in full gear, scrambling eggs at the stove, when Alec and Kate arrived in the kitchen. She urged them to sit down and have another cup of tea, and Isabel, fully recovered now, laid a platter of hot bannochs, oat cakes, in front of them.

Alec buttered one, drizzled honey on it and presented it to Kate. "You must eat your bannochs, MacGillvray," he advised. "They're good for the gastrointestinal tract, the cardiovascular system, and whatever ails you."

Kate laughed. "You sound like my Gram MacGillvray. Though she has never set foot in Scotland, she has always preached the virtues of the oat. She used to keep a vigil behind my chair every morning until I'd finished my porridge.''

"Yes indeed, we Scots esteem the almighty oat. But I'm forced to wonder if any of us really like the filthy things.''

"Alec!'' Violet admonished from her stove.

"Blasphemy!'' he laughed, cramming a bannoch into his mouth.

The eggs were fluffy and delicious, prepared with a touch of cream and fresh-snipped chives, and Kate made short work of them, as well as three more oat-cakes. ''It's clear that the Campbells know their way around the kitchen,'' she said to Violet. ''The food in your brother's restaurant was also delicious.''

Violet laughed. ''I taught him everything he knows.''

"I seem to recall his claim that he had deigned to share his wisdom with you, Mum,'' Alec said.

Violet waved her hand in dismissal and dashed to the stove to fetch more eggs.

The breakfast chatter was brisk and lighthearted and Kate felt herself being drawn into it naturally. When they finally pushed away from the table and Alec strolled out of the room with Isabel, Kate turned to Violet. ''Thank you for your hospitality, Mrs. Lachlan,'' she said.

Violet waved her hand in what seemed to be a characteristic gesture. ''Call me Violet. And thank you, Kate MacGillvray,'' she answered softly. ''I've never seen Alec look so happy. You're the first girl he has brought home since. . . .''

"Tess?''

143

Violet nodded. "Alec needs a wife. We all knew she wasn't the woman for him. But you. . . .''

Kate felt her face flush. "Mrs. Lachlan, Violet, Alec and I just met. . . .'' It was a protest she had made several times during the past few days.

Violet's hand was in the air again. "I knew Alec's father was the man for me before I got close enough to ken the color of his eyes. When I saw him across the dance hall, I felt dizzy, confused, tongue-tied.'' She smiled at the memory. "And I never once doubted he was the man for me during all the thirty-five years we were married.''

"I'm sorry you lost him,'' Kate said, able to understand the other woman's pain in a way she couldn't have done four days earlier.

"I'm glad I found him,'' Violet answered. She looked down at the gold ring on her left hand, then she twisted it and yanked it off with an effort. She handed it to Kate.

"It's beautiful,'' Kate said, examining the heavy band. It was worn and dark with age.

"It will go to Alec's wife.''

Kate looked up in surprise.

"It couldn't go to Isabel, of course, because when she wed Jamie, my James was still . . . with us.''

"Don't you want to keep it?''

Violet shook her head. "It symbolizes a living love. It belonged to James's mother and her mother-in-law before her. I have no idea how long it has been since it was crafted. But it's very old. Try it on.''

Kate hesitated, then slipped it on the third finger of her left hand.

144

Violet lifted Kate's hand and examined it. "A perfect fit," she pronounced.

Kate suddenly felt like Cinderella. *If the glass slipper fits your foot, you'll marry the prince.* Was this the Lachlan version of the tale?

"Come on, then, Kate," Violet said, accepting her ring back and struggling to press it down onto her finger. "Alec will be saddling the horses."

It felt good to be astride a horse again, Kate noted, as she thundered across the paddock behind Alec and his stallion and the trio of excited dogs who had invited themselves along for the tour. The air was cooler than it had been the day before, but it felt good against her face. The sun was shining again. *"You brought the sunshine with you,"* Alec had suggested. But the sun couldn't shine every day, forever.

She spurred her horse forward, drew it up alongside Alec's. He looked over at her and smiled.

"You didn't exaggerate your prowess, MacGillvray. You're a born horsewoman."

"I'm a woman of many talents," she laughed.

"And I look forward to discovering every one of them."

She lowered her eyes. She needed to make him aware of *one* of them, before he heard about it from someone else. "Your Dun Buie is beautiful."

"Aye," he answered, glancing around. "I was lucky to grow up here. But I'm glad Jamie's the older son. He has more of a feel for the land than I do. Oh, I enjoy gardening, like my mother does, but

I could never give Dun Buie the devotion it requires."

They had discussed devotion before. It seemed like a lifetime ago. "You don't offer your devotion easily," she recalled softly.

"But when I do offer it, I'm more or less committed for life."

She nodded, sensing this was more than casual conversation.

"Kate. . . ."

He hesitated, appeared to reconsider what he had started to say, then he spurred his horse forward, toward the rolling hills.

" 'Dun Buie?' " she called finally, pulling her reins up short as she reached the top of the eponymous rise and guided her horse between the few remaining walls and blocks of masonry that declared it so. "There's not much left of your fort, and the little white flowers between the rocks give the hill more of a dappled gray color than yellow."

"I've often wondered if it was named for the color of the hill or the blokes who manned the fort," he said.

"Yellow Scotsmen? No way," she replied indignantly.

"Right you are, MacGillvray, there's never been a coward among us!" he laughed. "Just ask Jamie!" He gestured toward a building in the distance and brought his horse about. They raced across the field.

James emerged from the barn as they neared it. He watched them questioningly for a moment, recognized them, then waved and grinned. He spoke to the workmen who were tinkering with a large piece of motorized equipment and strode forward.

"Ailig! Returned home on the heels of the departure of the dreaded MacLeod clan, did you?"

Alec laughed as he climbed down from his horse and handed its reins to the other man, bowed to give each dog a fond pat. "Isabel's mother is a bit hard to take," he said, reaching up and lifting Kate out of her saddle. Though she was perfectly capable of dismounting her own horse, she relished this little bit of chivalry, and the opportunity, however brief, to lean against Alec's chest.

"What's your mum like?" he queried softly as he set her down.

"You'd like her," she said. And Anne MacGillvray would most definitely like Alec.

I've met the right man, Mom! Kate thought. *But he has sworn off love and marriage, hates female physicians and lives an ocean away for Philadelphia.*

She turned and looked up into James Lachlan's face. "We meet again," she said.

"Did you doubt that we would?" James answered, taking her hand and shaking it with enthusiasm. His gaze was politely appraising, as if it were his duty as laird to judge the attributes of his little brother's lady. "Angus had told us you were pretty. But even so, I was surprised when I finally saw you for myself."

"Telephone, telegraph and tell Angus," Alec laughed.

"Angus is a very gallant gentleman," she said. Scotland, it seemed, was full of gallant gentlemen.

"An honest one," James countered.

"You're a family of flatterers."

James shrugged. "I'm glad you didn't run off without giving me the chance to look you over again. We'd all like to see young Alec married, with a bairn or two."

"Or four," Alec interjected irritably. "Kate's not a mare to be added to the stable and I'm not a stallion to serve as her stud, brother."

"Perhaps Kate has an opinion on that last point." She laughed.

"I like her, brother. She's no prim miss. A doctor too, aren't you, Kate?" James asked.

Guessing that James and Dunc Knox had found the opportunity to discuss the subject at the wedding, she started to answer in the affirmative, unable to lie outright. The preceding day had passed in a dizzying haze, filled with the idle small talk of a new romance, but sooner or later, even Brigadoon's lovers had been forced to talk turkey. She wished Mr. Lundie were here to referee. "Actually . . ."

"If she was, I'd have left her on the Culloden moor where I found her!" Alec interrupted, his voice emphatic, and Kate winced.

James guffawed. "Get over it, Ailig," he said. Then he looked back at Kate. "Not Catriona, is it?"

She shook her head. "Katherine." Where had she heard that name before, pronounced the way James had pronounced it, with the rolling second syllable? Ca-*tri*-ona.

James's eyes widened. "There's a headstone over in the old kirkyard for one Catriona MacGillvray MacLachlan."

"That's a mouthful." Alec suddenly looked uncomfortable.

"Her husband died at Culloden. 'In service to his King,' it says on the stone. I assume it refers to the Stuart king, not the German one, because I daresay Hanover counted few MacLachlans among his sympathizers. In those days, our clan lived in the midst of the fierce Campbells, who were loyal to King George. We had to fight our way through their land in 1745 before we could join Prince Charles Edward's forces for the Battle of Prestonpans. After Culloden, Hanover's son, the Duke of Cumberland, ordered Edinburgh's public hangman to burn the MacLachlan colors on the scaffolding, in gratitude for our support."

Despite James's wry grin, something in his eyes made Kate guess he felt this last humiliation as keenly as he would have done had it occurred two and a half days, rather than two and a half centuries, earlier.

"Get over it, Hamish," Alec said. "The Stuart clan was responsible for visiting as much misery on Scotland as ever the English did."

"Catriona and her husband lived in Alec's cottage at the time of the Rising," James supplied, ignoring his brother.

Kate stared at him, memories of the oddly vivid dreams she had experienced in the cottage flooding back.

"You didn't tell her about that, Ailig?"

"It didn't seem to have much to do with the price of kine in Carlisle," Alec grumbled.

Kate glanced from brother to brother. "I'd like to

see the stone," she said. It suddenly seemed essential that she see the stone.

"You can ride on over there, as long as you're out," James suggested.

Alec didn't appear as eager to do this as Kate was, or as James was to have them do it, and she watched him questioningly.

"All right then, MacGillvray. Let's have at it. Jamie, I assume we'll see you back at the house for lunch. Kate wants to talk you into renaming Dun Buie."

"I have a few things I'd like to talk her into, as well," James said, with an odd smile.

Chapter Eight

The old kirkyard was spread out around a very old chapel, which was tiny and made of gray stones that seemed weighted down by the moss and vines covering them. The chapel's roof had long since disappeared. The headstones were weathered and fractured, leaning at precarious angles. The place didn't project an air of neglect, however. "It looks like it's being drawn back into the earth," Kate said, as Alec lifted her off her horse, which, for some reason, declined to take another step forward.

He followed her gaze. "Ashes to ashes, dust to dust. . . ."

She nodded. "Everything cycles. Build, abandon, rebuild. Birth, death, rebirth."

"You don't believe in all that, do you, MacGillvray?" he asked.

151

She raised her shoulders as she strode toward the graves, noting that the dogs had also deserted them at the remnants of the fence that once ringed the area. She wasn't so sure what she believed anymore. Most of the stones were so worn that it was a difficult task to decipher them, and she crawled from one to the next on her knees, running her fingers over shallow etchings. As she approached a marker made of fine marble, which looked as if it had been inscribed by a sculptor rather than the local stonecutter, she saw the scene clearly.

The woman was wearing a gown with stiff petticoats. Her light brown hair fell unbound over her hips and a circlet of flowers held it back from her face. She was walking toward the chapel.

"Alasdair," she said, holding her hand out.

The man was dressed in a vibrant kilt and fancy jacket. His long, dark hair was braided on one side, in the ancient fashion. He took her hand. "Today ye'll become mine," he said.

"I've always been yers," she answered.

"Ye always will be." He raised her hand to his lips and kissed it.

A brigade of mounted clansmen thundered into the clearing then, a large burly man at its fore. The woman flung herself against Alasdair. "Either my father's here to gi'e me to ye, or to take ye from me," she whispered.

Kate settled back on her heels, breathing heavily. "Alec!" she called. What was this all about? Why was this happening again?

Alec had been searching halfheartedly on the other side of the yard, and he seemed to come toward her as reluctantly. He kneeled beside her, curled his arm around her shoulder, laid his lips against her cheek, ignored the stone.

"Look at it," she urged.

He turned toward it, laid his hand against it. He closed his eyes and drew in a sigh that seemed to wrack his body. "Catriona MacGillvray MacLachlan," he said. "Born 21 June 1723. Died 28 December 1749."

She stared at him in surprise. "You knew it was here all the time?"

He met her eyes. "Aye," he said. "I never liked coming here. Jamie used to tease me about being afraid of ghosties when we were boys. But this place always made me feel . . . sad, melancholy actually, not afraid. It's the same way I feel on the Culloden moor." Then he looked back at the stone and scanned the rest of the information. "Loving mother of Alec and Jeremy MacLachlan. Beloved wife of Alexander MacLachlan. . . ."

Alexander, not Alasdair! Kate reminded herself.

". . . died 16 April 1746, in service to his King." He closed his eyes again. " '*You are so strongly in my purpose bred, That all the world besides methinks are dead,*' " he finished in a whisper.

She watched him carefully, unable to shake the certainty that he still knew more than he was telling. Was it possible he had seen and heard something, too? Was it possible that a wedding *had* been interrupted by the arrival of the bride's father and his clansmen, here, once upon a time, and that Alec knew something about it?

She laid her fingers against his newly shaved

cheek, studied his eyes. He turned his face quickly, dropped a kiss in her palm. "In Gaelic the word 'died'—*bhasaich*—is only used for animals. Human beings 'change' or *shiubhail*—'travel,' " he said.

"Really?"

"In the old days, the deceased was stretched out on a board and wrapped in linen. A wooden platter was placed on his chest. This contained soil and salt—not mixed; the soil represented the corruptible body, the salt the incorruptible spirit. On the evening following his death, his friends and relations would meet in his house to cry, but also to dance—his nearest of kin would be the first to take the floor. The women would sing a *coronach* lauding his bravery and good deeds. They celebrated his deliverance from this life of misery and mourned the hole his passing left in theirs, at the same time."

It wasn't really such an odd conversation to be having in a cemetery, Kate supposed, though it was doing nothing to soothe her jangled nerves. And she couldn't help but suspect he was trying to sidestep the subject of their previous conversation. "Catriona died so young," she said, steering him back.

He glanced at the stone. "Aye."

"Do you imagine she had a wake?"

"I shouldn't think so. There were so many dead during those years, and so few left to mourn them. Most of the stones from that time were probably cut at the parish's expense, so the dead wouldn't lie in unmarked graves."

"Not Catriona's. Hers is much finer than the rest. And those last words. . . ."

"Shakespeare."

She nodded. " 'You are so strongly in my purpose bred, That all the world besides methinks are dead.' That is the sentiment of a lover, someone who mourned her deeply, yet her husband was already gone. . . ."

His expression was grim and he showed no inclination to dignify her conjecture with an answer. She sighed. "I wonder how she died."

"She drowned in the loch." He stood up abruptly, brushing soil off his jeans. "So, do you want to see the chapel, or no?" he demanded.

She nodded, more surprised by his tone than the information he offered. But it was somehow reassuring to know that she wasn't the only one affected by this place.

"Come on, then," he urged grimly, pulling her to her feet, pulling her along, behaving like a man who was eager to put an unpleasant task behind him.

They stepped through an archway from which the doors had long ago been removed. Sunlight poured into the small space from above, warming it. A dozen rough-hewn benches were still in place on either side of a narrow aisle. A small panel of stained glass remained miraculously intact and its colors fell in bright bands on a simple marble altar at the far end of the room.

"Your family was Catholic?" she asked, striving for conversation, for ordinary words that might make their tour of an unexceptional historical site unexceptional again.

"We were all Catholic, once," he answered, his voice a reluctant whisper. "I imagine the Mac-Lachlans were mostly Episcopalians by then." She hadn't specified *when,* she realized.

"But to the Presbyterians, there was little difference between the two. And it was widely held that the Stuart allegiance to Rome was as solid as the Pope's gold. It was a complicated time. . . ."

"And a simple one."

"Aye," he agreed.

She looked toward the altar and for a split second she thought she saw a dark-haired man in kilt, standing there, waiting, his beautiful mouth stretched into a broad smile.

"Come on," Alec said, taking her hand again.

But he was no longer pulling her, Kate noted. Alec's pace had become as slow, as cautious, as her own. They halted at the bottom of the two steps that led up to the altar and they raised their eyes to the colorful window behind it. They stood there in silence for many minutes. Finally, he shrugged, as if in answer to an unspoken question, and drew her into his arms. He kissed her tenderly.

"What have you done to me, Catriona?" he murmured against her hair. This was apparently the question he had answered with a shrug in the moment before he spoke it, and his tone made it clear that the words hadn't been meant for her ears.

But she couldn't pretend she hadn't heard them, nor think past one of them to comprehend the rest. "You called me Catriona!"

"It's the Gaelic for Katherine," he said.

They galloped across the hills, around one side of the lake, enjoying the silence and the crisp, sweet air in their faces; then they slowed so that they could talk. They talked a great deal, about many things, important things and inconsequential things, easily, as only lovers can, as if their acquaintance could be measured in eons rather than hours. But, as if by mutual consent, they didn't discuss the chapel or anything that had happened there. And whenever Kate started to broach the subject of her work and the incident that had caused her to precipitously turn her back on it six days earlier, she felt ashamed, the words died, unspoken, in her mouth.

Alec put his hand on her horse's bridle finally and gentled it to a stop. He dismounted and went to her side, held his arms up to her. She curled her arms around his shoulders and allowed herself to be lifted out of her saddle and held tightly against the length of him.

"I want you so much," he whispered gruffly, his words warm against her ear.

She pressed closer, feeling the truth of this.

"I'll never stop wanting you." He buried his fingers in her hair, tilted her head back so that he could plunder her mouth with his tongue. She gripped him possessively, answering with parries and thrusts of her own.

"I can't wait until we get back to the hotel," he gasped.

"Let's not," she suggested. She glanced around. "Let's make love in the heather on the hill, like in Brigadoon."

He laughed. "There's not much heather on those hills yet, and I certainly can't wait until it blooms. How does a hayrack sound?"

"Like heaven," she answered.

Later, they strolled back toward the stables hand-in-hand, each free hand clutching a set of reins. They settled their horses leisurely, feeding them handfuls of oats and last season's apples as they removed saddles and tack, abandoning their efforts to behave with some measure of propriety, finally, and tumbling into the hay again. Then they continued on to the house.

Violet greeted them at the kitchen door. "Where have you two been?" she asked, ushering them to the sink to wash and then to the heavily laden table.

James leaned behind Kate's chair to pick a bit of straw out of Alec's hair. "Took a wrong turn, brother, did you?" he asked.

Kate felt her face flush and she concentrated her attention on the soup in her bowl.

"Aye," Alec said in a neutral voice, but when everyone else's attention was similarly directed toward their food, he discreetly picked a leaf off Kate's sweater. She turned to him, met his eyes, and his grin. "Let's get lost in the woods again after lunch," he whispered.

They had barely finished the meal when the beasties rolled into the room like a thunderstorm, pushing each other and shouting, looking for handouts from the table.

"You shouldn't have them begging from your plate like pups," Alec said.

"Why not?" James answered. "I'm thinking about building them a kennel. There's not a prayer they can be housebroken." A beautiful little girl with bright copper curls climbed into his lap then and wrapped her arms around his neck. "Is it your brothers' influence, wee Maggie, or were you born with the de'il in you as well?"

"It's my brothers," she said, sticking her tongue out at the pair.

Kate watched Andy and Michael roll around on the flagstones with small fists flailing.

"What size kennel were you thinking about building, brother?" Alec asked, leaning back in his chair and smiling smugly. Isabel swatted at him with her napkin.

James looked from his brother to his wife and his eyes widened. "No . . ." he groaned.

"It's really no more trouble to put in an extra cage, or two, Jamie," Alec continued. "I'll help you."

"You've helped quite enough," James said.

"*Och*, I think you got yourself into this without any help from me," Alec laughed.

Isabel broke away from her husband's accusing glare to clear the table, and Maggie escaped from her father's suddenly limp grasp to climb up into Kate's lap.

"You're Kat," the little girl said with confidence.

"Kate."

Maggie shook her head. "Kat. Shall I show you my kittens in the shed?"

"I'd like that," Kate said, allowing the girl to take her hand, bending to pet the other two redheads, who were oblivious to her.

"You like kiddies, MacGillvray," Alec said.

She looked at him in surprise. "Yes," she answered. It was the second time today that it had occurred to her. She couldn't remember ever thinking about it, one way or the other, before today.

"Let's go, Kat," Maggie said.

* * *

When Kate and Maggie returned to the kitchen, it was deserted. This seemed odd to Kate, who had already learned that the kitchen was the hub of this gracious house and was rarely empty. A pot of lentil soup was boiling over on the stove. She turned it off. She caught Maggie's hand again and they stepped into the hallway to investigate, peeking into empty rooms as they proceeded. Finally, the emerged into the foyer to find the front door wide open. They stepped through it and saw the rest of the family gathered outside.

The red flat-bed truck in the drive was familiar; Kate had noticed it at the cottage this morning. And the voice of the man who was standing at its side, a large open trunk at his feet, was similarly familiar.

Alec turned and met her eyes, held his hand out to her. Had something gone wrong at the cottage? she wondered as she stepped forward. Alec's face was pale and solemn. In their haste to leave this morning, had they forgotten to put the screen around the fireplace or. . . . "What is it?" she asked.

Alec gestured to the trunk.

She bent over it. Its contents looked innocuous enough, a pair of silver candlesticks which didn't match, and three paintings in gilt frames, two landscapes and a portrait of a woman. She looked up at Alec inquiringly.

"Joe found a priest hole under the bedroom floor when he was laying pipes. The trunk was inside it."

She nodded, still not understanding the urgency in his voice, on his face. She knew that during the volatile eighteenth century even humble cottages were built with secret rooms where valuables, and weapons, could be hidden from the English. She picked up one of the landscapes and studied it, impressed by the rugged beauty it depicted and the skill of the artist who had rendered it.

"Look at the portrait," he said.

She lifted it. It was in excellent repair, no doubt thanks to the tightly sealed trunk in which it had been contained. Its subject was pretty and rosy-cheeked, wearing a bright plaid over one shoulder. Her mouth was turned up sardonically at one corner, conveying the distinct impression that she had posed for the artist under duress. But the warmth in her eyes also showed that she had loved him. The year under his unreadable signature was 1744.

"She's lovely," Kate whispered. Catriona. She certainly knew the face, and now she recalled where she had heard the name, before James spoke it this morning, in the manner he had spoken it. Catriona. She had heard it in a dream.

"She's you," Maggie announced, looking from the picture to Kate and back.

Kate met Alec's eyes and he shrugged.

She looked back at the portrait in disbelief. There was a resemblance surely, one that might be heightened if she gained a few pounds and grew her hair long. And then she remembered the odd sensation that the emotions of the woman in her dream were her own.

Her finger had been skimming over the canvas, but suddenly it froze. *"Fortis et fidus,"* she gasped. Brave and faithful.

"What did you say?" James asked, his voice urgent.

Kate glanced from face to face. Even Andy and

Michael were standing straight and silent, watching her.

"It's the legend on a pin I own, and on the one in the portrait, as far as I can tell," she said, her finger moving to the familiar circle brooch on the woman's plaid. *"Fortis et fidus."*

"Brave and faithful. It's the motto of the Mac-Lachlan clan," Violet said, her face tense with surprise.

"What does it mean?" Kate begged, needing information beyond the motto's relevance to the Lachlan family, searching for it in Alec's face and in his eyes.

It was James Lachlan who answered. "It means that sometimes we just have to accept the gifts of God without asking questions." He drew Isabel into his arms and found her lips.

James and the workman who delivered the trunk finally carried it into the house. The rest of the family drifted after them, glancing back at Kate as they did so. She watched them go, feeling as if she should say something to them, anything, an explanation or an apology or a comment on the weather, but her lips wouldn't cooperate. Alec's hand tightened on her shoulder as a shiver coursed through her. She turned to him, pressed herself into his arms.

"It's just an old portrait," he said. "They're all acting like you came face-to-face with your fetch."

"With my . . ."

He chuckled, as he had done before when he remembered that many of the concepts as familiar to him as his name were new to her.

"Do you know the German word *doppelganger*?"

She nodded her head against his chest. "It's something like an astral projection, right? A person's spiritual double?"

"Aye. Well, Highlanders were always big ones for seeing fetches—particularly other peoples'. The appearance of one usually preceded its solid half's demise, though if it was spotted at a young lad or lass's side, it was possibly just his or her future spouse. But if someone met up with his own fetch, it always meant he was going to die."

His voice trailed off as she shivered again. "Buck up, MacGillvray. I was just trying to humor you. The painting doesn't look so very much like you, anyway."

She finally lifted her face. "Doesn't it?"

He shook his head, though she thought his expression belied the movement. "The Scots have a penchant for hyperbole and always prefer supernatural explanations to more pedestrian ones. 'We found an old portrait.' What kind of story is that for my mum to repeat to her cronies for the next ten years? 'On the day Alec brought my daughter-in-law home for the first time, a 250-year-old portrait she could have posed for was mysteriously delivered to our doorstep.' That has more of a ring to it, no?"

"Daughter-in-law?" she whispered, forgetting the rest of what he said.

He grinned. "Come now, Kate. They've done everything today but call in the parson. They want me married off rather badly, you see."

She did see that. "Why?"

"I suppose they want me very solidly rooted so that I can't just up and jump ship."

163

"Don't they know: 'If ye ha'e less gear, ye ha'e less care'?''

He laughed at her attempt to render his favorite proverb faithfully. "They want me loaded down with gear, the care be damned."

Or maybe they just thought he was lonely. Was he? She searched his green eyes, didn't see it there. "In America, men call their wives 'the old ball and chain.' "

"To their faces they do that? And I thought the Scots were brave."

She laughed too.

"I promised Jamie I'd help him work through a glitch in one of his computer programs this afternoon," he said.

Glitches? Programs? In Brigadoon?

"Yes, we do have computers here. And electrical current to hook them into. Do you feel like watching?"

She looked past him, at the thick woods and rolling hills. "I feel like walking." And she didn't want to read all those surmises in all those Lachlan green eyes, just yet.

"Well, be sure to head back before the sun goes down. The ghosties come out at dark. . . . I'm kidding, MacGillvray!"

Kate soon found herself deep in the woods. The sunlight that filtered through the branches and pine boughs overhead was soft and green-tinged. The smell of evergreen and damp mulch from last summer's perennials filled her nostrils, seemed to soak into her skin. It was part of Alec's scent, she realized suddenly, the comforting scent that lingered on his

clothes, in his hair. He loved to walk in the woods—
she had learned that much about him very shortly
after they met. She could almost see him running
among these trees, a thin, copper-haired boy, his
larger, darker brother in hot pursuit. Or was it the
son she and Alec could produce who was dodging
and weaving his way through her imagination? The
thought made her smile. Perhaps she was brave
enough to have a son and a lovely little copper-
haired daughter like Maggie.

A shadow moved behind a tree and she jumped.
She wished Alec had spared her his talk on doppel-
gangers. She hurried forward, glanced over her
shoulder in time to see a large rabbit lunge across
the trail. She chuckled. But hadn't Alec said
Highland witches moved about in the form of rabbits
and cats and crows?

Foolishness! She didn't believe in witches or
fetches or reincarnation. The portrait didn't look
anything like her. And hadn't her father once said
that every Scottish clan was related to every other
in some way? The MacGillvrays and MacLachlans
had doubtless joined in marriage, exchanged trin-
kets, many times over the centuries, and Catriona's
pin wasn't the only one like it ever forged. And her
husband's name had been Alexander, not Alasdair.
The Highlands simply gave one's imagination per-
mission to shift into overdrive, and her own had
gratefully leapt at the opportunity. It was like REM
rebound, she supposed, looking for a scientific analogy. Every individual required a certain amount of
rapid-eye-movement sleep—dreaming sleep. If this
was suppressed, by certain drugs for example, he
experienced vivid dreams, nightmares, once the drug

was withdrawn. It made perfect sense. She had been suppressing her imagination for quite a while. Her fantasy-rebound had thrust her straight into her own little Brigadoon.

She emerged from this satisfactory line of conjecture to notice that daylight had almost completely faded. She heard a branch crack—overhead or underfoot, under someone *else's* foot, she couldn't tell which. She froze, then spun in a small circle, peering into the gathering dusk. This pirouette only served to disorient her, she realized, as she halted again. She was no longer sure which way was *back*. "That way," she murmured, with as much conviction as she could muster, and she started walking again.

Within minutes it was pitch black and the woods were filled with an assortment of new, and unrecognizable, sounds, not the least of which was the infernal whistling of wind through the treetops, now louder and more sinister than before. She had gone from *Brigadoon* to a script of her own creation, a *City Slickers*–type farce in which an inept big-town neurotic finds herself wandering aimlessly through a freezing wilderness filled with rabbits and . . . What? Badgers? She didn't even know what a badger was. She stumbled over a fallen log and splashed to her hands and knees in a stream. "Don't panic!" she said, as she stood up and pushed wet hair out of her eyes, attempted to wring out the hem of her sweater. Don't panic? Start with something easy like don't breathe, she chided herself. Her boots were making an unpleasant sloshing noise as she walked, the feet inside them were getting numb. And the damned wind was getting louder. . . .

Was it the wind? It sounded almost like a voice,

a high, pure, feminine voice raised in a mournful dirge. Keening. Hadn't Alec told her it was women's work to lament the newly departed in song?

No one was dead! Yet.

She stumbled on. Hadn't Alec mentioned that Highlanders never say someone has died, but rather has *shiubhail*—traveled? That unfortunate Gaelic word sounded too much like *shovel* to be comforting.

Alec talked too much, she decided.

Had she traveled to her death, here, in this remote and unkind wilderness filled with . . . sheep? She still suspected wild sheep could be nasty.

There seemed to be a light up ahead!

And the keening was getting louder.

She emerged into a clearing, found herself at the top of a hill looking down on a familiar little cottage whose windows glowed with the faint yellow light of a candle burning within. Or with the reflected light from the slip of moon that had just emerged. Her gaze jerked to the loch, where she thought she had seen a tiny boat, out of the corner of her eye. She looked back to the shoals where she might have glimpsed two figures, one shining, as if lit from within, the other shadowy. And she definitely heard an urgent voice cry: "Katherine!"

Or did she?

She ran toward the cottage, not thinking about who might have lit the candle inside it. She couldn't be afraid there. It was warm and safe. It was . . .

Home.

She hesitated for just a heartbeat before she threw the door open. Who could possibly be here? she wondered belatedly.

No one.

It was as dark and silent as . . . an empty house. She stepped through the door, closed it behind her, edged her way toward the sideboard where she knew Alec kept a box of matches. She struck one, moved it toward the oil lamp, ignoring the shadows that leapt up the whitewashed wall. She lit the lamp, lifted it, held it forward as she moved cautiously around the room. She glanced into the narrow passage that would soon be a kitchen. She stepped into the bedroom, caught her breath as a rhythmic slapping sound greeted her ears. She spun to it. It was just the heavy tarp that draped the hole in the wall, moving in the wind.

The wind. Keening. She had studied the cottage from the top of the hill, had kept it squarely in her sight as she ran toward it. But she hadn't noticed the dumpster or bulldozer or Porto-San at its side! she realized.

Get a grip!

She chuckled uncomfortably, returned to the main room. She put the lantern on the mantel, picked the blanket up off the back of the couch and hugged it around herself.

She gasped when the scratching started, jumped when the door flew open with a bang, shrieked when three low, dark apparitions plunged through it. Followed by a taller one.

"Good Lord, MacGillvray! Where did you get to?"

"Alec?"

"Who were you expecting?"

She started toward him, tripped over one of the dogs, who were all dashing around excitedly, sniffing and yelping. He caught her.

"Oh, Alec, I was so afraid out there . . ."

He lifted an eyebrow, glanced behind him. "Out there? You weren't lost in the Antarctic. Barely two miles separate the big house from this one, and a major road, loaded down with lorries and vans, runs between the two. Didn't you hear the traffic?" he teased, drawing her against him.

Maybe she had. She wrapped her arms around his shoulders and the blanket fell to the floor.

"Took a swim, did you?" he asked.

She remembered her stumble into the stream. "I'm getting you all wet."

"Do you hear me complaining?" He held her closer, rocking her, warming her. "Sing something for me," he said, several minutes later.

She chuckled. "You *are* a glutton for punishment. It would be kinder on your ears to set your hounds to howling."

"In the old days, they used to believe a dog howling in a house meant one of its inhabitants was going to die."

She stiffened. He was positively fixated!

"It was just the wind, after all," he added, to himself.

A frisson of fear ran up her spine.

"Cat walked on your grave?" he asked.

She jumped back from him. And in the dim light, his hair looked darker, and longer, his button-down oxford shirt looked looser, grayer, and his jeans looked for all the world like a kilt. He seemed to glow, as if lit from within. And the metallic object tucked under his waistband looked like the butt of a pistol.

"What's that?" she begged, as he drew it out.

He wrinkled his nose in bemusement. "On this planet, I believe it's called a 'cell phone,' Mac-Gillvray," he said.

James had the Range Rover at the cottage within minutes and Kate, Alec and the three dogs inside it soon thereafter. He dodged lorries and vans on the road that led to Dun Buie, with aplomb to beat his brother's.

"I wasn't sure whether you were lost or had run away from young Alec," he said.

Kate laughed. "I was enjoying the woods, thinking about this and that, and before I knew it, it was dark. I was definitely lost."

"Told you so," Alec interjected from the back seat, where the dogs were whimpering and falling against him with every dip in the road. "She would have been colder if she hadn't made her way to the cottage. It's lucky she found it."

She considered this. Luck had very little to do with it. But what did?

Kate soon found herself toweling off from her second "bathe" in Dun Buie's guest bathroom, preparing to dress herself in Isabel's things—a nightgown, robe and slippers this time around, as Violet wouldn't hear of her returning to the hotel tonight. Everyone else had already eaten supper, so she joined Alec at the kitchen table for hot sandwiches and soup, which seemed the most delicious meal she had ever consumed. Then she followed him into a large, cheerful room filled with overstuffed furniture and the rest of the family. A warm fire blazed in the grate. James promptly dismissed the children, and Kate got her share of hugs from them before they went off to bed. Maggie paused at the door, then dashed back to whisper in her ear and get a whispered response. Over a head of silky copper curls, Kate saw Alec smile.

"What did she have to say?" he asked, when the little girl had disappeared.

Kate grinned. "Andy apparently told her her new brother or sister would come out of her mother the same way kittens come out of theirs. She wanted to know if it was true."

"Ah. What did you say?"

"I suggested she discuss it with you."

"Uhmm," Alec said.

"You'd better not tell her the baby will come out the same way it got in, Ailig!" James warned him, then turned to Kate. "Andy gets all his information from his uncle, you see."

"Well, he is a doctor," Kate said diplomatically, looking from brother to brother.

"That's one of his qualifications," James said.

"Jamie!" Isabel said. "You'll scare Kate off."

James laughed. "MacGillvrays don't scare easy."

As a rule, Kate thought, remembering her near-psychotic episode in a copse of trees surrounded by two houses, a major highway and an open field from which all three were visible.

Violet entered the room with a tea tray and a basket of freshly baked peanut butter cookies, and the conversation turned to less risqué subjects. About a half-hour later, Violet, James and Isabel pleaded exhaustion and went off to bed. Alec turned on the television, then settled back on the couch and drew

Kate into the crook of his arm. They watched one of the peculiarly British comedies she occasionally caught on the public broadcasting channel back home. It was such a normal, pedestrian thing to do, something millions of people who never considered the habits of the restless dead, or the secretions of overactive nerve endings, were doubtless doing at the very same moment. Thoughts of her recent escapade receded, seemed as ridiculous as the antics on the screen.

"What did people do for entertainment before *the telly*?" she asked, still chuckling after the show ended.

"The same thing they do now after it's turned off," Alec said, grinning mischievously. "In the words of the immortal Rabbie Burns: 'When Princes and Prelates and het-headed zealots, All Europe ha'e set in a lowe, The poor man lies down, nor envies a crown, And comforts himsel wi' a mowe.'"

"Mowe?" she asked.

He laid his finger against her lips to encourage more discretion, glanced apologetically toward the second story of the house before he answered: "It's a *verra* rude word for the sexual act."

"So you're saying people found ways to entertain each other."

He nodded. "Always did, always will. There will be no mowe for us tonight, MacGillvray, but perhaps I can entertain you with a thorough description of tomorrow's."

She settled back in his arms and listened. She had to admit she found his thorough description more entertaining than *The Benny Hill Show*.

Chapter Nine

"Did you fix your glitch?" Kate asked James over breakfast the next morning.

He shook his head mournfully. "And my brilliant brother wasn't much help. Pray we have better luck setting the tractor to rights this morning. I don't fancy having to buy a new one."

"Shall I drop you by the hotel before Jamie and I get to it, MacGillvray?" Alec asked.

"I'll hang around, if you don't mind. Why don't you tell me about your glitch and I'll see what I can make of it."

"She's a scientist," Alec advised the table at large.

"Well, actually—" Kate began.

James held up his hand to forestall her comment

and grinned. "Better she was a saint, to abide your foolheadedness, Ailig," he said.

Kate was ready to kick some microcircuited butt. Isabel had provided her with a fresh set of clothes, James and Alec with details of their technological nightmare, and Violet with a big mug of coffee. She settled down in front of the computer and familiar-ized herself with it, stopping sporadically to sip from her cup and look out over the fields through the win-dow at her left hand. She ran systems, reorganized programs and finally attempted to retrieve the doc-uments Jamie had given up for lost. They were still there, she knew. Like the human brain, impressions made on an electronic memory could never be com-pletely erased. With the proper prompting, they could be salvaged, intact and intelligible.

She had it! She sat back and stared at the screen in surprise as an intricately drawn MacLachlan fam-ily tree appeared. She started to scan through related documents, seeing hundreds of ancient maps and deeds and handwritten pages from diaries that had obviously been photographed and scanned to save them from the ravages of time. No wonder James had been so upset about losing these things, she re-marked to herself. The originals might already be beyond touching, locked away in some hermetically sealed display case in some historical society. She came upon James's narrative finally, which was in itself hundreds of pages long. She had no right to read it, and she didn't allow herself to proceed be-yond the opening paragraph, but it was so compel-ling, so touched with its author's wry humor, that she regretted closing it. He can make history come alive, she thought. They were an interesting pair of siblings, the Lachlan boys: James a farmer and a historian, Alec, a doctor and a poet. *"My father would have liked you,"* Alec had told her. She suspected she would have liked him, as well. She allowed herself one last foray backwards through the scanned documents. This time, a poorly preserved page of cramped writing caught her eye. She bowed her head to the screen, squinted at the words, reading them aloud: "I thought there was naught left of my heart to break, but that day I felt the last of it crumble into grit and mortar, like the walls of my father's keep under the power of English guns. . . ."

They weren't bairns anymore, she noted, watching the boys circumspectly as she packed up the last of their few possessions. She didn't want them to know she was studying them, she didn't want them to see her tears. They were thinner than they should be, shorter than their birthright would dictate, but at least they had been spared the rickets and the scurvy. Their father's planning had provided funds enough to keep them from starving, even during those terrible first months when so many did. And the work she had managed to secure at the English officer's house had provided for them thereafter. But now, the Colonel was leaving, all hope of procuring another position was gone, and she had no choice but to trust his wife to take the boys away from this cursed, beloved place, to a better life. And out of hers. She stiffened when the knock at the door came. She swallowed to hold back the tears, the cries of outrage, and went to open it.

"My lady," she said, making a graceful curtsey. She hadn't forgotten the lessons of her pampered girlhood, though they had been given a lifetime ago.

"I'll love them like they were my own. I swear it," the Colonel's lady said.

"Thank ye," she said, knowing it wasn't the threat of starvation that had driven her to this, but rather the unkindness of neighbors who insisted upon laying the sins of their mother at the boys' feet. She couldn't allow her sons to be made pariahs because of her weakness. She hugged each of them, with much less passion than she felt. She removed the brooch from her bodice and pinned it on her younger son's jacket. "Mind the lady. I'll follow as soon as I'm able." She offered the Englishwoman a sad smile that conveyed regret at speaking the lie, but the smile that answered her was understanding and compassionate.

"Come, lads," the lady said. Each boy lifted his bundle to follow his new mother, raised his other hand to bid his old one farewell.

Kate dashed away the tears that flowed down her cheeks. The writer of the page hadn't identified herself, or her sons, or the husband who had died and left them to fend for themselves. There had been thousands of such families after the '45, Kate knew. Her imagination had put Catriona's face on the heartbroken mother because it was the only face from the past that she knew. It had put them in Alec's cottage because it was the only Highland croft she had ever seen.

That was all there was to it. Chances were slim that this page had been written by Catriona. In fact, in his opening page, James had mentioned entries from the memoirs of a Highland woman whose identity he had never been able to ascertain.

But Kate had seen the scene so clearly. She had read between the lines of the terse journal entry to imbue it with details and dialogue not provided by its writer. And she had felt the woman's wrenching agony, her shame, as if it were her own.

They were simply words on a computer monitor and she could clear them with a click of the mouse. She did.

But the mind's eye can't be cleared as easily, and Kate sat stiff and silent, staring at the C-prompt, remembering the scene for a long time.

Kate walked around the house, poking her head in the kitchen and laundry, offering assistance to Isabel and Violet, both of whom rejected it. She wandered out into the yard, saw James and Alec in the distance, still busy with the tractor.

She didn't consciously decide to head for the Range Rover, but suddenly she found herself standing in front of it. The keys were in the ignition, she noted. She climbed in behind the wheel. Alec wouldn't mind if she did a little exploring, she assured herself, and looked for a bakery or florist where she could buy Violet a small token of her gratitude.

She had never driven on the left side of the road, and it was years since she had attempted the complicated coordination of clutch and gears called a manual transmission, but she turned the engine over nonetheless, fastened her seat belt and started down the winding drive, bucking and bolting, stalling out twice before she got the hang of it. When she reached the main road, she hesitated just a moment before she turned right. She drove for a long time, passing through a tiny village in which she stopped to buy a cake and some flowers. She stopped at a quaint little distillery where a famous whisky was made, and left with a bottle. She felt compelled to continue on, even though the twists and turns she was taking made it unlikely she would ever find her way back to Dun Buie. She sped around yet another curve in the road, promising herself she would turn back after she saw what lay beyond it, but the scene she encountered there made her pull up short. She watched two workmen lift a slab of etched granite into the back of a truck. She looked beyond them to the long, low building from which they had carried it, and she knew she had to go in there. She set the brake, climbed down from the car. Some impulse made her turn back to grab the liquor. Then she started toward the door beneath a sign that read MacGowan and Sons. Monuments.

She opened the door and stepped into the workroom, which echoed with the sounds of chisels and power tools. An older man wearing a leather apron came forward with an inquiring expression on his face. She attempted to explain her errand, but he pointed to his ear and shook his head. He ushered her into an office and shut the door, blocking out the noise. "Good day to ye," he said. "I'm Stewart MacGowan."

"Good day," she replied. She looked past him to the stone angels and wreaths that decorated the walls and stood on the floor around the room. Some of them looked very old. "My name is Kate Mac-Gillvray. I was hoping you might help me."

"Have ye lost someone, Miss MacGillvray?"

"No," she said, realizing that, in a manner of speaking, she had. But what was the likelihood she was going to find him here? "I'm trying to learn who ordered a stone I saw in a churchyard yesterday. It's very important to me."

The old man studied her, his expression saying he could tell it was.

"Has this business been in your family long?" she asked.

He shook his head. "Only about three hundred years."

She suppressed a smile, seeing that no humor had been intended. Three hundred years wasn't so very long in this corner of the world, she remembered. "The stone marks the grave of Catriona Mac-Lachlan, an ancestor of mine," she said, wondering why she had made this last claim when she wasn't at all sure it was true.

"Ah," the old man said. "When did she pass?"

She couldn't keep from smiling sheepishly now, seeing her fool's errand for what it was. Even if Catriona's headstone had been ordered from this particular concern, what was the likelihood they would have a record of the transaction so many years after the fact? "1749," she said.

Stewart MacGowan scratched his bald head as he considered the problem. "I'm afraid all I have from that long ago is an account ledger. It doesn't give the name of the deceased, just the name of the person who commissioned the stone and what he paid for it.''

"May I see it?'' she asked, anticipating a refusal, but the old man simply nodded and waved her toward his desk. He dug through a dusty cabinet until he found the book. He set it before her. She opened the heavy cover, expecting to find its pages in very poor repair, but the heavy paper had withstood the passage of time. The fate of its entries wasn't as promising; the ink was faded, the penmanship of its various authors poor. She carefully flipped to the entries from 1749, and scanned the accounts payable column. It had been a very bad year for stonecutters, she noted; most of the prices were in shillings, and even at that, there were precious few entries. One stood out, however. This headstone had cost twenty-two pounds. She caught her breath as she checked the date of the commission: December 29th, the day after Catriona died.

"This is it,'' Kate said, and Mr. MacGowan studied the entry over her shoulder.

"Is the monument still in good repair?'' he asked.

"Very good,'' she replied. The old man made a pleased sound in his throat, as if to congratulate his forebears on their workmanship. She squinted at the name of the man who'd paid for it: Charles Shelton. "But what do these letters before and after his name mean?''

She stepped aside to allow Mr. MacGowan a better view. His glasses were hanging around his neck on a chain and he placed them on his nose. "Ah,'' he said, "it seems Charles Shelton was a major in King George's army.''

"Why would an English officer pay for Catriona's headstone?" she mused. The old man turned away and busied himself at the desk to keep from addressing her question, but the stiffness about his shoulders gave her his answer and she knew, even now, centuries removed from the liaison, that Mr. MacGowan felt little sympathy for a woman who would sleep with the enemy.

"That's the sentiment of someone who loved her," Kate had said of the Shakespearean verse etched on the stone. Yes, Charles Shelton had loved Catriona. He had loved her enough to have her dead husband's name, and political affiliation, inscribed there too, despite his own differing viewpoint.

But had Catriona returned his love?

And if she did, had she been branded the kind of traitor Mr. MacGowan seemed to think her?

Kate remembered her fantasy about the Highland woman who sent her sons away to keep them from being painted with the same brush the community had used on their mother, suddenly certain the journal entry had been written by Catriona.

She caught herself before she started to defend Catriona's behavior to Stewart MacGowan. Was she crazy? What did any of this have to do with her? *Ah, that is the question*, she realized.

Instead, she thanked him for his help and handed him the bottle of whisky. He smiled in gratitude, apparently forgiving her her unfortunate taste in ancestors.

She started driving in what she hoped was the right direction, and considered what she had learned. Was

Major Charles Shelton the English officer for whom Catriona worked after the Rising, the husband of the lady who took Catriona's sons away—though hadn't Catriona given her employer's rank as "Colonel" in her journal? Had she been guilty of the double sin of giving aid and comfort to the enemy and adultery? But if Charles was *that* English officer, why hadn't he insisted on having Catriona continue on in her role of servant and accompany the family wherever they went? Kate shook her head. That part of the story was pure, unsubstantiated conjecture on her part, she reminded herself. She had absolutely no evidence to support it. All she knew for sure was that Catriona had lived and died—a portrait in which Catriona was vibrantly alive, a headstone that marked her grave, proved as much; Major Shelton had paid for the headstone. And he had loved her. " 'You are so strongly in my purpose bred, That all the world besides methinks are dead,' " Kate whispered.

She managed to find her way back to Dun Buie, despite the musings that kept her attendance to landmarks poor. Alec was rounding the side of the house just as she pulled up. "Where did you run off to?" he asked, as he helped her down and hugged her.

She considered this mutely for a moment before she remembered the cake and flowers. She opened the hatch, removed them and handed them to him in answer, guessing he wouldn't want to hear about her other errand. He looped his free arm around her and led her into the house, where the family was sitting down to lunch. Violet clucked happily over the flowers as she arranged them in a colorful pitcher and placed them on the table. She set the cake out on a plate on the sideboard.

"Any luck?" James asked, turning to Kate.

She stared at him in surprise, sent her spoon clattering into her soup bowl before she realized he was talking computers, not headstones. "Yes," she managed.

He sighed in relief. "Bless you."

The expression on his face made her smile. "I have three words of advice, Jamie," she said. "Or is it six? Back-up. Back-up. And back-up."

"Och, I've learned my lesson, Kate. And now I'm in your debt. What can I do to repay you? Give you my only brother's hand in marriage, perhaps?"

Kate glanced at Alec, who was pushing a piece of potato around his plate, looking far from amused. "If she wants your tongue, I'll be happy to cut it out for her."

"I'm certain she'd rather have yours."

"Jamie!" Violet interjected in alarm, waving her hands apologetically at Kate.

Isabel, Kate saw, was struggling to control a laugh.

"How about a final gallop around Dun Buie before we head back to the hotel, MacGillvray?" Alec asked.

She nodded in agreement, remarking at how final he made that "final gallop" sound.

Kate's riding skills had been acquired at a posh equestrian club outside Philadelphia, had been maintained on the very civilized bridle paths in the city's parks, so when Alec decided to take off across the rock-strewn hills at a full gallop, leaping fences as if they weren't there, she had little choice but to let him go. Why he felt the need to take off was something she didn't want to consider. She soon found herself riding around the loch, watching its shimmering water, thinking about Catriona and her husband, her sons. Her lover?

She caught sight of the cottage from the top of a hill, dismounted and settled down on the grass to study it, her heart swelling as she did so. She had never really noticed much about the places she lived beyond that they provided shelter from the elements and space to keep her things. The house she had grown up in was beautiful; she knew this more from being told so than from her own recollection. She had never complained about the tiny cinder-block dorm room at college. And she couldn't recall much about any of the apartments she had lived in since then—even the one she had left less than a week ago. But she felt as if she knew and loved every stone of Alec's cottage. She wandered down the hill so that she might see it from a different angle. She spotted the small rowboat tied to a wooden mooring and decided the middle of the lake would afford her a better perspective still. She stepped into the boat, cast off, settled herself on its bench and grasped the oars. She rowed it smoothly through the water, then raised the oars and let it drift. She studied the cottage for a while, then she relaxed back in the boat to watch the sky. The sun was warm on her face. She dozed off, smiling.

The sun was dropping behind the hills as she rowed out into the loch. She lifted the oars, balanced them inside the boat. She turned to keep the cottage squarely in her view, saw two men standing on the shore. Then she went over the side, into the freezing water, and as she sank down she heard one of them cry: "Katherine!"

"MacGillvray!"

Kate awoke with a start, sat up slowly and looked around, confused. Then she saw Alec on the shore, shouting through cupped hands. She waved to him. She rowed back toward the mooring as quickly as she could. He was there to catch her rope and secure it, to lift her out of the boat.

"You just aged me ten years," he said, holding her hard against him. "I saw your horse on the hill and the boat out there, drifting, and I . . ."

She glanced back at the lake, then up into his face. "I'm a very good swimmer," she assured him.

He shook his head. "Even the best swimmer would have frozen long before she reached the shore."

His use of the female pronoun in a sentence where the male was customary wasn't lost on her. She was freezing now, shivering as if she had gone over the side of a boat, into a frigid lake. "Like Catriona did?" she asked.

Alec released her, shrugged and turned away. "I wasn't there," he said.

They rode back to the house side-by-side, but without conversation. They settled their horses in silence. Kate glanced at the hay longingly but didn't speak the sensual overture that sprang to her lips. Alec didn't seem to be in the mood for a quickie. They went into the house to make their good-byes. Violet and Isabel flanked Alec as he walked through the house to the front door where the car was parked. Kate walked beside James. She laid her hand on his arm to detain him for a moment and he nodded, understanding, didn't speak until the others were out of earshot.

"Having trouble with young Alec?" he asked.

She glanced at her lover's retreating back. Was it obvious to everyone? Then she shrugged. "I need to ask you a favor."

"Want me to pummel him for you?"

She laughed, shook her head. "Do you think you might be able to find some information on a man named Charles Shelton, a major in the English army after the '45?"

James watched her carefully, but nodded in affirmation. "The English were rather compulsive about keeping records. After tracking down Scots who lived and died without benefit of a line in the family Bible, it should be easy. The name is familiar, though. I'm sure I've heard it somewhere. Who was he?"

"The man who paid for Catriona's headstone."

James whistled, impressed. "I've often wondered. . . ." Then he shook his head. "I should have you working for me, Kate. But a word of advice: Don't tell Alec about your newfound passion for historical sleuthing just yet. He has often suggested I quit digging up the dead."

The mysterious significance of the events over the past three days receded as Dun Buie did, and Kate found herself recalling them with varying degrees of embarrassment and chagrin. Her escapade in the haunted forest was the stuff of bad comedy. Her willingness to label ordinary, garden-variety day-dreams "visions" was absurd. She wished she hadn't told Jamie about her ridiculous attempt at ghost-busting. She could only hope that the whisky she had left Mr. MacGowan had obscured his memory of her visit.

She shrank down in the car seat, glanced at Alec, grateful that he hadn't learned about her attempt to make mystical mountains out of mundane molehills, to go for the gold in the psycho Olympics.

She was so involved in castigating herself, she failed to notice that Alec had also grown more distant as his home did.

He finally pulled the car up to the Munro House's gate, set the parking brake, turned off the ignition. He leaned back in his seat and closed his eyes. He had her full attention now. "Is something wrong?" she asked, an aching beneath the left side of her diaphragm accompanying the question. She was getting an ulcer, she decided. Stress was encouraging the release of hydrochloric acid into her empty stomach, and if Alec didn't answer her quickly, it was going to burn clean through her gastric mucosa, her stomach's lining.

He turned and looked at her. "What's wrong, MacGillvray, is that nothing's wrong," he answered cryptically.

"I don't understand," she murmured. She was certain it wasn't good news. The expression on his face was difficult to read, but it wasn't happy. He had galloped away from her this afternoon as if she were in the foreguard of Hanover's cavalry. He had barely spoken a dozen words to her during the ride back here. And now. . . .

This Scottish idyll is over.

"You'll be going home soon," he said.

She nodded. "I intend to hunt for souvenirs in Inverness tomorrow. Then I'm hiking the Cairngorms on Thursday. Then I'm taking a tour bus to Glasgow on Friday morning. My flight leaves from there on Friday afternoon." He hadn't asked for her entire itinerary, but she couldn't keep herself from giving it, in a brittle and anxious voice.

"I'll drive you to Glasgow, if you'd like. I have kin in Inveraray who've been begging for a visit."

"So I wouldn't be putting you out."

He watched her carefully, obviously not missing the tone of this statement.

She shook her head. She couldn't bear to have him see her off at the airport en route to fulfilling other obligations. "I'm already booked on the bus. It will stop at Loch Ness. Maybe I'll be able to tell my friends that I saw Nessie. I'll have to come back to Scotland, someday. There are so many things I won't get around to doing, this trip. . . ." Her words and her hydrochloric acid were flowing, fast and furious.

"I kept you from them. I'm sorry."

She looked at him in alarm. "No" was surprisingly all she could manage in answer.

"I'll take you to Loch Ness tomorrow morning, if you'd like," he began. "I'm due to meet with the credentialing board at the hospital in late afternoon, but that leaves us most of the day. MacGillvray. Kate. . . .''

Welcome back to the real world.

She reached over and took his hand. "It's OK. You don't have to take me anywhere and you certainly don't have to say anything more. I understand what you're getting at. You win some, you lose some, and some get rained out, right? I'll have Mrs. Munro launder Isabel's things and deliver them to Dun Buie. Thank Isabel for me. Please. And thank you, Alec.''

He made no move to stop her when she climbed out of the car. He didn't turn around when she opened the hatch to rescue her suit, shawl, shoes and bag. She paused at the wrought-iron gate and glanced back at him before she pushed through it. He was still leaning back in his seat, his eyes closed.

She paused outside the inn's door, wiping tears off her cheeks. If she entered in this state, the inquisitive Mrs. Munro would want to know what was wrong and she couldn't bring herself to talk about it now. She stared down at a burlap-covered flower bed as her tears dripped down onto it.

Suddenly the contents of the bundle she had been holding were lying at her feet and she was tight in Alec's arms. He hugged her against him and brushed away her tears, while he murmured words she couldn't understand.

"Speak English,'' she begged him.

'' 'You win some, you lose some, and some get rained out,' eh?'' He grinned. "I hate to disabuse you of your romantic notions, MacGillvray, but if you look carefully, you'll see a yellow streak running up this Highlander's back. You've rattled me—scared me to death, actually. Everything has happened so quickly. And I'm not an impulsive man.''

His mouth clamped shut with finality and she waited. ''Then do continue on in Gaelic and I'll ask Mrs. Munro to translate,'' she prompted.

He guffawed. ''Mrs. Munro is what's called a *sweetie wife* in Scotland.''

''A what?''

''A gossip. Someone who's more interested in other people's business than her own and can eavesdrop in ten languages. She'll be falling over herself to come out here and learn it all. . . .''

She blinked to clear her vision, then met his eyes again. ''All *what*, Alec?'' she pressed.

He kissed her lips in what seemed to be a delaying tactic, a bid for time. ''I don't want you to leave me.''

''Tonight,'' she said softly. It *had* been over twenty-four hours since their last *mowe*.

''Tonight or any night thereafter.''

She stared at him in surprise. It had sounded like the ashamed declaration of a schoolboy, and she suspected the gathering darkness was hiding flushed cheeks, maybe even red-tipped ears. ''Alec . . .'' she gasped. She wasn't sure what she had been expecting of him, but it hadn't been *this*.

He held up his hand. ''Let me finish, before I turn tail and bolt. I swore I'd never give another woman more than one night. But your night became two, then four, then suddenly, just now, faced with the prospect of a lifetime of nights without you, I realized I had to choose between keeping my old vow and taking some new ones."

Vows. She clung to him to keep herself from sinking to the ground. She squeezed her eyes shut to savor the familiar fantasy that played behind them. She was wearing cream-colored lace. Prince Charming was carrying her over the threshold. But now he had a face—a beautiful, angular, gold-toned face with just a sprinkling of freckles across the bridge of his nose. And his castle was a little stone crofter's cottage on a Scottish hillside.

"What do you say, Cheit? Will you give me your nights?"

"I'll give you anything you want," she said.

Chapter Ten

Alec pressed his lips into Kate's, tenderly, passion-ately, and she sensed no indecision in his kiss, no hint of regret. She pressed forward against him, sigh-ing happily as she encountered further proof of his satisfaction with the choice he had made.

"Whoa, MacGillvray!" he laughed, kissing her one last time before he set her aside and kneeled on the ground to collect her belongings.

"I still have to leave on Friday," she whispered, remembering.

He raised his head quickly. He settled back on his heels and waited.

"I have unfinished business in Philadelphia, a professional commitment I must honor," she began. Although the prospect of returning to the hospital in less than a week, as scheduled, was wrenching her insides, widening the yellow stripe down her own back, she knew she owed it to Alec, and herself, to do so. She couldn't keep running from her demons. Ignoring them wouldn't make them go away. She couldn't hide in Brigadoon forever. And she had once loved her work, she reminded herself, had been very good at it, couldn't have imagined her life without it. Perhaps, someday, after the demons had been vanquished, she and Alec would work side-by-side, in a hospital, or in a practice of their own—treating kiddies and adults, delivering a few babies, doing a bit of light surgery in a pinch. *Alec, what do you make of Mr. Crimmon's rash? Alec, would you mind taking a peek at this X-ray? Alec, please see my next patient while I feed our son.* "Let me explain a few things . . ."

"Just tell me how long you'll be away," he begged.

"Until July."

He groaned. "And promise you'll come back."

"I'll come back."

He stood up and offered her his arm. "Right, then, MacGillvray. Let's go inside. We haven't got a moment to waste."

Mrs. Munro, of course, was well aware of which two guests hadn't slept in their rooms for the past four nights, and she smiled knowingly when Kate and Alec stepped into the foyer, arm-in-arm. She descended on them, chattering happily, insisting on having tea sent up to Miss MacGillvray's room and calling for one of her obedient young porters to see to it.

193

"It's true what they say about Scotsmen, eh, Miss MacGillvray?" she whispered, as Alec fled up the stairs.

Kate turned to the landlady and raised a questioning eyebrow.

"They make the best lovers."

Kate couldn't say she had ever heard anyone make such a claim before, but she couldn't contain the contented grin that curled her lips.

"They make the best husbands, too, don't doubt it. And you'd be wise not to let that one get away," Mrs. Munro finished.

She had no intention of it! Kate walked up the stairs slowly, recalling Alec's words. They were beautiful, poetic words—ones that had surprised her in form, as well as content. There was a romantic hiding behind Alec's cynical facade, after all, she decided. What kind of providence had led her to Scotland to meet the love of her life? If Evan hadn't broken up with her, if the Diablos and Huns hadn't gone to war, if she hadn't reacted in such an exaggerated fashion to the death of one of their number, she would never have left Philadelphia, she would never have met Alec. Had fate thrown her into the middle of these disasters to prod her toward the man she was destined to marry? *Sort of a cosmic kick in the rear, MacGillvray? You are losing it,* she chided herself.

Her ruminations stopped abruptly when she entered her room and saw Alec standing at the window, the last light of sunset touching his auburn hair. Suddenly *how* she had found him seemed much less important than the fact that she had. She loved him, he loved her, and they were going to be married. What more did she need to know?

"MacGillvray," he said, turning to her.

She ran across the distance between them, threw herself against him and found his lips. His hands moved up under her sweater and blouse, caressing her back, pulling her closer.

"You're incredibly passionate," he murmured.

"Is it too much?" she asked, unaccountably shy again.

He held her away from him and shook his head.

"The man likes to be the aggressor," she said.

"Who filled your head with this nonsense, MacGillvray? I expect that you'll make love to me as often as I do it to you, and as aggressively."

"Tell me how," she begged.

He laughed. "You'll have me continue on in the role of despoiler of innocents, then?"

"You're good at it."

He raised his shoulders. "Should I take that as a compliment?"

"It was meant as one."

"Very well, MacGillvray, your next lesson will commence after we've taken some tea."

She was considerably less innocent by the time they sank into the bathtub together over an hour later. Alec leaned back in the hot, foamy water, his knees spread, and he settled her between them. She laid her head on his shoulder. The piper was serenading the sunset beneath the window. It seemed odd, and wonderful, to be sharing this tub with Alec. She had changed so much since the last time she had bathed in it, alone, and caught her first glimpse of the secrets of passion. Had it really been only four days ago? It seemed as if she had known Alec forever, had known the secrets of passion for longer than that. She stroked the damp, auburn pelt on his chest pensively, in wonder.

"Are you sure you'd never done *that* before, MacGillvray?" he murmured.

She grinned. "I'm fairly sure I would remember *that.*" And she couldn't stop thinking about it now. She had never before imagined doing the thing she had done, but it had happened so naturally, it had felt so wonderful. "Was it good?"

"It was better than good. You seem to have a natural talent for it." He traced her lips with his fingertip.

"And practice makes perfect, I'm told."

He groaned.

"Your guidance was indispensable. Thank you."

"You're quite welcome," he said, bowing his head to taste the lips that she guessed had banished the last traces of his innocence.

"Do you know what happened to Alec and Jeremy MacLachlan?" she asked softly, as Alec fished the sponge out of the water, soaped it up and began sliding it up and down her arm. She was trying once again to make sense of her odd experiences at Dun Buie. They all seemed so illogical, improbable now, here, away from the spell of Alec's cottage.

He was intent on his chore. "Uhmm? Catriona and Alasdair's sons?"

"Alasdair?" she asked, her voice quavering.

Alec didn't notice. "It's the Gaelic for Alexander. Their sons went to America."

She laid her hand on the sponge to still it. "How do you know?"

"My father was a great amateur historian. Jamie has followed in his footsteps—as you probably guessed this morning. They were always drawing family trees and ferreting out moldy church records. Jamie went on to read History at University." He chuckled, met her eyes. "I, on the other hand, got ill at the mention of Culloden or Catriona Mac-Gillvray MacLachlan."

"Do you think it's Catriona in the painting?"

He shrugged. "It's a MacLachlan wife. The legend on the pin proves that. The timing is right and she certainly bears a strong resemblance to one MacGillvray I know. Beyond that, we'll never know for sure."

"I don't like mysteries," she whispered.

"Ah, MacGillvray," he said, reaching for the soap again, "life's a mystery."

The room seemed lonely when Alec finally left it to dress for dinner—like her life had been before he entered it. Kate considered this as she readied herself to see him again. Why had she never realized it before? In four days, Alec had drawn her closer, physically and emotionally, than Evan had in four years. And for so long, during her years with Evan, and well before them, she had been filling every empty corner of her life with her work, with the pain and problems of other people. Perhaps she had needed

197

to put that aside for a time to recognize her own pain.

She donned a long, teal silk dress with a demure little collar. She pinned her silver brooch—the badge of a MacLachlan wife—between the points of the collar, with a smile. She pulled on delicate patterned hose and black suede boots. She hadn't worn a trace of makeup since Friday night, she realized, and she applied it now with a subtle but definite hand. She drew her hair back into a loose tail with a silk band.

He tapped at the door several minutes later. He was dressed in gray flannel slacks, a white shirt and a gray cashmere sweater. He looked very elegant, but she was apparently unable to keep her disappointment from showing on her face.

"What's wrong?" he asked.

"You didn't wear your kilt," she said.

He threw back his head and laughed. "So you only love me for my kilt," he said.

No, she corrected him silently. The kilt was really the least of it.

"I only own the one, MacGillvray. They haven't been a staple in the Scotsman's wardrobe since before—"

"Culloden," she whispered.

"Aye. Besides, if you had to look at my bare knees all the time, you'd soon grow very tired of them."

"Never," she said, stepping up to him and laying her hands on his flannel-covered knees. She looked up into his eyes.

He kissed her lips. "Ah. I see that yearning look in your eyes and I know what you're about now, you shameless wee hussy," he laughed. "In about ten seconds, you'll have me back in that bed and I'll get no dinner. Then when I'm weak with hunger, you'll really take advantage of me."

"I wouldn't know how!"

"I believe you picked up a few of the rudiments this afternoon."

She wrapped her arms around his shoulders. "I want to know more," she said.

"The insatiable thirst for knowledge," he murmured, then he signed with mock resignation. "All right. I'll give you another lesson after dinner."

Mrs. Munro treated them like visiting royalty, saw them seated in the deep, plush couch in front of the fire, urging the guests who had occupied it previously to move on into the dining room. She served tall glasses of chilled white wine. She stopped by frequently to inquire after Dr. Lachlan's needs and to wink conspiringly at Miss MacGillvray. When Alec excused himself for a moment, the landlady immediately appeared at Kate's side.

"I'm not wrong about that man."

Kate laughed. "Are you ever wrong about anything?"

Mrs. Munro shook her head. "Mark me, Miss MacGillvray, you could do worse than to have his ring on your finger and his bairn in your belly."

Kate smiled as the woman walked away. She might just see to getting both things accomplished as soon as possible.

"What kind of advice is our sweet landlady offering now?" Alec asked, returning in time to see

Mrs. Munro leave the room, a self-satisfied expression on her face.

Kate grinned. "She was just making a suggestion about what she'd like to see me wearing."

He sat down beside Kate and drew her into the crook of his arm. "Allow me to make a few suggestions about what you shouldn't be wearing later on this evening."

He lowered his mouth to her ear and by the time he finished his recitation, she was bent double in mirth, and her cheeks were damp with tears. "You always make me laugh," she managed.

He caught one of her tears on the tip of his finger and studied it for a long moment. "It broke my heart to see I'd made you cry, earlier."

"I don't know what got into me, Alec. I've never been a crier." A disquieting thought occurred to her then. "I hope it wasn't the waterworks that prompted you to say what you said, *earlier*."

He took her hand, studied her face. "They made me realize how mistrustful I'd grown of my own feelings. They made me want to rip the lid off the crate where I'd packed away my own tears and let them roll down my face again. They made me realize how close I'd come to watching you walk away, instead of opening myself up to you, owning up to what I feel for you."

She leaned toward him, gathered him against her. "I love you, Alec," she said.

And she felt him stiffen, silently, in her arms.

They ate a delicious meal in the inn's superb dining room. Mrs. Munro brought her chef out of the kitchen to meet them, and when the man discovered he was feeding Angus Campbell's nephew, he insisted upon personally delivering a shortbread and lemon curd concoction of his own invention to their table. They finished every spoonful of this.

"Are you happy, MacGillvray?" Alec asked.

"I've never been happier in my life," Kate answered, meeting his green eyes in the candlelight, extending her hand toward him. "Are you?"

He nodded and took her hand, appeared to be studying her nails. Then he bowed his head to lay a kiss in her palm. "We'll need to work out the logistics of our arrangement as soon as possible," he said.

The logistics of their arrangement were simple: They would marry and live happily ever after. Perhaps he had said *engagement*, not *arrangement*. . . .

"We need to decide where you're going to live, that sort of thing."

She swallowed the gasp that rose to her lips, felt her heart begin to thump against her ribs. She would live in the cottage, with him, of course, with his ring on her finger and his bairn in her belly. They would love each other madly and eventually she might even get him to tell her so. . . .

"I propose to let you a small flat in town, near where I'll be working, so that I can visit you easily in the evenings."

This was an entirely different proposal from the one she had unhesitantly and, in retrospect, naively accepted. He had asked for her nights, not her days! she realized in dismay. Alec Lachlan had asked her to be his mistress, not his wife! She had gone from being a woman who couldn't please one man in bed, to one who couldn't please another anywhere else. And she had made the unpardonable mistake of telling him she loved him! She watched him through the blur of tears, praying she could keep herself from bawling like a bairn and making her humiliation complete. How could she have been so ridiculously puerile, so hopelessly old-fashioned? In this day and age, she should have known men didn't propose marriage hastily. Or at all. But, with the exception of rulers of small Arab states and U.S. senators, she couldn't possibly have guessed they still kept mistresses! She lifted her glass and took a gulp of wine, had trouble getting it past the lump in her throat.

"It's difficult for foreigners to get jobs here, at first, and I'm not a wealthy man, but I can certainly afford to keep you in comfort, if not grand style. Later on, you'll be able to work, if you want to. But in the meantime, I'll be happy to see to all your needs. . . ."

She tried to work up some righteous anger. Had she done anything to make Alec believe she would ever be party to such an arrangement, that she was the kind of woman to whom such arrangements were proposed? She cringed as she considered this, felt her face begin to flame. Although they hadn't had sex during their first night together, they had certainly talked about having it. She had blithely peeled off her clothes and jumped naked into a lake with him the next morning. Then they had engaged in all manner of sensual dalliance until they finally consummated their relationship the following day, about forty-eight hours after they first laid eyes on each other. And since then, she had behaved like a woman possessed, like a wanton, a lightskirt. A mistress. She groaned aloud. Perhaps she shouldn't reject Alec's offer out of hand. After all, the only marketable skills she had, aside from those cultivated with him during the past two days, were those she had acquired on hospital wards. If she wasn't able to reclaim her nerve, and her profession, she might need to call on those new-found skills to keep herself from starving!

"Of course, I do work long hours, but I'm sure you'll be able to find ways to amuse yourself between my visits."

How did mistresses usually amuse themselves? she wondered. They shopped, groomed themselves incessantly, like odalisques in a seraglio, and waited.

"It will be convenient, having you in town, I must say. It will save me a drive when I'm in dire need of a little *doss*."

Doss! She had never heard *it* called *that* before. "Alec!"

"Och, I've tried doing it in the car, when I've been desperate, but even in the Range Rover it's difficult to find a comfortable position—you know, feet against the windscreen and shift knob up your—"

"Alec!"

"And you don't strike me as the kind of lass who would expect a suffering man to engage in small talk and buy her dinner first, while his more urgent needs went unattended—"

"No. I'm not that kind of lass."

"It will be worth the cost of the flat to be able to

simply drop my breeks and slip into your nice, warm *kip*."

Her nice, warm. . . . This was a nightmare! "Cut right to the chase, huh?" she demanded.

He laughed. "It was a short chase, MacGillvray, but I caught you. And I'll never let you go."

She shook her head in disbelief. "Alec, we need to talk—" she began.

He leaned toward her, ran his knuckles back and forth across her cheekbone, studied her lips intently before he ran his tongue along his. "Later, Cheit," he said. "I'm afraid it's time for your next lesson— we can't have you falling behind in your studies, can we?"

Alec pulled Kate against him as soon as her room's door closed behind them, and he found her lips. He kissed her until she couldn't think of anything but having the aching need inside her satisfied.

"I can't get enough of you, *an gradh*," he whispered. He pulled her dress off over her head and tossed it away. He surveyed her underclothes for a moment, then peeled them off. He settled her down on the edge of the bed, kneeled before her and removed her boots and stockings. He reached up and removed the band from her hair. "Ready to be edified, MacGillvray?" he asked.

She nodded breathlessly.

He stood up and discarded his own clothes, then he recaptured her in his arms. He caressed the nape of her neck silently, for a long time. Finally he spoke in her ear. "Do you remember your fantasy about the flock of sheep?"

"Yes," she gasped.

"Let's talk about that one again," he said, running his hand down over her smooth, bare spine.

So much for the missionary position, Kate thought, as she collapsed face-down on the braided rug, in the circle of light cast by a table lamp, an indeterminable number of minutes or hours later. Her body was slick with sweat, her heart was hammering against her ribs, her insides were pulsing in time with her heartbeat.

Her temperature must be considerably above 98.6, she mused absently, in the manner of one incapable of sequential thought. The bedroom air felt cool against her skin, and she wondered if condensation might be visible around her, like hot breath on a winter day. Alec's hands felt like ice against her fevered shoulders when he finally roused himself to grasp them and turn her onto her back.

His eyes raked over her face, as if he were attempting to find the answer to a puzzling question there, then they locked with hers. "I want to look at you this time," he said.

This time? Her gaze dropped to the proof of his renewed readiness, and she drew in a gasp of surprise that trailed off into a moan when he thrust himself into her in one smooth motion. Her spine bowed in the instinctual gesture of feminine acceptance, allowing him even deeper access, allowing him to touch her cervix, and her soul.

He braced his arms on either side of her head, lifting the weight of his chest off hers, his focus drifting down to her breasts for a long, appreciative moment before it returned to her face. Then he began to move.

She had imagined her desire fully drained by their last coupling, but suddenly, again, she was in a frenzy of need. The rug beneath her was abrading her restless buttocks as she searched for the next plateau, creating discomfort that somehow drove her pleasure onward and upward. And all the while, his intense green gaze insured that here, now, there could be no secrets between them, no misunderstandings. Here, now, they both wanted the same thing.

She smiled then, suddenly understanding the extent of her female power. His face was as bare as she imagined her own to be, as readable. It was taut with hunger, with need. His mouth was a tight slash, as if he were pressing his lips together to keep them trembling. And his green eyes ... As she studied them, they lost their brittle, glittering acuity, grew glazed, then closed, and she knew he was approaching the limit of his control. She wrapped her arms around his straining shoulders, pulled herself up against him, burying her breasts in the forest of crisp hair on his chest, finding his lips, forcing them apart with her tongue.

As he growled deep in his throat and began to buck atop her, she lost the last of her own control. The brief seconds during which she had been able to study him with clinical detachment came to a screeching, shuddering halt as she began to convulse around him, milking him dry.

* * *

She was dead weight in his arms when he finally eased himself away from her. She didn't want him to leave, but she was incapable of making him stay, with actions or words. She couldn't lift a finger or utter an appeal. Even her chest seemed unnaturally still, as if her diaphragm had ceased to rise and fall, as if her lungs had ceased to fill and empty. Only the poignant pain between her thighs, the aching fullness in the region of her heart, convinced her she was still alive.

She was only vaguely aware of being lifted into his arms and laid on the bed, of having him join her there. She was completely malleable, pliable, and he easily arranged for the hollows and hillocks of her body to settle into the hillocks and hollows of his.

"Sleep for a bit, MacGillvray," he murmured against her hair.

For a bit? The directive echoed in her mind as she drifted into a heavy, sated slumber. So they weren't finished for the night. She would have thought they had already covered all the bases.

The lamp had been turned out, and the room was dark when Kate awoke to the rasp of Alec's tongue on her nipples, to the rasp of his callused fingertips on the swollen folds of her sex, and between them. His thumb found its target, which apparently had never quite fallen asleep. It was wide awake before the rest of her, greedy, ready for more. And Alec obliged, rubbing it gently but insistently. By the time he replaced his thumb with his tongue, Kate was completely with him, whimpering helplessly, involuntary tears streaming down her cheeks. This time, she came in gentle undulations, like lazy waves breaking on some tranquil Caribbean beach, without definite beginning or end.

When he kissed her, she tasted herself, and the two of them, on his lips. It was an intoxicating flavor, and she savored it. Then she felt him, patient but eager, against her leg, and she wanted more. She spent a long time cultivating the talent Alec had praised that afternoon, led on by her imagination and the rhythm of his breathing, until he urged her away. But she wanted to taste that too.

Then they clung together, kissing and whispering, until they drifted off to sleep. They were still in each other's arms when they awoke to sunlight streaming in through the window, onto the bed.

And he took her hard and fast, as if to put an exclamation mark to their night of pleasure. She responded the same way.

"Stud," she murmured afterwards. "I thought men reached their sexual prime at eighteen."

He chuckled. "I think I reached my sexual prime when I met you, MacGillvray."

Chapter Eleven

Kate studied Alec's profile as he scanned the road ahead of him, guiding his car through the lingering fog. She longed to touch him, kept herself from doing it by force of will, as a test of her restraint. She couldn't stop thinking about the peaks of quivering pleasure to which he had taken her last night, and well into this morning, peaks that had driven her beyond not knowing where she ended and he began, into a place where nothing had form but desire and satisfaction. And she still felt utterly pleased with life, still wonderfully free of volition, like a helium balloon drifting far above the workaday world, incapable of dissent, ready to agree to anything. . . .

Like being Alec's mistress?

Well, she certainly wasn't ready to turn him down cold.

Did all men know how to turn women into dish-rags, she wondered, or was Alec among the chosen few to be made privy to that wisdom, somewhere between the secret handshake and the mystical word, in some secret, sexual brotherhood? If the Masons wore rings inscribed with a triangle and protractor to proclaim their calling, then Alec's lodge would have to wear rings featuring a—

"What are you looking at, MacGillvray?"

"Your fingers." They were strong and beautiful, but quite ringless, manipulating the steering wheel with assurance.

They had manipulated her with as much assurance.

She caught her breath, leaned forward in her seat with what she hoped was insouciance. But he glanced at her and smiled knowingly, and the magnificent discomfort between her legs trebled. Naughty boy. . . .

Yes, he was a naughty boy, one who meant to set her up in a scandalous little love nest where he could obtain sexual first aid whenever he needed it.

And administer it whenever she needed it.

Think about your future, not last night! she commanded herself. And the helium began to hiss out of her balloon.

She couldn't think about a future without him.

Yes, she wanted to sleep with him, and *not* sleep with him, but she wanted to do it with his ring finger and, eventually, his bairn in her belly. She wanted to practice medicine with him and accompany him to his mother's house for Sunday dinner.

You can't always get what you want, she reminded herself.

She had been Alec's bride, and his medical partner, only in her fantasies, and only for the space of the few hours between the moment when she misunderstood his proposal and the one when he clarified it.

"I'll never fall in love again and I'll certainly never get married." He had made his position very clear, shortly after they met. A few days with a woman was unlikely to make a man forget such a pledge, even if sex with her was phenomenal.

Get your mind out of the bed! You can't spend the rest of your life there! Or can you?

Evan had promised her marriage, a lifetime of love, but he had reneged and walked away without a backward glance. Alec had simply asked her to be his mistress, without any mention of love. Yet his proposal had felt more permanent than anything Evan had ever offered. In fact, at one point yesterday, she had been sure she could taste forever in Alec's kisses, see it in his eyes.

Was it possible *forever* simply hadn't registered in his brain yet?

And wasn't being with Alec under less than perfect circumstances, for however long they had, better than being without him?

It reminded her of the story line from another of those old romances—*Edifying the Earl* or *Coaching the Count*, maybe? In it, the sensuous, brooding misogynist protected his once-broken heart by vowing never to marry. The beautiful, innocent girl who loved him agreed to become his mistress, despite the ridicule and condemnation this brought her, because she knew she could bear anything except being without him.

She eventually taught him that love didn't have to hurt.

Kate seemed to recall that the pair married and lived happily ever after.

I can teach Alec that love doesn't have to hurt. I can make him want me for his wife, as well as his lover, she decided.

But could she serve as his mistress in the meantime?

She was an old-fashioned girl, faced with a new-fangled dilemma. Perhaps she needed to adjust her attitudes.

Or perhaps she just needed to adjust Alec's.

Either way, no adjustments would be possible if she ran away.

She didn't want to run.

She hadn't dreamed in two nights, but the dreams she had had in Alec's cottage were still vivid in her memory. They could almost make her believe she had loved Alec in another time and would never love anyone else. They could almost make her believe he was her destiny, whatever the name of their relationship.

Who was she to fight fate?

She reached out and laid her hand on his knee, losing this fight, failing this test. He grinned.

"I'll be taking lessons from you soon, Mac-Gillvray," he said.

"We do seem . . . compatible," she ventured.

"Compatible? We complement and supplement

and make each other complete. We're magic.''

Magic. A short time ago, she had been ready to believe that magic had caused her path and Alec Lachlan's to cross, could account for the sudden unearthing of a centuries-old portrait she might have posed for and a beaten-silver circle pin that had traveled across hundreds of years and thousands of miles to arrive in her hands.

She couldn't come up with a better explanation today.

"We're bound to see Nessie, you know," he said. "I always thought it would be easier to find the Loch Ness monster than a woman who could make me feel the way you do."

"You enjoy me in bed," she answered, attempting to temper the edge in her voice. She needed to hear him say he enjoyed her as much out of it.

His next glance was odd, unreadable. "Ah. That I do. . . . And you enjoy me . . . in bed."

She watched him warily. *Don't blow it again, Kate. Don't show him that you need to grow up— about three hundred years. No declarations!* She cautioned herself, as a string of romantic promises rose to her lips. "Very much," she answered.

"Ah." He looked at her again and for a moment she thought she saw disappointment in his eyes, a plea for the words she had spoken once, had just kept herself from speaking, but his gaze moved back to the road before she could be sure.

"St. Columba is credited with being the first person to have had concourse with Nessie. His power over the beastie reportedly convinced a number of Picts to convert to Christianity," he said.

213

She laughed.

"Since then, there have been hundreds of sightings, most by very credible witnesses. And their descriptions of her are very much alike: She's about forty feet long, she has a small head, a long neck and powerful flippers. Skeletons of plesiosaurs found in other parts of Britain suggest they looked very much like our Nessie."

"Is it possible that Nessie is a plesiosaur?"

Alec raised his shoulders vaguely, keeping his eyes on the road. "Until the 1960s, scientists thought the coelacanth had been extinct for seventy million years. Since then, over two dozens of them have been caught in the South Atlantic. To quote a wise man named Mr. Lundie, anything is possible."

If you love someone enough, anything is possible.

Kate hoped Alec Lachlan, and Mr. Lundie, were right.

The sun obligingly broke through the clouds as they headed over rolling hills toward the ruined Urquhart Castle on the edge of the loch. Kate walked quickly to keep up with Alec's long-legged stride, looking up often to see the sun touch his cheekbones and glint in his auburn hair. *I can bear anything but being without him*, she thought. But she was suddenly filled with the oddest fear that she was going to lose him, whatever she did or didn't do, that he was going to be torn away from her, abruptly, irrevocably. *The choice is yours. The future is in your hands*, she reminded herself. She grabbed his hand and hung onto it, to ward off the premonition and to keep him at her side.

"Moving too fast for you, am I, MacGillvray?" he asked, with a gentle smile.

She shook her head. She had already concluded that if anyone's timing was off, it was her own. She had expected too much, too soon. She had shown him half a woman and expected him to respond by offering his whole heart. He had carried the pain of betrayal around with him for years and she had expected him to cast it off in one magical moment, like the hero from a stupid romance. But she would come back in July, with her courage restored, with her demons defeated, and give him as much time as he needed. She would teach him that love didn't have to hurt.

While she was his mistress?

"You'll be disappointed if we don't spot Nessie," Alec said, squeezing her hand.

She breathed in the cool air deeply, looked out over the blue-black water to the hills on its opposite bank, then up into his green eyes. "We'll spot her," she answered. Anything was possible.

He grinned. "The depth of the loch is said to be twice the mean depth of the North Sea just there," he said, pointing. "Millions of years ago it was connected to the sea by a fault that is now known as the Great Glen. Some people believe prehistoric sea creatures were making their home here when Ness became landlocked and have lived and bred here ever since."

She sidled up closer to him, stared at the murky water.

"A few divers have gone down. One lot reported black caves with very warm water, not what you would expect to find deep in a lake whose average temperature is just above freezing.''

"It's all very mysterious," she said.

"Ah, Cheit, Scotland's a *verra* mysterious place," he answered, drawing her into his arms, bowing his head to hers.

She jolted upright suddenly, pulled away from him and pointed. "I saw her!" she said.

Alec followed the line of her finger, then looked back down into her face. "Daft or drunk, Mac-Gillvray?" he asked, laughing.

Seeing the Loch Ness monster was no more farfetched than anything else that had happened to her during this holiday. "Well, I'm not drunk," she answered.

Alec parked the car in the center of town and rescued a tie and jacket from its trunk. He pulled these on impatiently, then turned to Kate. "How do I look?" he asked.

She studied him for a long moment, straightened his tie. "I don't want to be responsible for swelling your head."

"Just for swelling my—"

"Alec!"

He laughed and looped his arm around her waist, urging her onward.

She had seen the huge sandstone castle that dominated Inverness's horizon on the day she arrived in town, but it had been raining then and she had been alone. Today, as she walked along the River Ness in the sunshine, arm-in-arm with the man she loved, it looked like the centerpiece in a fairy tale. "We don't

A Case of Nerves

have many castles in America," she said happily. Perhaps she had succeeded in letting her dilemma disappear into the loch as completely as the magical monster who lived there.

"Well, we have a load of them here. If you like castles, you'll love living in Inverness, Mac-Gillvray."

Her dilemma buoyed to the surface like a cork. *Adjust your attitudes*, she reminded herself. But she didn't want to think about the circumstances that would surround her relocation to Inverness right now. She didn't want to accept Alec's proposal. Or reject it. She wanted to think about true love and fairy tales and Nessie for a little while, not about what her mother would say when she was apprised of the proposed arrangement. Anne MacGillvray hadn't raised her daughter to be a man's mistress, and she wasn't going to like it one bit.

"We haven't much time before you leave. Shall we look at a few flats after my interview this afternoon?" Alec asked.

Kate nodded halfheartedly.

"But first, we'll eat, and then I'll take you frock-shopping, lest you be tempted to entertain Mrs. Munro's sartorial advice. I fancy you in something leather—a tight little skirt, perhaps."

"What about some naughty nighties?" she asked, her voice as tight as the skirt she envisioned.

He halted, grasped her shoulders with his hands. "Rule number one: You wear nothing at all to bed. Agreed?"

"Agreed." *How many rules are there going to be?* she wondered. And it was clear that Alec wasn't

217

going to grant her a reprieve. He was determined to begin her lessons in the etiquette of being a mistress as soon as possible.

They entered a welcoming little pub and were shown to a quiet corner booth. Alec slid in beside Kate and slipped his arm behind her. He ordered ale and food. When the drinks arrived, she sipped at her glass gingerly, recalling her first experience with whisky, but this brew required less practice and she loved its rich, nutty flavor from her first mouthful. An adjuvant for attitude adjustment, she thought, swallowing it eagerly. Soon she was relaxing back against his shoulder, resolving to enjoy every moment of the next three days to the fullest, whatever her decision about the days, months and years that would follow. She accepted a tidbit of food from his fingertips with a laugh. "It feels so decadent to be fed by you," she said.

"I want to feed you and bathe you and dress you, MacGillvray," he murmured against her ear. "I want to possess you."

"Like an odalisque in a seraglio," she said, feeling the tension return to her shoulders, unable to keep herself from repeating the analogy that had occurred to her the evening before.

He glanced down at her. "I like the sound of being your own personal sultan, sometimes. But mostly, I just want to know that I'm the most important person in the world to you. I want you to know that everything I give you is given in . . . affection."

"And not for services rendered."

He drew away from her slightly and watched her face. "Is something bothering you, MacGillvray?"

She shook her head vaguely. *Grow up*, she reminded herself.

He touched his lips to hers. "Having second thoughts, are you?" he guessed. "If I hadn't been faced with your imminent departure, I would never have asked for your commitment so soon, or in such a forthright manner. I know you were brought up to expect things to happen differently, certainly more slowly. I would have been glad to indulge you in a wee bit of courtship before I got down to the nuts and bolts of our arrangement, had there been time."

"Would you have?"

"Aye." He stroked her hair back from her forehead. "You haven't decided that you'd rather not be my lady after all, have you?"

She considered this for the time it took her to assimilate his words. Whatever questions she had, the answer to this one had been clear since the moment she met him. "I want to be your lady more than I've ever wanted anything in my life," she said.

Kate examined herself critically in the dressing room mirror. The suede skirt was as soft and supple, nearly as lightweight, as silk. It was also very short and quite tight.

"Let me see you," Alec called.

She looked back at her reflection. The skirt was shorter than any she had ever worn, or at least during the past twenty years. "I'm not coming out," she answered.

"Then I'm coming in," he laughed.

He pushed into the small room and walked around her, studying her from every angle. "You look great in that," he pronounced finally.

"It makes me look like a tart."

He touched her cheek. "You're my tart," he said.

She considered this silently, while the remains of her straightlaced morality screamed in protest. *Either tell him you're not going to be his tart, or stop shuddering every time he mentions it!* "Alec, I'm a . . . professional . . ." she began.

"A scientist."

On second thought, this wasn't the time or place for revelations. "Let's just say I've had a lot of education. I've achieved a level of success that requires a certain dignity of me, that entitles me to a certain amount of respect. . . ."

He looked down at her in confusion. "What the devil are you talking about, MacGillvray? You'll appear as dignified in that skirt as your First Lady does in her Chanel suit. I respect you with every fiber of my being—"

He had yet to demonstrate that one to her satisfaction.

"And I'm not suggesting you go about town in a G-string and pasties."

"Thank God for small favors!" she said, turning her back on him, but the mirror made it impossible for her to hide her face. "It's not very practical, Alec. In a few weeks, I'll have to pack it away until fall."

"We're not talking about practicalities here." He curled his arms around her shoulders from behind and studied their reflection. "There's more to sensuality than enjoying the touch of my hands in the privacy of a bedroom," he said quietly. "The fabrics you wear against your skin when we're apart, when you're in America and I'm here, will heighten your awareness of your body and remind you of me."

"Will they?" she whispered. His hands were moving very lightly over her shoulders and she started to tremble.

He nodded. "I'll be thinking about you in this skirt, MacGillvray. I can picture you wearing it with a very proper silk sweater, under your very proper lab coat, as you go about your hospital on your first day back. Only I will know that your breasts are bare under the sweater and that your lovely pink nipples are thrusting forward in hard, little nubs against it. Only I will know that you're wearing tiny silk panties under your skirt and that they're rubbing you quite provocatively, *here*." His hand slipped down over black suede. "And that those sensations will remind you of—"

"*This*," she gasped, pushing back instinctively, feeling his arousal against her buttocks.

"Aye. This," he agreed, moving against her.

She turned into his arms and met his lips.

"How much time did you say you'll need at home, *mo breagha*?" he asked.

"Ten weeks," she murmured.

"Lord. It will feel like a lifetime. I'll try to get over to see you, but I can't promise I'll be able to get the time off. I miss you already."

The obliging young saleswoman peeked into the dressing room then. "Does it fit nicely?" she asked.

221

Alec glanced down at the skirt. "Like a glove," he answered.

The *very proper* silk sweater Alec picked out was anything but. It was a muted rose color, exquisitely soft and quite abbreviated, its neckline low, its boxy hem barely covering the waistband of the skirt. When she lifted her arms, it bared a strip of her midriff. What was he going to pick out next? she wondered. A navel ring?

"Very sexy," Alec pronounced with satisfaction. "We'll have to take that one, too."

Kate watched him for a moment, then peeled off the sweater and skirt and handed them to him, blushing under his scrutiny as she did this.

"Will you always blush when I see you in your scanties?" he laughed.

"When it's in a public place like this, *yes*, probably."

He considered this for a moment. "I see," he said. "You're ashamed to have it be known that you're mine."

That wasn't exactly the way of it, she realized, though it was close. She pulled on her jeans and sweater, laced up her boots, avoiding his gaze.

He handed the skirt and sweater to the clerk, telling her to wrap them up.

Kate felt her face flush anew and she busied herself studying trendy little dresses on a nearly hidden rack. She glanced up when Alec joined her there. "This shop is outrageously expensive. I really can't afford those things, you know," she said, examining the sequins on a silver evening dress with feigned interest.

"You don't have to. They're gifts. From me."

She spun to him. "You don't have to buy me gifts."

He snorted. "Don't I, MacGillvray? It's my responsibility."

"Your *responsibility*?" she asked.

"And my pleasure," he amended.

"Did you feel the same responsibility toward Tess?"

"No. Of course not. The nature of our relationship was never the same as this . . ."

"Wasn't it?" she asked, struggling to keep the sharp edge out of her voice.

"Not even close," he said.

She watched his eyes. "This isn't really different from offering me cash," she finished, gesturing vaguely at the luxurious wares around her. The main difference between a mistress and a whore was the form of payment, she decided.

"I'd offer cash, but I have to admit my credit is better than my cash flow at the moment. Will you take plastic?"

"I'm serious!"

"Unfortunately, so am I."

"So you can't afford these things either?"

He guffawed. "I'll wince when I'm presented with the accounting, MacGillvray, but I'll just remind myself how much I'm saving on *not* having to buy you a wedding ring," he said.

You don't pull any punches, do you? she thought,

as she watched Alec saunter toward the waiting clerk.

Alec checked his watch and suggested they begin their search for the perfect postcard before they headed over to the hospital. They continued on down the High Street, looking in windows, holding hands. Kate bought a dozen postcards, half of which depicted a cottage very much like Alec's—and she found she couldn't look at these without feeling a twinge of longing for the magic she had left there. She bought a tartan muffler for her father, a tartan tam o'shanter for her mother and a big mug with Bonnie Prince Charlie on its side for her grandmother.

She held the mug up to the sunlight that poured through the shop's window. The man depicted on it was lean and straight, dressed in a red kilt, a princely cutaway jacket and a flowing plaid. His face was angular and beautiful, with a long, thin nose and full lips. His red-gold hair was held back with a ribbon, but a long curl fell forward over his shoulder. "Do you really believe he was this good-looking?" she asked.

Alec squinted at the image and raised his shoulders.

Suddenly, she was dizzy and tingling. She saw the scene, full-blown, in that moment.

The streets were narrow and thronged with people. She had never been in a city before, and the crowd, the tall, close-packed buildings, and the stench that billowed from both, sickened her. She laid her hand on her child-swollen belly, drew closer to Alasdair. The boy perched atop her husband's shoulders giggled with glee. Wee Alec was enjoying the trip to Edinburgh much more than his mother was.

"Here he comes!" Alasdair shouted. His great height put him head and shoulders above the people who were pressing in around them, and he was the first to see the approach of Prince Charles Edward and his entourage. "Ye'll always remember this day, Catriona," he assured her.

The cheering was deafening and she caught a glimpse of the prince through the wall of people who stood between her and the center of the road. He was mounted on a white horse. He was as beautiful as a girl, she decided, with flowing curls and a face that looked as if it had never been subjected to a razor. He held his head high, his chin proudly, and his vibrant plaid was draped gracefully across his collarbones.

"Someday, he will be yer king, wee Alec," Alasdair said.

Kate gasped, blinked her eyes. She was shivering; her arms were covered with goosebumps. The other visions had come to her while she was sleeping, or nearly so, after she had drunk something considerably more potent than a half-glass of ale, in the afterglow of her first orgasm, or as she explored an ancient graveyard and chapel that would make even the most pragmatic person fey. This one had come in broad daylight, in a touristy gift shop, in the middle of a bustling city. Daft or drunk? *Well, I'm not drunk.* . . . "Do you think Alasdair MacLachlan ever saw him?" she managed in a tremulous voice, holding the cup away from her with a rigid arm, not looking at it.

Alec watched her. "Possibly at a distance. Foot soldiers didn't rub elbows with princes in those days."

"Or in these."

"Quite right," he said. "I doubt the present Prince Charles has many friends among the rank and file of Britain's military. But somehow, I can't picture him being present on the battlefield at that bloody defeat either, or having to be forced away from it in tears when his own life was in jeopardy."

"Your Thearlaich did that?"

"Aye. Someone called him a cowardly Italian after Culloden—he was born in Italy, of course, because his father James was in exile there. But I think in the end, he proved he was a Scot, with more courage than common sense."

Kate reluctantly returned her gaze to the dashing figure painted on white ceramic. "Do you think Gram will like it?"

"She'll love it," he assured her. "The Mac-Gillvrays have always had a soft spot in their hearts for the Bonnie Prince."

Alec parked the car outside the hospital, which was tall and modern, located on the outskirts of town. "It's the largest medical facility north of Edinburgh," he explained. "I shouldn't be long in there. My interview with the committee is just a formality. Take the car, now that you've gotten the hang of handling it. Collect me later."

She wasn't sure that was a good idea.

"You're looking pale. Are you all right?" he asked.

"Fine," she said, with as much conviction as she could muster. She glanced at the hospital again. "Did you ever want to be anything but a doctor?"

He shook his head. "I've always thought I'd have been a charmer had I been born in another century."

"You're a charmer in this one," she assured him.

He laughed. "The men and women who practiced folk medicine in the old days were called 'charmers.' They offered some sound treatment—like willow-bark tea for fever, the active ingredient of which turns out to be salicylic acid, aspirin, or foxglove for congestive heart failure, which just happens to contain the active principle of digitalis, but their real specialty was making charms—*eolas*—to ward off illness and bad luck."

"Can't hurt, I guess."

"Exactly," he said. "Have you ever heard the Hippocratic oath?"

"Yes." She had heard it and taken it.

"Its most important line is 'First, do no harm.' Sure, the charmers prescribed drinking holy water from the skull cap of a suicide as treatment for epilepsy, but in a time when trained physicians treated it by performing lobotomies through their patients' nostrils with filthy probes, that wasn't so far off."

"I suppose not," she agreed.

"Making a patient believe he's going to recover is as important to his recovery as any medicine you can give him. If he thinks a charm is going to help him, it's going to help him."

She smiled slowly. She liked Alec's brand of

medicine. "You'd better not let the committee know you're apt to start handing out charms."

"There's a place near Drumossie called St. Mary's well. Many a local still believes that if he ties a *cloutie*—a rag—on one of the branches overhanging it, walks around it three times widdershins, then leaves an offering, his ailment will fade away as the cloth rots away. If I suspect that kind of ritual will make my patient believe he's going to recover, I'll hand him the cloutie myself. You see, Mac-Gillvray, we have so many of the answers right inside us. Sometimes it takes a charm to help us find them."

Or a charmer, she thought.

He kissed her forehead and the tip of her nose. "Collect me back here in an hour and a half."

She watched him disappear into the building.

She didn't consciously decide to follow him, but in the next moment she was walking through the hospital's front doors. If the answers were, indeed, buried inside her, she was going to need a charmer to help her dig them out. And she would rather know for sure that she was crazy than waste any more time worrying about the possibility.

Hospitals smelled the same the world over, she thought as she glanced around inquiringly. The familiar feeling of dread grabbed her then, settling in her chest and her bowels. The medical staff looked the same to her as she had once looked to newcomers to her hospital, she guessed, alien, forbidding, preoccupied and harried, moving quickly through the lobby on their way to more important matters, stethoscopes slung carelessly around their necks, white coats flaring out behind them. This was the first time she had ever arrived at a place like this seeking help, instead of offering it, she realized. She joined the line in front of the reception desk. But when it was her turn to approach the ancient receptionist, she had second thoughts about what she planned to do.

"Good afternoon," the woman said.

It was too late to escape. Kate coughed, glanced back at the line of people waiting behind her, suddenly feeling as if every one of them was wondering if she was daft. *Awa' wi' the fairies*, as Alec would say.

"Good afternoon!"

Kate ran her tongue along her dry lips and leaned closer to the old woman. "I would like to see Dr. Elizabeth MacDonald," she said, very softly.

"Speak up! Dr. MacDonald, you say?"

"Yes."

"Psychiatry. Second floor," the receptionist said, in a tone of voice that would be better suited to announcing train arrivals at the Thirtieth Street Station.

"Thank you," Kate murmured, feeling her face redden. She bowed her head, hunched her shoulders and fled across the lobby. She climbed the stairs to the second floor. She traversed the long hallway quickly. But when she arrived at a frosted-glass door that bore Elizabeth's name, she froze, lost her nerve, turned to walk away. The door flew open.

"*Dr*. MacGillvray!" Elizabeth said meaningfully.

Kate smiled. The Scots grapevine was alive and well and Elizabeth's husband, she suspected, was at its root. But no one had yet seen fit to edify Alec.

229

And she recalled that she had promised to do so herself, a full two days ago.

"What a nice surprise, Kate! Are you here to see me?" Elizabeth queried.

"Alec is meeting with the credentialing board now, so I found myself in the neighborhood. I did want to tell you how much I enjoyed your wedding. Thanks for having me."

"It was a grand affair. I quite enjoyed it myself. And we all loved meeting you."

"It must have been anticlimactic to return to work right away."

Elizabeth shook her head. "I'll be looking forward to Majorca in June. We'll lie in the sun and we won't drink anything that's not served in a coconut. Maybe you and Alec can join us!" She seemed pleased with this inspiration and a broad grin split her lovely face.

"On your honeymoon?"

"It can be your honeymoon too!"

Would she ever have a honeymoon? Kate wondered. "Alec and I just met. . . ."

Elizabeth laughed. "You can't argue with the shortbread, Kate. You got the biggest bit."

Perhaps everyone in Scotland was daft. No wonder she felt right at home here.

Elizabeth glanced at her watch. "I've got a free hour. I was just going across the hall to fetch a cup of coffee. Would you like one?"

Kate nodded.

"Make yourself at home," Elizabeth directed, gesturing toward her office. "I'll just be a minute."

Elizabeth's greeting had been warm and friendly,

but Kate settled into a large chair uncomfortably. She stared at the spines of the books that lined the shelves behind the desk, wondering if Elizabeth would be as eager to see Alec married off when she learned that the bride-to-be was one scone short of a picnic.

"Cheers," Elizabeth said, handing Kate a cup of coffee and raising her own.

"Cheers," Kate agreed, then took a long sip of the drink.

Elizabeth settled down on an old tattered couch against the wall. "If this was a professional visit, you'd get the couch," she teased.

Kate smiled sheepishly. "It is professional, in a way," she started.

The other woman sobered, put her coffee down, stood up and hugged Kate's shoulder. "Is something wrong?" she asked.

"I was hoping you might be able to tell me."

Elizabeth listened quietly as Kate outlined the unusual events of the previous days.

"There," Kate said, drawing in a sigh. "Dizziness, breathlessness, numbness, tingling. Hallucinations. Vivid dreams. A sense of déjà vu. It's like I'm this Catriona, and Alec, Alasdair. What's my diagnosis? Am I . . ."

"Two squares short of a Tobberlone?" The psychiatrist shook her head. "I suppose one might call this a karmic conversion disorder."

"A *what*?"

Elizabeth smiled, settled back in the couch. "Do you recall your Freud from med school?"

"I remember that his patients included more than

a few women with sudden, unexplained blindness, paralysis of limbs, muteness . . ."

Elizabeth nodded. "When he wasn't able to discover a physiologic cause for their afflictions, he began to suspect that their *egos* had fabricated neurological symptoms to cover up unacceptable *id* impulses. . . ."

"Sex and aggression," Kate said. They were the universal unacceptable id—primitive, instinct-driven—impulses.

"He began to suspect that the women were unconsciously *converting* one set of symptoms into another, more socially appropriate, set."

"And when he helped his patients confront their true conflicts, the symptoms disappeared."

Elizabeth met her eyes for a long moment. "Your tingling, numbness and altered level of consciousness certainly sound like conversion symptoms."

"But you mentioned 'karma.' "

"It's the notion that one's essence returns to flesh repeatedly to rectify sins, of commission and omission—sort of a remedial study program for the soul. Souls supposedly evolve with each incarnation, and they tend to reincarnate together, so past debts can be paid." Elizabeth looked past her, hesitated before she said: "I think your conflicts may be rooted in a past life."

"I'm not hypnotizable," Kate protested as she lay down on the couch, but suddenly she found herself more relaxed than she could ever remember being, found herself losing awareness of everything but Elizabeth's soft, persuasive voice.

"You're standing at the top of a flight of ten steps now. There's an open door at the bottom. Start walking toward it. Ten, nine, eight. As you descend, you'll find yourself moving further away from this time and closer to that. Seven, six, five, four. With each step down, you'll find yourself becoming more relaxed, more open to what you'll find beyond the door. Three, two, one. You're standing in front of it now. Just step through it and tell me what you see. . . ."

Chapter Twelve

The great hall was filled with people. Banners hung on the stone walls and torches burned brightly in dozens of sconces. The evening meal had just been cleared away and the fiddlers and pipers launched into a jaunty tune.

"Dance wi' me, mo nighean," her father said, taking her hand and leading her into the clearing in the center of the room where her brothers and their ladies were waiting.

She smiled up into the old warrior's eyes, curtsied gracefully, then joined him, and the other three couples, in a spirited reel.

"Ye're as lovely and as graceful as yer mother was at yer age," he said wistfully, as the guests joined them on the dance floor.

"Ye still miss her, Da."

"I always will."

She considered this. "Ye're young enough to marry again and have a dozen more bairns."

He shook his head. "Ye'll gi'e me grandchildren, a Chatriona."

She snorted. "I'll be nay man's chattel. I'm no capable of being a biddable wife. Ye've long been complaining about how poorly I play the role of laird's daughter. And a husband would nay doubt be a tougher taskmaster than ye."

"Ye're a regular hoyden, lass! Yer brothers thought it great fun to teach ye to ride bareback and fight like a man, and I ne'er had the heart to tell ye nay. I must say, though, I'd no hesitate to fight wi'ye at my back! But wi' the right opponent, ye'd nay doubt soon be as skilled at the face-to-face skirmishes waged between men and women—"

"Da!" she protested.

He chuckled. "Determined to die a virgin, are ye, Catriona?"

It had never reached the level of a determination. It was simply an assumption that she had never doubted. After all, she was nearing her twentieth year and she had never been kissed. All the castle lasses with whom she had grown up had long since married; most of them had more than one bairn. She knew the other girls whispered about her, said she wasn't natural. Perhaps she wasn't. She didn't care.

"Shall I look into dowering ye to one of those fancy convents in France? Perhaps ye're better suited to a contemplative life," he said, his lips twitching.

She threw back her head and laughed. "Eager to be rid of me, are ye?"

He shook his head. "Dance wi' young Mac-Lachlan," he said, spinning her to a halt in front of a tall, dark-haired man and departing abruptly.

The laughter died in her throat as she looked up into MacLachlan's green eyes.

"Alasdair MacLachlan," the man said, with a shallow bow. "Dance wi' me, a Chatriona Nic-Gillebhrath."

It was a command and she found herself powerless to resist it. She moved into the circle of his arms, jolted, as if she had been struck, when he took her limp hand into his, when he settled his other hand on her hip.

"Ye've got to move, lass," he murmured near her ear. "Dancing nearly always requires it."

She nodded and began to move, woodenly, uncertainly, as if she had never danced before.

"I noticed ye this afternoon, Catriona, training in the courtyard wi' yer father's tacksmen," he said. "Ye're quite skilled wi' a dirk."

In a blur, she lifted the hem of her gown, drew her sgian dhu out from under the cuff of her fancy boot and held its needle-sharp point under his chin. "It's no a skill many men appreciate in a woman," she offered boldly.

He extracted the tiny dagger from her fingers without missing a dance step and tucked it safely into his sporran. "I'm no many men."

She met his eyes, guessed this was true. "King James will need the martial skills of every man, and woman, when the next Rising comes, unless we're *prepared to be beaten down like we were in the '15. I will be ready to fight."*

He laughed. "Will ye? I had suspected the MacGillvrays were Jacobites to a man, and a woman."

"So ye dinna support our king's righteous claim to the throne of England and Scotland? Ye're a traitor to yer people," she said in disgust.

"I'm nay traitor. But I do object to having my people slaughtered for naught," he answered.

"I dinna dance wi' traitors or cowards."

She broke away from his grasp, but he pulled her back into his arms effortlessly. "It sometimes takes a braver man to wait out the first fervor, to weigh the options before pledging himself, and his men, to die."

His voice betrayed no anger; it had taken on the tone of a tutor repeating a lesson to an obtuse student, and she didn't like it. "I'm no afraid to die!"

He grinned knowingly then. "It's more important that ye no be afraid to live, Catriona."

She considered this, then she nodded in grudging agreement. She suspected that this man would see past any bravado she could muster, that she could hide little from his perceptive eyes. He was an unusual man, in appearance as well as manner. He was broad-shouldered and lean. He was uncommonly tall, taller than her father and her brothers even, and she had to tilt her head back to study his face, which was tanned and finely chiseled. His long mouth was quite provocative, she decided. She couldn't move her attention away from his mouth.

"What are ye looking at?" he demanded.

She reluctantly raised her eyes to his. "Has anyone ever told ye that ye ha'e a lovely mouth?"

"No lately," he said, laughing. "Ye were peering at it as if ye'd ne'er seen a man's mouth before."

"I hadna," she whispered.

He narrowed his eyes and studied her, his gaze appreciative. "Will ye allow me to paint ye?"

"What color?"

He laughed. "I'm a fair artist, I assure ye, at the risk o' sounding vain. I'm considerably better at wielding a brush than a claymore."

It took a brave man to admit as much here, in a room filled with men who esteemed martial skills well above godliness and cleanliness, and she knew he wasn't a coward, whatever his position on the reinstatement of the Stuart monarchy. She glanced around uneasily, hoping none of the gathered warriors had overheard the comment. "I dinna think I should care to be immortalized."

His smile suggested that although he might allow the matter of her portrait to rest for the time being, she hadn't heard the last of it.

"Are ye spoken for, a Chatriona?"

No man had ever looked at her the way Alasdair MacLachlan was looking at her now. It made her aware, suddenly, of the weight of her breasts, of the slimness of her waist, of the texture of the hair that hung far down her back. "My father was just talking about wedding me to Christ," she answered.

He chortled. "Ye need a husband wi' lovelier lips," he said as he bowed his head to hers, brushed his mouth over hers, lightly, quickly.

The room started spinning and she lost time with

the music, stepped hard on his foot. She felt her face flush. "That was my first kiss," she explained, in apology.

He laughed. "Wasna much of a kiss to remembering for the rest of yer life," he said, halting in the middle of the dancing crowd, capturing her hand, drawing her toward the nearest door.

"Where are ye taking me?" she queried, willing herself to resist him when there didn't seem to be a resistive bone left in her body.

"I believe I'll be taking ye to the altar, eventually, but for now, I'll just take ye somewhere to gi'e ye a proper kissing."

She dug her heels into the floor. "I believe ye ha'e something in there that I want," she said, remembering her dagger, nodding at his sporran. "Gi'e it o'er before ye remove yerself from my father's hall."

"Ah, I'll gi'e ye that too, Catriona. Soon," he promised.

"Move forward." Kate heard the command as if from a great distance, across the lengthy miles of time, and she complied.

The moss was soft and very green, like a velvet blanket on the banks of the lake. . . .

His hair was jet-colored silk and it hung forward around his face as he straddled her, as he dipped his face down to hers.

"Ye could ha'e any woman ye want," she whispered, pressing the palms of her hands up against the hard slabs of muscle, the crisp, dark fur of his chest. It didn't feel odd to be lying naked beneath this man, to have him naked above her, to feel his rigid, throbbing arousal against her thigh. It was as

if it had all happened before. Somewhere.

"I want only ye."

She met his green eyes, smiled up into his beautiful face. He was an honest man. He saw no point in feigning humility and demurring at her assertion. He could have any woman he wanted. "Why me?" she asked.

He studied her. "Because ye're lovely and proud and strong. Because when I'm wi' ye I feel whole. . . ." He looked up, stared across the loch for a moment. "Until I laid my eyes on ye, a Chatriona, I was restless, searching. . . . When I drew ye into my arms, I knew what I had been searching for, what I had been waiting for, all my life. . . ."

"Alasdair. . . ."

"Ye werena meant to stay a maiden, love, and ye certainly werena destined for a convent. There's too much passion in ye. I will show ye what it means to be a woman, to be my woman."

"Now?" She attempted to quell the cowardly panic in her voice.

He nodded. He concentrated on her lower lip then, brushing it with his own, touching it with his tongue, over and over, until she was moaning in need. Only then did he kiss her full on the mouth, only then did he slip his tongue into the cavern of her mouth.

He bowed his head to her breasts, touched her nipples lightly, teasingly, with his tongue, again and again. They jutted forward in approval. Then he took one into his mouth, drew on it until she was arching up under him and begging him to take more, until she was tangling her fingers in his long hair and pulling him against her to encourage him to take more.

Just when she decided that there could be no sensations more exquisite than the ones he was inciting in her, his fingers slipped down to gently pull at the curls that shielded her sex, to part them and find the aching bud within.

"Now!" she begged finally, speaking the only coherent word that was left her, feeling herself damp and urgent against his fingers. Ready.

He nodded, positioned himself, and thrust forward. He took her cry of pain into his own mouth, drew it into his own lungs. Then he halted, his powerful arms trembling on either side of her head as he lifted the weight of his upper body off hers, as he waited for her to become accustomed to the feel of him deep inside her.

The burning pain quickly became a burning need, one that was communicated from her body to his, and back, and she lifted her hips against his, instinctually, hungrily, asking a question for which words were inadequate. It was answered in the next moment, in kind, when he began to move, and the sensations he stirred in her dwarfed all the others that had come before. She caught the rhythm and moved with him, allowed him to direct her down the path whose end she could almost glimpse, could almost touch. . . .

"Alasdair," she cried when her body convulsed on his, before she sank into a shadowy void in which the echo of his name was the only sound.

"Catriona," he gasped as his own release consumed him, as he gathered her against him, held her

against the sweating, shuddering length of his body.

They lay entwined and silent for many minutes afterwards. She resisted the movement when he finally broke away from her and stood up. She looked up at his powerful, dark body, outlined by the blue sky behind him. "Where are ye going, Alasdair?" she asked.

"To find a maiden who'll wed wi' me," he said.

She laughed then, until she was curled into a ball on the green moss and tears were rolling down her cheeks. He sank down beside her, drew her into his lap, rocked her gently against him.

"Ye always make me laugh," she gasped, laying her hand against his cheek.

He turned his face to place a kiss in her palm. "I pray God, love, I'll ne'er make ye cry," he said.

"Move forward." The command came again and again Kate obeyed.

She shifted uncomfortably on the tall stool, but froze when she heard Alasdair's voice boom across the space between them.

"Quit yer fidgeting, Catriona!" He glanced from the canvas that was balanced on the easel before him, to his model, and back, before he jabbed his brush forward.

"Canna ye content yerself wi' immortalizing the loch again?" she groaned. The child was low and heavy in her belly and she regretted not *posing for Alasdair when he'd first asked her to do it, a year earlier. She should have known he would get his way, sooner or later.*

"Nay. But if ye dinna sit still and smile prettily,

I'll immortalize ye wi' a huge wart on the tip o' yer nose.''

"Do that, if ye dinna mind being remembered as the artist wi' the ugly wife!"

"E'en if ye had a wart the size of Ben Nevis on yer nose, yer husband would think ye the most beautiful woman in the world,'' he murmured, painting furiously in the dwindling light.

She smiled prettily, despite her best effort not to.

"Move forward.''

Pale sunlight fell on the bed through the latticed window behind it.

The pain was unbearable. She had never been afraid of pain, she had never wanted to die, but suddenly she was begging for death, for release from the searing agony that was threatening to tear her in two.

"Ye're almost there, mo Chatriona,*'' Alasdair said, encouraging her to squeeze his hand as the next contraction wrenched her lower body, twisted her cruelly and made her cry out.*

"On the next one, bear down hard,'' the midwife between her knees directed.

She squeezed Alasdair's hand as the pain wrenched her again.

"Bear down hard. Now,'' he urged.

It was a timeless, painless moment during which everything inside her seemed to gush out. It was a sightless and silent moment and she was certain that she had, indeed, died. But then she heard a loud, lusty baby's cry and she knew she would live forever.

"Ye've gi'en me a son,'' Alasdair murmured, kissing her hands and her face.

She saw the tears on his cheeks and she touched them in wonder. She had never before seen him shed a tear.

"What will we call him, love?"

"Alexander," she whispered. "Of course."

He smiled in gratitude. "Da!" he bellowed then, taking his blood-and-muck-covered son from the midwife, wrapping him in a plaid blanket.

She raised her head up as her father appeared in the archway and she gave him a tired grin.

"Ye've a fine, braw grandson," Alasdair said, offering his tiny bundle to the older man. "His name is Alexander. Of course."

She swallowed a sob. She had never before seen tears on her father's cheeks, either.

"Move forward."

The last of the summer flowers were blooming around the cottage and the sun was shimmering on the loch. Her belly was rounded with the child she would bear after Michaelmas, and she held wee Alec's hand as they watched Alasdair bound up the path.

"A Chatriona!" Alasdair called, his voice tinged with excitement. He swept her into his arms and kissed her passionately, patted her belly to greet his second child, then kneeled to give his first, wee Alec, a lengthy hug.

"What has happened?" she demanded.

He looked up at her and grinned. "Prince Charles Edward has taken Edinburgh for his father. The clans are massing there. We'll march south until we hit Westminster and we willna leave until we've seen

James Stuart crowned King of England and Scotland!''

Her heart sank. "Ye mustna go,'' she whispered. It wasn't a cause that Alasdair had ever wholeheartedly avowed. "I can fight my own battles.''

He patted her belly again. "Ye're in nay shape to fight yer battles, love. I'll just ha'e to do it for ye.''

She shook her head mutely, laid her hand on his soft, black hair. She fought back the tears that were threatening to roll down her cheeks.

"There's a lovely lass who once told me she didna dance wi' cowards or traitors. Since she's the only woman I want to dance wi' for the rest of my life, I'll just ha'e to prove to her that I'm neither.''

"Don't go, Alasdair,'' she begged.

"Pack up a few things, Catriona, and we'll all go to Edinburgh to greet the Bonnie Prince! I'll ha'e one of yer father's men escort ye back here before my clan heads south.''

She shook her head mutely.

"Smile, a Chatriona. I'll bring ye back a gee-gaw from London.''

"I'm going to count from one to five. With each count, you'll come closer and closer to full awareness. At five, you'll awaken feeling refreshed and peaceful. You'll remember everything. One, two, three, four, five.''

Kate sat up and stared at Elizabeth for a long minute.

"I think that will take care of your symptoms. Do you feel better?''

Kate considered this. "Much better,'' she said, in surprise. "It all seemed so real, the laughter and the tears, the pain. . . . Do you believe those images were coming from a past life?''

Elizabeth raised her shoulders vaguely. "I think it was Voltaire who said: 'Being born twice is no more remarkable than being born once.' " She shrugged again. "Whether we're really tapping into past lives, or just creating fantasies that constructively work through, and resolve, deep-seated conflicts, no one can say for sure. All I know is that people often feel better after they've been regressed. People seem to find their answers more easily after they've been regressed. What was the emotion that drew you back to that particular lifetime?''

"Alasdair joined the Jacobites to please me. It was my fault that he was killed at Culloden." Kate recalled the words of Attila's girlfriend and understood why that incident had sent her into such a panic. *It's my fault he's dead. He wanted to paint, not fight. He joined the Huns to prove himself to me.*''

"Guilt. It's a powerful emotion."

Kate nodded. It was apparently one that could survive two and half centuries. She stood up and stretched, glanced at her watch. She hugged the other woman. "Thank you for your time. It has been a pleasure knowing you."

"We'll meet again. Maybe in Scotland. Maybe in Majorca. Or maybe in a place much further afield than either," Elizabeth said, with confidence. "You've seen the past. Now it's time to embrace the future," she added, very softly, failing to completely temper the note of warning in her voice.

Kate started toward the door, but halted and

turned back to Elizabeth's hesitant summons.

"My husband says it's up to Alec to discuss his past with you, that it's not my place to do it, but now I think I understand . . ."

"What?"

"Like Catriona, you're afraid to appear weak, vulnerable. You're afraid to let anyone see beyond that warrior-woman facade. You haven't told Alec the things you told Dunc because you believe he'll think less of you for them. Alec is a very brave man and he respects courage, but you might find that his definition of the word is different from yours."

Elizabeth looked down into her lap for a moment before she continued. "Alec once threw in the towel after he failed to resuscitate a young father who had been badly mangled in a motor vehicle accident. The man's two wee sons had been belted in the back seat and weren't hurt seriously. Alec kept saying: 'Two boys will have to grow up without their father because of me.' Never mind that their father had gotten into his Morris after taking at least two drams too many and, but for the grace of God, might have killed the boys himself. Never mind that their father was dead before Alec ever laid eyes on him."

"Alec told me he had never been afraid to do his job!"

"It wasn't fear, exactly, that kept him from it then. It was guilt and a profound sadness. I thought it might help you to know."

It did help. All of it. The thought of returning to work on Monday wasn't making her stomach ache anymore, Kate realized as she hurried down the stairs with a crowd of white-coated young men. She would miss Alec dreadfully, of course, but she was suddenly more confident of her ability to finish her residency, to respond appropriately in a crisis, to someday be an equal partner in a small, Scottish medical practice.

"I'm not afraid," she whispered in satisfaction when several beepers began to screech in unison and a handful of doctors took off at a run. The acid test would come with the next medical emergency, she knew, with the next shattered glass or ill-managed knife. With the next spilled blood. But she was once again proud to acknowledge she was a physician. And she was suddenly anxious to tell Alec.

On several occasions she had remarked at how little Alec knew about her, but she realized only now how little she actually knew about him, about the things that had hurt him and moved him in the past, about the things he felt in his heart. She had doubted his capacity to appreciate the incident that had driven her away from Philadelphia a week ago—when he had, in fact, had an almost identical experience in his own career. She had questioned his ability to love her. Could her judgment be as faulty in the second instance as it had proved to be in the first?

As she traversed the hospital's lobby, she considered the love Alasdair had felt for Catriona. She could almost believe that such a love might survive their deaths. But it was a quantum leap to believe that Alasdair's soul was now Alec's, that Catriona's was now her own, and that they could pick up their relationship right about where they had left it off two hundred fifty years ago. She and Alec would simply have to forge something new—something in keeping with their times, attitudes, priorities. Something that might just turn out to be as strong as anything Alasdair and Catriona had known.

She stepped through the front doors, remembering Elizabeth's advice to look forward, not back. She saw her future leaning against a street lamp, the offending necktie already removed and tucked into his pocket, and she ran forward to embrace him.

"That's some greeting, MacGillvray," Alec laughed. "We've only been apart for an hour."

"It seemed much longer," she said.

The small flat to which the eager rental agent took them was just slightly removed from the heart of town, on a quiet, tree-lined street. It was furnished simply but tastefully. Kate strolled around the main room, peeking into the tiny but well-appointed galley kitchen and bathroom, into the cozy bedroom.

"I like it," she pronounced finally. "There are certain advantages in having to refer my family to Mrs. Munro's when they come to visit."

"Mrs. Munro's?" Alec asked. "You'll refer them to Mrs. Lachlan's."

"That would be quite a presumption," she said.

"Why? Whenever Isabel's family descends on Inverness they're made welcome at Dun Buie."

She lowered her eyes. "There's a big difference between Isabel's family and mine."

She looked up to see his lips twitching, knew he was suppressing a grin with an effort. "Ah," he said, "the MacGillvrays use cutlery at table, do they?"

249

She laughed.

"Does the flat suit your purposes, Dr. Lachlan?" the agent asked, stepping toward them.

Their purposes . . . Kate felt her face begin to burn as she remembered exactly what their purposes were, and she couldn't meet the young woman's eyes. *Get current!* she chided herself. *Catriona's attitude toward sex was probably more modern than yours.* She walked away as casually as she was able, made her way into the bedroom. She found herself on a postage-stamp-sized balcony that overlooked a small garden. She leaned against the balcony's railing and studied the bare plots beneath her. She had felt as awkward just now as she had when Alec insisted on paying for the skirt and sweater in the fancy boutique. Being regressed hadn't relaxed the rigid sense of right and wrong—*superego*, she recalled, feeling as if she and Freud were old friends—that was as much a part of her as her backbone. She had felt like a kept woman, had been sure the salesgirl, and now the rental agent, could identify her as such. She had always wanted to belong to a man, but never to be owned by one, lock, stock and barrel.

She didn't want to be Alec Lachlan's mistress.

What would Catriona have done in a situation like this? Kate closed her eyes to summon up the image of the strong-willed, passionate woman with the well-honed dirk in her boot. She would have made her desires very clear. She wouldn't have allowed herself to be pressured into something that made her uncomfortable. *"People seem to find their answers more easily after they've been regressed,"* Elizabeth had said. And the answer occurred to Kate easily in that moment. She would apply for professional privileges here immediately and probably get them, eventually—even in Scotland there had to be some shortage of well-trained doctors—but in the meantime she would pay her own way, somehow. Short of candy and flowers, today's gifts were the last ones she could accept from Alec. She would encourage him to court her, in the time-honored manner. And she would make him love her. *I can teach him that love doesn't have to hurt. I can make him want me for his wife.* She would show him that she was a strong, competent woman, a worthy mate, and if he couldn't see clear of his battle scars to appreciate that, well, she would just wish him better luck in his next life and be on her way.

She squinted at the weeping cherry tree in the garden. It was beginning to bud, she noted. Would it bloom in July? Would she be here to see it happen? Alec had been pleased with the idea of having a mistress. Would he be as pleased with the idea of pursuing a traditional courtship, leading to traditional matrimony? Could he handle the idea of having a lover who was his equal, who was capable of paying her own way, leading her own life? Or would he simply opt to find another *lass* who wouldn't insist on dinner and small talk *first*?

Hadn't she felt forever in his kiss, hadn't she seen it in his eyes? Maybe.

Perhaps this wasn't the lifetime in which Alasdair and Catriona were destined to grow old together.

Perhaps she would wait until tomorrow to set Alec straight.

*   *   *

Kate leaned back in the Range Rover's passenger seat and watched the road.

"You're quiet, MacGillvray," Alec offered, glancing at her.

She nodded.

"Did you like the flat?"

"It's beautiful."

"It's small," he said, "but adequate. What did you think of that kitchen?"

She turned to look at him, hearing the eagerness in his voice. "It seemed very well-equipped—not that I'd know what to do with half the gadgets in it."

"Not much of a cook, are you?"

"I make pretty good soup—I'm sure the place comes with a can opener."

He laughed. "Well, don't bother yourself about it. I'm my mother's son. I'll teach you how."

"Will you?" She couldn't shake the feeling that she had taken her last lesson from Alec Lachlan. "You're a regular Henry Higgins, aren't you?"

"Who?" he asked.

"Pygmalion."

"Oh, aye," he said, understanding the second reference. "But I'm only as good as my raw material."

It was easier to make a dream woman from scratch, she supposed, than to remake one with thirty years of bad habits, stubborn opinions, inflexible expectations. How was Alec going to react when he discovered she wasn't quite as moldable as she had seemed?

"Yes, indeed, MacGillvray. I'll have you cooking straightaway. By the time I'm finished with you,

you'll make some lucky man a fine wife.''

He seemed pleased with his jest and laughed heartily. But somehow Kate couldn't bring herself to join in.

It had been a thoroughly confusing day. Kate settled back in the bathtub, glad that Alec had gone directly to his room, allowing her time to pull herself together before she had to face him again. It had been difficult to keep him in the context of the here and now during the brief hours since she'd left Elizabeth's office, and numerous times Kate had stopped herself just short of telling him things, of making little gestures, that were inappropriately intimate. Alec wasn't her husband, or the father of her children. He might never be. He wasn't Alasdair.

And yet he was.

She closed her eyes and suddenly she was standing in a stone-walled room, in the arms of a man with the loveliest lips she had ever seen.

Alec or Alasdair?

She was lying on the banks of the loch, her legs and arms spread, while he settled between them and dipped his head to possess her mouth.

Alec?

He was whispering in her ear, while she tried to control the guffaw that was swelling in her chest. *''You always make me laugh. . . .''*

Alasdair?

And he was battering her down into a warm, soundless void. She was a limp mass of flesh surrounding a core that was vigilant, pulsating, on the verge of clenching like a fist around the steel it sheltered.

Alec!

Alasdair?

She groaned and sat up, started scrubbing at her skin with a loofa sponge. "So what's your point?" she whispered.

Alec and Alasdair had a lot in common.

Did that mean Alec was likely to welcome the prospect of a respectable courtship?

Or that she was going to lose him—as abruptly, as irrevocably, as Catriona had Alasdair?

"Damn!" she muttered, realizing that the aggressive sponge had left a raw, sore patch on her upper arm. She flung it down.

And it hovered, a dark hump on the surface of the water for just a moment before it disappeared, leaving behind only a certainty.

Anything is possible.

Chapter Thirteen

Kate descended to the parlor, found Alec sitting on the couch in front of the fireplace. He had bathed and shaved, was wearing flannel pants and a tweed jacket with a casual taupe sweater beneath it.

"You look beautiful, MacGillvray," he said as she came to stand in front of him. His gaze moved up over her simple black dress to her eyes. "I could barely stand to be away from you for the past hour. How am I going to get through the next ten weeks?"

He took her hand, pulled her down onto the couch beside him. His hands were buried in her hair then and his lips were against hers. She moaned when his tongue breached her mouth, as if he hadn't done this in years, rather than hours.

"Alec . . ."

Hé looked down into her eyes. "I love to hear my name on your lips," he said.

"Say mine," she whispered.

"Catriona," he gasped. "*Mo* Chatriona, *mo bhean*."

"*Mo bhean*?" she asked.

He smiled. "Not yet, MacGillvray. But soon. Very soon."

After dinner they returned to the same couch, agreeing to Mrs. Munro's proposal that they have a cordial in front of the fire. She presented them with a plate of homemade truffles to go with the brandy. They watched the flickering fire, sipped their drinks.

"I told Miss Lindsay we would take the flat, beginning July," Alec said.

Kate had hoped the subject wouldn't come up again tonight, but there it was. She sighed. "How much is the rent?"

"Don't bother yourself with that."

"Don't bother myself with that?" It was time to take the bull by the horns, like it or not. "It will be my apartment. It's not as if we'll be married and living there as husband and wife."

"No. We won't be," he agreed quickly.

"So I don't want you to pay the rent."

"Can you afford to pay it?"

She had anticipated this question. A resident's salary was paltry, and the trip and the other extravagant purchases she had recently made had put her squarely into debt. "No. But I'll borrow from my family until I'm able to get a job."

"I can afford to keep you. I don't want your family to think otherwise. I've got my pride.''

''And I've got mine,'' she answered, more harshly than she had intended. Alasdair's attitude toward women had undoubtedly been more liberal than his twentieth-century counterpart's. How was Alec going to react to the rest of her ultimatum?

He glanced at her again. ''This was never meant to be a long-term situation, you know,'' he said, his tone conveying his confusion.

Her heart lurched. ''Wasn't it?'' she asked.

He snorted. ''Of course not, MacGillvray. I give it two or three months, if we can stick it out that long. Surely you can allow a man who's not your husband to keep you for that period of time. We'll be leasing the flat month-by-month and can keep it longer, if we want to. But I doubt we'll want to.''

''Won't we?'' she whispered.

''We're not indecisive, either one of us. We'll see no point in prolonging an unnatural situation, one that's bound to have grown tiresome for both of us, one that won't meet with the approval of either one of our families.''

She had tasted forever in his kiss, she had seen it in his eyes . . .

Hadn't she?

She lifted her chin, choked back the tears that threatened to roll down her cheeks. The bull's horns had gored her squarely in the gut. Alec had set her straight before she had the chance to do it to him. ''Why are we bothering with it in the first place?'' she asked, her voice a hoarse whisper.

He patted her knee and grinned. ''At the moment, our hormones are calling the tune,'' he said.

And her heart, she guessed, would be paying the piper.

Alec had taken the wind out of her sails and Kate sat beside him stiffly, silently, staring into the fire, trying to regroup. It had been romantic to believe he was so swept away by love that he'd proposed marriage after spending one long weekend with her. It had been equally so to cast him in the role of love-scarred cynic and herself as the mistress who could heal him. The truth wasn't nearly as romantic. It had to do with hormones. And pheromones, perhaps. Together, she and this sensuous, brooding misogynist created physiologic magic in bed, and he hadn't had his fill of it. Yet. She felt her face begin to flame with silent humiliation. And while she had been waxing melodramatic over a fantasy entitled *happily ever after*, he had been simply orchestrating an amusing summertime romp! It was a pity she couldn't find a way to put her imagination to more constructive use.

"What are you thinking about, MacGillvray?" Alec asked.

"I'm thinking about writing a novel," she grumbled.

"That's great! What kind of novel will you write?"

She turned to him sullenly, but met his boyish grin and couldn't keep her own lips from softening in answer. The bitter words she had been about to speak died on her tongue, and the love she felt for him, even now, staggered her. It wasn't his fault that she had imagined commitment where none existed, had accepted forever when it hadn't been offered.

Every second she had left with Alec was precious, she realized. The clock was ticking. The day of her departure was looming ever nearer. *Don't waste time with regrets*, she urged herself. *If you have only this week with him, at least you had this week with him!* "I used to love reading historical romances," she managed. It was an admission she had never made before. "Maybe I have one of those inside me."

"Ah," he said. "The saucy Saxon wench and the Norman knight who conquers her, that sort of thing?"

She studied him carefully, laid her hand on his hair, which, for just a moment, in the dim light of the sitting room, had once again taken on the look of jet-colored silk. "How about a saucy Highland wench whose father, brothers and husband go off to fight for King James . . ." The images were still clear and vivid in her mind, the emotions still simmered inside her.

He took her hand. "And what happens?"

"The men all die on Culloden field and she's left alone with two small children."

He laughed. "I don't want to argue with your literary vision, MacGillvray, but I think the genre requires a happy ending."

She smiled then. "Maybe I can figure out a way to make it end happily," she said.

After they had finished brandy and chocolates, they held hands silently for a long time.

"Alec," Kate said.

"Uh-huh?"

It was actually much simpler now. She didn't need

to draw Alec into the wife-versus-mistress debate, because he had never intended to make her either. All that remained to be determined was whether or not she would be back for their summertime fling. But perhaps he would withdraw even that offer when he learned exactly what kind of science she practiced. *"I intend to avoid them like the plague, for the rest of my life,"* he had said about female physicians. It seemed likely that their physical compatibility would grow less magical in the light of her next admission.

Maybe she would tell him tomorrow.

Catriona would have told him six days ago! she thought. She swallowed hard, steeling herself. "I have a small confession to make. It's something I've wanted to tell you since our first conversation, but somehow the timing was never right."

He sat upright and studied her face in mock dismay. "Just tell me you did it in self-defense."

She considered this, then laughed, understanding. "No, I'm not a serial killer, or an international spy or the mother of triplets. It's just that I . . ."

"You're shaking, MacGillvray," he said, seriously now, holding up her hand. He raised it to his lips and kissed it. "No confessions for you tonight. There's nothing you can tell me that could make me want you less, anyway. Tomorrow night, after we've hiked to Lairig Ghru and back, we won't really be up to much more than lying in bed and listening to each other's confessions. Will it all keep until then?"

She nodded. Even Catriona would have allowed

herself to be derailed by the invitation in those green eyes.

"Good. Now let me give you a brief overview of your next lesson, Cheit," he said. "I've kept a trick or two up my sleeve."

Kate studied Alec intently as he removed the last of his clothes, almost hoping he had developed a blemish or love-handle since she last saw him naked, but he was still perfect, lean and firmly muscled with broad shoulders and a magnificent set of buns. Then he turned around . . .

That was just about the way she remembered it, too.

He followed the angle of her gaze and grinned. "You've got me walking about in a perpetual state of excitation," he explained.

"I see," she said.

"Do you?"

"It's a bit hard to miss."

He chuckled, came forward and drew her into his arms. "The male member lends itself to puns."

She felt it settle against her belly, and the multitude of puns that had been on the tip of her tongue escaped her.

His hands roved over her shoulders, down her back, closed on her buttocks, pulling her nearer. His lips roved lightly over her face, then paused near her ear. "I was just thinking about a colleague from Edinburgh . . ."

Not Tess, she hoped.

". . . an Indian chap named Rao. He used to wax on about something called tantric sex . . ."

Kate caught her breath in anticipation.

261

"He seemed to believe that each person possesses a set of *chakra*, which I take it are like wee radio receivers tuned in to pick up the universal power called *prana*." He took a step back from her. "There are five major ones—head, throat, chest, navel and genitalia." His hand moved down from her forehead, demonstrating the location of each, lingering at the last.

"The head chakra, which corresponds to the Third Eye, or seat of the soul, is the most important. When it's wide open, one can glimpse the meaning of life," he finished.

"How do you open it?"

He grinned. "Oh, you know, fasting, meditation, lying on beds of nails, that sort of thing. Or you can line up all your chakras to create an open channel between top and bottom, then stimulate the bottom." His finger found that particular chakra.

"That will open my Third Eye?" she asked breathlessly.

"MacGillvray, if I do it right, it will blow the top of your head off."

He sat down on the rug, drew her down to face him. "Wrap your legs about my waist and your arms about my shoulders," he instructed.

She did it. Then he crossed his legs behind her, closed his arms around her. "It takes a good deal of upper body strength to keep those buggers in a straight line," he warned, before he lifted her up, then lowered her into position.

"You just touched my navel chakra," she gasped.

He chuckled. "Ready?"

She nodded. But as he began to move within her,

she knew she was more than ready. She tightened her arms and legs around him, drew herself up hard against him to straighten the channel. Soon, she was no longer aware of him thrusting into her, or of her core grasping him eagerly. She couldn't tell whether it was his upper body strength or her own that was lifting them off the floor. They were one body, fused, floating.

She struggled for breath when her chest chakra opened. She cried out when her throat chakra opened. And then. . . .

The top of her head blew off.

She thought she glimpsed the meaning of life in the moment before she squeezed her eyes shut and drifted away on a sea of prana.

She had selfishly pursued her own pleasure without a thought for Alec's, she chided herself as she regained cognizance some time later to find herself still thoroughly entwined with him, but one look at his face told her he hadn't been short-changed.

"So what did you think of that, MacGillvray?" he asked gruffly.

"I can't wait to see the trick you're keeping up your sleeve," she answered.

The minibus pulled up in front of the inn just as the sun was beginning to rise the next morning. Kate glanced around the foyer anxiously, certain Alec had stumbled to his room to dress for this excursion, then promptly fallen back to sleep. She wouldn't go to Lairig Ghru without him, she decided. She could force herself to live for the moment, in the present, until she left tomorrow, but she couldn't force herself away from his side until then. She was determined to make this day the most memorable of her life.

He was beside her when she turned around, dressed in hiking boots and warm layered clothing, topped off with a red windbreaker. His backpack was in his hand. He accepted the bagged lunch proffered by a wide-awake Mrs. Munro and tucked it away. Then she handed him a tall thermos and another sack. "Tea and scones. For the bus ride," she explained.

"Thank you, Mrs. Munro," he said, with a charming smile that caused the landlady to walk away with a blush on her cheeks.

"Are you sure you're up to a twenty-six-mile hike, MacGillvray?" he asked, hugging Kate against him as they walked toward the van.

She grinned. "You're looking a bit worn around the edges yourself. Too much *doss* for you?"

He snorted. "Not near enough. I'm a glutton for it, you understand. I'll take as much as I can get."

"You're amazing," she whispered, impressed.

"I can do it all through the night, then through the better part of the next day. In fact, if I'd given in to my natural urges back in my room a few minutes ago, you'd be heading into the mountains without me. Once I get started with it, I have a tough time stopping."

"You would have done it without me?" she demanded.

He shrugged. "I'd rather do it with you, of course, but I managed to get enough for a good number of years before I met you, and still remember how to go about it. I needed it so badly this morning, I could have done it with anybody." He helped her mount the vehicle's step, then slid into the seat beside her, slipped his arm around her shoulder.

"*Anybody?*"

"Well, maybe not with Dunc," he laughed. "The noise he makes while he's doing it is a bit off-putting. If we had been flatmates for another six months, I'd be stone deaf right now."

Kate gasped, dropped her gaze to her lap, not able to look at him, not knowing what to say.

He chucked her under the chin. "I love the sounds you make while you're doing it, Kate: soft, wee sighs, murmured words I can't quite make out. Oh, I've done it with more people than I care to recollect, but—"

"I get the idea!" she interrupted. She didn't want to hear another word about it. "When the object is dossing, one kip's pretty much like any other!"

"Maybe so, MacGillvray," he answered softly, taking her hand. "But the best thing about sleeping in your bed is that you're the first thing I see when I wake up."

Kate considered his last words and the foregoing part of this brief conversation. She recalled the similarly outrageous one they had shared in front of the sitting room's fireplace two nights ago. The she started to laugh. "Let me see if I've got this straight, Alec. A *kip* is a bed . . ." she chortled.

He nodded his head, his left eyebrow arched questioningly.

"And *doss*?"

"Sleep! For pity's sake, MacGillvray, what did

you think they meant? And how much of what I've said to you during the past six days has gone right over your head for want of a translation?"

"I'm beginning to wonder," she managed; then she laughed until she was completely out of breath.

Since their inn was south of the city, nearer the Cairngorms than Inverness, they were the last of the hikers to be collected. They offered greetings to the van's seven other occupants, most of whom seemed to be German tourists, and all serious mountaineers, by the look of their high-tech boots and expensive thermal clothing. The only other woman in the crowd was Ilsa, the hale and hearty mother of the teenage boy who sat beside her. Her English was excellent, but Kate was surprised to hear Alec address her in German.

"You're full of surprises," Kate said.

"Believe me, MacGillvray, if you can speak Gaelic, you can speak anything," Alec answered. He handed her a scone and poured tea into the thermos cup. "Maybe I should give you a working knowledge of the language before you get on your plane tomorrow, since we've apparently been having some trouble communicating in English."

She lifted a doubting eyebrow. "You might find I don't take to these lessons quite as quickly as I did to your others. French was the only class I ever flunked."

He grinned. "But I intend to employ an unusual method of teaching you, Cheit, one that calls heavily upon your success in my other course of instruction—"

"What?"

He smoothed a loose strand of her hair back to the barrette that was restraining the rest, then laid the back of his hand on her cheek. "First you'll learn the words for all the things I'm doing to you, and you'll understand everything I'm saying while I do them. When I hear you screaming out your satisfaction in Gaelic, I'll know you're ready to move on to more mundane lessons, like how to offer polite greetings to strangers or order haggis in a restaurant."

She laughed. "The language of love?"

"Just so," he said. "Now let me tell you what I plan to do to you tonight."

He put his lips against her ear and whispered in soft melodic Gaelic, and somehow she thought she was beginning to understand.

The minibus dropped the hikers off at the bottom of a wide marked trail. One of their number stepped forward and introduced himself as George Ross, the guide. He was tall and handsome, young, bearded, obviously an outdoorsman. He wore his long blond hair drawn back in a tail.

"The driver will collect us at the other end of the trail, in Braemar, in about eight hours," George said, glancing at his watch, then up at the gray sky in an appraising manner. "You will have to keep up the pace, unless you're of a mind to spend the night on the mountain, without the equipment to do so. Does anyone want to get back in the van before I send it off?"

"Well, MacGillvray?" Alec asked.

She shook her head.

The guide looked at them and spoke a brief sentiment in Gaelic.

Kate winced as she realized the guide had been sitting behind them in the bus and had probably heard most of their conversation. "What did he say?" she asked Alec.

He laughed, then bent to her ear and whispered: "He said he doubted you'd have any trouble keeping up with me."

The trail was steep in places and rocky, but well marked. The first several hours of their trek seemed grueling to Kate and she found herself digging into her raisin-and-nut trail mix frequently in an effort to find some energy. But just as she noticed the blanket of snow on the ground between the tall pine trees, she hit her stride. Suddenly the beauty of the place struck her full force and she was captivated by it. There were fierce outcroppings of rock and tumbling brooks. The air was the freshest she had ever breathed. She spotted a red deer through the trees and called out to Alec in delight as it leapt gracefully away.

"Aye, they're beautiful," Alec said, following her gaze. "But there are too many of them. They're upsetting the balance of plants and other animals in the Eastern Highlands."

"The balance of nature is delicate," George agreed, dropping back to join them, as he had several times since the beginning of the hike. He walked on Kate's side of the trail and seemed to be pointedly directing his comments to her. "Our famous

Highland heather, for example, is becoming scarce. It's not a particularly hardy plant and when its root system is destroyed by over-grazing, it's replaced by lichen and ferns the next season. Since red grouse will only nest in heather, their population has been dropping steadily.''

Kate considered this grimly. Even paradise could be threatened, she supposed.

''When they built the ski lifts into these mountains, more people came and more rubbish came and then more scavenging birds came. They've interfered with the ground-breeding birds, like the dotterel. And the skiing itself has eroded the slopes,'' George continued.

''I suppose it was man who threw off the red deer's natural population controls in the first place,'' Kate ventured.

George nodded. ''The deer's natural predators, like the lynx and the wolf, have been killed or driven away by man.''

''Since the Romans demolished the Caledonian forest nearly two thousand years ago, the Highlands have been at the mercy of men's greed and indifference,'' Alec offered.

George glanced at him and nodded grudgingly.

Ilsa called to Alec in German. He excused himself and walked forward to join her.

''You're very beautiful, Kate,'' George said softly.

She looked at him in surprise. ''Thank you,'' she said.

''Are you and Alec promised?''

''*Promised*?''

269

"You know, engaged to be married, engaged to be engaged, that sort of thing."

Kate considered this, then shook her head. They were neither of those things.

"Can I take you out for a meal and some dancing tonight?"

Alec's timely return saved her from having to answer. And his glare encouraged the other man to return to his post at the fore of the hiking phalanx.

"What did he want?" Alec asked.

"He wanted to know if we were promised."

He nodded. "And what did you say?"

She raised her chin, hearing the jealousy in his voice, seeing that his teeth were clenched together behind his lips. "I said we weren't."

He nodded again. "So what in hell did you imagine you were agreeing to the other day when I asked you not to leave me?"

His voice was soft and dangerously controlled. She stopped walking and looked up into his eyes. She couldn't bring herself to tell him about the first fantasy she had entertained after his unexpected declaration, the one that involved cream-colored lace, the threshold of a Highland castle and a prince named Alec. "I thought I was agreeing to be your mistress."

"My mistress!"

His tone struck a compromise between righteous indignation and incredulous disbelief, and she knew she had picked the wrong answer. Either asking her to become his mistress was a long-term commitment compared to what he had actually wanted of her. . . .

Or she had understood his intentions perfectly in the first place.

"So you were willing to assume the role of mistress?"

She raised her chin, deciding to brazen it out. "I considered it," she said. "But I never thought to describe it as 'a promise.' "

Then he started to laugh, uproariously, loudly, until a half-dozen German tourists had stopped in their tracks and turned around to stare back at him.

"What's so funny?" she demanded.

"I'm thinking about the expression on Violet Lachlan's face when she learns her fair-haired son entered into negotiations to engage himself a mistress."

Kate couldn't help smiling at the image that filled her mind. She could practically see Violet's beautiful, friendly face, wide-eyed and open-mouthed with shock. "Yes, well, I knew we'd have to be discreet. That small, pleasant flat you let for me isn't nearly far enough removed from the mainstream to be appropriate."

"We'll have to take certain precautions, I suppose," he said. "I might press the buzzer three short times to let you know it's me. And you might let me up quickly lest someone see me there. Of course, I will expect to find you bathed, perfumed and lying naked on the bed when I step through the door, so I can be out and about quickly."

"Well, I'm not the kind of lass who will expect dinner and small talk, first," she said pointedly. "When you find yourself in need of a little doss, all you have to do is drop your breeks and slip right into my nice, warm kip.''

He hooted in mirth, obviously understanding the magnitude of their communication problem in that moment.

''Will you want the lights on or off?'' she queried.

''On. I want the place lit up like a bloody fitba' stadium when I arrive, but I'll shut them all off before I steal out into the night.'' He shook his head and tried to control the laughter that was shaking his voice. ''Kate, I should have started your Gaelic lessons in Walker's pub! You know I never wanted you to be my mistress, don't you?''

''I know now,'' she said softly, forcing herself to ignore the small glimmer of excitement that was suddenly building inside her. *What if I understood his intentions perfectly in the first place*? She continued up the trail to hide her face, to keep from looking at his.

''MacGillvray,'' he called.

She turned back to him. ''Yes?''

''You're a piece of work,'' he said, wiping tears from his eyes with his coat sleeve.

She held her hand out to him, loving him so much that she knew she would never love anyone the same way again, and, still chuckling, he jogged forward to take it.

The sun fell in dappled shards through the pine needles overhead. It grew increasingly colder as they proceeded upward, but the increased exertion caused Kate to start removing layers of clothing and tucking them into her pack. When she reached the rugged pass, Lairig Ghru, at the top of the mountain, she was ready to remove even her windbreaker, but Alec cautioned against this. They stood together, looking at the mist-and-snow-covered peaks around them, gray shadows against the blue sky, outlined in pink and purple; then they turned to look at each other.

"What do you say, MacGillvray?" he asked.

"I've never seen a place so magnificent," she said. Words seemed inadequate to describe it. "And yet, it's as if I've seen it before, somewhere . . ."

He drew her against him. "You know, it's said that wherever in the world a Highlander travels, he can feel these mountains drawing him back, he can hear them calling out to him, bidding him *a' tilleadh*."

She gasped. "Attila?" And she remembered where she had seen these mountains before: They had been painted on the back of a blood-stained leather jacket.

"Return," he said.

She was suddenly dizzy, sure she was going to faint. "Alec!"

"Come on," he said, taking her hand and leading her to a tall black stone at the mouth of the pass. He eased her pack off her limp shoulders, then dropped it, and his own, on the ground.

Kate sank back against the stone, unable to keep herself standing upright, allowing heels and buttocks, shoulder blades, occiput and the palms of her hands to press into cold, solid granite. Then Alec was beside her. The wind blew strong against her face and she narrowed her eyes in a fruitless effort to bring the mountains into focus. But when his fingertips touched hers, the scene before her grew crystal clear.

She was standing in the kaleyard as the sun came up. She had passed her arisaid between her legs and secured it to hold the hem of her skirt up out of the moist soil. She was wearing a kertch on her head. She was holding a hoe in her hand.

It was static, like a single frame from a movie, or a photograph from a book. Kate jerked her hand off the stone, away from Alec's, abruptly. But he reached out and curled his fingers through hers to keep her from escaping. And suddenly she could feel the emotions behind the image. Suddenly its characters came alive.

The ground was half-frozen, but even so, she was swinging the hoe with more violence than the job required. Then she lifted her eyes to the mountain peaks in the distance, stared at them through the blur of tears. There was nothing she could do to prevent what was bound to happen. Alasdair was here, but soon he would be gone. Forever. And it was all her fault. He would die fighting her battles. She hurled the hoe, with all her strength, like a javelin, watched it sail across the neat brown furrows. And she sank to her knees.

"A Chatriona," Alasdair whispered, drawing her to her feet and against him. "Mo bhean."

"I canna bear it," she sobbed against his sark. "I love ye so much."

"And I love ye."

"Dinna go," she begged. "Ye mustna fight this battle on my account. Ye need prove naught to me."

He held her away from him and watched her in-

quiringly. "What are ye saying, Catriona?"

"Ye joined the Jacobites at my urging. Ye'll die by my hand on Culloden moor as surely as if I was there to plunge my dirk into yer heart."

He grinned slowly, sadly. "Is that what ye think, love?" *He shook his head in disbelief.* "I'm willing to die for ye, Catriona, but I'd no ask my clansmen to do it, and I'll be urging three hundred of them onto that moor just a few days hence. This is nay longer a battle to determine which monarch will sit the throne of England. We're fighting for our way of life, for our land. And for our dignity. We're fighting because we have nay choice. Do ye ken me?"

She nodded, unconvinced. Could it be so? Alasdair had never lied to her.

He touched her face. "I must go. I left written instructions for ye in the strongbox."

A will. "Ye seem certain ye'll nay be back." *As certain as she was.*

He kissed her deeply in answer, holding the length of her body against his; then he pulled away.

"I packed some food in yer sporran," *she said, reminding herself to be brave, brushing tears off her cheeks.*

"No too much, I hope. Ye'll need it."

And I won't. The unspoken codicil to his statement hung in the air between them and brought a fresh flood of tears to her eyes.

"Yer father will be leading his men into the fray. Any word for him?"

"Tell him I love him. Tell him good-bye . . ."

Alasdair nodded and drew her tight against him again, kissed her lips one last time. "Tell my lads *how much they meant to me. Tell them why I left them—when they're old enough to ken."*

"Aye," she said, wondering if it was a promise she could keep.

He studied her face for a final moment, then he turned. He started down the path.

She kept herself from screaming his name with an effort. She had to be brave, for the bravest man she had ever known. *"Till we're together again, my love,"* she whispered.

Chapter Fourteen

"Alasdair! Come back!" Kate cried.

She found herself tight in Alec's arms. "I'm here, love," he murmured, rocking her against him. "I'm here, *a* Chatriona. I'll never leave you again."

"It was as if I was at the cottage . . ." she began, realizing, only after she had spoken the words, that she had identified the woman in the scene as herself—Kate, not Catriona. And that Alec had done the same thing.

"I know," he whispered. "I saw it too. You had used your arisaid to bind up your dress and your hair was tucked under a cap."

It was tucked into Alasdair's sporran, Kate guessed, wondering if, in the end, that gesture had given Catriona's husband more pain than comfort. Then she smiled, feeling lighter, somehow, feeling

277

freer. Alasdair had died bravely, in service to an ideal. He had gone of his own will, despite his wife's pleas that he remain at home. Catriona couldn't have stopped him, Kate was sure, whatever she believed before he went, whatever guilt she felt in the years that followed. He was proud and stubborn, like Alec. They weren't perfect men, just perfect for the women who loved them.

And Kate suddenly understood what drew tourists to Culloden moor two hundred fifty years later, what still caused Scottish fathers, and fathers like her own, who were many generations removed from Scotland, to relate the tale of that terrible, pivotal battle to their children. They weren't glorifying warfare or the cause that inspired this tragic bit of history. They were asking their sons and daughters to lay claim to the faith and courage that were their birthright.

"Brave and faithful," Kate said, looking up into Alec's eyes.

"I can't promise I'll always be brave," he said, smiling.

"You know I didn't want you to be my mistress, don't you?" he had asked. She knew it now. There was only one thing she could ever have been to Alec, and they had probably both known what it was, from the moment they met. *Mo bhean.* . . . She met his lips.

George Ross was beside them then and chuckling softly. "I've had people swear they've conversed with the wee folks and William Wallace," he said smugly. "It's the combination of exertion and altitude."

Alec held Kate, and their eyes locked. They

couldn't explain it, but they knew it was no such thing.

They chose one of the many boulders atop the summit plateau and settled there to eat lunch and drink from their water bottles. Kate redonned every layer she had discarded and wished she had more as the chilly wind blew through the pass.

"Is there anything more over there you want me to taste?" she asked suggestively, as she rewrapped her uneaten sandwich and gestured with her chin toward the bag on his lap. She was filled with wonder and giddy happiness and she doubted she would ever require food again.

He laughed. "With your teeth chattering like that? I'd have to have a death wish." He drew her toward him, rubbed his hands briskly up and down her arms to warm her, then hugged her against him.

"For at least the past ten years, people have been telling me how pragmatic, unemotional and down-to-earth I am," she said, against his chest. "And it wasn't usually offered in the tone of a compliment. Evan once said I was incapable of appreciating anything that couldn't be poured into a test tube."

"Evan didn't know a thing about you," he answered.

She bowed her head slightly in agreement. "What does it all mean, Alec?" she whispered urgently. "The portrait and the images that filled our minds a few minutes ago. The way we met on the Culloden moor and the way—"

"The way we recognized each other right off," he finished for her.

He *had* felt it too. "Yes."

He pulled away from her, stared off toward a distant mountain top, as if he thought to find his answer there. The peak was outlined by pale blue sky, shrouded by roiling clouds. A beam of sunlight pierced the clouds, illuminating the peak from behind.

"This scene could have been set by Cecil B. DeMille," she remarked lightly, to hide the awe she was feeling, "though he would have thrown in an angelic chorus right about now."

Alec grinned, "*Bod an Diabhoil*," he said, pointing to the peak.

"Diablo . . ." She heard her voice falter, felt her stomach lurch.

"Devil's Point."

A shiver coursed through her and she could almost hear the chorus swell.

"There's magic everywhere," he began.

She stared at him, unable to look away.

"It's magic that we're alive, that we're in a place as beautiful as this, together. It's magic that we . . . feel for each other what we do. . . ."

"Yes." He didn't have to say it, not until he was ready.

"We, each of us, has a history stretching back through thousands and thousands of years, back to the days when these mountains were closer to the volcanic eruptions that created them. We, each of us, holds a piece, maybe just a cell, of the people who made us, who made them, back to the beginning. . . ."

She had come here to learn this, she guessed, here

to Devil's Point where she was filled with a sense of being part of everything around her, where she felt as ancient as the mountains and as young as the fragile sprigs of grass that were breaking through the snow.

"Perhaps there's a gene in each of those cells that contains a trace of memory, an image, an emotion. Perhaps the emotions people experience in a place continue to resonate there after they've gone, leave an imprint there."

His voice was growing softer and more hesitant and she struggled to hear every word he was speaking.

"Or perhaps our souls *are* immortal and simply keep seeking new, and more evolutionary appropriate, vessels through the years."

He looked into her eyes and his voice came strong again. "But none of that changes that fact that we're here, now, on the brink of the twenty-first century, and that we have a whole new set of emotions to experience, experiences to live through. You can study the past, but you can't live in it without wasting the present. And you can't build a modern relationship on intangibles from the past. Our age has so much to offer—technology and space travel, art, literature, music. Medical advances—transplants, neurosurgery, the total eradication of infectious diseases that have plagued mankind throughout time. We will marvel at these things together . . ." He touched her face in a promise. "You know, MacGillvray, there's a dark side to every gift and I see the dark side to these—pollution, overpopulation, dwindling ties with the earth and the Power that made it. But I never doubt they're gifts.''

'' 'Sometimes you just have to accept the gifts of God without asking questions,' '' she murmured, quoting James Lachlan's words. It wasn't advice she could swallow without a struggle, even now.

"Aye," Alec said.

"But doesn't it seem likely that I . . . that you . . ."

"I don't know."

"Don't you believe that Catriona and Alasdair's love was strong enough to . . ."

He raised his shoulders.

"If you love someone enough, *anything*, even miracles, are possible!" she finished helplessly.

He smiled and drew her back into his arms. "Och, I do believe in miracles, MacGillvray," he said.

Several minutes later, they started downhill. In many ways, the hike down the rocky trail was more difficult than the hike up, but Kate felt energetic and peaceful, content with her hand in Alec's. She was filled with the sensation of having arrived at the destination to which she had been heading all her life, and her need for explanations seemed to melt away, like the snow on the ground as they descended past the arctic line.

He paused, several hours later, and drew her against him. "There's something I've been trying to say to you since that first night, Kate," he whispered. "I love you. I never thought I'd be able to say those words again, and I never thought I'd mean them the way I mean them now."

"Alec," she answered, clutching his sinewy arms

through his windbreaker. "I love you. Forever."

He kissed her passionately, his hands roving up under her backpack, and he pulled her closer. He groaned with pleasure when she slipped her tongue into his mouth, thrust her hips forward to meet his. "You would have made one hell of a mistress, MacGillvray," he gasped.

She smiled happily. She would make a much better wife.

The sun was low in the sky and they were finally nearing the bottom of the trail.

"What happened after Harry Beaton died?" Alec asked suddenly.

Kate glanced at him and laughed. "Your memory is amazing."

He snorted. "It's *Brigadoon*, not brain surgery."

"Well, while Harry is on the loose, running for the border, and Brigadoon is in danger of disappearing forever, Gene Kelly realizes he's in love with Fiona."

"Ah. Some laddies make their best realizations at the edge of a claymore."

"Anyway, when the alarm is over, he goes running to find her. Meanwhile, she's afraid he has already left, and she's running around trying to find him. They enter the ruins of an old church from opposite sides. They freeze, stare at each other in the moonlight, each reading the truth about the other's feelings in his/her eyes—"

"His/her eyes? Ah, well, it is nearly the twenty-first century, I suppose. Sexist speech is passé."

"Then they run toward each other, embrace, kiss.

And then they do what their bodies have been urging them to do all day—"

"You mean they—"

"Yes! They dance!"

"Ah," Alec said.

"But the question still remains: Does he love her enough to give up everything for her? And it's getting pretty late—"

Ilsa's scream interrupted the telling of the rest.

Kate had been absently watching the woman's son, Gregor, settle down on a ledge, pointing his camera up to get photos of the peak from which they had come. She saw him go over the edge in the same instant his mother did, his hands grasping for a purchase as his feet kicked out helplessly at the empty space beneath them.

Alec saw it too. He didn't hesitate.

"There's method to their madness," Dunc Knox had said.

Kate knew this was true as she watched Alec hurl himself, belly-down, onto the ledge, reach down to grasp the teenager's elbows. She watched Alec's muscles swell, his face contort, as the boy's tenuous grip on the rock faltered and his entire body weight was borne by his rescuer. Then, in the next moment, the boy was lying prone on the rock, his mother was running forward to hold him, and Alec was gone.

Kate screamed, all the horror she had experienced during the brief moments of this interlude flowing out at its unexpected conclusion, but her own instincts took over, and she sprinted to the rock's edge. She peered into the ravine, squinted at its bottom at least a hundred feet below. Then she saw Alec lying crumpled and still on a narrow outcropping about ten feet down. "Alec!" she begged.

He didn't respond. She didn't hesitate.

She stumbled down a more gradual slope some feet distant. She negotiated a slender ledge that led to the plateau on which Alec was lying, gripping the cold gray rocks with her fingertips, pressing her body weight forward against them to keep from pitching backwards into the ravine. Finally, she kneeled at his side, examined him quickly, not doubting her ability to help him, but her ability ever to leave this mountain if he was beyond help. *Pulse strong and regular,* she told herself. *Respiration shallow. A closed fracture of the right tibia and fibula*, she noted, running her hands over his lower arm. *A closed occipital swelling, rapidly taking on the dimensions of a ping-pong ball.* She touched this gingerly. *Contusion on the right cheek and a deep bloody laceration above the right eye.* Spilled blood. But her movements were quick and confident. The only thing she was afraid of now was losing Alec. She forced his uncooperative eyelids open. *Pupils equal, round and reactive.* He would live. He was going to be all right. She squeezed her eyes shut for a second, saying her first prayer in many years, then she set to work.

"I need two long flat pieces of wood," she called up to George Ross, who saluted and disappeared.

She slipped Alec's windbreaker off his right arm, slipped his pack off his back and surveyed its contents. He had brought bandages, a suture kit, antiseptic, acetaminophen. She pressed a gauze pad over the oozing gash in his forehead, dampened another

285

with his water bottle and sponged the blood off his face. If she was lucky, she could set his arm before he regained consciousness, she decided. She lifted his limp hand, noted the unnatural angle at which it was hanging. She grasped his elbow firmly in one hand, grasped his wrist with the other, then pulled and twisted with one movement. The separated bone ends snapped together, rendering the line of his arm smooth again. George handed the requested slats down to her. She laid one against the front of Alec's arm, one against the back, and twined bandages tightly around the pair, immobilizing the joints above and below the break.

His eyelids were beginning to flicker.

She lifted the gauze pad off his forehead and examined the wound again. She shielded his eyes with additional pads, irrigated it with the water bottle, floating out bits of soil. Then she cleaned it with antiseptic. She opened the suture kit, threaded a needle, laid scissors and forceps on her lap.

"What in hell are you doing, MacGillvray?" Alec asked.

His eyes were open and he was struggling to sit up.

"Don't move!" she commanded. "Those aren't the best splints I've ever seen."

He looked down at his right arm, then up at her questioningly.

"You have a broken arm. I set and splinted it. Don't lean on that hand!" He laid back.

"You'll need to have it X-rayed and properly casted as soon as possible."

His gaze was relentless. She took a deep breath

and continued. "You have multiple contusions and probably a mild concussion—you've got quite a bump on the back of your head." He laid his left palm against this and winced.

"It seems pretty unlikely, but you'll need a skull X-ray to completely rule out the possibility of a fracture or subdural bleed, though a CAT scan would be better." His arched eyebrow informed her that they did, indeed, have CAT scans in Inverness.

"There's a deep laceration above your right eye that will require three or four stitches. I've irrigated it and I'm ready to suture it. It looks clean, but you'll need to get a tetanus booster, just in case."

"Kate?" he whispered.

"I'm a physician, Alec. Now let me do what I have to do so that we can get off this mountain before it gets dark, or I'll have to add frostbite and hypothermia to your list of maladies."

He watched her for a long, silent moment, then nodded. "Gregor?" he asked.

"He's fine," she said. "You saved his life."

Alec nodded again and squeezed his eyes shut. He didn't flinch as she stitched his forehead. He didn't open his eyes until she was finished. She shook three Tylenol out of the vial and extended them to him. "You'll need these," she said. He nodded, swallowed them, washed them down with water from the canteen she offered. Then he allowed her to help him stand, to tuck his windbreaker around him. She slung his pack over her own shoulder. He had difficulty navigating the narrow ledge with only one hand to use for gripping and balance, but she pressed her hand against his back, moved crab-style beside him until he reached the slope. George and a large German came down the hill to help him ascend it, slipping strong arms under each of his.

When Kate finally reached the trail, she was greeted with sincere accolades, but Alec was the real hero and Ilsa was hugging him, Gregor was shaking his good hand, and a group of appreciative hikers were gathered around him, urging him to sit and rest and drink from their canteens. Even George Ross fled to Alec's side after offering Kate a quick, "Good job." Alec seemed oblivious to all of this. He was looking past the hikers to her, his expression anything but grateful. She stepped toward him to re-settle the loose sleeve of his windbreaker around his shoulders, but he jerked away and dropped his gaze.

He set off down the trail, disregarding everyone's protests, not waiting for Kate to join him. She hur-ried to catch up, fell in step beside him, despite the fact that he didn't speak or acknowledge her pres-ence when she did so. She walked silently at his side for several minutes, feeling awkward and insecure, unsure what to do.

"The Life and Times of Katherine MacGillvray," she said finally, glancing up at his profile. She saw a muscle at the angle of his jaw jump in response. "Where should I begin?" When it became clear that he had no intention of offering an opinion, she opted to begin at the beginning, in a modestly gracious house in suburban Philadelphia, in the year 1966. The words came tumbling out, flowing out, and she was barely conscious of speaking them. She talked about her parents, her brothers, her teachers; she talked about her dreams, the books and movies she had loved. She described her college in detail. She talked about medical school, the long years of her residency, and the friends she had made during the two stints, people, she had avoided telling him about before lest she slip and mention where she'd met them. She talked about Evan. She talked about the day the Diablos fought the Huns and she realized the foe she was battling was more savage, more frightening, than death.

"I had seen so many horrible things before: battered and abused children, women raped and left for dead, painful, lingering illnesses that made me wish I could hurry death along. I had learned the importance of maintaining distance, of detaching myself from a situation emotionally so that I could deal with it professionally—God, did I learn how to do that!" She considered this silently for a few minutes as she walked. "Maybe I was shaken by the sheer number of casualties that were suddenly piling up around me, or their youth, or the senselessness of what had brought them there. . . . No. I was more shaken by hearing the survivors talk. They had no remorse about it, no regrets, and absolutely no reason. I realized that the boys in either gang would just as soon have killed their own as the *enemy*, that the only thing marking one boy as another's enemy was the name on his jacket. They had no respect for life, or beauty, or authority, or even themselves. I found myself wondering if this was a generation of children born without souls, and I was suddenly scared as hell of losing mine. I tried to save one boy who I sensed was different—an artist who had painted the most incredible landscape on the back of his gang jacket.

But he was lost before I ever laid my eyes on him . . .''

"No one is born without a soul," Alec said.

She glanced over at him, but his gaze was directed straight ahead. She waited, but his comment obviously hadn't been the opening line in a conversation, so she continued. "I had to get away from there. I'm still not sure why I felt compelled to come here. . . .''

He stepped aside to allow her to mount the step to the minibus.

"You should have told me," he said, behind her.

She froze, but she didn't turn to look at him. And she didn't need to ask him what omission he meant. "I intended to."

"When?"

She raised her shoulders. "I started to tell you last night. You convinced me to hold my confession for tonight, but it couldn't wait that long, under the circumstances."

"You should have told me," he repeated.

She spun to him then. "It doesn't change anything, Alec," she said.

"Doesn't it?" he asked, his lips curling mirthlessly. "I can accept your being a physician. I can't accept your being a fraud and a liar. How do I know that anything you told me is true? How can I trust that what happened between us is real?"

She considered this as she climbed into the van, slid onto a bench, watched Alec negotiate his entry with a helpful hand from George. He met her eyes, hesitated for a moment, then seated himself beside Ilsa. Kate stared out the window into the darkness, fighting back tears. She didn't move a muscle until the van pulled up in front of the inn. She stood up as George obligingly slid the door open and jumped to the ground. She looked back at Alec before she took George's hand. "Aren't you coming?" she asked.

Alec shook his head. "There's the little matter of a tetanus injection and a few radiograms," he offered. "Or a CAT scan, if they can figure out how to work all those wee dials and knobs. Doctor's orders."

"I'll drive you to the hospital."

"I'll have the van driver drop me there."

"I'll come with you."

"No," he said. "I can manage without you."

The uncertainty she heard in his last statement wrenched her heart. She allowed George to help her down, and he walked silently beside her to the door of the Munro House.

"It will be all right," he offered.

She looked at him. "Will it?"

He raised his shoulders vaguely. "If you need to talk to me, you can reach me at the tour company."

She nodded, watched him start away. "George," she called.

He turned back to her.

"*Bhean,*" she said, recalling the word Alec had said to her the night before, that Alasdair had said to Catriona as he held her in his arms for the last time. "*Mo bhean.* What does it mean?" she asked, guessing she already knew, needing to hear it spoken aloud, in *English*, so that she could be sure she hadn't imagined it, that Alec had really addressed her as such. Once.

He watched her quizzically. "It means *my wife*."

He hurried toward the minibus and climbed in. Its door slid shut with a responding metallic bang. She watched its headlights disappear around the curve in the road. She stared into the night for a long time, shivering in the chilly air. My wife. Everything made sense now, perfect sense, in twenty-twenty hindsight. Alec Lachlan wasn't the kind of man who would live with a woman without benefit of marriage. The lease on the flat in Inverness had been short-term because he was planning to have her move into his cottage, as his wife, at the end of the summer. "*I give it two or three months, if we can stick it out that long*," he had said. That was long enough to plan a wedding and invite her family and friends from the States to attend it. "*I'll remind myself how much I'm saving by not having to buy you a wedding ring*." He was planning to give her his mother's, she knew, recalling the heavy gold band she had worn on her left hand for just a heartbeat, the poignant conversation she had had with the woman who was so eager to forfeit it to Alec's wife. "*Our hormones are calling the tune*," he had said. He wasn't the kind of man who could make love to his fiancée under his mother's roof, nor embrace celibacy easily, or he would have invited her to become his family's house guest until the nuptials could be performed.

She reached toward the inn's door, but drew her hand back before she opened it. She couldn't go in there yet, into the place where she and Alec had danced so joyously to the tune of their hormones, just the night before. Despite the fact that she had just returned from a hike to Lairig Ghru, she decided she needed a long walk. "You win some, you lose some, and some get rained out," she murmured, as a cold rain began to fall.

Chapter Fifteen

Kate returned to the inn finally, dripping wet, physically and emotionally exhausted, her feet and fingertips frozen. Could she make Alec understand why she hadn't told him the truth? Was he ever going to give her the chance to try?

"Miss MacGillvray," Mrs. Munro said in a low hiss, glancing around surreptitiously as she approached, glancing past Kate pointedly before she spoke. "Dr. Lachlan isn't with you, then?"

"No," Kate answered. Mrs. Munro had been as eager as the Lachlan family to see Alec married off, counted herself responsible, in some way, for his romance with her American guest. She was going to be disappointed.

The landlady seemed to draw in a sigh of relief, however. "Your fiancé arrived this morning."

Fiancé!

"Katie! Where in the world have you been all day?"

She heard Evan's voice, spun toward it. She stared at him in disbelief, watched him stride across the distance between them. He was wearing jeans and a heavy sweater. He tossed a strand of glossy dark hair back from his forehead. There was irritation in his milk-chocolate eyes.

"What are you doing here? And by what right do you question my comings and goings? Shouldn't you be back in Philadelphia checking up on your little friend, Jenna? And how did you find me, anyway?"

"Keep your voice down," he urged, looking over his shoulder to meet Mrs. Munro's interested, and not altogether friendly, gaze. "Our travel agent gave me your itinerary. Come on. Let's sit in the parlor."

She reluctantly allowed herself to be led into the adjoining room. She sank down into a comfortable chair across from the one Evan chose for himself. They watched each other warily, silently, taking each other's measure, as if from the plate and mound before the first pitch.

"I've already cleared the tea away," Mrs. Munro said, coming forward. "But I'll brew up a fresh pot, if you'd like. Or a sherry, perhaps—"

"Whisky, please," Kate said.

"Katie!" Evan said.

Mrs. Munro smiled knowingly, and went to fetch the requested libation.

"I don't remember ever seeing you look this angry, Kate," he said.

"I've never been quite this angry," she assured him.

"You weren't happy when I called off our engagement."

"I wasn't happy when you called it off. I'm very happy about it now. But I'm not happy to see you here."

He shook his head in resignation. "I'm sorry. I love you, not her. It was just a case of nerves, of pre-wedding jitters. Everyone gets them, I'm told."

"And the treatment of choice is to find yourself an obliging little medical student and screw her until it passes?"

"Katie!"

Mrs. Munro was standing behind him with a towel in one hand and a generously filled glass in the other, absorbing every word, nodding in concurrence. Kate extended her hand toward the towel, mopped her face and head with it, then accepted the glass. She took a long swallow of whisky before she thanked her hostess in as dismissive a tone as she could muster. The landlady didn't budge.

"She didn't mean anything to me, Katie," Evan said, giving it another try.

"You told me you loved her! As I recall, you praised her skill in bed and graciously hoped I might one day find passion to match hers!"

They both turned to the low clucking noise behind Evan's chair to find Mrs. Munro still holding her ground. "Another dram, Miss MacGillvray?" the woman asked sympathetically.

Kate drained her glass and thrust it at her. "Yes, please."

"I should never have said those things, Kate. I didn't mean them." He leaned toward her. "We're still expected at the church on the last Saturday in June. We still have the fairway ballroom at the country club reserved for our reception. The invitations are ready to go out. . . ."

Kate took her refilled glass and sipped from it.

"Mother is planning a big party in New York the weekend before," Evan continued, glancing back at Mrs. Munro. "We'll check into the Plaza Hotel on Saturday morning, then you'll go for the final fitting of your gown with Mother. She's planning on spending the rest of the afternoon with you, at her salon—"

"What?" Kate demanded.

"You know, they'll give you a head-to-toe make-over, skin, hair, nails—"

She snorted. This man had dumped her unceremoniously for another woman ten days ago, and now, without prelude or anything close to a reasonable explanation for his behavior, he was discussing her prenuptial grooming! "I won't be going to your mother's salon. I won't be marrying you, Evan. In fact, I find I'm in love with another man."

Mrs. Munro gave a supportive cluck.

"You've got to be kidding, Kate," he laughed. "I know for a fact that you've never looked at another man. Your constancy, your purity, are among the things that make me love you!"

Kate was truly angry now, could feeling it bubbling up inside her and threatening to explode. "You listen to me, you pompous ass," she said, leaning toward him, wishing she had a dirk in her boot so she could unsheathe it now, "I'm in love with another man. I slept with him the day I met him." Her voice was getting louder, but Mrs. Munro was the only other person in the room, and she was bound not to miss a word, no matter what the tone in which it was delivered. "I clawed his back as I screamed his name!"

Mrs. Munro made a noise that sounded like the rapid expulsion of a long-held breath.

Evan shook his head. "God, Katie. Don't humiliate yourself like this. Don't fabricate fantasies for my benefit. I never should have said those things to you. I didn't mean them. I've never expected you to behave like a bitch in heat. I never will."

Kate finished her whisky wordlessly. This was futile. Evan was never going to believe her. Perhaps later, after she had spoken to Alec and begged his forgiveness, after they descended to the parlor, arm-in-arm, to sit in front of the fireplace and plan their future together, Evan would. But she guessed *that* scenario might be quite some time in coming. *Maybe in my next life*, she thought, frowning down into her empty glass.

"You're not the kind of woman who can jump into bed with any stranger who asks."

Kate heard the bitterness in this statement and understood. "Ah," she said, grinning, handing her glass to Mrs. Munro. "The truth comes out. Your passionate little medical student cheated on you!"

"She was a slut!"

"And I?"

"You're a lady, Katie."

"And never the twain shall meet." Kate took a

deep breath, searched herself for the words to make Evan understand that his brand of subtle misogyny had always made her feel asexual, inadequate and ashamed. Perhaps she would simply try again to tell him about the stranger's bed into which she had so gratefully jumped just the night before.

"Why do you think I want to marry you? Why do you think I want you to be the mother of my children? You're not the kind of woman who could run off with another man and leave her small son despondent and confused. . . ."

Kate felt sorry for Evan in that moment. Hadn't he once told her that his mother, Madeline, had divorced his father when he was only five? So Evan had chosen Kate MacGillvray because he saw her as a paragon of virtue and fidelity, rather than a passionate and three-dimensional woman. And she had become what he wanted her to be. She shrugged. He hadn't done it willfully, she realized; it was merely the reflection of a hurt so deeply buried that he could never see it for what it was. And had her reasons for choosing Evan been any more noble or psychologically mature? She had cast him in the role of neuter companion and housemate. She had agreed to marry him so that she wouldn't have to go home to an empty house. It would have been healthier, and more honest, to go out and buy herself a dog! The dynamics between her and Alec, on the other hand, were adult, three-dimensional and very passionate. . . . She saw the flash of a red windbreaker at the parlor door.

Alec.

His right arm was in a cast and sling, his right jacket sleeve was hanging empty at his side. His left arm was being clutched possessively by a beautiful blonde. Tess.

Mrs. Munro followed her gaze and emitted the gasp that Kate couldn't bring herself to voice.

Tess was wearing a simple plaid jumper, black turtleneck, black tights and shoes—another schoolgirl outfit that made her look like anything but. She appeared to be listening to every word Alec was pronouncing with unflagging interest. Her tinkling laughter floated across the room.

Kate was going to vomit.

She stood up unsteadily. Alec lifted his eyes from his companion's then, met Kate's in surprise. He freed himself from Tess's grip and started across the room.

Kate was dizzy and breathless. Swooning . . .

She sank into the darkness, not fighting it.

She was first aware of the hard surface on which she was lying, then of the bright lights that were shining in her eyes as she forced them open. She attempted to focus on the face hovering over hers. Evan.

"Are you all right, Katie?" he asked.

Kate nodded, struggling into a sitting position. "I don't know what's the matter with me."

"You drank a lot of whisky, very fast," he said. Softly and sympathetically.

"Yes," she agreed.

Mrs. Munro and Tess were standing behind Evan, their expressions concerned. Alec was standing behind them. His face was misshapen; one eye was swollen shut. The red bruise on his right cheekbone would be black and blue by morning, Kate guessed.

His expression was unreadable. She allowed Evan to help her back into her chair.

"Vasovagal syncope. Hypoglycemia. Coupled with a very rapid rise in the blood alcohol level," Evan offered by way of diagnoses. "You'll be fine in a few minutes."

Would she? "Alec," she said.

He stepped forward and inclined his head slightly in answer to her summons. "It's fortunate that your fiancé is a physician too, Dr. MacGillvray, since you're prone to these . . . spells—"

"My fiancé?"

Alec nodded in a collegial manner at Evan. "Dr. Hall was kind enough to introduce himself and explain the nature of your relationship while we were waiting for you to *come to*. Though since he's a surgeon, in Scotland he could more properly be addressed as *Mr*. Hall."

"Evan. Just call me Evan," Dr./Mr. Hall offered magnanimously.

Kate shook her head, feeling like Alice newly emerged through the looking glass. She focused on Alec again. "How's your arm?" she whispered.

He glanced down at his sling. "Expertly set. And I had the opportunity to look in a mirror as I passed through the foyer. Your stitching is commendable too, Dr. MacGillvray," he answered, his voice bitter. "You're a credit to your profession and your sex," he added through clenched teeth.

"Alec—"

He raised his hand to stop her next sentiment.

"Well, you're looking much better, Katie," Evan said. "I say we shouldn't let this coincidence slip away: two bright, young American physicians meeting up with two bright, young Scots physicians. I imagine we have a lot in common. Tess, Alec, will you join us for dinner in about an hour?''

Kate felt as if she were going to pass out again. Evan's proposed dinner companions had more in common than he could begin to imagine.

"We'd love to," Tess answered, before Alec could respond.

Kate entered her room and looked around it in dismay, seeing evidence of Evan's unpacking everywhere. He sat down on the bed, the bed in which she and Alec had made love throughout the preceding night. It seemed like sacrilege of some sort.

"You look different, Kate," he offered, watching her.

"Do I?"

He nodded. "Sexier, somehow. More . . . knowing." He patted the bed beside him in invitation. "Come sit with me, Katie."

The invitation was in his eyes as well.

"I've been hiking all day, Evan. I'm soaked to the bone. And I just fainted. I need a hot bath."

"Just a kiss, then," he said, coming to her, taking her shoulders in his hands, lowering his mouth to hers.

Nothing. She felt absolutely nothing.

"Let's get the first plane out of this godforsaken place in the morning," he said. "There's an early flight out of Inverness that will get us into Glasgow in time for the nonstop to New York."

She pulled away. She couldn't leave before she

attempted to make things right with Alec. At that moment, the Munro House sunset piper, probably tired of waiting for the rain to stop, decided to hold forth in the Munro House lobby.

"Good God!" Evan said, clamping his hands over his ears. "It sounds like he's killing something down there, beating it to death with a big plaid bag."

If a big plaid bag had been close at hand, Kate would have beaten him with it.

Kate had applied her makeup with a heavy hand. Her foundation and powder were just this side of Kabuki, her mascara just *that* of Tammy Fay. Her lips were outlined in brick and glossed in rose. She brushed her hair furiously now, more to relieve her frustration than to relieve it of tangles. She piled it on her head, leaving a few curls loose in the back. She pulled the rose-colored sweater on over her new Wonderbra. She squeezed into the short black suede skirt. She pulled on black stockings, slipped on black heels. She surveyed her reflection appraisingly. Cheap? Sexy? Competition for the incomparable Tess? None of the above? If she wanted to compete with Tess tonight, she would probably be better advised to put knee socks on her feet and pigtails in her hair, she decided.

"Kate." Evan whistled as she stepped out of the bathroom. The expression in his eyes was easy to read; she didn't need to wonder whether he was plugging her into the lady or the slut pigeonhole at the moment. He stood up, dropping the book that had been perched on his lap.

"Let's go," she said. She didn't need compliments or comments from Evan. "I'm starving."

Their dinner companions had already claimed a table near a window by the time Evan and Kate arrived in the dining room. Kate stared across the room for a long moment before she worked up the courage to walk toward them. Alec stood up when she arrived. What did she see in his green eyes? Sadness? Anger? Memories of the intimacy they had shared such a short time ago? She shivered as his disapproving gaze swept down over her outfit. She could practically hear the words he had spoken on the mountain this afternoon: *I love you, Kate.*

"Dr. MacGillvray," he said now, bowing his head politely.

"Dr. Lachlan," she answered.

Tess laughed. "Why so formal? We've too many doctors at this table to stand on ceremony. Besides, Kate, Alec told me what you did this afternoon. He had me floor my petrol pedal all the way from Inverness so that he could get back here to properly thank you for it. In some cultures, saving a man's life binds him to you for eternity."

And in others, it doesn't. But how could he properly thank her for lying to him and breaking his heart? Kate wondered. She forced herself to smile as Evan pushed her chair in toward the table. "So what do bright, young physicians talk about when they find themselves coincidentally thrown together?" she asked, her voice brittle, her gaze moving from face to face. "Why did we all go into medicine?"

"To save lives," Evan said, watching her questioningly.

"To save lives," Tess agreed, her expression confused.

"To cheat death," Alec said. "Wine?"

"Please," Kate whispered, considering Alec's answer. Perhaps the lesson they had learned was that death could never really be cheated.

"Kate," Evan warned as she gulped the wine; then he raised her hand to his lips and kissed it. "Where's your ring, darling?" he asked.

"I didn't bring it with me," she answered.

He laughed. "Afraid the airline was going to charge excess baggage for it? It's quite a chunk of glass!"

Alec's grin was unpleasant. "When's the wedding, Evan?"

"June 29th," Evan said, draping his arm across the back of Kate's chair. "The day after Katie finishes her residency. I can't wait. I've wanted to make this lady my wife since the day I met her. Soon she'll belong to me."

I'll always belong to you, Kate thought, meeting Alec's eyes.

"Well, let's drink a toast to the happy couple," Alec suggested, his gaze not leaving hers. He raised his glass.

Kate finished her wine before Alec could speak the toast.

Tess glanced at the empty glass, then at the woman who was holding it, in surprise. "It's so refreshing to meet a man who's ready to embrace marriage with both arms," she said finally, with a husky laugh. "Perhaps, Evan, you can convince Alec to give it a try."

"Not bloody likely," Alec said, draining his own glass. "Besides, I've only got one arm capable of embracing anything at the moment."

"I've never gotten over you. I'd take you with all five limbs in plaster, dearie," Tess said, laying her hand against the angle of Alec's jaw.

Kate reined in the desire to slap Tess's face. "So you decided to stay on in Inverness to reunite with your old flame?" she asked, unable to keep the nasty edge out of her voice.

Tess laughed again. "Actually, I stayed on for a medical conference. A colleague asked me to stop by the hospital with him this evening to review some unusual Roentgenograms. Imagine my surprise when Alec walked into the Radiology suite with his arm in splints."

"Imagine it!" Kate said.

"I had been scheduled to stay the night in medical staff lodging, but Alec's offer sounded so much more . . . comfortable . . ."

"I can believe it did," Kate said, extending her glass to Alec for a refill.

"Kate," Evan admonished.

The room was spinning again. But it didn't matter. She didn't care if she passed out. She didn't care if she died. Anything was better than sitting here and watching Tess rub the smooth, soft skin under Alec's ear.

"I heartily approve of the Scots fondness for dinner dancing," Evan said, glancing from one woman to the other, obviously unsure what to make of the tone of this conversation. "The last time I was here, every hotel dining room and nearly every restaurant had made some kind of provision for it. We don't have that in the States. I love to shake a leg."

"You're a regular Gene Kelly, I imagine," Alec said.

Kate winced.

Evan shrugged modestly. "Tess, would you care to dance? I don't think my fiancée is up to it."

Tess looked at Kate and then, apparently agreeing with the assessment, stood up and offered Evan her hand. They disappeared into the adjoining music room.

"More wine, MacGillvray?" Alec asked.

Kate nodded, pushed her empty glass toward him yet again, flinched in embarrassment when it teetered and fell over.

"On second thought, let's dance."

She looked up in surprise. "You don't dance."

"It's the only way I'm going to get to hold you again." He pushed his chair away from the table, held his hand out to her. She rose, like someone in a trance, and glided into the next room beside him.

He stood awkwardly in the midst of about a half-dozen dancing couples. There was no welcome in his expression. "I only have the one arm, MacGillvray. Loop yours around my neck and I'll hold onto you at the waist."

She did as he suggested and they began to move.

He was so tall and he felt so right in her arms. She allowed her fingers to touch the short hair at the back of his neck, but she felt him stiffen. The place on her hip where his hand was resting, lightly, impersonally, was tingling, and she thought, with an aching loss, of the hungers he had stirred, and satisfied, during their brief time together.

"Have you always been a liar, MacGillvray, or did you take it up recently?" he asked after a few minutes.

"I'm not a liar," she protested, with little conviction. She had always prided herself on her honesty. But she hadn't been forthright with Alec, or Evan, and now she was going to pay for it.

He sighed. "Why didn't you tell me you were a physician?"

"You made your opinions about female doctors well known before I got a chance to tell you."

"Do I strike you as the kind of man who would be threatened by having an intelligent, accomplished lover? And you don't strike me as the kind of woman who's incapable of telling me to take my sexist and misbegotten pronouncements and shove them up the back side of my kilt."

She laughed, despite herself. "I thought you wanted a woman from another time. Female doctors are rather a recent phenomenon . . ."

"I wanted you, a modern woman with some old-fashioned values . . . Or rather, I wanted what I thought you were," he amended. "Why did you tell me you and Evan had broken up, when he was actually due to join you here?"

"I wasn't expecting him! We did break up!"

"Evan doesn't believe that's the case."

"Evan believes what he wants to believe."

"There's a lot of that going around," Alec said, dropping his gaze. "Did you give Evan back his ring, or are you still in possession of the Hope Diamond?''

"I've still got it, but . . ." She had been too upset, too confused to give it back. There hadn't been time to give it back.

"Did you cancel *the church* and *the country club*?'' Alec asked. His excellent imitation of Evan's Main Line Philadelphia accent would have made her giggle under other circumstances.

"No, but . . ."

He laughed unpleasantly. ''You know, MacGillvray, when I first laid my eyes on you, I felt like I was going to faint. I felt weak-kneed and dizzy. I was afraid I was losing my faculties . . .''

Misperceptions. Confusion.

"And when I touched you . . . it was as if I suddenly understood why I had been born, what my own personal reason for populating this planet was—to love you. I understood why I had always held something of myself back from other women—I was saving it for you. I understood why I felt such a compulsion to make that cottage perfect—so that it would be a fit threshold over which to carry my perfect bride. I was ready to put my mother's ring on your finger. . . .''

His bride. She realized again, with blistering clarity, how close she had come to getting everything she had ever wanted. "Alec . . ." she whispered.

"I had almost been ready to accept the fact that fate, or destiny, or God himself had brought you here, now, for me. I had even entertained the ridiculous possibility that we were being given another chance to enjoy a love that Bonnie Prince Charlie had interrupted rather abruptly two and a half centuries ago. . . .''

"You've got to—"

He shook his head. "I doubt that Catriona MacGillvray MacLachlan ever lied to Alasdair. I doubt she ever failed to tell him the truth. That first afternoon, in Walker's pub, why didn't you simply tell me everything?"

She wanted to tell him the truth now. It was essential that she tell him the truth now. "I was afraid you wouldn't make love to me if I did . . ." she started.

"Ah," he answered quickly. "So despite your pretty protestations to the contrary, it was all sex from the beginning, the all-powerful urge to merge." He snorted and then was silent for a long time. When he finally spoke again his voice was barely a whisper. "And you couldn't be content to just have me give you a good *mowe*. You had to make me believe in Brigadoon."

"Alec. . . ."

He stopped dancing, lifted his hand off her hip, held it up. "Don't say another word about it, Doctor," he warned. "I don't want to embarrass you, but if you so much as open your mouth to speak, I'll leave you standing here in the middle of this room, alone, and I'll go to your fiancé and describe to him in detail how you spent the last six days."

Kate felt the tears begin to trickle down her face, and she made no attempt to stop them. Pride alone kept her from falling to her knees now and begging him to listen to her.

She allowed Alec to lead her back to the dining

room, to which Evan and Tess had already returned, but she didn't sit down in the chair he held out for her. "If I'm going to make that early flight, I'd better get to bed now," she said to the table-at-large, not lifting her eyes. She turned and walked away.

She could feel Alec's gaze following her across the room. Like a touch.

"MacGillvray," he called.

She froze when she heard his voice, stood motionless on the step she had just mounted, but she didn't turn.

"Oh, Dr. Lachlan," Mrs. Munro said, coming after him and laying a restraining hand on his sleeve. "I have a few important things to tell you."

He shook off the landlady's hand rudely. "MacGillvray," he said again.

Kate turned then, clutching the banister to keep herself from pitching forward, and she gazed down at him. He was so tall and handsome. He was the man she had been walking toward since she was a little girl, every time she donned the kitchen curtains and promenaded across the porch, every time she turned down a date with a boy who couldn't come close to matching her fantasy, even when she finally stopped looking for Brigadoon and agreed to marry Evan. Alec Lachlan was the love of her life, she had no doubt about that, and she had lost him. "Yes?" she croaked, feeling the tears constricting her throat, taking away her ability to speak.

"What did he finally decide?" he asked.

She stared at him without comprehension. "Who?"

"Gene Kelly," he said. "At the end of the day,

311

when he had to decide whether to stay in Brigadoon forever or go back to America, what did he do?''

The tears were flowing freely now, blazing black mascara trails down her face. "He went back to America."

He appeared to consider this, and then he nodded his head. "Good-bye, MacGillvray," he said, turning away.

Mrs. Munro's hand was on his sleeve again. "Dr. Lachlan! I must speak to you," she said urgently.

"Maybe tomorrow. Right now I have some serious drinking to do," he said.

"Strike three," Kate whispered, watching him disappear into the dining room. And she hadn't even gone down swinging.

Despite her exhaustion and overindulgence in spirits, Kate had been unable to sleep, and by the time Evan awoke, she was packed, dressed and sitting at the window, watching the sun come up.

"Eager to get going, Katie?"

She turned to look at him. He was incredibly handsome. But she wasn't in love with him. She had never been in love with him. And he had never really been in love with her. "Yes," she said. "I need to stop somewhere before we go to the airport."

He sat up. "Where?"

"Culloden moor," she said.

Mrs. Munro never seemed to sleep and she was busy fluffing pillows in the front parlor when Kate and Evan descended to the foyer with their bags a half-hour later.

"We're going, Mrs. Munro," Kate said.

The landlady made sad clucking noises as she hugged her departing guest.

"Mr. Hall, perhaps you'll come with me to settle your account. Miss MacGillvray, why don't you have a peek through the far parlor window at the wild orchids? They're already beginning to bloom, I think, despite the ghastly winter we had this year."

Kate nodded halfheartedly. She had no interest in Mrs. Munro's flowers. She wanted to be far away from this place, as soon as possible.

She glanced out the window, not seeing anything that faintly resembled an orchid. Then she heard a low groan behind her and she spun toward it.

Alec.

He was sprawled out on the couch, dressed in the clothes he had worn to dinner the night before. His rich auburn hair was tousled and standing out in spikes. His mouth was partially open. He was snoring loudly. Fumes of Scotch whisky seemed to hang around him like a cloud. He hadn't slept with Tess, she remarked to herself with some satisfaction. But there was always tonight.

She kneeled beside him and studied his bruised face for a long moment, memorizing it. When she put her lips on the stitched gash in his forehead, his nose twitched and he drew in a deep sigh, but he didn't awaken. "I'll never forget you, my love," she whispered.

Evan climbed out of the car. He raised the collar of his shearling coat and glanced up at the gray sky before he scanned the deserted field with distaste.

"What's today's date?" Kate asked, following his gaze.

He lifted his wrist to examine the Breitling chronograph there. "It's April 19th," he said.

Two hundred fifty years and three days since the battle that claimed Alasdair's life, she remarked silently, laying her fingertip against her lips. Yet it seemed like only minutes since she'd kissed him good-bye. . . .

"Mind if I wait here?" Evan asked.

She shook her head. She had been planning to suggest it.

Ignoring Evan's startled shout of protest, she climbed over the fence that was meant to keep people off the moor until the Visitors' Center was open and the price of admission could be collected. Without a wasted movement, she found the boulder where Alec's hand had first touched hers, a week earlier. Without surprise, she regarded one of the names carved there: MacLachlan. It was second from the top, right under the name MacGillvray.

The condensation on the boulder looked like teardrops, she noted. She sank to her knees. She laid her cheek against the cold, gray stone. And her tears trickled down to coalesce with those the morning, or three hundred dead Highlanders, had already shed. Time heals all wounds? *Maybe we'll get it right next time*, she thought. "Till we're together again, Alasdair," she whispered.

Chapter Sixteen

Before Kate had left for Scotland, she had been a contender for the job of Assistant Director of Emergency Services. When she returned, she wiped out the competition. "Dr. MacGillvray's a machine," she heard one of the medical students whisper with awe, when she arrived in the E.R. on her night off, in time to successfully resuscitate the latest cardiac arrest to be wheeled through the door. She had almost wished the student was right. Machines weren't given to internal bleeding.

And no one seemed to notice that she had taken to lingering around after the fireworks stopped, talking to families and the patients themselves, soothing them, searching for their souls and feeding her own.

It was easier when she kept busy, she had discovered. Working her usual 60-hour week left 108 empty hours. It wasn't wise to listen to the bagpipe tapes, or the ones in Gaelic she had purchased in the Glasgow airport. It was difficult to sleep—though she could swear she hadn't dreamed since Scotland—and she had very little interest in eating. The start of the baseball season had come and gone, unnoticed by her. And the wedding had taken on a life of its own, the plans proceeding full-speed ahead without much need for her input.

Her relationship with Evan had become unexpectedly tender, though no more passionate, and was as easily carried on inside the hospital as out. The deficits in it struck her only when she remembered how she had felt with Alec.

Alec. She avoided thinking about him at all costs.

She was flipping through the channels in the middle of the night nearly two months after her return, when a familiar scene flashed on the screen: Gene Kelly and Cyd Charisse, dancing amidst Scottish ruins in the moonlight. She quickly turned off the set. Over Sunday dinner the next day, Gram repeated the question she had asked a hundred times before: "How was Scotland?"

And Kate gave her usual reply: "Chilly."

"If you ask me," Evan offered, "you're all lucky that potato famine or civil war or *whatever* drove your family out of Scotland way back when. I couldn't wait to get out of there."

Gram's expression said: Who asked you? And Mom's: When are you going to get out of here?

They both turned questioning eyes to Kate, who simply raised her shoulders and pretended to eat the lamb stew on her plate.

She discovered the envelope in her mailbox early the next morning as she left for the hospital. How long had it been there? she wondered, turning it over and over in shaking hands, afraid to open it. The stamp and postmark screamed its place of origin: Scotland. She wasn't sure if the handwriting on it identified its sender as clearly.

And the stanched wound in her chest began to bleed.

She became dizzy and breathless, there in the tiny vestibule of her apartment building. She tore it open, though the light in the space wasn't conducive to reading, pulled out the thick sheaf of papers and scanned down to the signature on the first one: James Lachlan. She swallowed heavily as she began to read the terse, impersonal missive. "I finally remembered where I had seen Charles Shelton's name. It was mentioned in the anonymous Highland woman's memoirs which I came upon years ago and have quoted from extensively in my book. Thanks to you, she's anonymous no more." She fanned the papers behind it, seeing that he had enclosed copies from the woman's—from Catriona's!—memoirs. She folded them clumsily and shoved them in her bag, stalked out into the darkness to her car and the long day ahead of her.

There was a forty-year-old man with chest pain awaiting her attention after she pushed her jacket and bag into her locker, took out her white coat and put it on. She examined him, scanned his EKG, sent bloods off to the lab and called Cardiology stat. After that, there was a young asthmatic woman, in moderate distress. Kate listened to her chest, drew blood gases, administered a shot of epinephrine and called Respiratory Therapy. Cookbook. She left the medical students to review the charts and follow up on the blood work.

She wasn't certain if she was grateful for the lull that followed.

She soon found herself back at her locker and, a moment later, en route to a vacant treatment room with the thick envelope in her pocket. She accepted the cup of coffee one of the students offered her, but didn't ask him to join her. He eventually got the hint and disappeared. She settled down on the edge of a stretcher, took a sip of coffee and pulled the papers out. She set Jamie's letter aside, smoothed the other pages absently before she started reading.

"I often thank God Alasdair is in heaven, unable to bear witness to the hell he left behind . . ."

Kate caught her breath. She wasn't up to this now. But she couldn't bring herself to put it down.

"His beloved land was plundered and burned. So few of his friends and kin came home, and those who did were wounded and afraid, hunted down like dogs."

Not quite *Brigadoon*, Kate thought, with a laugh that sounded suspiciously like a sob.

" 'Twas kinder that Alasdair died on the field of battle where he went willing, than that he lived to be dragged from his home in humiliation, as defenseless as a lamb at slaughter, and murdered in front of his bairns. 'Tis odd the things for which one can find oneself grateful. . . ."

Like a barrel of oats stored in a tiny root cellar

dug under the bedroom floor. Like a female goat, muzzled and lowered down beside the barrel when the soldiers came to search the house for anything worth taking. These were more precious than the sterling silver also hidden there. During the long months that followed Culloden, there was no one to buy the silver, and nothing to buy with the proceeds even if it could be sold.

Like a debt owed Alasdair by an English colonel named Fitzwilliam.

"Pride has always been one of my sins, and I waited as long as I could before I went to Inverness to throw myself on the Englishman's mercy, leaving the bairns with Alasdair's aunt Mor, who arrived at our cottage in those horrible first weeks, injured and near demented, after her own house had been burned. Mor was another of the things for which I was grateful, for she helped me keep my own reason intact, as I helped her regain hers.

"It was unlike me to bow my head before the enemy, and if not for wee Alec and Jemmie, I would have starved first. But duty sent me on my way, and I kneeled on the conqueror's doorstep for their sake. I was surprised when the Colonel's lady raised me to my feet and drew me into her arms. 'Alexander spared my Ronald's life, early on in the conflict,' she told me. 'Even on the field of battle, he behaved as an honorable man.' Alasdair had never mentioned the incident, nor, indeed, the Colonel's name. I learned it in the papers he left behind that last morning.

"I was in no position to ask details of the debt, but simply accepted the lady's offer of work in her

house, with a day and a half off each week during which I could return to my bairns.

"I was worked hard, even by my standards, but it kept me from thinking, remembering. And I went home each week with food from the Englishman's table—eggs, a bit of bacon, day-old bread . . ."

"Dr. MacGillvray! There's a patient in Six."

Kate looked up with a start, knocked the remains of her coffee on the floor. "Coming," she said, pushing the papers in her pocket.

She saw a migraine headache, a gunshot wound, a pneumocystis pneumonia and a decompensated schizophrenia. Demerol IM. Call Surgery. Bloods, O-two by nasal cannula, start a line and antibiotics. Call Psych. Cookbook.

The chest pain went to CCU. The asthma went home.

She gave the students the promised rundown on IV solutions, her mind far away from the chalkboard on which she was writing; then she saw a fever of unknown origin. Complete blood profile, bloods for culture and sensitivity, urinalysis and urine for culture and sensitivity, chest X-ray, Tylenol.

She had lunch with Evan.

"You're looking fried, Katie," he said.

She picked the bacon off her BLT and crunched it. "You're not so bad yourself," she said.

"Seriously," he said, "you're pushing yourself too hard, you're losing weight. I don't want my bride to pass out at the altar two weeks from now."

Two weeks? Fourteen days? No, twelve! she realized. The wedding would be two weeks from this past Saturday. She coughed the bacon into her napkin and set it aside, her stomach knotted with panic. Yet she would have been willing to rush off to Vegas with Alec ten minutes after he asked her to marry him. . . .

Alec.

"Let me take care of you."

She met milk-chocolate eyes across the table. "I can take care of myself."

"Of course you can," he said, softly and sympathetically; then he looked up and grinned at the beautiful girl who was standing beside him, balancing a tray on her beautiful hands. "Well, hello there. Dr. Kate MacGillvray, I'd like you to meet Deirdre Doucette. She's the new medical student on my service. . . ."

The rest of the day was busy, but not crazy, and for once, Kate signed out to the night shift on time. She hurried home, guessing Evan was going to find himself in the middle of a "surgical emergency" named Deirdre Doucette this evening and would be forced to cancel their dinner out.

She was in pajamas, in bed with a cup of tea and Catriona's Xeroxed memoirs, before seven. The phone rang. She accepted Evan's apologies and wished him good luck in the operating room before she hung up—though personally, she thought it was a lousy place to take a date.

She began to read.

It was a different world within the confines of the Colonel's house, a world where people did not have to huddle around peat fires for warmth because their tartans had been confiscated and burned, where they went to soft beds with full bellies, not sparing a thought—leastwise not a kind one—for the starving children outside their safe shelter.

"Or so I believed, at first.

"I soon learned that the Colonel's lady loved children, and cried when she was alone at her failure to conceive one. I soon learned that she spent a good part of each day working at the makeshift orphanage she had founded soon after the English victory, giving food and warmth and affection to the little ones whose lives had been torn asunder by her countrymen. The ladies who came to call at the house did not always look kindly on this endeavor, some likening Scottish children to vermin, calling them Jacobites-in-the-making who were best put down early. Mrs. Fitzwilliam never allowed such comments to pass unremarked, and I often marveled at her bravery.

"Though the only familiarity she ever allowed me was the hug I received upon arriving at her door, I never heard her speak an unkind word to me or any of the other servants. And though I could never like her—the bitterness in my breast would never allow such a thing—I came to respect her.

"Her husband was seen about the house but rarely. He was a bluff, jovial man who had doubtless driven his bayonet through many a Scottish heart. And yet, Alasdair had spared his life. At times I felt compelled to correct Alasdair's mistake; not in response to any specific transgression of the Colonel's, but just to see blood darken his red coat. I did not attempt to drive out these murderous, unchristian

fantasies, but rather nourished them. Hatred was, after all, the only passion left me.

"Or so I believed.

"Several years after I came to the house, the Colonel and his lady decided to hold a great ball. I was required to cancel my visit home to assist in preparations for it, and did so grudgingly, as my lads were growing so quickly, and I saw them so rarely. By that time, grain and meat and game were more plentiful, at least to the English, and there were huge haunches of beef to be turned, long splits of fowl to be basted, mounds and mounds of dough to be kneaded. I spent most of the week before the event in the kitchen, so 'tis not surprising that is the place where I first encountered Mrs. Fitzwilliam's brother, Charles.

"He was also a soldier, dressed in regimental red, and my enemy, I vowed, as I studied him across the kitchen. But the unexpected heat that flooded my loins belied the vow, and I turned my hatred toward myself, ashamed. Such sensations belonged only to my husband, and now, by rights, should be as dead as he was, surely not bubbling up at the sight of a man who could easily be the one who killed him.

"That last possibility, at least, was ruled out in the next moment when I heard the man talk about his home in America, addressing his remarks to his sister's Scottish servants as if they were friends and helping himself to samples of everything that was being prepared.

"He looked up from a plate of roasted mushrooms and met my eyes, and I had difficulty catching my breath. . . ."

Kate was suddenly very tired and she slipped down against her pillows, allowing the sheaf of papers to fall to the floor.

Catriona wiped her hands on her apron and turned away quickly, feeling the telltale warmth flood her cheeks. She fled from the kitchen, and from his eyes, slipped out the door, into the yard. But the tingle that ran down her spine told her he had followed her.

"Your name?" he begged.

She spun to him. "Catherine, sir," she said, remembering to use the requisite English version, curtsying, keeping her gaze properly lowered. The lives of her sons depended upon her keeping her position in this household.

He raised her chin with his fingertip, studied her face. "Catherine," he murmured. "Is it possible we've met before?"

"Nay, sir," she said, still not looking at him.

"Uhmm. I suppose you're right, and yet . . ."

He maintained his grip on her chin and the gentle pressure seemed to surge down her body. She struggled to keep herself from trembling beneath his touch.

"Do you fear Englishmen?" he asked.

She did raise her eyes then. "Never! I . . ." She stopped, remembering her manners and her duty, swallowing her pride, but apparently not in time to keep the sentiment from registering on her face. He dropped his hand to his side, stepped back.

"Ah. I see. You hate us, and with just cause, from what I've heard, but I cannot permit you to feel so about me."

"Forgi'e me, sir. Please. I ha'e two young sons who will starve if I'm let go."

"Let go? Catherine, I'm quite sure I'll never let you go," he said.

She lifted her eyes again, quickly, expecting to see something lascivious in his, but they were warm, solemn, echoing the promise she had heard in his words. "I dinna understand," she whispered.

He took her hand. "Nor do I. But believe me when I say, I mean to. Now sit with me and tell me everything there is to know about you."

Kate rolled over, opened her eyes, squinted against the brightness. She hadn't turned off the light, she realized. Had she been dreaming? She must have been, because Catriona's diary hadn't offered much in the way of dialogue, and now she recalled not only words, as one might after reading a novel, but inflections of voice, as one would if one had overheard a conversation, or been a part of it. Catriona's diary hadn't provided her with a description of the Colonel's house, yet Kate had clearly visualized the scene unfolding in a place she knew as the Munro House hotel. It hadn't provided a description of Catriona herself, but Kate knew the woman had looked older, thinner, sadder at the time it was written, than she had when she posed for the portrait now in the Lachlan family's possession. And Major Charles Shelton . . .

Funny. The dream had been as vivid as any she had had in Scotland and yet she couldn't for the life of her remember Charles Shelton's face.

She rescued the pages and began to read again.

"The ball was a grand affair for the English. They

dined on the fare served by Scots, danced to the music played by Scots, in a land that had once belonged to the Scots. I must admit, Major Shelton looked handsome in his hateful red coat, and every other woman in the room seemed to think so, too. However, each time he joined one in a dance, he looked toward me, with what seemed to be an apology. I had done nothing to encourage this attention, except, perhaps, comply with his request for information about my life on the previous day, with as few details as he would allow. I realized again that I could do nothing to suppress the purely physical reaction he roused in me just by being in the same room. And he spent a great deal of time at the buffet table behind which I was posted. Each time he happened by, he told me something more about himself, about America and the land he owned in a place called South Carolina, about the home he had built upon it. He required no response from me, and I gave him none.

"At one point, I retreated to the kitchen with an empty platter, refilled it and turned, only to find him behind me. He rescued the platter that nearly fell from my nerveless hands, laid it on the counter, then very circumspectly drew me toward a darkened hallway. I did not protest, for fear of attracting the attention, and animosity, of my peers. He took me in his arms, and my attempts to rebuff him were cursory at best. He was neither as large nor as strong as Alasdair, but he was solid, unquestionably manly, and the kisses he showered across my brow rendered me dizzy, unsteady on my feet. When his lips finally *met mine, I was powerless to keep from kissing him back.''*

Kate glanced at her alarm clock. She was due at the hospital in less than five hours. She reluctantly laid down Catriona's recitation and shut off the light.

It was still dark when she pulled into the hospital parking lot the next morning. She was exhausted—she needed coffee, and lots of it, before she tackled this day. She hadn't dreamed about Catriona and Major Shelton again. But she had dreamed about Alec.

She was lying on the uncut grass, amid weeds and dead flowers, Catriona's tombstone at her head. Alec was kissing her, deeply and thoroughly, his hand stealing up under her wedding gown to tease the wet, eager place between her legs. "Soon I'll be yours," she said.

"You've always been mine," he answered; then he drew her to her feet, prodded her toward the door of the ramshackle chapel.

She spun to question him, but he had disappeared. She hesitated on the threshold, looked toward the altar where a man waited. "Alec?" she called, and the guests in the pews laid their fingers against their lips to silence her. The glare through the stained-glass window blinded her and she stumbled down the aisle, using the pews to guide her, unseen hands pushing her forward helpfully until a strong male hand closed around hers, signaling her arrival at her destination.

"What have you done to me, Katherine?" he asked.

And then she realized he was wearing a red coat and that he had no face. . . .

She had awoken breathless and trembling, her heart, and that lower part of her body, throbbing. And she hadn't been able to fall back to sleep. She had finally decided to shower and head for work, rather than lie there and miss Alec.

It was the first time she had dreamed about him since Scotland. It was the first time she had allowed herself to think about him beyond the involuntary, momentary flashes of memory that crept to her awareness before she could suppress them. And it didn't feel good.

Catriona's memoirs were to blame, Kate guessed.

She climbed out of the car, grabbed her pocketbook, remembering the pages she had shoved in there before she left her apartment. She would stop in Medical Records and run them through the shredder, she decided. *"Quit digging up the dead."* She could bury Catriona, and Alec Lachlan, with the switch of a button.

The sound of her heels echoed in the silent hospital corridor. She walked past Medical Records without stopping. The cafeteria was also nearly deserted. She took a tray, pushed it along the stainless-steel tray ledge, pausing to consider danish and bagels, the steam table upon which fresh bacon, sausage and scrambled eggs were displayed. "You don't want all that cholesterol, doc," Lonnie, the hairnetted man behind the counter, said, waving a huge serving spoon dismissively over his offerings.

"They look good," she said. Surprisingly good, in fact. The eggs wouldn't turn to plastic and the sausage to rubber until they had been steaming for another few hours, Kate supposed. "How's the oatmeal?"

"Nasty," Lonnie said, demonstrating this by scooping up a ladleful of the stuff and grimacing as it plopped back into the pot.

"OK," she said. She started to fill a tall Styrofoam cup with coffee.

"Coffee's better in the doctors' lounge—I made it myself. And it's free."

Kate looked at the man askance, then finished filling her cup, put it on her tray and continued on to pay for it. What had gotten into Lonnie? He usually acted as if this place were Maxim's.

"Coffee's free in the doctors' lounge, doc," Grace, the cashier, offered.

"And better too, I'm told."

Grace nodded in ready agreement, not cracking a smile. She took Kate's money with what seemed to be reluctance.

If she didn't know better, Kate would think they'd poisoned the coffee and she had happened along instead of the intended victim.

When she reemerged into the cafeteria, her friend Rose Lefarge was waiting for her.

"I'm sitting over there, Katie," she said, steering Kate toward a corner table and urging her down into a chair that faced the window. "You're early today. Keeping surgeons' hours?" She grimaced, and Kate wondered if she had been taking lessons from Lonnie.

"And you're talkative for so early in the day. Where's the woman who used to threaten me with bodily harm if I spoke to her before she had her coffee?''

Rose laughed uncomfortably. ''Speaking of coffee, it's better in the medical staff lounge.''

''And free, too.'' Kate took a sip of the cafeteria's bitter brew, pulled her own version of the grimace of the day, and spun around to nab a sugar packet from an adjoining table. Then she saw them: Evan and his med student on the other side of the room, sitting close together, looking into each other's eyes. He was wearing the same clothes he had been wearing yesterday, an unpardonable sin in his book. And she knew what was really better in the doctors' lounge. The view.

''Does everyone in the hospital know?''

Rose shrugged. ''*General Hospital* has nothing on this place. Look, Katie, I got a new dress for your wedding and the prettiest dancing shoes you've ever seen, but they're returnable. Go on over there, slap his face and give him back his damned ring. Salvage your pride. He's not worth your tears.''

''I'm not crying.'' And she didn't have much pride to salvage at this point if even casual acquaintances like Lonnie and Grace were attempting to protect her from the truth. Kate put the lid on her coffee. ''I'll see you later.''

She went to the lounge, which was empty. She sank down into a chair, uncovered her coffee, forgetting her brief brush with humiliation and the scene she had witnessed. She took Catriona's story out of her bag and found the place where she had left off.

''When I arrived home the following Saturday, I

330

A Case of Nerves

found that Mor was ill, had been ill for at least a week. She had been caring for the lads as best she could, and wee Alec, being nearly five, had been looking out for his brother. But that day, she was barely able to get out of bed, and her face was burning with fever. I sponged her with cool water, and sent Alec to fetch the charmer, as there had been no doctor living nearby since before the Rising.

"The charmer brewed a willow-bark tea, and prepared an eola, which seemed to afford Mor some relief, but by Monday morning, my friend and kinswoman was much worse, and I feared for her life. Circumstances did not permit me to forget, however, that I had been due back at the Colonel's house on the preceding evening, and my sorrow was augmented by the knowledge that I had almost certainly lost my livelihood.

"I was surprised when I heard hoofbeats beyond the cottage door. I followed the boys out into the daylight and saw Major Shelton there, atop a fine stallion.

"I assumed he had come at his sister's behest, to discharge me, without benefit of my last fortnight's wages, no doubt, but he quickly assured me he had come out of concern when I failed to arrive back as scheduled.

"He examined Mor, stating he had seen much sickness during his years in the military. He was sympathetic and gentle, but could offer nothing more than his fear that she would not see another dawn. He insisted he would fetch a proper doctor. And he insisted on taking the lads away with him, to avoid contagion if, indeed, Mor's ailment was contagious,

331

and to permit me the freedom to attend her more vigilantly. I guessed he meant to take them to the orphanage, and refused the suggestion, but he assured me he meant for them to be guests in his sister's home, with her own attention to their amusement. I could do nothing but thank him for his kindness. I saw the lads settled atop his horse, Alec against the pommel and Jemmie wedged securely between his brother and the Major, and I waved as they disappeared down the path.

"By the time the Major returned with the doctor, Mor was gone.

"The doctor assured us the illness had not been contagious, and left straightaway. The charmer helped me wash and prepare the body; then she returned to her home. It was quite late by that time, and the grief I had forestalled with frenetic activity suddenly overwhelmed me. Major Shelton held me as I cried for Mor, and soon I was telling him about Alasdair and the horrible months after he died, shedding all the tears I had not allowed myself to shed at the time. And soon he was telling me about his own losses: a wife and daughter to the smallpox several years before, his best friend to a red Indian raid just eight months before.

"Our lips met quite naturally, as we tried to comfort each other. The events that followed occurred as naturally. It had been years since I knew a man's embrace, and I responded to that English soldier as fervently as I ever had to Alasdair, in Alasdair's house, in the bed I had shared with Alasdair.

"And then, as he slept beside me, I was overcome

with guilt and self-hatred, and I vowed I would never allow it to happen again.''

The beeper screeched and Kate jumped. She poured herself a new cup of coffee before she headed off to the E.R. It *was* better than the cafeteria's.

Kate advised Rose that she was sure Evan was just sowing the last of his wild oats; then she avoided her as much as possible, not wanting the pity she saw in her friend's eyes. She thought about Catriona's concerns every time she found her mind free from the more immediate concerns of her patients. Catriona had loved Alasdair—Kate couldn't forget the love she had witnessed, touched, during those strange brushes with the past during those strange days in Scotland. She wanted to believe she had imagined the odd events, but the emotions inside her refused to agree. She knew Catriona's entire world had been destroyed by the English; her husband had been killed by them. She knew it would have been difficult indeed for Catriona to give herself up to loving an English soldier.

Did she ever do it?

Kate decided she had to know. She wasn't going to feed the paper shredder just yet.

She met Evan at lunchtime, as usual. He was as attentive as ever, embraced her as she slipped into a chair beside him at the same table he had shared with his latest medical student at breakfast. There was nothing remarkable in his demeanor, and he talked about the wedding with an eagerness that fascinated her. She was also fascinated by her own lack of malice. They were like actors playing two carefully rehearsed roles, motivated by a script, not the emotions that really existed deep inside them.

The afternoon and evening hours were long and hectic. When she signed out at midnight, Kate decided she was too tired to drive home and settled into one of the on-call rooms for the night. Though the cot was narrow and lumpy, and the room smelled of antiseptic, she fell asleep immediately. She dreamed of Catriona and Charles.

Catriona felt many eyes upon her as she walked across the kirkyard at Major Shelton's side. One man, whose many years of defeat and heartache were etched on his face, was not as successful as the others at holding his tongue, and he spoke the epithet she had seen in the others' eyes.

"What is he saying?" Charles asked.

She glanced up at him. There was no need to spare him this information, because the old man had spoken nothing but the truth. "He called me 'the Englishman's whore.'"

Charles turned as if to lunge at her tormentor. Catriona laid her hand on his arm to restrain him. "For so I am," she assured him levelly.

And he turned angry eyes on her. "You're more of a lady than any of the ladies I've seen you serve. The indignities you have suffered have only made you stronger, yet have left you with the capacity to understand other people's pain. I can no longer abide the company of women without that capacity."

He removed his hat, raked his fingers through his hair in exasperation. "Did I force myself upon you, Catherine, or threaten your position if you refused me, or offer you payment for obliging me?"

She shook her head. He had paid to have her kins-woman buried today, but she knew he would have done so whether or not she had lain with him.

"Did you pretend your response last night?"

She shook her head again, felt guilt twist her insides as she recalled the magnitude of that response. "But ye'll ne'er get it again."

He clutched her upper arms urgently. "What are you saying?"

"I gave myself to ye in a moment of weakness which I'll nay allow myself to repeat. Ye're my enemy, and I betrayed my people and my sons and my husband's memory last night. I'll die before I do it again."

He drew her against him, there amidst the grave-stones and the gasps of outrage that rose from their audience. She stiffened in his arms, but didn't pull away. "I love you, Catherine. I want you to marry me. I want to make your sons my own. I'm returning to America at week's end. Say you'll come with me."

"I canna," she whispered.

Kate awoke before the alarm clock advised her it was time to do so. She had a splitting headache and she was filled with a sense of despair. She removed the papers from her bag and scanned them quickly, reading Catriona's brief recitation of Mor's burial, Major Shelton's proposal, her own refusal of it. Charles apparently returned to America soon thereafter, and Mrs. Fitzwilliam allowed Catriona's sons to live in the house where their mother worked. The MacLachlans returned to the cottage rarely, but when they did they were the object of their neighbors' ridicule and censor.

"The Englishman's whore," Kate whispered, though Catriona had never written those particular words. She could feel the woman's humiliation, her desire to protect her sons from it.

Then Colonel Fitzwilliam received word of his transfer to the Colonies. His lady offered to take Catriona's sons there, to raise them as her own. And Catriona agreed.

"I thought there was naught left of my heart to break, but that day I felt the last of it crumble into grit and mortar, like the walls of my father's keep under the power of English guns . . ."

She wiped the tears off her cheeks and made her way into the room's tiny shower stall, let the water run on her face for a long time, trying to wash away old memories that should, indeed, never have been dug up.

She dressed in the change of clothes she always kept in her locker. She got a cup of coffee and gulped down half of it before she read James Lachlan's addendum to the tale.

"Catriona drowned in a fishing accident a year after her sons went to America with the Fitzwilliams. The Colonel and his wife apparently died from yellow fever in South Carolina. Charles Shelton married the daughter of a local planter and raised the boys as his own, though both kept the MacLachlan name. In his declining years, Shelton served as an advisor to the Continental Army. Jeremy MacLachlan distinguished himself fighting for the patriot

cause. He later rose to a position of authority in the new government in Philadelphia.''

Philadelphia.

''Alec MacLachlan returned to Scotland a wealthy man, to reclaim his ancestral land. He built himself a house he named Dun Buie, and had a half dozen children.''

Kate finished her coffee and tossed the cup in the trash can. She gathered up the papers and headed to Medical Records. She guided them into the shredder and pushed its button.

Case closed. End of story.

Her beeper went off.

Chapter Seventeen

Kate stood in her stockings on the plush white carpet, pirouetting obediently in front of a bank of mirrors, under an elaborate chandelier.

The dressmaker got up off her knees with a sigh and lifted her shoulders. She removed the pins from between her lips so that she could deliver her ruling to the attractive middle-aged woman in the thousand-dollar suit who was sitting on the sofa. "There's nothing more I can do without ruining the lines of the gown, madame," she said. "My seamstresses will absolutely refuse to cut this beautiful fabric again."

Madeline Whiting pursed her lips in resignation and stood up to appraise the situation herself. She walked slowly, silently, around her soon-to-be daughter-in-law, studying her critically. "Oh, dear," she said finally. "I do see what you mean, Paulina. Exactly how much weight have you lost, Katherine?"

Kate shrugged. She had no idea. All she knew was that she had had no appetite since she returned from Scotland. "*Running on nerves alone,*" her mother had said.

"I would guess she has lost twenty pounds since the first fitting, and she was slender to start with," Paulina accused.

Kate regarded the fashionable wedding-gown designer blandly. What's the big whoop? she felt like asking, but had no trouble staying the impulse. The equanimity she was feeling today was a welcome surprise. It was as if all this were happening to another woman.

"Katherine, perhaps I can convince you to live on chocolate bars between now and the ceremony next Saturday," Madeline said.

"Chocolate makes my face break out," she answered, with perverse pleasure. Perhaps she *would* pick up a few pounds from Godiva after she left here.

Madeline threw up her hands. "Forget I said it! Paulina, is the headpiece ready?"

Paulina nodded and quit the room, returned a few minutes later with a large flat box which she laid open on a low table.

"Beautiful," Madeline breathed, shaking the confection of lace and beads out reverently. "She'll need to wear her hair gathered up high so the pearl circlet fits around it, but we'll leave a few artful curls

339

loose to tumble onto the lace in the back. Don't you think so, Paulina?''

Paulina considered this. "It's the only way," she agreed.

They didn't ask Kate's opinion, which was just as well, because she didn't have one. Funny, but she couldn't really remember ever voicing an opinion on the headpiece, or the gown for that matter, though she supposed she must have.

"Smile, Katherine!" Madeline said brightly. "You'll be a beautiful bride, a fitting bride for my beautiful son." She turned to the dressmaker. "Do what you can with the gown, Paulina. Everyone knows you're a wizard. I'll get her over to my salon and see what they can do about the rest of her," she added in a stage whisper.

I'm dumb, not deaf, Kate thought.

"*Oui*, madame," Paulina sighed.

Even in New York, a city where there were always many more people who wanted cabs than there were cabs to carry them, Madeline Whiting managed to hail one as soon as she emerged onto the street. She led a charmed life.

"I had the opposite problem before my first wedding," she confided, after she slid in beside Kate and spoke a terse "Fifty-fifth and Fifth," to the driver.

"Oh yes?"

"When I'm nervous, I eat. Before I married Evan's father, I ate everything that wasn't nailed down. My gown had to be let out not once but three times."

"I'm not nervous," Kate said. And she wasn't.

She was marrying a man to whom she would probably never respond physically, who would almost certainly cheat on her constantly. Yet she couldn't seem to work up more than a little indifference. She yawned.

"Am I keeping you awake?"

Kate glanced at her companion. "Sorry. I worked all night. Evan suggested I sleep in the car on the way here, but I couldn't seem to doze off."

"Well, I hope you're not planning to work next Friday night. Those shadows under your eyes are quite unattractive. They'll ruin the wedding pictures."

You can touch up the pictures, but not the marriage, Kate thought. "I'm off Friday."

"Good! And you won't be starting that emergency-room thing until you get back from your honeymoon."

Honeymoon. Where *were* they going? Aruba, Tortuga, Barbuda . . . or was it the Grand Canyon? And Kate didn't mind Madeline referring to her amazing professional coup as *that emergency-room thing*. She was sick of everyone acting as if they expected her next feat to involve crossing the Schuylkill without benefit of boat.

"You are looking pretty peaked, if you don't mind my saying so."

Kate didn't mind.

"If you had gone off to India or Africa in April, I'd suspect you'd picked up one of those nasty tapeworms. But they don't have tropical scourges in Scotland."

Scotland. She didn't know what they had there.

341

The interlude seemed more like a fantasy, a dream, than an experience now, and yet . . . " 'Sometimes the things you believe in become more real to you than the things you can see and hear and touch.' "

Madeline's expression said, *say what*?

"It's a line from *Brigadoon*. Gene Kelly is back in New York, back to his usual life-style. He's in a crowded restaurant where everyone is smoking and tossing back martinis and talking about unimportant things as if they mattered in the scheme of things. That's what he tells Van Johnson when Van asks how he can believe in ghosts—or in places like Brigadoon."

"Of course. Now, *Rent*, that's a great show. Shall I try to pull a few strings and get you a couple of tickets for tomorrow's matinee?"

"No, thanks."

"But listen to me, running on, making diagnoses for a board-certified internist. You'd know if you were sick, wouldn't you?"

"I'm not sick." Not physically, at least, Kate amended to herself. "*You're sick at heart*," her mother had said.

"Well, I suppose it's fashionable to be stick-thin. I wish I could lose a few pounds. 'You can never be too thin or too rich,' right?"

"Right."

"Evan tells me you've never had a good head-to-toe pampering. I say it's inhumane to deprive a woman of her God-given week at the spa at least once a year!"

Things were tough all over.

"Who does your hair?"

"You wouldn't know her," Kate said with a thin, rich, dirt-eating grimace.

"Well, you're going to love my hairdresser, Gerard. He's truly an *artiste*."

The way Madeline exaggerated the first syllable of the man's name, Kate had momentarily suspected it was going to turn out to be Gee-Whiz.

"You'll be a new woman when this day is over!"

Kate certainly hoped so. Her old self couldn't find the energy to tell the cabbie to pull over so she could get out.

The leg and bikini wax was painful. The manicure and pedicure were boring, but painless, and Kate was beyond pain by then anyway. The facial left her skin feeling smooth and fresh, but when she looked in the mirror afterwards, she saw that she was sporting angry splotches. "The irritation will be gone before your party this evening," the esthicienne assured her. It had long since become apparent to Kate that everyone in the salon knew her business. She raised her shoulders in answer. A few splotches weren't going to make any difference.

She gave herself up to the massage gratefully, feeling her tired muscles turn to jelly under the masseuse's skilled fingers. Then she was wrapped up tight in damp, herb-scented bandages, like a mummy, and was left in the darkened room with soft New Age music for company. She dozed.

The loch lay serene and inviting before her, the remnants of daylight making it glimmer like a Christmas garland. She sighed, with resolve, not sadness. The predominant emotion inside her was relief. She glanced back at the cottage that had once been her home. It wasn't now. Alasdair wasn't there. The lads weren't there. It was just a pile of stone and thatch that shielded her from the elements she would rather embrace. The loch would be her home now.

She could simply walk into the water. It would be a simple thing to walk until it reached her waist, her chin, until its surface was the new roof over her head. But that would leave no room for uncertainty about her intentions when her body finally washed up on the shoals. She would just as soon not be buried at the crossroads with the witches and hanged men. And suicides.

A fishing accident, her boys would be told, if they were told at all. She had placed a line and hook in the rowboat that would insure she merited a marker in the kirkyard where they could mourn, should they ever return to Scotland and feel the need to do so. But they were young, and an English colonel and his lady were their parents now. They would probably forget the woman from whose body they had been born. They had long since forgotten the artist and warrior who was their father.

She pushed the boat off. The water was cold about her knees. She climbed in and took the oars in her hands. She considered the movement of the muscles in her arms as she rowed. She considered the feel of splintered wood against her palms. She didn't consider what it would be like to drown. It couldn't feel worse than bidding Alasdair farewell, than seeing her land raped, than entrusting her sons to the enemy.

She finally pulled the oars into the boat, braced them against its sides—it was a sturdy craft and someone else could make use of it. She stood up, turned for a final glance at the cottage, saw two figures standing at the water's edge. The first was instantly recognizable, glowing as if lit from within, his sark snowy white, the folds of his kilt hanging to his knees, his dark hair hanging to his shoulders. The second was shrouded by the gathering dusk. "Come to me," the first man said, though his lips didn't appear to move. A beam of sunlight broke through the clouds on the horizon and touched the second man's face.

"Catherine!" he shouted as she hit the water and plunged down to meet Alasdair. Her choice had long since been made.

Kate awoke with a start, with the claustrophobic sense that she was being buried alive. She sat up, looked around, remembering where she was and why she was being primped and pampered and lulled to sleep with hypnotic music. She remembered that the man she was scheduled to meet after her makeover wasn't Alasdair, but the other man in her dream. . . .

"Evan."

She lay back, squeezed her eyes shut. It wasn't difficult to imagine Major Charles Shelton's horror when he visited his sister's new home in America and found Catriona's boys there. He had no doubt hightailed it back to Scotland, suspecting the worst— and finding it. Catriona hadn't been able to forgive herself for wanting Charles. She couldn't allow herself to love him. To do so would have been disloyal to Alasdair.

"Fortis et fidus," Kate whispered.

Catriona had died faithful, but how brave had she actually been? She had taken the easy way out, clinging to a dead man rather than daring to love another.

Kate sat up again, recalling the saying about pots calling kettles black. She realized, with sudden, staggering insight, that Alec was the only reason she hadn't broken her engagement with Evan. Revenge was a worse reason for marrying than wanting someone in the house when she came home to it.

Clinging to the wrong live man was just as cowardly as clinging to the right dead one.

Going through with the wedding was the easy way out for her.

But did she have the courage to call the whole thing off at this late date?

And she didn't have Alec waiting in the wings. He didn't want her. He hadn't really loved her. He hadn't trusted her. He had tried and convicted her on circumstantial evidence, never allowing her to speak in her own defense. And he had made no attempt to contact her during the many weeks since she'd seen him last. He was probably still as smugly satisfied with his verdict as he had been then.

If she dumped Evan, she would probably wind up an old maid, after all.

She was unwrapped and hosed down, bundled into a plush robe and escorted into a comfortable room for lunch. Madeline was similarly gowned and splotchy, Kate noted with some satisfaction, as she surveyed the food that was set before her, food that looked as if it should be served to rabbits. She had no appetite in any case. But the small glass of white wine was just what the doctor ordered: a little something to settle her nerves. Liquid courage. She drained it in a swallow, evading Madeline's disapproving gaze.

She was next scheduled to see the colorist, who evaluated her locks and prescribed highlights. *An upgrade to dirty blond*, Kate thought wryly. She watched her reflection in the mirror as strips of aluminum foil and brown goop were applied to her head. She chuckled briefly, and it was the first time she could recall being honestly amused in over two months. What with the silver plates, the dark circles under her eyes and the spotty skin, she looked like a refugee from a UFO. This day of beauty was working wonders.

She endured these ministrations with more patience than she had mustered earlier, suddenly grateful for the time to think. The decisions she made today could very well determine the course of the rest of her life.

She was shampooed and rinsed and deposited in a different chair.

She studied her eyes in the mirror, seeing something in them that hadn't been there in a while, a spark, a fire. She saw passion in her eyes and courage enough to steer a woman through at least one lifetime filled with love and loss, triumphs and disappointments, friendships and hardships—and, she hoped, the next few hours.

She spoke softly to Gerard, who was pulling a comb through her hair. She saw his eyes widen in surprise behind her reflection, and his voice was horrified. He chattered nervously about her wedding and her headpiece and his dear friend Mrs. Whiting—the woman from whom he was apparently taking his marching orders.

Kate interrupted him, repeating her own instructions in a tone that would make even Evan's mother stand up and take notice. And she smiled as the first artful curls tumbled onto the pink marble floor.

She was feeling light-headed and considerably more light-hearted when she finally emerged into the anteroom to meet Madeline. It felt good to do something even slightly madcap and impetuous again, to make even a frivolous departure from the status quo. She laughed when she saw Madeline's jaw drop.

"My God, Katherine," she murmured. "Whatever were you thinking?"

Kate raised her shoulders and tossed her headful of curls, liking the way they felt against her temples and the nape of her neck. Gee-Whiz was, indeed, an *artiste*.

"It will never work with your headpiece. I don't suppose you'd consider wearing a hairpiece?" the older woman queried hopefully as they were led into a brightly lit room stocked with pots and vials and tubes of colored sludge.

"No, I wouldn't," Kate answered, grinning, allowing a young man with brushes in hand to usher her to a chair and commence her repainting. She had just decided she wouldn't be wearing the headpiece either.

*   *   *

Kate bought a new dress in Bergdorf's on her way home from the salon, dismissing Madeline at the doors of the celebrated department store with words that brooked no refusal. It was short and black, sleeveless, covered with tiny beads. And when she finally got it back to the hotel and slipped it on in front of the full-length mirror, she congratulated herself on her decision not to wear the matronly silk suit Madeline had approved the evening before. Her waxed legs looked very sleek, Kate noted, turning sideways, kicking up one heel, then the other. She slipped her feet into delicate gold sandals and wiggled her painted toes. She did feel like a new woman. She hadn't been surprised to find Evan gone from their suite when she returned to it. However, his absence left her with no choice but to break off their engagement during the party.

She rode the gilded elevator down to the ballroom. She wasn't looking forward to what she had to do. In fact, her stomach was aching and she was afraid she was going to throw up. But it would all be over soon and that thought drove her forward. She had lost Alec—she didn't doubt it. Though the memories of the brief days they shared were still poignant and would probably always be so, the despair that had hung over her like a rain cloud for the past months felt more like righteous anger this evening.

She was suddenly ashamed of the way she had fled Scotland, meek and silent, with her tail between her legs, never insisting on being heard. She would go back to Inverness and set Alec straight, once and for all, she decided, force him to listen to the truth and take some responsibility for the end of their relationship. She wouldn't allow him to use Kate MacGillvray the way he had used Tess, as an anecdote, as a convenient excuse to keep his heart out of bounds indefinitely. *Kate did cure me of one thing, though. I'll never fall in love again and I'll certainly never get married.* She couldn't bear to have what had happened between them served up in the rewrite of Alec's seduction-without-commitment speech. She would go back to Scotland and gouge enough of a chink in his armor so that someday he might allow himself to fall in love again. And, thanks to the chinks he had already left in hers, perhaps someday she might allow herself to do the same.

She paused outside the ballroom from which the sound of music and people's voices flowed. She attempted to rally her resolve. Then she saw her mother emerge from the ladies' room down the long carpeted hallway. She rushed toward her, hugged her tightly. "You were right, Mom," she whispered.

"Again?" Anne MacGillvray said, surveying Kate from head to foot, surprise and approval in her expression. "What are we talking about?"

"Evan's not the right man. I'm not going to marry him."

Anne held her daughter away from her. "You might have listened to me sooner! Madeline has over a hundred people in there."

"She's going to be livid."

Anne laughed. "That's the good news. How did Evan take it?"

"I haven't told him yet. But he'll get over it," Kate answered with certainty.

* * *

Kate hesitated on the threshold of the ballroom and scanned the crowd. She spotted Evan on the other side of the room, talking to a beautiful and exotic dark-haired woman, gesturing in his usual animated manner. The woman was no doubt the flavor of the day. He looked toward Kate then, met her gaze. His expression was murderous as he made apologies to his companion and started across the room. Kate stepped back out into the hallway. There was no reason why a hundred people had to hear this conversation.

"Where have you been? The party started almost an hour ago. And what the hell did you do to your hair?" he demanded as he came to a halt in front of her.

"I didn't do it."

"You're more likely to be mistaken for a lost waif than a blushing bride. Don't you care what you look like?"

"I like what I look like."

She saw him clench his teeth in an attempt to control his anger. "Well, there's not much to be done about it at this point, is there?"

"We can call off the wedding," she answered.

He looked taken aback. "That's like throwing out the baby with the bath water. You can wear a hat."

A hat wasn't going to fix this. "I don't want to marry you. I'm sorry I didn't have the nerve to tell you this sooner, but I suppose it's better coming to-night than next Saturday night."

His eyes were wide in disbelief. "This is about Jenna, isn't it?"

351

She shook her head. "This is about you and me."

"Katie, I'm sorry about the other women. You don't understand how it hurts me to know you don't want me . . ."

She understood it more clearly now than she ever had. They had a long shared history of guilt, of desire denied, repressed. But appreciation for the karmic travails his eighteenth-century soul endured didn't soften the fact that the twentieth-century Evan was a selfish bastard.

"Don't get me wrong, Katie. I never wanted you to act like . . ."

A whore? The Englishman's whore? Did a small part of him remember what succumbing to such urges had cost her—and him—once?

"Jenna. You're going to think this sounds weird . . ."

She doubted it.

". . . but since the day I met you, I've felt I was destined to spend my life with you."

"Not this life," she said gently, taking the Hope Diamond off her finger and handing it to him.

During the entire flight to Scotland, Kate had worried that she wouldn't be able to find Alec's house again, that it would have evaporated into the mist like the village of Brigadoon. Now that she saw it atop the next rise, she wasn't sure she had the courage to approach it. She pulled the rented car into a bay at the side of the road and got out. He might not be home, she speculated, staring up at the white cottage. Or worse, he might be there with another woman, enjoying an early-summer Sunday afternoon tryst. Perhaps she would find them skinny-dipping in the loch. She turned back to her car. It had been foolish for her to come here. Alec had given her no reason to believe he was interested in anything she had to say. She gripped the door handle fiercely, but didn't pull it. She was being a coward. She would simply start walking toward his house right now. Or perhaps she would just stand here until it got dark and chilly and she was forced to get back in her car and find a hotel for the night. She looked down at her short jeans skirt. She wasn't dressed to confront Alec anyway. If she had really intended to set him straight, she would have taken a room first and changed into something more sophisticated, more authoritative, something that made her feel more self-confident than the tank top, faded skirt and dirty tennis shoes she was wearing.

She shrugged, knotted her baggy cotton sweater around her waist and started toward the hill. Confidence came from the inside, she supposed. Clothes couldn't give it to you if you didn't have it, or hide it if you did.

She hesitated at the bottom of the narrow dirt path. *No declarations!* she warned herself. Just tell him you found yourself in Inverness and stopped by to see how the renovations on his house turned out. Just tell him you wanted to clarify a few things about what happened in April. Just tell him . . .

Damn it! She had no idea what she was going to tell him.

She searched herself for the indignation that had gotten her aboard the plane this morning. Alec hadn't trusted her. He hadn't loved her enough to listen to her, to give her the benefit of the doubt. He had probably reduced their relationship to the subject of provocative banter over glasses of Scotch whisky in Walker's pub! That did it. She nodded resolutely, started up the path, repeating this indictment over and over in her head, in rhythm with her steps.

But when she saw him, finally, bent over a flower bed under his front window, a small shovel in his hand, a large, battle-scarred orange cat on the step at his side, her anger melted away as if it had never existed. She walked toward Alec mindlessly, silently, watching the sunlight turn his bowed auburn head copper, watching the muscles in his forearms tighten and relax as he dug out weeds and tossed them away, listening to him murmur to the cat from time to time. And she was filled with a sense of love so profound that it left her trembling.

She shouldn't have come back here!

Her heart had survived her first trip to Scotland. She doubted it would survive the second. A week ago, she had grudgingly acknowledged the chinks Alec had left in her armor. She realized only now that he had actually demolished the whole suit of it, leaving her bare, defenseless and vulnerable. But it wasn't too late to beat a hasty retreat. . . .

I can feel it like a touch.

He must have felt her gaze then, because he turned quickly and looked up at her. "MacGillvray," he whispered.

"*Ciamar a tha thu?*" she asked, with bravado she didn't feel, practicing Unit One from the "Teach Yourself Gaelic" tapes. How are you?

354

"And speaking Gaelic too! Now I know I'm hallucinating."

She couldn't help smiling, recalling the similar explanation she had made for his appearance on a foggy moor one April afternoon. "Who's this?" she asked, bending to scratch the cat's huge head, which butted up to meet her fingers eagerly, then jerked to one side in response to rustling in the tall grass.

"Tom."

"Original," she said, watching the tabby streak off to investigate the disturbance in the garden.

Alec stood up, wiping his hands on his chinos as he did so. Was he going to order her away without hearing her out?

"How are the Phillies faring?" he asked.

"Last I heard, they were in last place."

"Bad luck," he said as he took a step toward her. He looked down into her eyes for a long moment and she shivered under his scrutiny.

"Your arm's all healed," she said, dropping her gaze to his right forearm, which flexed involuntarily in response to her observation.

"Good as new," he agreed. "You cut off all your hair."

She nodded, raised her left hand to push a cropped curl back from her eyes as his hand moved to do the same thing.

Fifty thousand volts of electricity! She was dizzy and light-headed, unsteady on her feet. *Swooning.*

He grabbed her hand roughly and stared at it for a long minute. "It's the 30th of June," he said finally. "You were supposed to marry Evan on the 29th."

She looked up into his green eyes and all the words she had practiced disappeared from her repertoire. *No declarations!* she warned herself. "I love *you*," she said.

He raised her hand to his lips, closed his eyes, kissed it. "Let me show you the house," he said neutrally, retaining his grip on her hand.

The main room was much the way she remembered it, except that the planked floor had been stripped and buffed, the peat-smoke-blackened ceiling had been painted white. There was a large, vibrant modern painting hanging over the sideboard and a smaller one of a MacLachlan wife, in red plaid arisaid and beaten silver circle pin, hanging over the mantel. The couch was the same. She touched it longingly as she passed it, noting the low pine table that stood in front of it now and the pair of mismatched silver candlesticks that stood atop that. The dining table had been carefully refinished and it gleamed under the electric lights in the ancient wrought-iron chandelier that hung above it. The chairs had been upholstered in gold silk.

She watched Alec bow his head as he passed through the archway that led to the bedroom. She followed behind him with a heavy heart. It would probably be easier for her if she called a halt to the grand tour right now, if she didn't see how beautifully everything had turned out, if she didn't remember how close she had come to being the bride carried over this house's threshold.

This room was dominated by a massive bed that was covered in a brightly patterned quilt. Sunlight spilled in through the latticed windows above the bed and through the two new archways situated on either side of it. She couldn't bear to look at it. It made her think of the women who had, who would, share it with Alec.

"The bathroom?" she asked, looking away, gesturing to the passage on the left, attempting to recall the blueprints she had studied.

"Go on and have a look," he suggested.

She gasped as she did so. It was a bathroom, huge and modern, tiled in white. The tub looked more like a small swimming pool and was tucked into an alcove made entirely from glass.

"You can look at the loch from the bathtub," she murmured in awe.

"I thought you'd like that," he said, coming to stand behind her.

She spun to him, met his eyes. "You thought about me, then?"

He chuckled. "To tell the truth, MacGillvray, I've thought about precious little else since the last time I saw you."

"Alec—"

"Come on, there's more," he said, pulling her out of the bathroom and across the bedroom to the opposite archway.

"This wasn't in your plans," she said as he drew her into a modern hallway with a floor-to-ceiling window at its far end and two doors off it.

"My plans needed changing," he said.

She laid a shaking hand on one knob, took a deep breath and flung the door open. She stepped into a bright modern room filled with books, television and stereo components, computer equipment and a huge comfortable couch, above which a familiar Highland landscape had been hung.

"This is where you'll write your book," he said. "This is where I'll sleep when you toss me out of the bedroom."

The room was spinning. Vertigo. She was dizzy and breathing rapidly, the victim of a veritable flood of neurotransmitter into her synapses. Misperceptions. Confusion. "What?" she whispered.

He held his hand out to her and she took it, felt it warm and strong and very real in her own. A bridge across a synapse. He drew her back into the hall and gestured to the second door. She watched him for a moment, then pushed it open. She stepped into a room as bright and new as the one before, but quite empty. She turned back to him questioningly.

"The nursery," he said, "if you'll agree to be my wife and bear my beasties. Otherwise I'll just leave it as is—a monument to the pride and arrogance that drove you away."

"You want me to be your wife?" she whispered.

"And I could use your help in my practice. The National Health doesn't pay very well, but as my partner you would enjoy certain perquisites . . ."

"Such as?"

He drew her against him in answer, bent his head to hers and found her lips in answer, kissed her until she was limp in the circle of his arms.

"Is that all?" she murmured against his lips.

He shook his head, lifted her into his arms and carried her to the quilt-covered bed. He laid her down on it and watched her for a long moment before he unknotted her tennis shoes and pulled them off. Then he very thoroughly kissed her feet.

"And?" she asked.

He grinned as he dove onto the bed and pushed her skirt up around her waist in a single movement. He peeled away her panties and tossed them on the floor. "Your partner giveth and he taketh away."

"Giveth!" she laughed and she felt his soft auburn hair tickle the inside of her thighs in compliance. Then she was melting. She had forgotten what it felt like, she had resigned herself to never feeling it again, but now, suddenly, she was aching, burning, begging him to end her torture. And it was the most exquisite torture she had ever imagined.

"I need . . ." she groaned.

"I know what you need, MacGillvray," he said, looking up from his task. "But you'll not get it until you say you'll marry me."

She watched him drop his trousers, saw him hard and eager beneath the hem of his polo shirt, ready to relieve her suffering. "I'll marry you," she said.

"Then I believe we have a bargain," he said, thrusting into her smoothly, deeply, repeatedly, until there was no pain.

She lay tangled in his arms, in her clothes, afterwards, studying his profile, stroking the velvety stubble on his cheek, up and back. "I love you, Alec," she whispered. "I never thought I could love someone the way I love you."

"Nor did I."

She considered this, remembering her righteous anger. "Jamie managed to get my address . . ."

"Yes," he agreed. The tone in which the word

was spoken told her he also knew what his brother's communiqué had contained and had probably objected to its being sent. Quit digging up the dead? She could live with that, but Alec had practically plowed under their chances this time around!

"Why didn't you write to me? Why didn't you call?"

He raised his head. "I was too ashamed of myself, I suppose. All the way to the hospital after our ill-fated trip to Lairig Ghru, a vanload of Germans regaled me with the tale of your decisive action while I was lying oblivious on a ledge. I found myself feeling very proud to love the heroine of the day and I decided that any woman who was brave enough to scale the side of a hundred-foot gorge to pull a thorn out of this wounded lion's paw was destined to become a MacLachlan."

"More courage than common sense?"

He grimaced. "I talked Tess into driving me back to the inn at full throttle that evening so I could beg your forgiveness for acting like such an ass, but before I could do it, you pitched to the floor in a heap and I made Evan's acquaintance over your prostrate body."

She groaned.

"I never gave you a chance to explain. I was too hurt to listen to any explanations from you. And by the time I deigned to hear what Mrs. Munro had tried her damnedest to tell me all night, you were gone."

"Mrs. Munro?"

"Well, it seems our favorite sweetie wife has total recall of the conversations on which she eavesdrops, and she recited one between you and Evan, verbatim, I would guess.''

"Ah," she said, recalling the conversation in question well.

"Then Tess advised me that your Evan had made some rather *interesting* proposals to her while they were dancing, and I guessed the 'Jenna' Mrs. Munro had mentioned wasn't Evan's first, or last, infidelity.''

"You got that right," she murmured. "How *is* Tess?" She couldn't keep the jealous edge out of her voice.

He chuckled knowingly. "She's marrying Hugh Knox in September. And no, I didn't sleep with her that night, in a drunken rage, to hurt you for hurting me.

"But Tess did offer me a shoulder to cry on the next morning, one that became considerably colder as I related my tale of woe. As I recall, she cursed me for a chauvinistic pig before she stormed out of the sitting room. I doubt I'll be invited to her wedding," Alec continued. "Of course, Tess was on the phone to Elizabeth before I had sobered up from my evening of debauchery, and Elizabeth was on the phone to Isabel soon thereafter. Pregnancy makes our Isabel rather testy. She went directly to my mother. None of these charming ladies has spoken more than two civil words to me since."

Kate smiled, thinking about the strong-willed and opinionated women who would become her friends. "I have quite a Scottish fan club," she said.

"I'm its chairman and founding member."

"But why didn't you try to reach me? I almost married Evan."

He rolled onto his back and stared at the ceiling. "I convinced myself that you would be better off if you did marry him, a man who could take proper care of you, a rich American surgeon and a good-looking fellow, if I'm any judge of such things, carrying considerably less gear about than I do . . ."

Perhaps someday she would tell Alec about the gear Evan had been carrying about. Or perhaps not.

". . . an even-tempered man who doesn't wear the scars from his past failures . . ."

Time heals all wounds. "But I wasn't in love with him!" She straddled Alec, braced a hand on either side of his head, studied his face.

He sighed, met her gaze. "I was afraid one day you would stop loving me."

"That day will never come," she promised.

"I was afraid one day you would find someone else—"

"Never," she vowed. "*Fortis et fidus*, remember?" Brave and faithful. She would be a Mac-Lachlan soon.

He considered this for a long moment, then nodded. "I will love you until the day I die, *mo* Chatriona. And possibly longer."

"I believe you will," she said. Brave and faithful. He was a MacLachlan too.

He raked his fingers through her hair. "And I love this. It's very modern. I wondered what you would look like with your hair short."

He had wondered about it for two hundred fifty years, she guessed. "Well, I hope you're handy with a pair of scissors, since I'll be living three thousand miles away from Gerard.''

"Who in hell is Gee-rard?" he demanded.

She grinned happily, loving her lover's possessive tone. "He's a hairdresser."

Alec relaxed. "We have hairdressers in Inverness. This isn't Brigadoon."

"Isn't it?" she asked.

He pulled her down on top of him and kissed her. "It's a pity he decided to leave."

"Gerard?"

"Gene Kelly."

She laughed against his mouth. "He came back."

"But the whole thing was gone and wasn't due to return for another ninety-nine years!"

"You forget, *if you love someone enough, anything is possible.*"

"How could I forget that!" he crowed.

"So the American and the Scot were reunited and they lived happily ever after."

"Ah, MacGillvray," he said, rolling her onto her back, settling himself atop her, claiming her lips again, "I love a happy ending."

Golden Man

Evelyn Rogers

Steven Marshall is the kind of guy who makes a woman think of satin sheets and steamy nights, of wild fantasies involving hot tubs and whipped cream—and then brass bands, waving flags, and Fourth of July parades. All-American terrific, that's what he is; tall and bronzed, with hair the color of the sun, thick-lashed blue eyes, and a killer grin slanted against a square jaw—a true Golden Man. He is even single. Unfortunately, he is also the President of the United States. So when average citizen Ginny Baxter finds herself his date for a diplomatic reception, she doesn't know if she is the luckiest woman in the country, or the victim of a practical joke. Either way, she is in for the ride of her life . . . and the man of her dreams.

___52295-0 $5.99 US/$6.99 CAN